Dysplasia

Brad Lewis

Authors Choice Press

San Jose New York Lincoln Shanghai

Dysplasia

Authors Choice Press
an imprint of iUniverse.com, Inc.

For information address:
iUniverse.com, Inc.
5220 S 16th, Ste. 200
Lincoln, NE 68512
www.iuniverse.com

ISBN: 0-595-14566-3

Printed in the United States of America

Dysplasia

ACKNOWLEDGMENTS

∞

Paperchase, a service of Beth Israel Deaconess Medical Center, a major teaching hospital of the Harvard Medical School for its Medline biomedical database including *HealthSTAR, CANCERLIT, Index Medicus*, and the *American Hospital Association's Hospital index.*

L-Hed Enterprises

Dan Smith, of *Smith Publicity*, a unique, talented, and dedicated friend to authors.

Editor Janis Uhley of *Top Drawer.*

And to *iUniverse.com, Inc.* for making *Authors Choice Press* a reality.

For my family, then and now.

PROLOGUE

JUNE, 2000

They stood outside the hospital, yelling and jumping around like those rioters on the television. Every twenty minutes for the last few hours, CNN proudly displayed footage from South Africa. That's what CNN would do when it had a new story. Repeat. Repeat. Repeat. Anyone killing time by watching CNN would know the story cold, even if they weren't listening. It was some weird form of communication osmosis, absorption of information via satellite and screen.

Dr. Donald Gardner glanced at the television, then the window. He would alternate quickly. Through the window he could see a mob of people crowded on the sidewalk. A lot carried signs with long sticks. The printing on the signs looked as if the artist had deliberately tried to make the signs look sloppy, like they were homemade. Several tapped the sticks rhythmically on the concrete. Don could hear the tapping just enough to get his attention.

By this time the crowd had swelled. The mob could easily be mistaken for the old guard marching in the streets of Johannesburg on the television. The regular group of locals raised hell every time there was a racial problem north of 110th Street in New York. Now they had a new reason.

Don made the common mistake of killing time by watching television. The show on CNN did little to quiet his nerves. He stared at the television, never once noticing the rusty wall mount. It was installed twenty years earlier, when the hospital "refurbished" the doctors' cafeteria.

It was getting dark. He waited for the announcement. Maybe there wouldn't be one. The segment was now the "evening news," that had taken on a completely different life from the days Don watched the Huntley-Brinkley Report with his parents. They sat in front of an over-sized RCA television and listened to the news as if Huntley was the local rabbi and Brinkley the town priest. Don let his mind take him back to his childhood.

"Educational," Don's father Robert used to say emphatically. "This is the only goddamned educational show we got on."

Robert Gardner sold ties to hoards of small-time retailers in New Jersey. "Haberdashers," was how Robert referred to his clientele.

"Don. You stick with these guys, 'Huntford' and 'Brinkiman', and keep hitting the books, and you'll become a damned smart doctor."

Don's father never got names right. But he was right about the fact that Don became a doctor, and by most people's estimation, a damned good doctor. He never thought about it before. Perhaps his father was correct. The national Huntley-Brinkley Report was a good foundation for life.

"A damned smart doctor." Don heard his father's voice a second time. But at that moment, Don was feeling anything but smart.

He looked at the television and wondered if he would end up in one of those violent scenes shown on hundreds of cable stations. Simultaneously all over the world. His mind twisted his thoughts until he played out the last moments of his life. People would see him die on the evening news. The final moments of his existence would be no more than one violent electronic signal. That would be it. Then he would be gone.

His scientific background often played games with his rational mind. He thought of his years of training. Late nights studying neurology in the old Basic Sciences Building at New York University. The mind game was on. He envisioned the inner workings of his own body. A complex system of millions of microscopic electrical and chemical connections that worked together to make one human being function. The huge chemical and electrical outpouring of energy could be snuffed out in a second. At the moment it would end, his own last electrical impulse would be captured and displayed by the electronic media. From millions of personal impulses inside his body to one detached vision of him on a television. His image could be seen in a shopping mall, in someone's bathroom, or in a brothel in Thailand.

He didn't want to see his life snuffed out incidentally. Particularly now. He was young. He was intelligent. Above all, he was scared, a kind of fear few men ever experience. He fantasized that the mob would beat him into a bloody pulp. He would be left to rot on the sidewalk. He wondered how long the television cameras would keep recording. Perhaps they would leave one camera on him so they could flash back periodically to check on his decomposition. A public monument to his violent demise.

Creepy things had always gone on in hospitals. And the public was more aware than ever before. The newspapers were full of articles critical of doctors. Doctors make mistakes. Doctors cover up for one another. Doctors don't deliver the best care possible. It was endless.

Dysplasia

ⓢ

The mind game continued. One blink and the viewer would miss his electronic passage on the tube. Maybe CNN would run the story so millions would see the bloody heap on the sidewalk.

"How could this be happening to me?" was all he could think.

He was an observer as they finally performed his autopsy. He looked up from the autopsy table as the medical examiner revved up the engine on a circular saw. Like a segment from "This Old House." Don saw himself rise from the table. The autopsy room nurse backed away in horror.

"You idiot. Can't you see? They beat me to death. You guys never see the obvious. No wonder you messed up the O.J. thing in California." Don displayed his battered parts to the doctors. "I died from trauma. Get it?"

Don still had his sense of humor, albeit a bit warped. It was helping him get through the night that seemed to go on forever. The mind game lapsed after a few moments.

Don watched impassively. The reporter spoke the voiceover while a film clip featuring hundreds of opposition locals marched proudly through Johannesburg to protest the killing of a black leader. They continued past barbed wire barricades that separated them from the local conservative "cowboys" who taunted them at every turn. Perhaps hoping to squeeze off a few rounds in the interest of historic preservation. The similarities in the faces of the two mobs on television and outside were unmistakable.

Don yelled nervously from his sticky plastic-coated chair. He sat near the old frame windows. The doctor's cafeteria was deserted. "Hey. Hey. Is there anyone back there? Hey? Can you shut the television?" He had enough. No sense waiting to hear the obvious. He only needed to look outside.

Don's voice sounded weak. He felt like having a drink. Several drinks. Enough so he could erase any awareness of his predicament.

Brad Lewis

Don got up from his chair. He felt his white lab coat stick slightly to the grease-imbedded chair. He walked to the counter. Three long stainless steel bars separated it from the dining area. They created a path next to the inadequately refrigerated food counter.

No one left on the food line, the only activity in the kitchen. As Don neared the counter, he heard a symphony of banging pots and pans interspersed with Puerto Rican music.

The music was a clear reminder. Don was not in South Africa but in Manhattan. Manhattan! At his hospital. His hospital! Morningside Hospital. Where he worked for almost six years.

"Can you turn off the television?" The music was his only answer. He abandoned the quest to eliminate the mob on the television. He moved back to the windows.

Now the crowd outside shouted his name. Even through the windows on the seventh floor, Don could hear them, "Gardner. Gardner." They drew his name out in long syllables so that it sounded like "Gaaaaard nerrrrrrr". Of course, the overzealous local politicians organized them. Don knew that. These people didn't know him. He was just another white doctor at the hospital. The fact that it was in Morningside Heights did not help matters any. It was an area familiar to the early news because of its fair share of city violence. Tonight, they had a national story and a patsy to go with it. But they were not after some criminal, they were after him. One of the staff surgical obstetricians. He probably worked on the families and friends of some of the protesters. The situation seemed incredulous to Don. He was their friend, not just their doctor. He had always tried to help them.

Don's mind wandered back to the years of long hours in stinking, understaffed wings of the hospital. He had given them the best years of his life and now they were shouting against him. They wanted to take everything away. Everything he had built.

Dysplasia

Don slumped back into his sticky chair. He sat huddled at a cafeteria table by himself. His hands almost hid a Styrofoam cup of coffee like it was his last. He couldn't remember how the coffee got into his hands.

While he was in school he hated the taste of coffee, but he ended up drinking it for most of his six years on staff. He often thought it was the taste of Styrofoam that gave him that extra high. He rushed thousands of times from this very same cafeteria to get to the O.R. in time for his morning surgery. Sort of a Pavlovian response. The rat in the Skinner box who got high on Styrofoam coated coffee. Doctors were full of bad habits in their own lives, and bad habits dealing with their patients. That's the part of medical practice Don didn't like. He never came to terms with the dark side of his profession. It was the part that made doctors human, with their own foibles and malicious intentions.

Perhaps he developed a slow immune reaction to some component of Styrofoam. Perhaps he was being destroyed by an autoimmune response. He would die anyway. His own cells would gang up on him for repeatedly dousing them with caffeine and the odor of freshly produced Styrofoam. He let go of the cup and moved to the window. His hands turned into fists as they dangled at his sides. He could feel the moist, cold sweat on his hands. He touched his hand to his cheek and felt the cold moisture as he clenched his teeth. The movement made his thick masseter muscles flex on each cheek. Caffeine was an awful habit.

He wanted that drink. He thought of malt scotch and laughed silently to himself. Malt scotch? Here? His throat was parched. He wanted to make believe none of this had happened. He parted the old Venetian blinds in one corner of the room so he could look out onto 114th street without being seen. As soon as he touched the blinds, the thick dust encapsulated his fingertips. Dusting the cafeteria was a low priority for a hospital always trying to save a buck. He automatically wiped his hands on his white lab coat. It was an uncleanly habit at best. He always made sure to get a fresh coat before making rounds, a habit he wished his colleagues shared.

When he first took a job on staff he was very naïve. He never would have dreamed that most of the doctors on staff were not there to make any sort of medical contribution to the community. It was a plug. Another feather in the professional cap. It was good P.R. to hang around in one of the last great vestiges of good ol' boy hospitals in New York. Doctors put in their time very graciously. The hospital appointment went hand in hand with their posh practices in the suburbs where they could boast about their big deal appointment at the hospital and university. Aside from prestige, a position here could bring in at least a couple of new referrals a month. Once in a while a patient showed up in the hospital with a high quality insurance plan or, miracle of miracles, they could afford to pay cash. That signaled the attending physician to whisk them like hell out of the clinic and place them quickly in his private patient roster. The patient often saw such an activity as an element of luck. Dr. Suburbia or Dr. Fifth Avenue was on call and the patient was so lucky to get his care instead of one of the residents. The quality of care often was a little better, but always better than the care that the non insurance patients or patients on city insurance received by the same suburban doctors. It's not that the medical profession conspired to do it that way. That's just how the system evolved. It got so bad that many of the welfare patients were not even offered full diagnoses. There were no alternatives or second opinions. Everyone got what his coverage allowed. Like HMOs and managed care facilities, the range of medical services was getting smaller for the "low end" patient. More often than not, the treatment decisions were in the hands of administrators.

If the city was paying for the case, you could be sure the patient would get the no frills version of whatever was needed, from a PAP smear all the way up the line to an abdominal hysterectomy. It was only fair to "let the city get what it pays for. These people should be damn glad they get any kind of care at all." So said many doctors in the privacy of the coatroom. Business was business. And hospital business had its own set of unwritten rules and regulations.

This kind of thinking always disturbed Don. Against his own morality, he continued on in the system. He thought he could do good for the community. Even if it were just some good, it would be worth the effort. But he got caught up in the system. When he tried to correct it, his efforts were too little and too late. He felt stupid to think he could have made a change. He was naïve to think he could have done any good at all.

The first bad habit a doctor learned in a big city was "going along with the system." Like thousands before him Don went along as best he could. Now he was paying for his "mistake" of bucking that system.

Old visions, sights and sounds, flashed in and out of his mind, still trying to make sense out of how it all happened. He recalled when his life first changed. It was the day he met his senior partner. He fixed on the old sights and sounds.

Don wasn't one of the Lexus and Land Rover crowds from the suburbs. He hung out with the elite. The upper echelon. The world-renowned doctors. It had to be that way. That's the way he came up. He was groomed by one of the best in the city, his senior partner, Dr. Henry "Call Me Hank" Chessman. Chessman was the popular leader of the most highbrow international OB-GYN practice in New York. Because of Chessman, Don had become something he had never planned to be, one of the "great white doctors" of Fifth Avenue, a title that often led to more bad habits.

Brad Lewis

꙰

Don thought about the day he met Chessman. The noisy crowd quickly distracted Don. He looked out. He envisioned how he would eventually get to his car to speed away from this nightmare.

There were probably no more than one hundred people at the entrance. A smaller group blocked the entrance to the parking lot. How they knew that his car was parked across the street was beyond him. Don had grown more and more paranoid over the last few months. But now it seemed justified. Spies everywhere.

He zeroed in on one toothless black woman screaming loudly. He couldn't hear the words, but it was clear that she was chanting, "Hang Gardner. Hang Gardner." That's how he saw it. "Not very creative," he thought. It summed up his local popularity. The rest of the people were either African-Americans or Hispanics. Today he was their target. A skinny Jewish boy from Queens whose parents wanted only one thing for him, to be a doctor. That was his ticket out of the cozy apartment maze. Out of the dreary suburbs and into the city. He would leave behind the embarrassment his relatives had for his Uncle Max, selling meat in Bedford Stuyvesant. He would leave behind his own embarrassment, the silly but ever present insecurities that stayed with him to this day. He had dreamt of other careers, but was too afraid to try, too afraid to tell his parents, and too afraid to fail. After all this time, he found himself in the greatest untenable situation of his life because he became one of the "great white doctors" of Fifth Avenue. He kept hammering himself with the phrase "Great White Doctor."

"Dr. Gardner. Are you Dr. Gardner?" a deep voice bellowed from across the cafeteria floor.

Don turned to see a rather squat, young black policeman. He waddled along the cracked tile floor. He smiled as he approached.

"Yes, I'm Dr. Gardner," Don answered directly.

Dysplasia

The man was direct and calm. "Patrolman Brown. I've been assigned to escort you out of the building. If you'll come with me, we can get your things and then I'm taking you out of the building."

Don looked squarely at him and wanted to say, "Just you?" He couldn't bring himself to question him or his authority. He was glad to get the hell away. Soon he would be safe. Then he could stop the mental torture.

After the day he had, he was in no shape to question anything. It was his questioning that got him into this trouble in the first place. More trouble than he ever thought possible, more than he could handle.

He wanted to get home. He wished he could turn back the clock. Start over with his wife before the trappings of his success corrupted her. Once out of the hospital everything would be okay. He had lived through the worst day of his life, a day that might totally destroy his career and leave his life in shambles.

"Okay. Just give me a minute," he mumbled to his single police escort.

Don moved back to the cafeteria table and took another sip of coffee. He had no idea why.

Reality hit him hard. There was no way to get things back in order. No way to get a sense of what to do. He could start throwing money at attorneys. His best friend Robert Kronen was an attorney. He was the one who warned him. Even Kronen had no idea that this was what would happen. They could find the "right" attorneys and pay outrageous fees. That's the way things went in the new millennium. Throw money at attorneys. Hope for the best.

Don looked back at Patrolman Brown. He waited patiently. Don wanted to run like a coward, a sniveling worm with no vertebrae, a fearful little man who overstepped his social and professional boundaries. Now he was the victim of his own activities. He was stuck in the dreariest, murkiest, sullied existence. He succeeded in overcoming his own familiar prejudices. Did the protestors somehow secretly know that his own family showed a dislike towards African-Americans and other minorities? Did they find out about Uncle Max's stories from Bedford Stuyvesant?

"You have to have a special knack to deal with them schvartzes." Uncle Max was proud of his talent. He could size them up. He knew the good from the bad. Uncle Max was king of the schvartzes.

When he got older, Don would cringe as Uncle Max told his litany of schvartzes' stories and jokes. It was as if he were giving a Biblical history of the Bed-Stuy section. Many said it was the worst black neighborhood in the city. Don found it odd that a Jewish man would make his living on such dangerous turf. Even when Don tried to show disinterest, Uncle Max would continue on about his illustrious career. The main meat purveyor to the blacks was a hero in his own life.

"Them Schvartzes were afraid of us. They would see the long knives we kept in the front of the store and almost turn white." That was one of his favorites. It got big laughs at the Thanksgiving table. Uncle Max would tell the story while he brandished the extra long carving knives for the turkey. Even Don's mother would continue to laugh at that classic. The stories would go on long after Uncle Max sold his store.

"Uncle Max. What a time to think about him," Don thought as he again found himself nervously sipping his coffee. It was cold. He could smell the Styrofoam.

Don looked at Patrolman Brown. The smile was gone from his face. He rocked forward and backward, heel to toes, ever so slightly impatient. Neither man spoke.

Don took one last look out the window at the crowd below. A news truck had pulled up alongside, partially blocking the emergency entrance ramp. A policeman signaled for the news truck to move further down the road. Too late. The Eyewitness News Team, including the driver, had already exited the familiar white van on their way into the crowd. It was feeding time at the media zoo. This crew was sent to cook up and serve the appetizer. The frenzy had started.

Don was glad CNN didn't show. If his morbid fantasy came to fruition he would exit the world at a local level. Most of his friends would miss the show. At the same time, it made him feel less important. Why wasn't CNN covering the story? It was New York. Maybe East Coast doctors had fallen into the same category as East Coast intellectuals.

"Because they're anti-Semites." That's how Uncle Max saw these situations. Or any others that didn't fit his sense of right and wrong.

Don thought what a great shot it would make if he crawled out on the ledge and executed his best swan dive. Splat onto the concrete. Suicide had always been a recurring thought, brought on from the dreams of his childhood. In each dream, instead of falling to his death, he would fly like Superman. All-powerful, all omnipotent. He would spy as he flew over the neighborhood. He could look in the neighbor's window and see the Rabbi's daughter doing her stretching exercises to reduce the cellulite on her jelly roll rear. He would spy on his parents and overhear them plotting his future. "The boy is creative. Maybe he should take some time off before he goes to medical school," his mother would say in the dream. She recognized that Don would rather fly into Greenwich Village in time to perform his role in a play. Sometimes to see his plays performed, plays that he didn't dare let anyone read. Then the dream would sour. It was his father's voice.

"Do you know how much we spent on his education? The boy is going to graduate free and clear. Do you know how many friggin' ties that is?" Don's father would also say this in real life. Too many times for Don to forget. "Free and clear. And I don't think he gives a good goddamn about what I've done for him."

Don wanted to dream that flying dream again. He would jump out of the hospital window. Fly high over the crowd and then loop north to

Central Park, again avoiding death. He would become the all seeing, all-knowing, and flying god of his youth. Don saw himself as omnipotent. A god of words and sensitive expression. An inner being that conflicted with the carnal man who got him into so much trouble.

Don walked over to Patrolman Brown like a man being summoned by his executioner for the walk down Death Row.

"Dead Man Walking" is what he thought he would hear. Instead he heard his own voice. He sounded better. More secure. Everything might turn out okay.

"Right. My things are on the second floor. In the doctor's coat room." His voice didn't reflect his fear.

When he reached Patrolman Brown the officer abruptly stepped in front of Donald. The Patrolman was eager to play his role as protector.

They moved towards the elevator in single file. Brown rhythmically waddled in front of Don, like they were in a long procession.

Patrolman Brown pushed the button to summon the elevator. The old huge Otis monster rumbled into motion. Patrolman Brown turned and looked squarely in Don's face.

"Doc, did you kill that girl like they say you did?" It was not an expected question.

There was no hostility in the question. He asked it as simply and directly as "Do you think it will rain tonight?"

How did he know that's what the committee decided to pursue? The hearing was only two hours ago. Don felt betrayed.

It didn't start out as a hearing, but that's how it ended. A hearing for Don. News did travel fast.

Don stared at Patrolman Brown. He spoke as calmly and controlled as possible, "Don't be ridiculous. I'm a doctor. We don't kill people." It seemed like a prepared statement. Don knew that statement was a false

Dysplasia

one. Doctors and hospitals did kill people. Don always held himself out as one of the exceptions.

It didn't matter whether Patrolman Brown believed him or not. Don was already thinking about the absurdity of his response. "I'm a doctor. We don't kill people." He decided not to use the statement again. At that point it didn't matter that Don knew that doctors kill patients. Everyone knew it. From the *Wall Street Journal* articles down to the local precinct in Morningside Heights.

One thought crystallized. "Bam," said Emeril, the showman chef from cable television. "After this break we're going to kick it up a notch. I'm going to tell you who committed the murder." That was it. Don knew who the real killer was. He was sure of it, but who would believe him under the circumstances? After what he just went through, his reputation was already destroyed. Less than two hours after he left the committee room, the local police were leaked the committee findings. So much for the rumored confidentiality amongst doctors.

The elevator doors opened. They stepped inside. The door closed slowly. Don readied himself for the slowest elevator ride of his life. Not another word was spoken. Don heard an inner voice count backwards as they passed each floor. It was his voice at age four. His eyes welled with tears. His throat felt thick, like he had swallowed cotton. He tried a hard swallow. It was so dry it made him cough. He wished he had taken the Styrofoam coffee with him.

Don paused to urinate before leaving the doctor's coatroom. He could see his face clearly in the tarnished framed mirror that hung over the urinal.

How many times had he stood there and pissed proudly into the cracked white porcelain? The old guard never intimidated Don: the 60,

70, and sometimes 80-year-old hospital warriors in white lab coats. Relics from the era before insurance and HMOs. Each coat had the doctor's name embroidered in red. Doctors would pace the room, check the stats on the bulletin board, and then saunter inside to stand urinal to urinal with Don, another great white doctor.

Don studied his image in the mirror. He thought he looked a little haggard, but not bad for a man in his mid 40s. He used to jog to the office, but not lately. He was still wearing his tuxedo. He had put on his tuxedo earlier today so he wouldn't have to change for an awards dinner he was supposed to attend with Chessman. Chessman was playing the Israeli side of his connections by attending an evening for Technion, the Israeli version of MIT. Chessman would do that for any of his "buddies" at the drop of a hat. Providing the hat was filled to the brim with financial goodies. Charity was fine if it included entry to the rich and famous.

Don needed to shave again. He was always careful about his cleanliness. But he didn't care at this point because he had no special destination. Not then. Possibly not the rest of his life. His hair was slightly thinner than when he came to Morningside. It didn't bother him much since many of his colleagues looked like hell by their mid 40s. By 50 a lot of them became part of the burned out core group, the pot bellied, balding, alcohol and drug abusing zombies of the profession. This last year Don saw his own score on alcohol abuse take a significant rise.

He zipped up his fly and pulled back his lab coat to expose a medium frame, still firm enough to fit comfortably inside a size 36 belt. Don stood nearly six feet, and probably could have modeled when he was younger. He had blue-green eyes and olive skin, both from his mother. In the midst of his turmoil, he shocked himself with his own audacity to wink at himself in the old, giant mirror. Then he smirked as if to say, "You jerk. What have you gotten into now?" Of course he would blame himself. He had a masochistic way of thinking. His self-esteem ran low. Even during the best of times, he thought slightly less of himself than he should have, a fact he clearly felt contributed strongly to his fall into the darkness that surrounded him.

He hung up his lab coat on the old, thick, wooden hangers. "Were they mahogany?" He had no idea, and berated himself further for never finding out. That is how Don always treated Don. That is how Don's father always treated Don. With his lab coat now on the hanger, Don walked slowly past the hideously faded green leather chairs, the kind with the blackened gold-colored tacks.

He stopped to look at the old ashtrays. They were never removed, even after smoking was outlawed. He looked back at the narrow hall of lab coats, glanced at his watch. He made a calculated decision that he was not—. He paused and repeated the words "was not." He was not going to let this happen to him.

He flung his Zegna black tuxedo jacket over his shoulder with the authority of a man who wasn't going to go down easily. After hours of lamenting his own demise, his wallow in self-pity was over.

He pulled himself up to his full height and marched into the hall. Patrolman Brown stood ready to get him out.

Don had to fight. If he were to go down, he would go down fighting. He nervously adjusted his bow tie, finally pulling it off. He hated ties, something for which he blamed his father.

He had one more short elevator ride to go. It would leave them off near the street level exit. That ride would feel longer than the first.

CHAPTER ONE

CHRISTMAS, 1999

It was a cold, windy day in New York. The side streets just off Fifth Avenue were still jammed like a parking lot. The vehicles waited to turn onto Fifth, an unwise decision for vehicular travel at that time of the day unless it was absolutely necessary.

Don finished a routine day of practice. He showered and dressed in the office. His wife recently bought him a new gold collar bar from Tiffany. It was a pain in the ass to get into place. Don was determined to get it right. Thinking back, he never thought that his "uniform" for work would be like that of an investment banker, white collared shirt, rep tie, suspenders, designer suit, and now a gold collar bar.

Don left himself extra time to fiddle with his new gift. It had a pin and ball arrangement. Don knew if he didn't take his time, he would probably end up with a Swiss cheese pattern around the white collar of his expensive shirt. He started copying his senior partner Chessman, and was even buying white collared Turnbull & Asser shirts from Bergdorf Goodman. Chessman's were made in London, and since Don only had two, it was easier for him to purchase them at the sole New York department store that sold them. Both had bold colored stripes. Today he was wearing his blue and green model. His other was red and blue. White collars and French cuffs. The colors of a Turnbull & Asser leaped from the shirt, making them clearly visible across a room. It was a power shirt, like Ascot Chang. Shirts known to Fifth Avenue addresses.

Don checked himself in the mirror and was generally pleased with his image. Looking deep into his own eyes, he reminded himself that something was wrong, something deep inside, something that was troubling him for some time. He abandoned the thought. He grabbed his coat and scarf, opting to walk to the Christmas party further up Fifth Avenue. As he waited for the chrome and glass elevator, the thought he was trying to avoid hit him hard. It hit a conscious level and Don hashed it over in his mind, hoping to get it out of the way so that he could enjoy the rest of the evening.

The thoughts were simple. Don was beginning to have doubts about his life. The usual doubts. About his marriage. About his practice. But Don was having more extreme thoughts about the nature of his marriage, the nature of his practice. He essentially was beginning to dislike himself, and subsequently was picking everything apart. Worst of all, he thought he had made a mistake about the practice. He didn't like the way his partners practiced, the way they treated women, both socially and professionally. He was drawn in to their style of practice. He endured their professional philosophies. Basically he practiced the way they did. They didn't have a problem with it, but he did. It seemed to go against his grain. He became aware of it early on, but he felt he could control it, practice the way he wanted, balance his inner feelings with how the practice was already run, and reach a happy medium. This wasn't the way it happened. He was doing procedures to women that he felt were basically unnecessary, and he was giving out information to women that was basically untrue. In his heart this made him both a butcher and a liar. Plenty to develop some more self-hatred. Plenty to stimulate any basically moral doctor to reevaluate his methods. Yet there were plenty of seductions, combined with barricades to keep the ruse going. He felt trapped in his marriage and in his practice. He abandoned thinking about his marriage. He didn't want to go over it again. At least not now. He made a mental note to stop torturing himself and try to enjoy the party. He knew it would be tough. Fifth Avenue parties could be very exciting or very boring. There seemed to be no in between. And this was a Christmas party for business, one of the many opportunities for all the "great white doctors" to get together, to tell hunting stories. Being a successful doctor was all about conquests. Who had the new hot dot-com stock? Who went to the ball game with Donald Trump? Whose house was only a few miles from the new Clinton house? These were the questions that begged for answers when the cocktails flowed on Fifth Avenue.

Don left the building via a side entrance and turned west to walk the half block to Fifth. Fifth Avenue. How proud his family was when he told them he was going to practice on Fifth Avenue. He wasn't totally sure he should have told them. At family gatherings, Don's parents would proudly bring up the location of Don's practice.

"Huh. Fifth Avenue. I'll tell ya. The kid has really made it. Fifth Avenue. Right across from the Park. Schmuck! Central Park. What are you, some kind of idiot, you don't know Central Park?" Don's father was merciless, but he did it with a twisted love. Don always kept silent, and let his father mouth off the words "Fifth Avenue", letting the words roll out with a mysterious ring of power. Don's mother would stare and nod, repeating "Fifth Avenue" to verify the truth in case there were any nonbelievers listening.

Dysplasia

∾

Don's parents would raise the same subject at deli counters, gas stations, and department stores. Anyone who would listen would learn that the Gardners had a boy who practiced on Fifth Avenue.

It was a big turnaround for Don. In the beginning he had other ideas, ideas about being a playwright, ideas about practicing in the West Village, around New York University, around the artists, away from the chic. It didn't work out that way. He blamed himself for being weak, for being seduced. After all, this was America, and shouldn't he take the opportunities presented to him? That was the American way, the American dream. He only needed to remind himself of the fortunes made in the computer industry. One day working in a garage and the next day having a company capitalized in the billions. If he wanted to really hurt himself, he could look at the salaries of sports figures. Right? Doctors were educated, hard working people. In school until almost age 30. And Fred Couples made a million in three events after the regular season golf tour. But that was still nothing compared to baseball, basketball, and football. Don was entitled to his fair share. He worked hard to get where he was. He just didn't like the way he was making the money. His parents couldn't relate to his dilemma. He once made the mistake of criticizing Chessman to his father.

"Don't look a gift horse in the mouth," Don's father would scream. "Politics, it's all politics. It's not what you know, it's who you know, and you better damn not forget it!"

Don had heard that since he was born. "Get connected. Everyone successful is connected." Don knew his father meant well.

All Don's colleagues would have gladly given up any chance for future procreation in exchange for "the deal Don got." Or so he thought. Perhaps incorrectly. At the time of the contract, things happened fast. A whirlwind courtship. Prestige. Power. Oh, and money. Lots and lots of money. It was an occupational goal of doctors, just like any other successful businessman. The higher you went up on the practice ladder, the more money you made. Don and his partners were on the top. The money was always pouring in. It made it harder to think about doing anything else.

His childhood friend Kronen told him early on that "You're not the Fifth Avenue type."

"Kronen, what do you know about Fifth Avenue?" Don always called him Kronen. It stuck since they were kids.

"Duh, isn't Fifth just after Fourth?" Kronen knew there was no Fourth Avenue in New York, but loved to provoke anyone he could with his unique sense of humor, a humor that irritated as many as it pleased.

Kronen followed up on his advice periodically. This included buying books for Don with titles like "How To Swim With The Sharks," and subjects like White Collar Crime in America. Kronen was never subtle if he wanted to get a point across.

There was clean snow on the ground, not yet desecrated by the black soot that would find its way from the cars to the pristine white covering. It looked pretty. Don watched his feet as they sank about a half-inch into the soft, white carpet. The oncoming headlights blurred his vision just enough to give a surrealistic feel to his view of the barren tree limbs and giant buildings that loomed over him.

He never wore rubbers. He didn't care if he ruined his shoes. He would buy a new pair. He wore Church's or Johnston & Murphy, full last, wide shoes, to help cover his double E foot. Don never thought he would be spending $300 on shoes. His partners either wore Gucci loafers or Bruno Magli dress shoes. Ferragamo was in, too. He thought about Bruno Magli shoes in the Simpson trial. How Simpson was prosecuted in the civil case. The picture of him with the shoes was unmistakable. But California had its own kind of justice. New Yorkers would never have stood for the first trial.

Dysplasia

∞

He couldn't focus on anything positive. Don was worried about the hospital, how it was being run, and how he had to do something about the bad treatment of the city welfare patients. It would be a lot simpler if Don's senior partner Chessman was not head of the hospital department where Don had his appointment. It would be a lot simpler if Don were not making tons of money in the same office, the office Chessman seduced Don to move into seven years ago.

Don thought about the money. What would happen in the office if Don made a stink at the hospital? He felt he had to do something. He could at least do some good for the hospital patients. He wouldn't dare address how his own partners practiced in the office. Doctors got into modes of practice. They stood by them, backed up by their professional cronies, pharmaceutical companies, and manufacturing companies. That's who determined how "upscale" medicine was practiced in the United States. The result was extremely high fees for patients, and extremely high profits for everyone connected to health care delivery. Overtreatment and overprescription were the willing partners of any upper echelon private practice.

Don was making more money than he needed or wanted. His wife was not shy about spending a lot more when it became available. In the beginning of his financial windfall, Don liked to see her spend money. He was happy to see Linda enjoying things she otherwise would have avoided in the past. Now it was part of their lives. The central wheel in their Rube Goldberg life. The overspending was like having a third person in the relationship. Don. Linda. And the things the money could buy.

The three were not getting along. Don liked to delude himself by claiming he could go back to a simpler life, but there was no way Linda was going to give up the money. Who was he kidding, anyway? He liked the perks. Nobody would give up a Fifth Avenue practice. When wealthy doctors sat around bitching, everyone would have the same answer.

Why go through it all? Money. Power. Prestige. Few said it that way, but most thought of it that way. Most would leave out "prestige" and insert money a second time. Why practice at the top? Money. Power. Money. Prestige and accolades could be bought at charity functions and professional awards dinners. There was no room at the top for false liberal stands or altruism. If you were in with the big boys, you had better share their motives.

When Don was in medical school, the uniform was all jeans and T-shirts. Now Linda would come home carrying shopping bags from Saks, Ferragamo, and names that Don had trouble pronouncing. He loved to mock the names of the designers by making up ordinary real names. This made Linda laugh nervously, as if Don had violated some sacred order of designers. They often fell down in the heap of shopping bags to make love on the spot; their writhing bodies interspersed with new shoes, lingerie, and an occasional pants suit. The hanger proved to be an annoying obstacle.

Henri Bendel was Henry Bendowitz. Ferragamo was Frank Regamo. Valentino was Val and Tinos. Gucci was Goo Che, "the Tao Boa instructor." It was an endless game they could often play at cocktail parties, to keep from getting bored. Linda stopped playing those games when the money started getting seriously big. She didn't like to hear Don's jokes when she was talking it up in public. Linda felt she had a role to play at functions, a role Don could only describe as "wife of a great white doctor." Linda didn't want to offend anyone, most of all one of the social elite that liked to keep his doctor in his designer pockets.

Don thought about the old routines.

"Isn't that a Valentino?" Linda would ask.

"No," replied Don, "that's from Val and Tinos on Delancey Street, corner Essex."

Dysplasia

∞

It never ceased to get a laugh in medical school. Many of the students were second and third generation New York City Jews. Another large group was Italian. All shared the same "New York" humor. Anyone could do "shtick". Most everyone, from the doormen to the taxi drivers, spoke the same language. Shtick, oy vai! and schmuck were heard as often as a knish was eaten.

Once he began practice, Don learned to be careful. Occasionally someone would become offended. In the past, it never mattered. It was just a joke. But language had to be tempered and designed to fit the moment. These were no longer jokes, but elements of scripted lives. Chessman had his set battery of jokes. Don knew every one. It took a little less than six months to run through all the possible scenarios. Patients. Politicians. Billionaires. Celebrities. Nobodies. That just about covered the Chessman humor audience. Don and one of the other partners, Lou Benjamin, would mouth the punch lines to each other as soon as Chessman would start a joke.

Don was taught to worry about offending the doctors that sent him patients. The referral base. It was how the practice machine kept going. Internists, family practice doctors, schleps eking out a living by teaching medicine, and physicians that stopped doing the OB part of OB-GYN, all sent them patients. Of course they had their political connections, connections that brought them patients from all over the world. Word of mouth still worked. It worked big time for Don and his partners. They were part of the international buzz.

Chessman warned Don early on. "The referral base in New York would like to have an image of their young specialists as being poor, eager, hungry, and most of all humble. You fulfill those ideals for them and they will send you patients."

But that was only the local part of the Chessman formula. "That's if you want to be a bread and butter specialist. The rest of the world wants you to be well dressed, and I don't mean off the rack from

Bloomingdale's, a little arrogant and aggressive. People are not going to fly here from Qatar or South Africa because they think you are a local shlepper."

Chessman was the kind of salesman that probably would have given Ross Johnson, the former RJR Nabisco boss, a run for his money. Chessman counted Ross as one of his buddies. He also counted his other Ross, Perot, as a "close, personal friend." Chessman pretended to know everyone. "FOC" was the inside joke word in the office. The partners would hear a name and say "FOC". The letters stood for "friend of Chessman". Over the years he had contributed to both major parties. He raised money for the Clintons. Recently he arranged for a group of New York doctors to attend a fundraiser for Bill Bradley at Madison Square Garden. If asked, Bradley was "a good friend" and all of the retired Knicks were also FOC. When Chessman was done with a celebrity, the past tense was used. "Oh, he's FOCed." The sound was deliberate. No one ever said it to Chessman's face.

Chessman was not shy about his social and political power. The envious would call him "starfucker". "Once you get them beholden—and you can learn a variety of traps to get them beholden—you turn the tables and piss on them. You become a star in their lives."

Chessman was right. Don had become a star, just like his other partners. He carved out a part for himself, a part that made him the envy of all the young doctors in his field. Don understood what Chessman originally meant by "turning the tables." Don was constantly getting calls to socialize with the referring doctors. "Let's get together with the wives." The other doctors and their wives loved to hear anything about celebrity patients. It made sense. If shows like *Hard Copy* and the *Enquirer* were hits, it proved our entire society was locked into yearning for the secrets of the wealthy, powerful, and famous. Don had a key to that world, or at least that's what it looked like from the outside. By pursuing Don, an outsider might get entry into that unique world.

Chessman had been Don's advisor, guru, role model, and chief seducer. Now Don was thinking about leaving. Each day that Don did nothing, he was pulled deeper into a life that was beginning to look like a dark abyss. Don's star shined bright on Fifth Avenue along with other self made luminaries. Chessman predicted his rise. Could he sense that Don wanted it to end?

Chessman did not look or act like a doctor. Not for one second, ever. The only place he acted with "doctorly" respect was in the hospital. Chessman was born Jewish, like the rest of his partners, but was very careful to conceal it from the rest of the medical profession and most of his business contacts. He dressed like a WASP, ate in the fanciest restaurants in town, a fixture at Le Cerc for lunch, and was active in all non-denominational cultural activities. For all practical purposes, he had made the assimilation quite well. He could weave his way in and out undetected. It was in sharp contrast from the world of the hard working Jewish boy who becomes a doctor in the world of blue blood socialites. The latter could provide business and social connections afforded to few, particularly a self made Jew. Chessman created his own entry to that world.

Surely those connections were never afforded to the son of a Jewish tie salesman. Don's father never expected him to have lunch at the Pierre, the old Mortimers, or the newer Daniel's. And to this day, Don's father continued to give him advice on the very same subject. It bothered Don's father. It was hard for him to accept the lifestyle that went with the Fifth Avenue trappings. In a way it made him uncomfortable, and almost pushed his relationship with Don to that of estrangement.

"Stop showing off. You can get a good lunch sandwich at the Carnegie Deli. If you don't want to walk over there, you can go to Wolf's on 57th. You know, Wolf doesn't own it anymore. He builds 'em up and sells 'em. That's what he does. The corned beef suffers a little with that kind of switchin' around. Now you ain't in that kind of business. That's what's good about your business. You're protected from that sort of thing." He could see in Don's eyes that the advice was wasted. Don's father had a need to help, and Don just didn't need his help anymore. Don was made to feel guilty for being successful. It was a classic Catch 22 of the dysfunctional Jewish family. We want you to be successful but not too successful because we also want you to be dependent on us. It was a hard role to fill.

Don's father loved to say "ain't" and other slang words to make his point. "Coin your money. Don't waste it on any friggin' restaurants." That was the topper.

On many occasions, Don would reply that he and his three partners had an expense account that was part of the budget. They also had a retirement account where money was allocated into a tax-deferred account. Expensive lunches were part of the life. They had to entertain. Sometimes just be seen.

Don put away over $400,000 in the last five years. He could have put away more, but he went on a spending spree with Linda. Cars, vacations, clothes, and Cristal Champagne. Linda would only drink Cristal. There were endless long weekends to Atlantic City, North Miami, Stockbridge, Tanglewood, and of course, the Hamptons, an area Don dreaded and Linda loved. That was the big number. The summer rental. Chessman had his own house. Linda insisted that the Gardners get a foothold in the Hamptons. Someday they planned to "buy in". All someone had to do was mention an "in" vacation spot and Linda wanted to go. "Just for a little weekend," she would coo while stroking Don's penis.

Dysplasia

∞

"Her timing is impeccable," Don would joke to Kronen. The "little weekends," never cost less than $2000 if airfare was involved. If they went by car, it was always cheaper, but Linda would make up for it by buying some expensive bric-a-brac. Don and Linda would often leave on Friday morning, sometimes driving back early Monday, dropping Don off at the hospital in time for morning rounds.

His very first year he netted $95,000 in income after taxes and expenses. After his health club membership, two deductible trips, one to Acapulco, where he lectured to the Connecticut State Society of Obstetricians, and one to Atlanta, where the American Association of Obstreticians had their annual meeting. After hundreds of two-hour lunches where Don would sit with Chessman and his partners and listen to horrendous jokes, plan strategies, and at every single luncheon meeting, watch Chessman consume no less than two martinis with exactly four onions. "On the same skewer." This often took some humorous explaining if the waiter didn't understand the drink order.

Sometimes he would order a skewer of onions on the side, but never in the drink. He still called it a martini even though he asked for extra vermouth. No one ever told Chessman that he was drinking Gibsons. He wasn't receptive to this type of learning. It was a clue to the man's character, a small but evident failing. He wouldn't want the new information. Don's father was just like Chessman. If someone presented information that would refute his point of reference, both would become angry and dismiss the invading party with a profanity. Chessman's favorite was a plain, simple "go fuck yourself." He would utter it slowly, with all the charm of someone saying, "I love you." He would flash his pearly bonded teeth and blow a kiss through his pursed lips.

Like the referring doctors, Don's father preferred his son to be poor, hungry, eager, and humble his whole life. Every time Don would say something positive about his income, his father would change the subject back to where Don should go for the good corned beef or the ever-present charmer, "You don't call your mother as often as you used too. She worries about you a lot. And the shiksa too." Don's father thought he accepted Don's wife, but by calling her "the shiksa," it hardly made her part of Don's family.

In the beginning of his marriage, everyone in Don's family made an effort to be friendly to Linda, her mother, and stepfather. The beginning lasted about one year. Some families have nothing in common, and this was a classic case. The Thanksgiving dinners were painful and staid. The forced "Happy Chanukah" juxtaposed the somewhat uncomfortable "Merry Christmas". Linda's stepfather still pronounced the "Ch" with a strong accent, as in "charmed". Don thought he did it on purpose.

When Don turned the corner on East 61st street a gust of wind found its way under his new Aquascutum topcoat and all wool Zegna suit jacket with matching vest, and shot a chill up his behind. He felt a cold spot. He envisioned it where his ancestor's prehistoric tail used to be located. Maybe that's why it was more susceptible to cold.

Once more he thought about the money. It caused him to smirk. He shouldn't complain. He was earning it and he was spending it. He wasn't going entirely wild with the money. His wife wanted a new Mercedes, "like Hank's, with twelve cylinders." She unhappily had to settle for Don's six year old BMW, a savings of over $100,000. Lately she was lobbying for an Infiniti or Lexus. The moneyed crowd was lining up for Lexuses like they were obligated. The Jews adopted the Lexus along with the Polo insignia.

Don tried to convince himself that he hadn't hung around for the money. But he was human, and he knew the money was a big influence. It had to be the money. The rush of being called "doctor" wore off years ago. The flirtatious encounter with patients, the best tables in restaurants, frontrow seats at Knicks games behind Woody Allen, had all worn off. He was staying for the money. At least he admitted it to himself. He would have to come to terms with his own character if he were ever going to resolve his negative feelings about his practice. Otherwise his life would remain the same. He would continue to drift through life ignoring his inner instincts, lost in the common sea of complacency.

Don looked at his watch as he moved past the front of his building. He waved to the white-gloved doorman, Pierre Dessieux, who loved to say, "Pierre's corner is across from the Pierre." He meant the hotel. Across the street on the same side of the avenue. Pierre guarded the entrance to the building with a quiet dignity and noticeable authority. It was his corner. He took pride in his job. He wore the uniform of the building, a brown service suit with cadet styled hat, and a heavy, matching brown topcoat with a fake fur collar. The hat came down low on his forehead. The shiny brim masked part of his nose. He looked like he might be part of the honor guard in some wealthy third world nation. In a strange way, he was. The Fifth Avenue honor guard.

Don thought it odd that his patients would pass by the white-gloved doorman only to be faced upstairs, perhaps only a few minutes later, by another man wearing gloves. It gave the building its own sterile look. The stone flooring always sparkled. Even on a cloudy day, the metallic chips imbedded in the stone would glisten. The perfect slabs were bordered by chrome instead of darker mortar.

Don liked to take a quick look at the brass address plate. It reassured him each time he entered the building that he was at the top of his profession. 799 Fifth Avenue. Just off the corner. There was one ground floor space with its own entrance. The rent was so high that only an art gallery with megabucks could afford the space. It seemed like they never sold anything. Chessman was often inside negotiating the prices anyway, hoping to "get a deal", because "you never know whose shoe is hurting." Chessman could embarrass anyone in his company when he became Chessman the great white horse trader. Don felt the gallery people secretly mocked him when he was in the gallery. Don wondered if Chessman knew it. After getting to know Chessman, it was apparent that no one could hurt his feelings. There were no feelings to hurt. Not when it came to getting a deal. The public Chessman was immune from personal pain of any kind.

The residential part of the building was filled with a mix of the rich and famous. A famous Hollywood manager owned two top floor condominiums. A few of his clients sought health care in the building, making the early morning elevator trips a who's who of Hollywood. It was rumored that Donald Trump once lived in the building on the same floor with Tom Brokaw.

Don was a few blocks further up Fifth Avenue, in the higher 800 numbers. Snow was beginning to fall. Don proudly flipped up his large Aquascutum collar and moved the famous patterned scarf over the collar. He became the walking model for the winter look. His only regret was that passersby could not see the matching pattern on the coat lining. He liked clothes again. He had become fond of three piece suits, outfits he hadn't worn since he was about four. Chessman had done a fine job of molding Don from a part time doctor, to a full time medical animal with all the frills.

Don was an Associate Professor at Columbia University, a very impressive perk to go with his hospital appointment at Morningside Hospital Center. Prestige was flung at him as soon as Chessman got him under his wing. It happened quickly, just after Don signed a long-term partnership agreement in which Don's income would increase each year based on a complicated series of staggered payments and bonuses. It was not unlike that of a professional athlete. Instead of yards rushing, Don's bonuses were based on things like performing new surgeries on the uterine lining to prevent the spread of cancer. Medical offices worried about "production," the same way that Chrysler or Apple did. The more procedures, the more money. Costs were calculated to the penny, supplies were "rationed" in accordance with fees, and each member of the practice received a bimonthly production breakdown, complete with net cost of their individual activity as a percentage of the entire practice.

When a new laser device became available for use in the office, Chessman insisted that the practice buy it. The office had the best equipment in the world. As soon as the accountants amortized the cost, Chessman would raise fees. The patients covered all the increases.

"Insurance will pay us $900 for each time you zap 'em in the pussy with this thing." He said "pussy" because he knew it irritated his partners. "We all know the bullshit statistics on these dysplasia deals. Let's make your cut fifty-fifty. Get in there and clean up those nasty pussy cells. The world will be a safer place when you're through."

"Hank," Lou would moan. Lou knew Chessman for a long time. He knew Chessman thought the misogynist remarks were meant to be funny. "Come on."

Chessman always followed up these remarks with a laugh from deep inside his bowels, a somewhat hideous laugh against everyone and everything. That's one of the things Don could not stand about Chessman. In private Chessman was a classic misogynist. He probably hated women. Socially, Chessman knew how to charm everyone, including women, and he knew which women would tolerate his "good ol' boy" vulgarities. He seemed to get away with it, despite the fact that Don thought he really meant a lot of what he said about women. It was remarkable that a man like Chessman would choose OB-GYN for his specialty.

Don discussed his pop psychology theories with Linda. Maybe Chessman was getting even with women through his work. It gave him power over them. Control of their sex lives. They went over all the obvious ones.

In the early days, Chessman could make Don laugh with vulgar speeches. It came off as cheap locker room stuff. If only he wasn't a women's doctor. Chessman was actually a funny man, a man who was as much at home having cocktails at the Kissingers' or sitting on the dais at a celebrity roast at the Friars Club. Chessman was there when they went after little Jerry Stiller. Jerry wasn't a big fan of the word "fuck" or any jokes that used that word or anatomical slang. The group let him have it. Chessman roared.

Chessman was also a good businessman. He knew he had to get the best of everyone, never admitting that he might have the upper hand. He always complained about business, citing that production had to pick up, complaining to his partners about their huge malpractice costs, and always making his partners feel guilty for taking a nickel out of the office. It was quite a trick to pull off, and Chessman did it. One time Chessman agreed to reduce a fee for a long standing "friend", someone who sent Chessman several wives and girlfriends. Chessman looked him in the eye and said, "Okay. But I'm not making a dime on this." Everyone knew Chessman was wealthy. Especially his friend. It was just the idea that Chessman could say it.

Don was getting a percentage of collections on most of his "in office" billings, the rest going to the "office" for expenses. The more work he did, the more money he made, and the more money the office made. Don realized that he was doing most of the laser procedures, and that his production was well above the national average. He would rationalize it by thinking they were the most capable. Better than the rest of the country. It didn't take Don long to realize that they did more procedures simply because they had the machine.

Dysplasia

There wasn't anything illegal about doing the extra procedures. It was a recognized procedure from the American Medical Association. Don was encouraged to recommend the procedure, both from a standpoint of better safe than sorry, and also to protect himself and his partners from being sued for not offering the new procedures. That's how medical practice evolved during the last part of the century. Many extra procedures were introduced under the guise of prevention. The new work increased liability. Protecting yourself went right along with protecting the patient.

Don had become the same kind of elitist he made fun of when he was in school, the artificial egalitarian, helping the world, while filling up his own pockets. It was beginning to creep up on him, in ways that made him very uncomfortable.

Lately, Don was having bizarre nightmares. The scariest one took place in Disneyland. Linda sat by his side. They were riding on Space Mountain, the indoor roller coaster that shoots the rider around the rails like a marble in a Rube Goldberg device. Suddenly the lights go on, and Don is standing naked on top of the ride. His hands are covered with blood and human tissue. Everyone is laughing at him.

"I had to do it. She needed a radical." Even in that nightmare, Chessman made it sound like he saved Linda.

Don sees his wife laying lifeless on the rail beside him. A large black circle covers the area where Don had performed the surgery, the kind they use on the evening news to block out part of a person or thing.

"I can fix it," shouts Don as he moves closer to his wife.

Don kneels next to the black circle, but he sees only a dark void.

Linda is gone. Her body is replaced by Chessman. Chessman is sprawled out nude from the waist down. His hands support his erect penis. The top of Chessman's penis is covered with a jack-in-the-box-styled clown head. It bobs back and forth as Chessman flagellates himself in a rhythmic ritual.

"I'm ready for you," gurgles Chessman. "I'm all yours!"

"No. No more," shouts Don. "You botched another surgery."

Don jumps over the protective frame, doomed to tumble and splatter as soon as his body hits the twisted rails. He sees himself bouncing to his death. Now would be a good time to fly. He tries to fly, but keeps falling. He screams and wakes up in a cold sweat.

CHAPTER TWO

⚭

The entrance to Dr. Stu Beitleman's office was a few steps down and to the left of the residential entrance. It was one of many buildings on Fifth Avenue that housed the medical elite of the world. It was a compact linear presentation that served no function other than making it easy for the office managers to give directions to patients.

"We're right across from the park. Two blocks up from your gynecologist." Not that any of their high paying patients would have anything to do with Central Park. Perhaps three generations ago, their grandparents might have planned a visit to the doctor with a stroll in the park on the same day. Most of the patients came by taxi. The upper crust would be driven either in a privately owned vehicle or one of the many "chauffeured sedan" services. The older money might still use the old family limo, a bare-bones extension of the basic yet historic Fleetwood. Paranoia mixed with harsh doses of reality saw the Fleetwood limos and old Rolls Royces all but disappear from doctor's row. Manhattan still had its share of fancy cars, but most of them belonged to dot-com investors from Wall Street or some rich Generation X kids that thought of sports cars as bracelets for the ass. Every time Chessman saw a new Ferrari double parked outside the office, he would look at Pierre and say "computer nerd." Pierre would always laugh and nod in agreement.

Stu had plans to expand his office, renaming it Uptown Integrated Health Care. It would include doctors who just did laser surgery and liposuction all day. Stu was even negotiating to lease space to a well-known cosmetic dentist. Stu knew he needed to do more procedures for cash, procedures that were not covered by insurance. Stu's waiting room was always filled with a well-groomed crowd and enough cell phones, beepers, and laptops to open an electronics store.

Don walked inside the opulent setting. The office was packed. At that time of year, there were usually six or seven parties to go to each week, sometimes two or three in one evening.

Stu Beitleman was one of the best referral sources for Chessman, Benjamin, Gross, and Gardner, P.C., a Professional Corporation. Stu was extremely young to be so successful, and Chessman made a point of telling Don to "kiss his ass in Macy's window if Stu asks you." Don replied quickly with "it's not his ass he'd like kissed." Don pointed to his penis to make sure Chessman got his point. Chessman replied without hesitation. "I don't care how you bring in the business, so long as you bring in the business. You might like it." It was said with Chessman's way of making his remarks appear funny, even though there was nothing funny about his intentions. It was abundantly clear that Stu Beitleman meant a great deal to the Chessman practice. That was another small adjustment the partners made. Chessman was the focal point. The main partner. Many doctors also called the group "the Chessman group" or "the Chessman office."

Chessman and Beitleman were as different as day and night. Stu Beitelman was a much younger man. He dressed in a gregarious but stylish fashion. The common appeal for each other had to be bound up in the fact that they were both business animals. Both had created themselves. Chessman was born in the Bronx, but only referred to his childhood in a more upscale area named "Riverdale". Riverdale was

Dysplasia

North of Mosholou Parkway and Pelham Parkway, where Chessman actually spent his youth. He was from the same "neighborhood" as Calvin Klein and Ralph Lauren. Chessman's father was a bank guard, a "security analyst for a major bank."

Beitelman went even further in inventing himself. He had diplomas made up from universities in case reporters reviewing his books would ever challenge his background. His book jacket bios were full of lofty academic credentials. Occasionally, a knowing colleague would force the issue of Stu's strange habit for falsifying his credentials. It was usually someone jealous of Stu. Stu was on the fast track. He was way ahead of the rest. He knew he had to make the jump from local obscurity to national fame. Underneath it all, Stu was colder and more calculating than anyone thought. He thought nothing of inventing extra credentials. What difference did it make whether he had an extra postdoctoral degree from Harvard? The information was used in "harmless" media publicity packets. Background checks went no further than the top line publicity firms did, and Stu used the best. Stu got caught once by an overzealous health columnist for the *New York Post*. Stu defended himself on *Good Morning America*. The segment made it appear that Stu was being picked on. Stu had a way to embrace the camera. "I did attend the medical postdoctoral program at Harvard. So the publisher called it a degree. Well, isn't it?" It was a summer session. Stu was right. Who really cared? The public loved his books. The book sold nearly one million copies and Stu was on the talk show circuit for months. Stu became very famous, very fast, and acted the role. He loved it. If Stu weren't a doctor, he would have done something in the entertainment business, possibly taking the job of one of the talk show hosts that interviewed him. Stu loved to go on Regis and Kathie Lee. Stu went toe to toe with Regis. The segments were funny. At the same time, he would plug his "how to stay healthy books," including the first, *The Macro Power Diet*.

The minor problem of the day was that Stu staged his holiday party the same night as did the Chessman office. They staggered the times by one hour. This caused a logistical problem. The parties could go on simultaneously, but the Chessman group had to attend both parties.

Chessman did nothing to help with any function, anywhere, anytime. Not only a great white doctor, but he was also a great white delegator, a master at avoiding any kind of detailed work. Tonight was no exception. Chessman felt his only job at holiday time was to show up. The rest was left to his partners.

Chessman was already at Stu's party. Don was assigned to fetch Chessman. Don had to tell Stu that he was brilliant, then get Chessman out of the party and back to 799 Fifth where Lou Benjamin and Harvey Gross were nervously holding the fort. It was a small pain in the ass, but Stu came first, and he knew it. Stu was quite the power broker. He was always out on the town with the celebrity of the moment. He could walk into Elaine's whenever he wanted and be guaranteed a good dinner. He often sat with Elaine, blabbing away at the table. Everyone liked Stu. He spoke as if he loved his listener, and perhaps he did. Unlike Chessman, Stu's connections ran deeper into the art and entertainment world.

The party at 799 Fifth was just getting underway. Lou Benjamin stood near the door and greeted the early arrivals. The first ones at these parties were usually the interns, who were always hungry, and the nurses that worked in the same building. They came straight from work. Lou loved to wear bow ties and button-down sweater vests. It was his trademark. Tonight was no exception. A bright red bow tie. A green vest with cables. A herringbone jacket with elbow pads. His handlebar moustache was waxed to sculptured perfection. Outdoors, he wore English trench coats and newspaper delivery boy caps.

Dysplasia

Lou kept his character flaws masked. There was only one exception. Lou was a drinker. He wasn't a fall-down drunk, but he was a pro. He was discreet and well informed about his tastes in alcohol. "Anyone can drink. If you drink, learn to enjoy it. Find out what you like. Pick them out carefully and they will be your friends." That was the advice Lou gave Don after the first partner's lunch. It came after the second round of martinis. Don was stunned. Surgery in the afternoon after martinis? Despite Lou's taste for adult drinks he was probably the best-liked OB-GYN in town. Don was in denial about Lou being an alcoholic. If Don used the definitions flashed on late night television by those small, private hospitals looking to seduce borderline people into treatment, everyone who wasn't a teetotaler was a drinker. The questions covered a broad base.

"Do you think about what type of drink you will have, later in the day?"

"Do you ever have a drink when you feel you need to calm down?"

"Do you feel you can't talk to strangers at a party without having a drink?"

Don usually answered yes to at least half-a-dozen questions. It was harder to make that judgment for Lou. Don wasn't home at Lou's every night. On the rare occasion where Don would see Lou at night, he would watch Lou and Elaine consume a bottle of scotch. Don had two or three shots before waltzing downstairs to get a cab home.

A bad side to Lou didn't exist. "Lou's a mensch" was the frequent comment when his name came up at meetings. That's how his peers referred to him. That's what the inner core thought about Lou. Lou was basically a nice man. It was a good reputation to have in New York circles. Most successful practices needed a doctor like Lou. He was the real cornerstone of the practice. Without Lou the office would unravel. Lou was much smarter than Chessman when it came to the nuts and bolts of OB-GYN.

"What's he doing with Chessman?" was runner up for the next most-frequent comment.

Lou functioned, as one of the referral sources was fond of saying, "as Chessman's shadow." Lou was comfortable in his position in the practice. Of course, so was Chessman. Lou was folded into Chessman perfectly. A dessert chef could not have folded the ingredients for an elegant soufflé any better. All small businesses had similar "partner" relationships. There was always a partner who really worked for the partnership. A tireless worker bee who didn't make waves. That was Lou. He knew it. There was no way he could ever have reached this level of practice on his own. Chessman was never shy about reminding him. He also functioned as Chessman's conscience, although most of the time he was bullied into going along with Chessman's decisions. Lou liked money and perks like the rest of the partners. Whatever moral underpinning Lou had, it wasn't strong enough to buck Chessman in any way.

Lou was a tall man with an abnormally large shock of reddish brown hair. It curled forward over his brow, courtesy of some hair club or some other new hair thing for men. Lou tried them all. Lately, he was using a spray material that he bought from Ron Popeil's company, the one that ran endless infomercials to sell its wares. Lou had a great sense of humor, particularly about himself.

"I got a great deal. I bought the hair material, the broiler, the pasta maker, and the new Popeil pocket fisherman. And you should see all the stuff Ron threw in. I got such a deal!" He emphasized the name "Ron" as if they were pals.

Lou was always changing his hair. His wife Elaine, a former singer turned rabbinical student, had problems being married to a bald man. Lou was created through a vision she had for him. That vision did not include a shiny scalp. Lou refused surgery to correct his lack of fur on the skull. He would have to hear his wife harangue him in front of his partners.

"I talked to Stu Beitleman and Stu said it was the easiest thing in the world. He'll do a scalp reduction and a series of plugs. You'll look great." Elaine wouldn't give up.

Plus Stu wouldn't charge them. Even though they were well-off financially, this still pleased Elaine. Lou was tempted to have the procedures done once he found out it was going to be free. The Benjamins could certainly afford the extra money. They lived in a simple one-bedroom apartment in the East 80s. It was rent controlled. Lou was proud of the fact he was able to save so much money. He was the opposite of Chessman. Chessman loved to spend, to collect, and to show off. Lou got pleasure out of being penurious.

Lou was comfortable leading a modest existence, by New York City standards for Great White Doctors. With the proper guidance from Chessman, Lou was a fairly well-known clinician. Lou had great skill and talent as a doctor. He also had a key ingredient that was missing in Chessman, although Chessman worked hard at masking his deficiency. The two complemented each other's styles in a way that worked well for marketing the practice. Lou was passionate about his work and was always reading the medical journals for any piece of information that might help him with his ability to practice. Lou could hold his own at meetings and annual scientific conventions. In contrast, Chessman had not read a journal article for over twenty years. Before computers, he assigned the residents at the hospital the task of making synopsis cards as part of their didactic course work. It was a common practice since the residents had to read so many articles. Chessman was content with the summaries. Chessman wasn't just a taker. He took the young residents out to lavish dinners, often leaving an open check at the bar even after leaving the restaurant. Chessman wasn't the only clinician who didn't read the journals. Lou was trying to teach Chessman to use the Internet. Abstracts were available online. If a question came up, Chessman had Lou retrieve the article from the Internet sources. A copy was left on Chessman's desk. He could phone back whomever he wanted to impress and throw in a little zinger. "By the way. Did you happen to see the article on cervical dysplasia in the NEJ?" (The New England Journal of Medicine.) He read off the abstract as if he was trying to recall the details.

Chessman had Lou to keep up with trends. Just ask Lou. Lou would fill Chessman in on the pertinent details, not just the articles, but politics and general gossip. Chessman was conversant on a decent level, good enough for professional society meetings. Chessman could fool a large percentage of doctors because they didn't read the new literature either. Chessman was smart enough to have people do it for him.

He also functioned as the peacemaker of the group. If Lou was the peacemaker, then Harvey Gross was the troublemaker, a very subtly styled troublemaker.

Harvey had a way of mumbling something in conversation and then say "forget it." Harvey still counted pennies, nickels, and dimes. He wanted the whole world to be balanced. It drove him crazy that the books never balanced, that Chessman would borrow hundreds of thousands of dollars from the group's pension fund, eventually pay it back without interest, and then write himself a new loan the next week. Chessman was always three paychecks ahead of the other guys. Harvey would say "that's not fair" and Chessman would swat him away like a fly by saying, "Life isn't fair. I need money. You live like a fucking monk or some derelict. What do you need money for?"

Don hoped that Harvey had some secret plan about retiring young. Then all of Harvey's behavior would make sense. Otherwise, Harvey was a pain in the ass. He was always worried about some insignificant detail of the practice, like the cost of local anesthetic carpules, the tiny glass containers that stored the anesthetic.

Harvey was more than ten years older than Don. He probably already had enough money to retire to an island paradise. But Harvey was locked more firmly into his life than Don could imagine. Harvey was another prisoner of New York City. Harvey only knew work. The single way to keep track of how much work he had done was to see how much money he had saved.

Unlike Harvey, Lou would look the other way as long as he got his check twice a month. Lou never questioned the amount and never asked to see the books. He shared one personal accountant with Chessman, something Don could never figure out. He guessed it was easy in some way for them.

Harvey was the machine of the practice. This little man with a funny goatee worked tirelessly. He could not sit still. He produced more income for the office than any of the partners, and never once asked that he be given a bigger share of the net money. "I think, therefore I work," was how Chessman would tease Harvey. He knew he was lousy at bringing in business and was satisfied to be the workhorse of the practice. Every good practice in Manhattan needed one. Harvey knew if he was going to be part of the Great White Doctors, he had to offer something other than just good clinical skill. His next best attribute fell in line with his work ethic. He was a good foot soldier. He never questioned anything. However Chessman voted, he would vote too. He came to the office early, didn't leave for lunch, and left late. Yet if asked, a nurse or one of the partners couldn't recall if he had hours in the office on a particular day. With Harvey there wasn't any small talk. A joke was taboo. Fooling around was not tolerated, at any level. Even to Don, Harvey was a bore.

Harvey's third best attribute was his willingness to focus on tiresome chores that were practice related but boring, like keeping track of all the employee healthcare expenses. Because of his accountant-like prowess, Harvey was the practice party planner. In other offices the responsibility was often shunted off to one of the wives. Harvey took pride in organizing the party his way. "Most of our guests don't know the difference between gravlax and belly lox. We don't need imported cheese 'doodles' on the trays. After a drink or two, all the food will taste fine." Harvey beamed when he reported the party costs to Chessman. Lou would remark privately to Don that "Chessman gave him the usual pat on the head and Harvey scampered off."

Even by party time Harvey was still checking. He nervously counted the number of jazz musicians, as if they would bother to short change the number from five to four. One was in the office powder room.

Harvey cared a great deal about being cheated. About what was right. It was important to him to let it be known when his morals were being compromised. Fortunately, he took stands on issues that were insignificant to Chessman. The favorite example was Harvey's objection to Chessman "overcharging" the wife of an ex-President. The discussions were endless. Chessman was clear on his position. "Her husband fucked us for eight years when he was in office. Now it's our turn." Even Don, who at that time had only been with the practice a short time, could see that Chessman was humoring Harvey. After verbal battles with Chessman, Harvey would go back to his corner and become the good foot soldier. But with great morals. Don pieced together bits of history about Harvey. Harvey was an ex-hippie who kept veering further and further to the right. One of Harvey's classmates in medical school alluded to the extensive pot parties and magic mushroom nights. It seemed to fit. The only thing Harvey could focus on was work. Maybe he was running from his past. Maybe Harvey didn't like what he had

Dysplasia

∽

become. Whatever the reason, Don felt a certain empathy for Harvey. Both of them were trapped in the practice.

Harvey's frugality made Lou look like a big spender. Harvey's penny pinching bordered on a full blown personality disorder, a disorder for which Chessman suggested he seek treatment. Harvey lived down in the 20s, "twenty-tird, near tird," above a Greek coffee shop. After passing through a vestibule that featured the urine stench of the month, it was a short trip up a flight of stairs. Chessman always asked Harvey if he charged rent to the local homeless who often slept in the building's vestibule. It was safe to say that Harvey probably lived in the worst accommodations of any OB-GYN in the city. Even the guys at the Veteran's Hospital lived in newer styled apartments, near First Avenue, that were owned by NYU. Harvey would buy mail order shoes to save ten dollars, which by itself is probably not a bad idea.

Many years ago, and for very little money, Harvey bought the pool house on an old estate near Monticello, New York. It didn't come with the pool. The place was such a dump he could only salvage the foundation and a few walls. For dozens of years he would go there and work his weekends, doing all the work himself. Labor costs were at a minimum that way. The place still needed a lot of work, but there was a usable kitchen and bath.

Harvey tried to rationalize that since he was already paying alimony and child support he couldn't afford to spend extra money. This was the best he could do. His new wife, Marilyn, rarely complained. Marilyn's only concern that conflicted with Harvey's fiscal policies was to have a child. They tried for years. Harvey refused any form of medical intervention. Marilyn had been going in regularly for attempts at in vitro fertilization. These procedures were making her a little edgy, a little hostile. Her lack of success compounded with her pain and suffering made her resent Harvey, his partners, and doctors in general. She had good reason. Even as an "insider", the system was failing her. Don was her treating physician and did the best he could. He also didn't mind listening to stories about the "that little shit Harvey."

Stu's office manger Sherry quickly grabbed Don's matching Aquascutum ensemble. Sherry was Stu's front person. She was good looking, bright, with a figure to match. She knew how to handle everyone. She had been in the trenches for years.

"Nice coat, Doc. Let's see. That's nine Burberrys and seven Aquascutums so far. It looks like it's going to be a good night."

"Hi, Sherry. Merry everything," Don shot back with a forced, close-lipped grin.

Sherry grabbed Don by the arm, "inadvertently" pressing her right, braless breast into Don's arm. "Boy those are firm," he thought. Some women were experts at that little turn maneuver. Sherry was well schooled, particularly with the older doctors. She had some believing they were the objects of her flirtations.

"Come on. We all get the blues during the holidays. Have a drink and then you won't mind all the assholes." Sherry could tell Don was out of sorts.

Sherry released her breast from place. Don was certain she must have had implants. Stu probably did them. He was always doing cosmetic "freebies" for his nurses. It was one of the perks that went with working for Stu. The girls were sometimes "actors" in infomercials, not mentioning that they worked for Stu.

Don liked Sherry. She worked hard for Stu. She was a pro who privately was just as cynical as the rest. It was a game she played well.

Dysplasia

⟨∞⟩

"Thanks, Sherry. I've got to go and do my advertising," Don said as he moved to give Sherry a peck on the cheek.

"I don't have to worry about lip gloss with you. Do I?" she joked.

Don kissed her cheek. "I don't think so."

As Don moved on Sherry teased him with, "Come back if you get bored. You married guys are getting more in demand."

Don acknowledged the remark with a wave. He continued on through the regular mix of the Gucci-shoed elite, who just hours before dressed in lab coats and surgical scrubs. Now, $3000 suits were the uniform. These doctors were equally comfortable in both garbs.

Don looked around the room. He knew many of the familiar faces. His mind reviewed each one as he passed by. "Nice Jewish boy from Flatbush. Nice Jewish boy from Woodmere, Long Island. Nice Italian boy from Valley Stream. Nice Irish Catholic girl from Chelsea." Not one of them resembled their pasts. Each one started out in a similar way. Just like Don. Parents thrilled at the prospect of having a doctor in the family. At least one parent offered unconditional love, while the other complained that the premed student had little time to work and therefore couldn't contribute to high tuition expenses. When it was all over, a strange thing happened. The new doctor could no longer relate to the role of "Nice whatever from wherever." Then the loving parent felt betrayed, while the more cynical ran around screaming, "We're not good enough for him anymore."

He passed by Kyle Bixler, a sweet, charming alcoholic plastic surgeon who loved to joke about his success. He was one of the well liked. But not by his father. Kyle's father worked long shifts at the old Delmonicos. The Bixlers lived above a bar frequented by Kyle's bullying father. The day he graduated from medical school, Kyle laid his father out flat following the usual exchange of harsh words. "I got him that one time. Up against his yearly Christmas beatings. He never spoke to me after that."

Kyle was a career American Medical Association politician. He would serve on any committee that would have him. "Providing there is an adequate cocktail hour included prior to each dinner meeting." Kyle wasn't shy about his lifestyle. He was a delegate to the AMA from the silk-stocking district in New York. Even though he was actually one of Stu's competitors, Stu invited him to the party anyway. A lot of doctors were paranoid when it came to competition, including the big corporations, HMOs, and local hospitals. Not Stu. He was the most secure doctor Don had ever met.

"Hey, Kyle. How's your stock in Corning doing?" Don said as he poked his fist gently into Kyle's roly-poly belly. It was a deliberate dig, alluding to a breast implant fiasco.

"I never buy stock in medical products. Who knows what kind of crap they make those things out of?" Kyle toasted Don. Then sipped his drink.

"So what kind of implants are you putting in?" Don asked the question much the same way a straight man sets up another comedian.

"I don't know. Whatever the detail guy sells me at discount. Isn't that how you do it?" Kyle said slowly, with a twinkle in his eye.

Don knew what he meant because the only materials Kyle could use were approved by the FDA Only the richest, most successful companies had any hope or interest in selling new materials to doctors.

"How's business?" Don asked. It was a common matter-of-fact remark.

"Same old shit. The young girls are knocking down the door. You should come with me some night to Pure Platinum and Scores. I've got over twenty pairs of dancing titties jiggling on the stage on any given night. You know I could show you where I close my cases so there's no visible scar. You'd have to get real close." This time Kyle poked Don in the stomach. The two laughed. Don didn't mind sharing a cheap chauvinist laugh with Kyle. Kyle liked women. He took good care of his patients. Don wished he felt the same way about Chessman.

"I'm a happily married man," said Don. "What a lie," he thought.

"Do you think I was implying anything that would breach your sacred vows?"

"No thanks. Tittie bars aren't my thing," added Don. He didn't want to insult Kyle. "You enjoy it."

"Then I drink to you," said Kyle as he raised his glass high in the air to begin one of his occasionally hysterical attempts at humor. "To my friend, Dr. Don Gardner. A man who has compromised his own existence by spending his life during the day inside the same cavern of joy he has to go home to at night, and then show respect with his tongue. God bless you, my son. I couldn't put my tongue in there after a hard day at the orifice."

"And Merry Christmas to you, Kyle." Don extended his hand. Kyle took it, squeezing firmly. Don didn't mind the sophomoric teasing. The higher up in medicine, the lower the humor. Don had to mingle before getting Chessman back to his office party.

"Have a nice Chanukah, boytshik," Kyle said with a sweet sincerity. The kind that always accompanied his third or fourth martini.

It was not unusual to hear more Yiddish expressions from the non-Jews than the Jews. Don took it as something that seemed particularly indigenous to New York, not unlike the actors in Hollywood who learned Yiddish even though they weren't Jewish. By that time Don had adjusted to it. He never questioned a non-Jew's interest in speaking Yiddish words. He simply felt it was a New York thing, even though a part of him still felt that some used the words with a patronizing quality. It went with the territory.

Don tossed from group to group. He kept his eye on the corner of the room—there stood Dr. Henry "call me Hank" Chessman. Chessman was a very handsome man, about six feet tall with dark hair and chiseled features. In a room of one hundred men, Chessman could easily be picked out as the best looking. He knew it and always used it to his best advantage. Even though he began putting on weight last year, he still caught the eye of the women who allowed themselves the politically incorrect luxury of scanning the room to see who was available. Lou loved to call Chessman "the Jewish Cary Grant." Chessman admitted to being "near sixty." Chessman's driver's license had one age while his professional bios had others.

Chessman's gold collar bar glistened as he jerked his head and neck around, craning to be sure everyone else in the room knew he was there. He was holding court, surrounded by a few young residents, a few doctors' wives, and several actors who Don didn't immediately recognize. Don assumed they were Chessman's friends from the current Broadway shows. Don had heard the stories many times, how Chessman would stay up all night, hitting Backstage, Charlies, and Joe Allens. The name-dropping was endless. Chessman was one of the original investors in *Fiddler on the Roof.*

Don checked his watch. He excused himself from chatting, careful to make sure he would get Chessman back to the office in time for a reasonable "photo op."

As he got closer to Chessman, now within earshot, he could hear Chessman telling one of his stock jokes. "My partner Lou was travelling on an airline next to a priest. The priest spent most of the trip doing a crossword puzzle. About halfway through the puzzle, the priest turned to Lou, and said, 'I need a four-letter word that ends in "unt". The clue is "woman."' Lou cringed. He couldn't say a bad word like that to the priest. What kind of crossword puzzle was he doing? Finally it hit Lou. '"Aunt," he shouted. "Aunt," he repeated.' He spelled the letters out loud. The priest looked puzzled. He turned to Lou and asked, 'Do you have an eraser?' A big laugh went up around Chessman. Don didn't know how he did it. It was a horrible antiwomen joke. At Stu's party? Why? But

Dysplasia

Chessman knew how to get away with it. Don hated that part of Chessman. Don had never heard Chessman tell the joke in public. He usually told all of his harsh four-letter-word jokes to smaller groups. Two or three old cronies in the corner of a cocktail party. A power lunch with his partners present.

Don recognized several of the foreign doctors as one of them tried to explain the joke to two others. They actually paid to follow Chessman around the city. Thousands of dollars were charged in advance to watch Chessman at the office and hospital. All with hope of learning how to be a Hank Chessman. It was a foolish endeavor, because the man was one of a kind. At that moment Don felt revulsion for Chessman. He wanted to warn the people to run away. Not laugh. Not coddle. Not be entertained. Chessman was evil.

Don's eyes met Chessman's. At that moment Don wanted to run away. He wished he had never met Chessman. He knew at that moment that he could no longer stomach Chessman. Don wasn't sure if hatred was the right word. He saw Chessman as a sick, perverse, cruel and malicious man, a man who probably hated all women. And yet he was a famous hero to thousands of them.

"Hey, Junior. Did you get my shirts back from the cleaners?" Another laugh for Chessman. The foreign doctors acted like Chessman was Jerry Seinfeld. Chessman always knew where and when he could be cruel. A master salesman. A master great white doctor.

"Okay, Hank. Have you seen Stu?" Don asked to end their very brief exchange. Don hated to call Chessman "Hank."

"I think he's buried in the back somewhere. I think he was trying to corner your wife." No laugh that time. It didn't translate as easily.

"As if that gay caballero had any interest in Linda," thought Don.

Chessman half nodded, indicating he was aware of his time constraints.

Sometimes at parties Stu would overdo it. Usually if he were around friends. Stu could play the part so far out that one of his friends once told him that he was getting bored. It was at a Chinese restaurant on the Upper Eastside, a birthday party for Stu. Don was in attendance with his partners. The friend stood up and threw his napkin down in the Moo Shoo Chicken.

Stu loved the attention. He was nonstop all night. Joking. Mugging. Flirting. Kissing.

"Stu, if you're going to act like a fag all night, I'm going home now." The friend said it as if he had been through the routine before.

Stu eventually diminished the act, but not before staging a funny mock fight. Stu challenged his friend with an angry Katharine Hepburn followed by a provocative Mae West, complete with the pickle-in-a pocket gag. When his friend was totally exasperated, Stu got up and grabbed a dessert tray from one of the waiters. He waltzed around the room serving everyone, yelling, "You likey dessert?" When the waiter tried to stop him, Stu gave the puzzled Chinese waiter a big kiss on the cheek. The situation was easily rectified when Stu pulled a hundred-dollar bill from his pocket and offered it to the waiter.

"Catch you later." Don slipped past the ogling young secretaries. Heads twisted to keep an eye on the door.

"Is that the actress who was in the movie with Arnold Schwarzenegger?" one girl asked the other in complete starstruck awe. Of course it was. They were on Fifth Avenue, where famous doctors mingled with movie stars. Several of the entertainment celebrities, politicians, and businessmen were there because of Chessman. They would attend both parties too.

Executives from drug companies also showed up. Chessman was a powerful political figure in the national societies. He had helped many research doctors and companies market their wares, providing Chessman got "my small piece of the action." Chessman made a career out of keeping in touch with anyone who had money, for any reason.

Dysplasia

෴

He didn't care how you got it, so long as you still had it. This included former casino owners who were thrown out of Las Vegas for ties with organized crime. Chessman would go out of his way to take them to "21" when they were in town, a restaurant where Chessman was almost as well known as the likes of old regulars like Irving "Swifty" Lazar. Chessman always called him Irving, a sign to Chessman that he was part of the inner circle. When Irving finally died, Chessman flew out to Beverly Hills, staying at the Peninsula one week beyond the funeral date.

Even the Mayor would stop by to pay homage. His wife and daughter were Chessman's patients. Chessman had access to City Hall, dating back to Mayors Wagner and Lindsay. Chessman had just as many friends in politics as he did in small social clubs in Little Italy. "Friends" from the setting sometimes asked Chessman to set up meetings with certain city officials.

A few people connected with the black-caucus Democrats from Manhattan mingled with two squat men in sharkskin suits, pinky rings, and loud $200 ties. Central casting could not have set the scene better.

Many doctors from the hospital were invited to both parties. Don and his partners were involved with teaching. They used the office party to pay their respects to "the fulltime teaching stiffs" and administrators. Chessman had tenure at Columbia University and Morningside Hospital, and was head of the department of Obstetrics and Gynecology. Lou Benjamin was a Research Associate at the Veteran's Hospital and taught at New York University. Harvey Gross taught at New York University and was famous for the record of most birth assists by a part time faculty member.

Stu Beitleman always wore the latest high-fashion clothes. At parties he would add a fashionable carnation to his lapel. Don walked over to Stu. As soon as Stu saw Don approaching, he launched into a tirade of introductions. Don took note that the carnation that evening was a bright Christmas red.

"Ladies, and of course, gentlemen. Here's Don Gardner, boy wonder. He's got the best hands in town. Next to mine of course. Don is delivering more than half of all the babies from my practice. All the girls love him. And guys, take note. He doesn't cheat on his wife. So don't worry." It was easy to like Stu. He was much more humble about his success than Chessman. Tonight Stu came off more like Regis Philbin. When he spoke to the Mayor, Stu launched into an all-butch mode. He was a real talent.

Don worked the room one last time. He looked for unshook hands. If they were going on to Don's party, he would grab them later. A few actors would probably never make the short walk back down Fifth. Stu had a knack for latching onto celebrities. He would engage them in conversations about their health, about his books, and stick on whatever subject worked. After an hour or so of free medical advice, the patient would be well on their way to becoming one of Stu's private flock. Stu was basically a good doctor, because he knew his limits. He was the best at diagnosis and then unfortunately at over treatment. But that's where he drew the line. He hardly did any procedures himself. Stu was trained as a dermatologist, but pretended to be a plastic surgeon. Two board certified plastic surgeons worked with him. Although Stu did take extra surgical training, he rarely got his hands wet. He also functioned as a general medical advisor to the rich and famous. Because of his books and on camera exposure he lifted himself out of the usual corner of being a specialist and made himself an expert on everything medical.

After starting a complicated case, he would use his diagnostic skills to direct the treatment. It usually meant bringing in specialists. Stu knew how to make Stu look like a hero. The nice part was that more than half of the time, Beitleman was actually helping people who were previously not getting the best medical care available. Stu would reach for the extra care, advice, and/or research. This could only happen by keeping abreast of who was doing what and where. The rest of the patients were no better off than before. But many felt better because of Stu's "bedside manner."

Beitleman was forever flying patients around the country so a specific doctor could do a specific procedure on the patient. Most doctors would privately say that what Beitleman did was bullshit. His patients thought he was a deity, and a genius to boot. They gladly paid the bills. Occasionally a disgruntled patient would complain. Some would even sue, but the public never got wind of those cases.

Don excused himself. It was time to get Chessman out of there. Don walked toward Stu.

"Merry everything, Dr. Beitleman!"
Stu grabbed Don's arm and pulled Don aside.
"I have to go to the coast tomorrow. They're having a book party for me in Beverly Hills," Stu said as if it happened every day. "I'd ask you to come with me, but I don't think you're ready for my crowd," he continued with a twinkle in his eye. My crowd could have meant the book-writing, television-appearing, jet-setting great white doctors or it could have simply meant Stu and his bisexual friends. Stu was married for "business reasons", but never traveled with his wife Cindy. With Stu it wasn't so much a matter of which sex, it was more a matter of just plain sex. At least that's how Don perceived Stu.

Cindy was involved in all aspects of Stu's business. She had an MBA from one of the local city colleges and put her knowledge to constant use.

"Beitleman. You're a hoot." Don laughed.

"Listen to me," Stu said as he grabbed Don's arm more tightly. "Don't do anything with the hospital thing until I get back." Stu's voice was firm and direct. The mock tone of seconds ago was gone.

Don was shocked. How could Stu have known anything about the hospital? Don realized he shouldn't have been surprised. Part of him still maintained a naïve approach to business things, even after his tutelage under Chessman.

"Stu. That's none of your business," Don shot back. "And besides, how did you know?"

Stu showed legitimate concern. He liked Don. Beyond that, Stu didn't want to see any disruptions in the Chessman office. Don was part of the referral system. In a way they were all unwritten partners.

"Business is my business. You'd be the biggest schmuck in town if you went around criticizing the hospital program. Chessman is a big shot there. Why would you fuck with it?" Stu looked worried.

"I want to make it better," Don said with all the sincerity he could put into six words.

Stu's words came more slowly. "Listen to me, asshole. Don't rock the boat. Do your deliveries. Work on maxing out your C sections. Stuff your retirement account. Get in and get out and live happily ever after. That's the drill. Business is business."

There was a strong sense of sincerity in Stu's speech. Don trusted Stu to a point.

"Did Hank put you up to this speech?" Don asked.

Now Stu was angry. "I shouldn't have to say this. I think you already know it. But if it's hand holding time, let's go for it. Hank Chessman is not my friend. I don't have to protect Hank Chessman. It's you, you little dickhead, that I'm worried about."

"Why?" was Don's only thought. "I'm one of them."

Stu saw the puzzled "why" expression look on Don's face.

Dysplasia

"Darling. Maybe it's my softer feminine side." Stu poked Don in the side and said, "Go on. Get out of here. Stop trying to fix the world. You're in great shape. Leave things alone. I'd hate to see another break up in your office." Stu was alluding to the fact that Chessman forced out an old partner about the same time Don was brought in.

"Okay," Don answered. He didn't want to take the matter any further. He still felt it was none of Stu's business. Don knew that everything Stu did had a self-serving component. This was no exception.

Don shook Stu's hand. Stu pulled Don close and kissed him on the cheek.

"Merry Christmas," said Stu. He smiled broadly.

"Okay. See you," said Don.

Don looked around for Chessman. He was gone. It figured. Chessman probably saw Stu talking with Don.

Don wondered how Stu knew about the hospital. Or exactly what he knew. Don was planning to complain to the head of the hospital about the short shrift the hospital staff made of the welfare cases. The public sort of suspected that for years. The media was always getting after doctors. But Morningside seemed immune. It was a combination of its great wealth, city history, and spin-doctor administrators.

CHAPTER THREE

The temperature outside had dropped markedly. Don purposely exhaled slowly so he could watch his breath leave his mouth. The streets were almost empty. The newly fallen snow left an inch or two on the sidewalk. The streets were wet with slush, a common New York scene during Christmas week.

Don turned up his collar. Now he was worried. If Stu knew, who else knew? Don's mind raced, trying to figure out the chain of gossip. Stu's wife got wind of it. That's it. Stu's wife had become friends with Harvey Gross's wife. Chessman must have mentioned it to Harvey, in some veiled yet pejorative way. That was Chessman's style. Always get someone else to do the dirty work. That's what Chessman did when he forced his ex-partner out of the office. The poor bastard was cornered in a Starbucks coffee shop early one Sunday morning. Lou was the messenger boy.

"You're out, Sid." That's all Lou said.

The intellectual Sid shook his head and smiled. "Out where? What are you talking about?" Sid had agreed to let his personal attorney work out the differences with the Chessman group's attorney.

"No. Harvey signed, too. That's it." Lou didn't want to hang around. Sid made sport of Lou for nineteen years.

Dysplasia

‿

Sid tried not to show any reaction. He knew that this was certainly a possibility. He also knew that money would change hands, more favorably on Chessman's side. Otherwise, Harvey would never have signed.

"Always the hatchet man, Lou. Not everyone can be a leader." Sid sipped his coffee.

Lou took the last insult in stride. The ex-partners wouldn't talk for years. At meetings, Sid always gave Don a dirty look, making him feel like he had something to do with Sid's leaving the practice. Don did, but not intentionally. Chessman had all the parameters figured in before he lowered the boom on Sid.

That's why it had to be Harvey. Chessman told Harvey what was going on in the hospital. Harvey panicked on cue. His thoughts always ran to the extreme. The gold mine would be shut down. He would be out on the streets, selling fake watches in front of the Plaza Hotel. Harvey immediately presented the information to Marilyn. His fears were embellished. Marilyn contacted Stu's wife Cindy either to commiserate or find out what she knew, or perhaps, and now Don was giving her a lot of credit, hoping Cindy would tell Stu in the belief that he would act as a peacemaker. Cindy had a lot to protect, just like Harvey's wife Karen, but Marilyn was not experienced in business like Cindy.

Cindy was clearly in it for the money. She even made that clear herself, although she made sure whom she told, usually in the form of a tag line to a joke. Marilyn felt an obligation to her husband and to her marriage. Don was sure she didn't view the practice beyond the effect it could have on her own marriage. A lot of the wives felt if anything bad happened to their husband's practice, it would have a direct effect on them. It was logical and realistic. They had seen it happen when partnerships broke up, or one member of a group got into drugs. It could take all of them down a few financial notches. Marilyn was already "living like a damned pauper. Some doctor's life she got." That's how Cindy described it. Marilyn had visions of what Harvey might do if his salary was reduced in any way.

Don thought it through again. It was more obvious the second time around. Chessman first told Stu what Don was planning about the hospital. Stu told Cindy, who blabbed it to Marilyn just to give her a dig. Even for the content Marilyn, the thought of "tightening their belts" put her in a panic. She told Harvey that she was scared, that Don was going to do something that Hank was against, and that was a terrible no-no in her world. Harvey ran to talk with Chessman, the originator of the story. Harvey knew that Chessman knew how to handle it. That's what Chessman wanted. Rile everyone up first. Play on their worst fears. That way nothing ever got out of hand.

Chessman never confronted anyone to take direct action. He would always manipulate someone to take care of it for him. Don's original instinct was correct. Now that he was away from Stu's seductive influence, the scenario was clear. Of course, co-starfucker Stu would do anything for Chessman, friend or no friend. It was business as usual. That's what Stu kept saying. Don felt so naïve. He could hear Chessman's words.

"Stu, you know what to say about these things much better than I do. Don likes you. He has a lot of respect for you. In a way, you've been a better mentor for him than I was. Don is still very young. He's a good man, but this hospital thing is a little out of line. I can't tell him even though the whole office is against it. I wasn't going to say anything, but Harvey is really upset. I haven't told Lou yet. He might drop dead on the spot. See what you can do. You know, let him know it's a bad idea, something like that. I'll leave it to you."

Stu hardly listened. He knew this play. He had seen it before. Business as usual.

Dysplasia

Don took his time walking back to his office. Even though the party was at full throttle, there was no rush. Chessman had always told Don that "nothing starts until we get there, so why rush?" Chessman had that attitude about almost everything, including his own patients. He loved to be late to the office and would deliberately rush through the waiting room, even though there were ample private entrances for the doctors. The patients forgave him when they saw how he was rushing. Even if Chessman was already in the office, and there was a delay for other reasons, he would still use the waiting room. Chessman would pretend he had just arrived. He would put on his outer clothes, exit through a side door, and make his entrance through the waiting room. "One day the same patient is going to see you come in twice," Harvey would comment.

Once in the waiting room, the bullshit would fly from Chessman's mouth. "Sorry. The Vice President's wife flew in this morning. Oh, it's nothing serious. But when duty calls, Dr. Chessman answers the call."

He would save that kind of patter for the older women. That was the crowd he still called "honey" and "sweetheart". No offense was taken. Their generation revered doctors, and despite whatever feminist attitudes they may have adopted as they became older, they still swooned for the likes of Dr. Henry "Call Me Hank" Chessman.

It wasn't clear whether Chessman was more lucky than calculating. Probably a good deal of each. Chessman evolved into an expert on dysfunctional uterine bleeding. This was an area that seemed to be overlooked by most of his colleagues. It was just something that OB-GYN guys took in stride. It was a part of the practice that usually didn't require any special attention. Chessman elevated it into an art form. By self-proclamation, he was probably the world's best authority on the subject. He picked that area because it is usually not life threatening, although it could cause disruption and discomfort to many women. It was naturally a source of great stress and anxiety. Enter the hero, Henry "Call Me Hank, Sweetheart" Chessman.

It was easy to treat. When necessary, Chessman poured on his suave bedside manner. The treatment was relatively simple. There were several nonsteroidal anti-inflammatory drugs (NSAID) that worked great when menstrual bleeding occurred. The drugs had relatively few side effects and usually worked for most cases.

Chessman became a hero simply by writing a prescription for one of the NSAID drugs. Then he followed up with several sympathetic, monitoring phone calls. Chessman was no stranger to house calls. He always alluded to the fact that he carried on sexual relationships with some of his patients. Before leaving, Chessman would make some dumb remark like, "I think she needs Hank's beef probe". The sick laugh followed. Then more of the crass humor. If I'm not back in one hour "tell the fire department to check the heels on my shoes where I left hooks so they can pull me out." Chessman had about a dozen versions of that line that dated back to when he was a child. During these exchanges, Lou had to turn his head away. Lou didn't really think that Chessman was still having sex with any of the patients. Don wasn't as certain.

If the case proved too complicated for Chessman's easy out therapy, he would sometimes combine the dose with some oral contraceptive. It was still a snap, especially if the patient required contraception. It afforded further reduction of menstrual flow.

There was also a surgical alternative. That was Chessman's bread and butter. The hysterectomy. It was a procedure Chessman recommended frequently. He had performed more of these procedures than he would like to admit. He clearly lied about the number of cases when confronted by colleagues. In recent years, overtreatment by hysterectomy

Dysplasia

became a political as well as a practical subject. To sound "politically correct", Chessman proclaimed he was cutting down. There was some truth to the fact that Chessman personally had cut down, but not for medical reasons that benefited the patient. He referred more of the bread-and-butter hysterectomies to Harvey. Harvey did them without question, like the good workhorse.

Don had a more modern approach. Since Don began practicing with the group, an endometrial resection was another option. Don learned it as part of his training. It was unheard of in Chessman's day.

"Bullshit. They'll end up needing a hysterectomy anyway" was how Chessman felt on the subject. He was either too lazy or too disinterested to change his practice patterns.

Chessman was a less-than-average surgeon. Chessman's anatomical acumen was limited to what he originally learned in school. He had forgotten most of it. Little of the background applied since there were actually only a few procedures he could do surgically. Despite concentrating on those few procedures, Chessman's technique was anything but neat or consistent. Don thought Chessman was sloppy at best.

It was a known fact in medical schools that the real klutzes, the guys who had two left hands, and sometimes the grades to match, steered away from surgery. The limitations showed up early. That worked as a general rule of thumb. Of course, there were ways to compensate for being clumsy. A great bedside manner, good looks, and good diagnostic skills. Most doctors who were good looking, had a great bedside manner, and were great diagnosticians, naturally gravitated away from strictly surgery.

Some doctors would never develop surgical skill and were smart to head in different directions early on. Some students with little natural talent stayed on. But they tried to improve by practicing certain procedures over and over again. It gave them better visual-motor coordination for surgery. Some got better and were adequate, so long as they stuck to a rigid technique, while some would always be less than adequate. A few of those would remain sloppy. Chessman's own arrogance led him to be inadequate and sloppy. It seemed like he cared less and less as he got older. He stopped doing hospital work with residents unless they did most of the work.

"Everything heals in the body or it doesn't" was another of his catchy excuses for rushing through a procedure. Many residents got their share of experience working with Chessman. There was plenty of action and plenty of mopping-up work. Chessman had little respect for arteries. The smaller the artery, the more insignificant. Worse, if the patient were a city welfare patient, it was easy to think that Chessman was working on a cadaver in the gross anatomy laboratory rather than a human being.

Don was blessed with an innate ability to perform surgery. The first time Chessman saw him work, Chessman made a calculated assault on Don to get him contractually bound to the Chessman group. Equal partnership followed soon.

"Golden hands," Chessman told Lou. "Let's make a little investment in this guy. Stroke him. You know. Let him know we like him."

Lou did just that. There were dozens of lunches, parties, Knicks tickets near Spike Lee, front-row orchestra seats for any Broadway show. The perks were extended to Don's friends, long before Don finished paying the cash for his share of the partnership.

Don's way of practice was markedly different than Chessman's. Chessman's basic approach was to scare patients with the threat of hysterectomy first. Then he could retreat to his hero position by treating the case easily, with mefenamic acid or indomethacin, two of the common anti-inflammatory drugs. "You have to give them the options. That's what the attorneys say." Chessman was referring to malpractice protocols.

Sometimes when Chessman pressed for a hysterectomy, an informed patient became upset with that course of action. Chessman would flip in a millisecond. He would back off by saying, "Well, you know I'm always researching new avenues for care. I've been in touch with some research scientists at Harvard, who have gotten good results with some of the new anti-inflammatory drugs. It's worth a try."

Chessman knew the show cold. He was as smooth as silk. Chessman would pick up the phone and call Harvard, Sloane Kettering or even China if he felt it would impress the patient. Chessman would hold a conversation with some doctor who was beholden to Chessman. "Yes. I think that's the best way to go. I agree with your idea, but don't you think we should vary the dose, to say, ten milligrams once a day?" He would make up something. Anything to make it sound like he was conferring as an equal with the world-renowned expert. Chessman's dose idea was always better and of course readily acceptable by the expert. "Next time you run your trial studies, try using the dose I use."

Because Chessman was well-known to the older crowd with money, he had a lot of patients over sixty. Chessman's other bread-and-butter procedure was the D & C, the dilation and curettage, a procedure that he routinely performed on patients with postmenopausal bleeding. Chessman always recommended the D & C because, as medical fashion would have it, the tendency was to rely on the results of the D & C rather than plain clinical judgment. Chessman knew where the money was.

It certainly wasn't in delivering babies, although with the invention of the fetal monitoring system, pregnant women were encouraged to stop in the office frequently. At $100 plus a visit, the fetus' heart rate was measured. If a patient was in her 30s, it was once each week, tacking an extra $3,000 to $5,000 to each birth.

Despite his "surgical bread-and-butter work", Chessman hung his clinical hat on cancer. Cancer phobia was a huge business, a business that the Chessman office milked for all it was worth. Frozen sections of tissue were taken out during the D & C and checked to see if there were any indications of malignancy. This was a common starting point for a ton of additional business. It all boiled down to dysplasia. Bad cells. Precancerous cells.

Dysplasia was a bad word that would terrify patients. But it could be cured. If there were areas of dysplasia, there was cause for going in and removing the offending cells. A laser was used to remove the cells. "The zapper" was what Chessman called it. Each "zap" resulting in another fee. If Chessman were in the room during one of these procedures, you could count on the average number of zaps being increased by two or three. Chessman told his patients how thorough he was.

Even if the D & C showed no malignancy, the bleeding often was a sign of more severe trouble. If the patient was obese or had other contributing factors like diabetes, that was enough of an indication for an abdominal hysterectomy.

Sometimes the patient would actually have some stage of endometrial cancer. Then Chessman was an even bigger hero. He could tell them how he saved them from additional procedures and risk by getting right to the problem.

"We took care of the dysplasia," Chessman would say, knowing the patient would ask what "dysplasia" meant. Chessman would launch into how some cells just become evil and then beat up on the good cells. Left unchecked, an evil dysplastic cell continued to become more and more evil, reproducing and bringing in other bad cells, until the good cells just couldn't take it anymore.

Don thought he could have been talking about himself. Chessman had become something of a bad cell, an evil cell.

Chessman had several versions of the explanation. The cell tissue was prepared in sections and examined under a microscope. The dysplastic cells were stained black. That gave Chessman the opportunity to launch into a cowboy scenario, about the evil bad-guy cowboys dressed all in black. The good cells wore white.

Chessman loved to use his clinical experience to make the diagnosis before getting the results of the pathology reports, including slides and blood work ups. Chessman often made his clinical judgments without any histologic slide examination.

"When you've done as many goddamned cases as I have, you know what to do. You don't need some nerd from the lab counting those fucking cells for you. I've forgotten ten times more than that nerd knows." It was true. Chessman had forgotten plenty. He just didn't care enough to replenish what was lost.

As Don approached his office, he continued to define Chessman in a new light. Don finally realized that Chessman wasn't a doctor. Don was always trying to describe Chessman in terms of what it meant to be a doctor. That was Don's clear mistake. Chessman was an entrepreneur, who happened to be licensed in New York State to practice obstetrics and gynecology. Don felt that he was taken in by the carnival barking of an American huckster, a salesman of extraordinary talent, a man who saw prey, hunted it, and wore the balls of his victims around his neck, like a phallic trophy. Don was beginning to feel like one of the prey.

Don and Lou spoke about two weeks before the holidays. Don believed he was confiding in Lou. Lou was far from a threatening presence. Don certainly could not confide in Harvey. Harvey would see Don as a threat to the financial stability of the practice. As soon as Lou understood Don's doubts about Chessman, he answered Don immediately.

"Hank likes you a lot. In a way, you're like Hank. You've got your own ideas and that's fine, but don't expect a man like Hank to do your bidding. The other day Hank confided that in me, and now I'm confiding in you." If one thing was true, it was that there was only room for one leader in the Chessman practice.

Lou paused to see if Don realized what he had just done. Lou always seemed sincere, caring, and appeared to want the best for everyone.

Don thought for a moment. The message was simple. Lou had broken a confidence with Chessman. However small, Lou must have thought it was important.

Don nodded that he understood. If Lou was to say anything else, then it could never get back to Chessman. Don said, "Okay. It's between us, Lou." Lou continued. It was a scenario Don did not expect.

"Hank told me that if we're not careful you might walk right up on over us."

Don laughed at this somewhat flattering version of himself. It was a version that changed the entire complexion of the office hierarchy. Now Don was to be viewed as the one the partners should fear. Not Chessman. What a manipulative move by Chessman.

Don realized that talking with Lou would not help the situation. The information he was passing on was designed to be passed on. Still, it always pleased Don to talk with Lou. Lou had a terrific sense of humor about everything and could calm Don down.

"Did you see how fucked up my wig was the other morning? If my wife doesn't help me with it, I can't get it on straight. It looked like an alley cat slept on my head."

Dysplasia

After one of those talks, Don and Lou would go out for drinks. A short time later, Don would end up feeling good about his professional life. Don wanted to believe that Lou was a friend, but knew that Lou was knotted to Chessman in ways that made Lou uncomfortable.

Don was a few blocks from his office. He stopped to stare at the park across the street. There was pure white snow on the bare tree limbs. A few lights from inside the park filtered through the limbs. The park benches had a fresh layer of snow, adding white stripes to the long thin slats. Don looked at the peaceful scene. He thought of the importance of snow as a child. For a moment, he felt that pure joy, the kind reserved for children. In a second it was gone.

Don accidentally flashed back to the day he met Chessman.

Don was working three days a week on 61st Street, right off of Lexington Avenue. It was a nice practice. A few hard-working residents got together just about the time they completed their training. All were from poor backgrounds. They were going to make a go of practice in New York. They graduated a few years before Don and were happy to include him in the mix. Don would do the OB-GYN work on a percentage, in exchange for rent and other office services. It was a good situation for Don to start building a little practice of his own.

Don was in love with Linda and Linda was in love with Don. No commitments, just love. It sounded good and both were young enough to still be happy. Linda was working as a model and actress, a combination not uncommon in New York. She had the dubious distinction of being the only model/actress whose boyfriend was a playwright and OB-GYN doctor. "How strange," thought Don. He hadn't thought about his writing for years. He had practically erased any memory of his writing days.

In those days, most of Linda's time was spent making the audition rounds for commercials. That meant dragging herself around the city, stopping at advertising agencies and casting director's offices. Another fairly remarkable distinction for Linda was that she was earning a living. She worked occasionally on the popular soap operas, *The Guiding Light* and *As The World Turns*. Linda knew a lot of people in New York acting circles. That included the theater, movies, and soaps.

It was because of Linda's contacts that Don met Chessman.

Don had written a play about a heart surgeon called *The Last Days of An Addicted Player*. It was avant-garde enough to attract the attention of the people at *The American Factory Theater*. A despot named Harold Winston ran it. He was popular, despite the fact that he probably destroyed several careers a week.

Winston sounded excited. "Your play was one of only twenty-five we select every year, out of thousands."

Don replied sheepishly, "Yes. Thank you very much." He was stunned.

Winston repeated himself several times and then launched into casting suggestions.

"Renee and Joe are on the coast, but Eli and Anne will be back from Canada and they can do the readings." Wow! Eli Wallach and Anne Jackson were going to be in Don's play. He had to ask Linda who Winston meant by Renee and Joe. She said automatically, as if Don were an idiot, "Renee Taylor and Joe Bologna—they wrote *Lovers and Other Strangers*."

Don was left with the impression that Winston was going to launch a full production of Don's play in the fall. Over time, Don would learn not to trust Winston. Nothing happened the way he said it would. There didn't appear to be a production, at least not anytime in the near future.

Dysplasia

Don asked around town. He quickly learned he couldn't count on Winston.

Don began a series of readings to attract interest in his play. One was held for Otto Preminger. Otto's publicist Alan Bader really liked the play. "It's got a Woody Allen kind of quality. It's funny."

Linda cast the parts for the reading. Linda cast her friend Trudy Campbell in the role of the Jewish Mother. Type-casting. The reading went well.

Trudy's husband was a rich but pleasant WASP from a long line of insurance people who had "strayed" by marrying Trudy. Trudy invited the entire cast to her house on New Year's Eve, an evening that would dramatically change the course of Don's life.

As the evening wore on, Don sat with Linda in the corner of the long living room. His hand was intertwined with hers. She had smooth white skin. Don loved to feel his skin against hers, even if it was just their hands. Trudy's husband Arthur stopped by to patronize two of his poorer guests. It was something he'd learned to stomach after marrying a theater addict.

"So, you're the writer?" slurred Arthur, who was well into his third gin and tonic. Arthur wore typical, plaid WASP trousers, filled with overlapping shades of green and yellow. The solid green blazer, embroidered with the shield from a Long Island country club, completed the uniform.

"Playwright" corrected Linda.

"How do you make a living? How do you eat?" Arthur demanded answers.

Don loved those kinds of questions. He answered them straight, quickly, without skipping a beat, because his answer usually brought dead silence.

"I'm a doctor, obstetrics and gynecology."

"You're a medical doctor?" Arthur almost shouted loud enough to be heard across the long room.

"Yes. Do you want to see my licenses?"

Now Don was having his version of a little fun. He reached into his pocket to get his I.D. Usually at this point, the person would stop him, but not Arthur. He wanted to inspect each and every I.D. that Don was willing to produce. After passing the cards back to Don one at a time, Arthur looked squarely at Don and launched into a discussion of health insurance costs that would have made an actuary proud.

"Son. We estimate that coverage per capita on the average in New York will go up between sixteen and eighteen percent by the year 2001. That means by practicing full time, you can expect the same kind of growth in your practice. Just like the kind that accepts an adequate cross section of health plans in your same practice catch basin." Arthur appeared proud of his remarks.

Don wasn't quite sure what Arthur was getting at. Don wondered if he really meant "catch basin", or some other phrase the insurance people were using to grapple the control of the medical profession out of the hands of the doctors and into the firm grasp of large corporations, "where it rightly belonged". It didn't matter. Don decided not to pursue the matter.

"Thank you very much for that information." Don turned to Linda. "Did you want more turkey, Linda?" He had had enough of Arthur.

"Yes. Isn't the cranberry sauce delicious?" cooed Linda taking Don's cue.

Dysplasia

The two excused themselves and had a little more wine interspersed with a few laughs at Arthur's expense. In those days, Linda was still rebellious. She saw her own, stiff, regimented upbringing as a joke. Arthur reminded her of her relatives.

While standing over the beautifully tanned turkey, Don looked up as Arthur made a beeline across the room with a well-dressed tall man in tow. The man had a winter tan that almost matched the turkey skin. Don immediately thought of Aspen and the Caribbean.

"I found another one. Can you believe it? I found another one?" Arthur was elated.

"Don. This is Dr. Henry Chessman, my wife's gynecologist."

"Call me Hank," the taller man said, and extended his hand. If anyone was out of place in the profession, it clearly was Chessman. He let Don know right away that he had friends in high places.

Within minutes of saying, "Call me Hank", Chessman rattled off the names of various billionaire families, a few token Hollywood stars, and several politicians. Gates. Beatty. Hillary. The names came out fast and furious. Somehow all connected to Chessman.

Arthur was acting as if he just introduced Michael Jordan to Magic Johnson.

"What are the chances of finding two of you at the same party?" Arthur continued, still thrilled with his incredible discovery.

That's how it started. Don and Linda were drunk. Stuffed on turkey. They were very receptive to being charmed. Chessman need only to hear the word "theater" once. Chessman knew the name of every play off-Broadway. He was friends with David Mamet, Christopher Durang, and played tennis with Neil Simon. "I have a lot of friends at the Beverly Hills Tennis Club."

The image of the tanned talking machine disappeared. Don took off one of his gloves. He touched his frosted cheek. He was getting cold. He didn't know how long he had been standing across from the park. Don turned to enter the outside alcove at 799 Fifth Avenue. He was stopped sooner than usual by two burly security guards in uniform.

"Invitation?" one asked. The other held his position, blocking Don's path.

"That's Dr. Gardner," yelled Pierre from inside the warmer vestibule. Like a security general Pierre walked between the two guards, who parted to let him through.

"Hey, Pierre. How's it going?" asked Don.

Pierre had excellent diction for a New York doorman. He had a slight accent, one that Don guessed was French or French Canadian. Something like that. He once told Don he was from New Orleans.

The guards backed off, standing at ease.

"Great. You know who just went upstairs?" asked Pierre. He loved to give everyone the celebrity rundown.

Pierre could not have found a better spot to work. He loved it. He was on the most popular corner in New York for hawking celebrities, albeit on their way to the doctors. It was also the sight of more daylight purse snatches, or so the police would have them believe. One perpetrator even followed Milton Berle's wife into the elevator and attempted to steal her necklace. What a mistake. It seemed she had some training in the Army. The guy got a little beat up before the elevator opened on the next floor.

Because of that and like incidents, the residents in the building hired the services of a private security firm. The corner was the most popular for Nike-clad thieves who would have the Gucci bags in hand in no time. Across to the park and they were gone. That situation was compounded by a series of automobile thefts, classic New York style. Always a little laughable. The garage attendant ended up with a gash on his leg. If the car was a Rolls Royce, a superficial blow to the side of the head was included. He was getting very rich and very punch drunk. It would have been a neat inside job if he didn't try it so many times.

"Who you got up there, Pierre?" Don asked in an almost patronizing manner. Even Don had outgrown his first few years of being starstruck. Now he and Lou would make jokes. If an actor mentioned his internist, he was met with a sophomoric retort. "Dr. Friedlander. Don? Is he back from Lompoc yet?"

Pierre eagerly continued. "The young Oriental girl. She was his daughter and now she's married to him. Whatshisname?"

Don thought for a moment.

"That funny guy. He plays the clarinet."

"Right" was all Don said as he made his way around the security guards.

Don chuckled to himself as he walked inside. Don's accountant Scott Fein had an uncanny resemblance to Woody Allen. Don figured Pierre mistook Scott for Woody Allen. Scott was dating a Chinese broker from Prudential.

"You mean Woody Allen," said Don as Pierre scooted ahead of Don to open the inside glass door.

"Yeah, yeah. That's the guy. He must be some coxman for a little nerd, right?"

"Must be," said Don.

"You still tellin' me you don't get a hard-on looking at all those tits and pussy. I know some of the old broads must look like hell, but the nice ones." He paused to savor the thought. "What about it, Doc?"

Don laughed, as he always did, at Pierre's sometimes vulgar remarks. Being on friendly terms with the doorman went with the territory. Pierre kept his patter good-natured. He never offered any of the low-down remarks in mixed company or with people he didn't know. Pierre was a pro. That's why he commanded such a good building.

Brad Lewis

The Fifth Avenue doormen were a special hip crowd. Some dressed the part, complete with gold Rolex watches and Gucci shoes. Pierre accessorized better than most of the doctors in the building. He was enjoying New York; the way he felt it should be enjoyed. After a few years in New York, he frequented all the places the beautiful people did. He learned the "in" spots from reading the *New York Post* and talking to the people who passed his doorway. He didn't make all that much money as a doorman, but was always doing odd jobs and errands for the tenants. There was plenty of extra cash floating around 799 Fifth. Pierre knew how to make the extra cash and spend it at the hot spots in town.

"See you later, Pierre." Don pressed the "up" button on the small chrome elevator.

"Enjoy the party, Doc," said Pierre as he turned to go back to his post inside the vestibule.

As Don waited for the elevator, he flashed back to that morning when he had last seen his wife Linda. They made love spontaneously, the moment they woke up. It was quick, but none-the-less pleasant. Sex had become a rarity in Don's life. He was thinking that he wasn't a good lover anymore and automatically blamed himself for the fact that the flame was flickering in his sex life.

Linda had just about given up on aspects of pleasing Don. Don was embarrassed to repeat himself. In the beginning, there was an erotic quality to Linda playing the student and Don the instructor. Over time it became clear to Don that Linda either couldn't recall or didn't care to recall the things Don liked. It's as if Linda had a selective sexual memory. Each time was from scratch. Like it was the first time. One thing was for certain. Linda explained that she never really liked giving oral sex. She did it to please Don, but she just didn't like doing it. Don was beginning to think that perhaps they were never

Dysplasia

really sexually compatible. Don's own memory played tricks on him. There used to be a lot of drinking with the foreplay. Maybe they deceived each other. Perhaps it was his entire fault. He didn't pay enough attention. He always thought he was being attentive. They discussed it many times, although not recently. Some of the conclusions were dismal. "None of the couples we know have great sex anymore." "We're getting older. This is what happens in long relationships." Don overthought sex, just like he did everything else.

Kronen's humor was cruel, but contemporary. "You're not even a DINS couple." He was referring to "double income, no sex."

Linda thought that Chessman was a great role model for their lives. If the Gardners had children soon, the children would be married or away at school by the time Don got to be as famous and as rich as Chessman. Linda could plan ahead. Since Don was making a good deal of money, Linda thought it was time to start a family. She spoke of the children going to the snooty Dalton private school. She knew all the "backups" too. Don was ready too, despite his overthinking the situation. There was one real problem. Chessman. Linda was aware of Don's doubts about Chessman. She blamed Don for not continuing her idolization of Chessman. Linda was furious that Don said he did not like Chessman anymore. "What's the matter with you? Hank Chessman set us up. Don't be an idiot." How could Don dislike the man who Linda wanted Don to emulate?

"You don't have to like him. Just find out as much as you can about how he operates, and eventually it will all be yours. Lou is a wimp and Harvey is a penny pinching Jew—woops." It was a common slip.

Years after they were married, Don found out that his wife was brought up around different gradients of anti-Semites. He didn't think she was, but occasionally the expressions she heard all too often during her youth would automatically pop out of her mouth. He endured endless remarks from her relatives, remarks designed to make the Jews more comfortable. "You've got your own Christmas, right—that Hava Nagila holiday, right?"

Don reviewed the morning sexual romp. When Don was about to ejaculate, he encouraged his sperm to do a good job. "Okay, boys. You know your mission. There's no turning back." Linda laughed, arching her back in such a way that thrust her firm, little pink rear high in the air. Don thought of her milky white-and-beige breasts standing firm.

"Ready. Aim. Fire." Don let go with a series of undulating thrusts; emphasized further by pulling Linda's hips as tight as possible against his.

She sighed as Don's miniature canon stopped firing. He reported the troop movements. "The troops are on their way swimming upstream to get at that egg."

Linda laughed. "Thank you, Colonel Gardner."

Don was never very secure about his own sexuality. His father neglected to talk to him about sex. When Don was old enough to understand the mechanics of sex, he was supplied a "how to" book. When Don was older, his father gave him many lectures on the value of women.

"Women are the enemy. The enemy. Never forget that and you'll be okay." Don laughed when he heard it. It was the best advice his father had to offer.

Don felt he liked women, at least more than his father did. During his first few sexual experiences, he mistook his ability to last a long time before ejaculating as a sign of being a good lover. He just pumped and pumped, as if the Energizer Bunny was in the saddle. He didn't get any complaints. None of the women he had sex with suggested to him to slow down, perhaps due to their own lack of knowledge or their own shyness about sexual matters.

Dysplasia

꩜

When he met Linda, she made him feel very insecure about his abilities because she stopped him the first time they were making love. She suggested that he just hold her for a few moments. He was all set to pound away for a new Energizer record.

She eventually introduced him to a variety of sexual positions he had never tried and he became very fond of sex on their sides, with his arms wrapped around Linda's breasts.

He realized after a few years that Linda was completely controlling their sex lives. Linda never let him do it the way he wanted, and occasionally he really just wanted to get back in the saddle and pound away. Don realized that he liked to exert force, and Linda was preventing him from ever doing that. He fantasized about forceful sex with other women, including bondage, which for Don would be an extraordinary and deviant experience. He could never mention this to Linda. Even though she used to be the creative one, she operated in a narrow frame of creativity. Don also didn't trust her because she sometimes shouted about how big his penis was, especially when they were in the throes of passion. Don knew he was average, and began to resent the fact that Linda probably said this to other men she had been with before Don. He once brought it up to her and she just laughed saying that Don felt very big to her. Well, that was a completely different story to Don. "Feeling big" to her and actually being big were two very different concepts.

"Well, I don't like it when you say I'm big," Don explained.

"You don't like it when I say you're big," Linda answered, almost mocking Don's tone. She found the conversion very amusing. Who wouldn't?

"Hey, don't make fun of me," he said.

"I'm not making fun of you," she answered.

Don was convinced he would get nowhere fast, trying to pursue a logical discussion about sex.

"Linda. Do you think I have an above-average-sized penis?" Don asked, demanding a serious answer.

"I don't know. Let me think about it," said Linda, adding to the confusion and ridiculousness of the entire episode.

"You're not sure?" Don didn't give up.

"I didn't say I wasn't sure. I said I didn't know for sure. Let me think about it. In the meantime, I won't mention it in bed. Okay?" She really hoped that would be a solution.

Don didn't have any more energy.

"Okay," he said, and never brought up the subject again.

That's how most of their sexual discussions ended. Each time a little more polarity was added to the mix. Now talk about sex was a thing of the past.

The elevator stopped on his floor. Don thought about how he was usually satisfied with what he considered "normal sex". He found nothing sexy about his work despite knowledge of how some of the OB-GYN doctors had affairs with patients. He questioned why they would want to in the first place. For a few, the occasional "blow job" from a patient went with the territory. After the Clinton ordeal, the usual stream of jokes was given new meaning.

Chessman would go further by telling stories like how he would put his hand on the head of his dick when he was out of a patient's sight.

"Just to remind myself what it's really all about."

"What it's all about?" was about as far removed from reality as anything Chessman ever said. Pressed further Chessman would wink and smile. As if all men were part of his twisted misogynist union.

There were always jokes about which patient was going to do it or how she would do it. Sometimes it broke up the boring routine of work, and at

Dysplasia

other times it was plain silly. It was no wonder to Don that women were fed up with men telling antiwomen jokes. Don had a hard time telling when Chessman was putting people on with his perverse stories.

That night Don would learn something new and personal about Chessman. Something Don would never have imagined. Chessman was more than perverse, more dangerous, and more twisted than Don thought possible. Chessman was unlike any man Don had ever known. When that night was over, Don's opinion of Chessman would be changed forever.

CHAPTER FOUR

There was a fancy brass rolling coat rack in the hall outside of the Chessman office, overstuffed with coats, and a few brightly wrapped packages for the holidays.

A pretty young black woman greeted Don. She was dressed in a hostess outfit, featuring scalloped white frills. A broad smile crossed her face as she welcomed Don to the party.

"Merry Christmas and Happy New Year. You look like a doctor to me."

"I didn't know it showed," said Don.

Chessman always insisted they hire "pretty model types" for the parties.

"It doesn't. But not in a bad way," she said. "What I mean is you look very handsome. There. I've gotten my foot out of my mouth."

She smiled again. That time a big wide toothy grin. It made her look sensual and juvenile at the same time.

"I'm Dr. Gardner," Don replied, returning the smile.

"I'm Susan. May I take your coat? You are pretty cute for a doc."

She had a slight accent. Don had heard it somewhere before, but he wasn't sure.

Dysplasia

Don let Susan help him off with his Aquascutum raincoat. He handed her his matching scarf. Don also had a matching rain hat that he kept in the pocket. He never wore it. It was too much of a look. Don reached for the scarf once his coat was off.

"I'll lock mine up inside. This looks like a rough crowd," Don said with a sarcastic ring to his words. He held onto his coat and placed the scarf in the inside sleeve.

"Wow. This is your office? You guys must be rich," Susan shot back.

"Rich we're not. My office, yes." Don walked with Susan to the front door of the office. He stopped to ask a polite, "How's the business treating you?"

"Okay. How'd you know?"

Don knew from his years of hanging around Off-Broadway with Linda that Susan was probably an actress. Every good-looking person in New York was somehow connected to modeling, acting, or hanging out with chic people, which ultimately lead back to the modeling and acting crowd. At least that's what Don thought. In this case he was right. The part-time employee pool for caterers was made up of a lot of show business types.

Don took a closer look at Susan. Susan had light, chocolate-brown skin, green eyes, and a thin frame accentuated by full, jutting breasts, which pressed against her tight servant's outfit. The scalloped frills hung over the area that would show her nipples. Don wondered if they were big and firm enough to be seen through the outfit.

Don always controlled his thoughts. He never cheated on his wife, although in his travels the subject would come up more frequently than he would have liked. If he ever was going to do anything sexual, it surely would not be with someone connected to the office. Don looked back at Susan as he entered the office. She was an extraordinarily beautiful woman.

Chessman always bragged about "mocha" being his favorite. He loved to categorize women by the color of their skin. That would enable him to launch into racial stereotypes, ranging from American Indian lust to promiscuity as an intrinsic cultural trait of Phillipinos. Chessman could sound like some horny anthropology professor, lecturing on what he thought were inherent sexual traits. Somehow he would always come back to the color.

"That sort of not-chocolate-not-white, just-enough-cream-in-my-coffee look. Mocha. That's my favorite." Lou would nod, verifying Chessman's color history with women.

Odds were high that Chessman would corner Susan. At some point during the evening, he would waltz over and exude all the charm he could muster. Chessman did his share of flirting with the women employees. If only half of his boasting and intimations were true, Chessman was also doing his share of philandering.

He traveled a great deal for a practicing physician. Like his habit of drawing extra paychecks, he was always well ahead of his partners when it came to vacation time. Chessman kept residences in Manzanilla, Nassau, and Haiti. Don always thought it was an odd combination.

On top of the out-of-town places, Chessman had a two-bedroom apartment in the same building as the office. It was high above the office floors. The apartment was listed as a corporate asset, but the partners accepted that it was really for Chessman. The large master bedroom was clearly Chessman's and only he had a key, leaving the door unlocked once a week when the room needed cleaning.

Over time, Don learned that the houses weren't very expensive. Don wouldn't have been surprised to learn that Chessman never laid out a nickel for any of them. Chessman never let a grateful patient forget him.

Dysplasia

The house in Manzanilla came out of a defunct business deal. A friend of Stu's in Beverly Hills, a businessman who also happened to be a physician, got Chessman interested in a new product that helped woman diagnose breast cancer by wearing some sort of shield. Like many of Stu's acquaintances, the Beverly Hills doctor had a close working relationship with the company that manufactured these devices. He convinced the CEO of the company to skew the research statistics in favor of the product. It was easy to twist the statistical results of a study. The company stock shot up, and Chessman and a few of the L.A. doctors sold shares before the FDA could pull the plug on the device. No harm. No foul. And a house in Manzanilla to bury some of the profits. Doctors interpret the same research in many different ways. If they bent the research results enough, sometimes they ended up with a house. It was a great deal, except for the shareholders that held onto their stock. The stock slipped back down when the rumors and buying frenzy was "nixed" by the FDA taking the product off the market.

Chessman was an "old friend" of Vern Roberts, a financier who fled the United States under charges of financial misdealing. Lou Benjamin would only tell Don that Roberts helped clear the way for the house in Nassau. Don thought the house was Robert's, and at one point, when the Bahamians asked Roberts to leave the Bahamas, Chessman stepped in "as a friend" and relieved Roberts of the home.

Chessman did these kinds of "favors" for friends.

The Haiti house was probably the only miscalculation of Chessman's life, at least to Don's knowledge. Chessman had friends on the board of General Tire and Rubber. They had a factory in Haiti. The old leader, Duvalier, had alliances with several types of American businesses. Oddly enough, professional, major-league baseballs were made in Haiti, along with Lacoste shirts. If an American with money would like to live like a king, he could do so in Haiti, particularly in Petionville. This environment was not popular to many American businessmen. Despite the highly leveraged financial benefits, Haiti was still the poorest country in the Western Hemisphere, and its cultural phenomenon like voodoo, mixed with the many political murders, didn't sit well with investors. Haiti was a political mess. It was a continual embarrassment to the United States, which still pretended that it could turn the little country into a democracy. Because of the political situation of the last few years, Chessman and his cronies got very little use from the mansion in Petionville. People were still getting killed in Haiti, despite the United States efforts to hold elections and train a new police force. When the return of the Cuban boy became an international cause, Haitians were slighted, stating that the U.S. government always sent them back to Haiti.

Don was impressed when he found out that part of his partnership deal was use of the house in the Bahamas, as well as part of the upstairs apartment. Recently he asked his own accountant Scott to look into who paid the expenses on the other houses. Scott asked the corporate accounting offices of Deloitte, who handled the office accounts, how much came off the top of the gross of the practice for taxes and services at the houses. It took about six months to get answers. The costs were lumped into everyone's travel and entertainment expenses and then taken off the top. Chessman and Lou got a twenty percent edge, since they were the senior members of the practice. It was no surprise that Don was really paying for those vacations, like his partners. It was just in a different form, and he was paying more than two of his partners. He wondered if Harvey knew what was going on. It wasn't like Harvey to stand for any inequities. He probably didn't know.

When Don joined the practice, his accountant was shown the previous two-year gross and net for the partners, amounts of money that

Dysplasia

❦

staggered what Don was making. Don looked no further, and signed aboard at Linda's urging.

"We're getting older and I want to have a family before I'm forty," said Linda. "According to this section about a Keogh plan, you'll be saving a fortune, and it's tax deferred."

Don was pleased that Linda was taking such an interest. She must have called Scott dozens of times during the contract period. She knew more about Don's contract than he did.

Linda was only 29 at the time, but was instrumental in pushing Don into the Fifth Avenue milieu. She was quick to give up her acting activities.

"Get it out of your system and then go back to school." That's the advice her parents gave her about acting.

Marrying Don was Linda's equivalent to going back to school. Once she was married, her parents never mentioned another word about school. A great education was afforded anyone who hung around Fifth Avenue medical practices.

Don spotted Linda across the huge waiting room. The office was the largest of its kind in New York, if not the entire East Coast. A group from Atlanta flew to New York a few years ago, to see the "Chessman set-up". Although they borrowed dozens of the technical layout ideas, it was impossible to duplicate the view of the park across the street. While other offices could copy the interior design, it was impossible to buy all the art that went with it. Few doctors could afford it, and even fewer would "waste" money on those kinds of "decorations." The office served its purpose, acting as a fifth member of the practice. The office sold itself, especially to those who wanted their doctor's office to reek of the excesses they enjoyed in their lives. To the rare patient, the office presentation was repellent. It clearly wasn't an environment for everyone.

The office was a monster. Very few people, rich or poor, famous or otherwise, would ever experience an office like that. When a patient exited the elevators, she was already in the office. It took up the entire tenth floor. The lower floors were filled with dermatologists, internists, cosmetic dentists, oral surgeons, and a group of dentists that did nothing but root canal work. Don couldn't believe that dentistry was more specialized than medicine. Specialists did one procedure all day long. "Fuzz" Schiff, one of the root canal guys, used to tease Don by saying, "On an hourly basis, we make more money than anyone else in the building." Don believed it.

The art also filled the waiting area, halls, and was strategically stationed so that if a patient had her head back and was in the dehumanizing stirrups, she could see the room art. If a patient wanted to completely tune out the art, she could watch the overhead VCR/TV. A popular movie or information about OB-GYN was readily available.

Linda learned to work a room with ease. She was always sneaking in a good word for Don. Devotion. Proud. Hard-working. Endless hours down at the hospital. She naturally downplayed the fact that he was spending more time with office patients and increasingly less on New York City Welfare patients.

He flashed on her. He saw her in a blue bikini. The bathing suit she wore when Don first moved into the practice. That year, Chessman took an entourage to Haiti for the reopening of the new Club Med. Things were quiet. The talk about AIDS was diminished. The facility built by Club Med was a spectacular oasis. It took over an hour from the airport at Port Au Prince. The group drove through the worst living conditions they had ever seen, only to arrive at a paradise. It was one of the best vacations the Gardners ever had. Between days at the Club Med and some dinners at Chessman's house in Petionville, it was hard to leave. In those days, Linda said that she could actually live the Club Med life.

Dysplasia

∞

Chessman was revered in Haiti. Don was impressed that his new partner's political and business associations were so expansive. A private army of security people protected Chessman's house. It was hard to tell who was a house servant and who was security. The house seemed to be off-limits to locals, and Don got the message from Lou that they were not welcome there without Chessman. Lou explained that the situation was "just Haiti". The only time Lou was invited to take an extended trip with Chessman, Chessman suggested Lou stay in a hotel in town. It was still very luxurious.

"It's safer for you," said Chessman.

Lou didn't need any further recommendations.

Linda latched onto the arm of the President of Morningside Hospital, Harry Rollins. A sort of roly-poly man from the South, Harry acted more like a house servant to the old hard-line WASP board at the hospital. Don always pictured Rollins wearing an all-white suit, holding a mint julep, standing on the rooftop of the hospital. Harry looked a little like the actor Ned Beatty.

"Hi, kid," Don said as he leaned in to kiss Linda.

She gave Don a Hollywood kiss, something she learned only in the last few years. Her lips just kissed the air next to Don's head.

Don noticed that her lipstick shade was getting redder and redder. He didn't like red lipstick. She knew that.

"Don, you know Harry Rollins, don't you?" she asked. It was automation.

Don actually did not know him well. But there was a matter that was troubling Don. Maybe this was his opportunity to discuss it with Rollins.

Morningside just merged with City Hospital. This was not an ordinary merger. Morningside was a private, venerable hospital attached to the University. City Hospital was one of the many hospitals going broke. The merger was worked out to the dismay of many of the older, WASP doctors at the Hospital. All the necessary assurances about autonomy, core curriculum, and hospital policy remained the same. The enticement for Morningside was simple, more beds. The Morningside people envisioned themselves "taking over" City. The Morningside Board was convinced they could run City better. Why not? Private-sector business was always giving government lessons.

Don learned first-hand how far the assurances were from the truth. City was backlogged with patients. Overbooking prevailed. All were on welfare. The extra patients were dumped on Morningside's lap. Morningside was now doing almost double the amount of welfare cases it had done the previous year. The OB-GYN unit of the hospital became a battleground. Doctors with private patients were fighting over the available beds. The welfare cases were treated like cattle.

"Harry, could I speak to you about something in private?" Don asked.

Before Harry could answer, Linda pulled Rollins by the arm and whisked him 180° south of Don. Linda didn't want Don discussing any business with Harry.

"Mr. Rollins, have you met Sigourney Weaver?" Linda cackled at the first celebrity face she could spot. Linda wasn't even sure if it was the actress, but it was as good of a guess as any. Linda wanted to get Rollins away from Don. She knew what was on Don's mind. Like Stu, she hoped Don would put it to rest.

Don shouted after them as Linda guided Rollins through the crowd towards the actress. "Harry, I'll catch up to you later," Don yelled not knowing if anyone heard him.

Don was feeling very insecure. At his own office party. He tried to discard the thought. A waiter walked by with a tray of appetizers.

Dysplasia

"What's this shit?" asked Don. It wasn't his nature to be so crass, but he felt uncomfortable.

"That shit, sir, is a miniature taco shell with shrimp. It's good shit, sir," said the young blond man, smiling at Don's glib question.

The waiter knew he gave the drop-dead New York answer. The kind that only waiters pick up somewhere in their on-the-job training.

"You want one?" the waiter asked. He extended his other hand, the one that was stacked with those little annoying cocktail napkins. The kind that stuck only to human skin.

Don grabbed one from the tray and ate it quickly. He grabbed two more and one of the napkins.

"Thanks," Don murmured through his full mouth. Don thought it was odd fare for Balducci's.

"You're welcome, sir," said the young man as he veered off, heading for an elegantly dressed group of four, including Chessman's wife.

Chessman's wife Joan wasn't happy with the catering service at Balducci's any longer. It had gotten too popular. "Everyone" was using Balducci's, and she found "this wonderful caterer" who also had offices in Los Angeles. "They do the studio parties," she would mutter.

Chessman was happy Joan had made some friends in Beverly Hills. It kept her busy. He encouraged her to visit as often as she liked. It kept their mockery of a marriage intact.

When word got back to Joan that Harvey was still insisting on Balducci's, she took a different approach.

"Why not let The Pierre do it? They're a block away." She knew Harvey did not want to hire the hotel caterers.

She then pressed for a compromise.

"Why not have two parties? Why not let The Pierre do the catering, with Balducci's serving during the late afternoon for people who couldn't come at night?"

Joan had a firm way of expressing her thoughts and a powerful presence. Don thought she would have made a great politician. She was bright, witty, and perceptive.

Harvey naturally balked at the extra expense for both The Pierre and Balducci's. Chessman's wife really wanted to try the new caterer to the stars. She usually got her way. On top of that, they had to put up with Joan singing her yearly Christmas medley. The one she got from the musical writing team of Kander and Ebb.

"They write for Liza, you know," a fact Joan would tell anyone willing to listen. Joan thought of Kander and Ebb as her personal composers.

That time of year was filled with more bullshit than Don could stand. During the first few years, it appeared interesting. Still novel. He was younger, eager, and preoccupied with his own success. Now he was harboring an inner pain, from deep within his soul, from someplace he had almost let die. It was almost forgotten. Somehow, he would get back what he had almost forgotten.

Don went over to the bar and asked for a double shot of whatever malt scotch they were serving. When Don developed into a scotch snob, the office staff made sure the caterer included malt scotch.

"We have Macallan," the bartender reported, like a corporate executive quoting from the company's product line.

"Is it the twelve-or eighteen-year-old Macallan?"

"The eighteen, sir. Shall I pour you some? In a shot glass?"

"No. In a bucket, and fill it up," Don answered in a flash.

Scotch was one of his newer pleasant perks. He took heavy gulps of the drink as he walked around the room, shaking hands, mugging a false smile, and thinking about Susan, the coat check girl. The scotch was doing its job. He was getting a buzz and thinking about sex. He wondered about the vulva on Susan's vagina, something he kept assuring himself was just a mental reflex, common to the life he had chosen to lead. Pink, surrounded by shades of brown. He thought of a few other color combinations, and laughed as he drank his scotch. "Perverse bastard," he said. He was enjoying his little mental indulgence. His changing visual image became a plain page in Gray's Anatomy. Now just a medical illustration, he turned the page. He saw himself with Susan, rolling on the hall coats, completely naked. As a guest left the party, Don and Susan rolled the coats over themselves and hid, continuing to make love, while people stood above them, searching for their belongings.

Don closed the book in his mind and made a beeline to grab the Mayor before he left the party. Don wanted to talk to him about the welfare patients at Morningside Hospital. Don was determined to do something about the problems in the hospital. The Mayor was hard to corner. Since crime in New York City was at an all-time low, the Mayor was enjoying bipartisan popularity.

An hour passed. During that time, Don succeeded in getting a little drunker. He slowly forgot about his personal unrest. He was enjoying a momentary peace. Alcohol did have its benefits.

He was able to chat up a storm with some of the young doctors that practiced Internal Medicine in the city. They were a good source of referrals for Don. Many of the doctors lived outside Manhattan in places like New Rochelle, Westport, Great Neck, and the Five Towns. They looked alike, dressed alike, and drove either a Lexus or a Range Rover. Their wives overdressed for parties like this because a party in Manhattan at 799 Fifth was something to brag about when they were home, car pooling or gossiping with the locals that loved to name drop.

"We went to a party on Fifth Avenue. The Mayor was there. Oh, and Arnold." They waited after saying "Arnold" to see if the listener mentally filled in the last name.

"Don, I hear you want to make the conditions better at the hospital?" Hal Karp asked, after reporting that he had his best year ever in practice, "knock on wood."

Don was caught off-guard. He was momentarily stunned to hear Hal ask him about the hospital. Did everyone know about Don's idea? First Stu. Linda couldn't get away fast enough, but he knew that Linda knew.

"Er, well, you know they rush the hell out of the welfare patients. In and out. In and out. But it's the same all over."

Don covered himself. He looked around to see if Stu landed at their party. Don thought that maybe Stu had spilled the beans after talking with him. It was a way to defuse any secrecy about Don's activities. It wasn't unlike Stu. Don wasn't discounting anything. It was easy for people to talk "off the record" at parties.

Stu was in sight in the corner of one of the hallways. He appeared pretty drunk. His face was flushed and his tie was crossed across his chest like an ammunition belt. He was blabbering away with a few book publishers, probably making up a book he hadn't even written. If the publishers bit, Stu would piece something together quickly, often paying a ghostwriter to fill in the blanks. Stu must have had a chat with the young Internal Medicine boys. Stu loved to stir things up. The earlier speech to Don was history.

Don saw Rollins about to leave and caught up with him at the door.

"Harry," said Don, as he moved closer to Rollins.

Before Don could say another word, Rollins reeled and spoke quickly and directly to Don.

"I hear you have some complaints about the system." It was friendly, but very direct.

"Not complaints, Harry. I, er..." Don stammered in disbelief.

Everyone knew everything. He still hadn't learned that he was part of a small, powerful hierarchy. He still hadn't learned that he could trust no one. Not even his wife. Did she talk to Rollins too? His head was spinning from the drinks, and he just wanted to go home to go to sleep.

"We have just hired a new team of consultants who specialize in cost-effective, intensive preconstruction planning. Project management by owners looking to control time and costs. We want to identify and solve scheduling, design coordination, cost and feasibility up front, not later. Before we can do that, we've got to clean house, so to speak, on our own, get a firm grasp of what's going on, in each unit. Hank Chessman recommended you personally to do the review for OB-GYN. He said you're the brightest, most capable doctor on staff. If you're willing to work for under the lowest bid we received, I think you could help us."

"Wow," thought Don. "That's a surprise."

"Don? What do you think?" said Harry, actually impatient that Don was thinking about it.

"Chessman did this?" thought Don. For a second he was skeptical. In an another instant, Don saw the whole situation differently. "Of course he did. Chessman was right." Don saw himself as the most capable doctor on staff, and damn it, most everyone knew it. By having Don involved, Chessman would have an ally reviewing the OB-GYN unit.

"Thank you. I'm very flattered," Don politely responded and leaned back against the wall, almost knocking over one of Chessman's giant Neiman lithographs. "Can I let you know for certain after the holidays?"

"Sure," said Rollins.

The warning from Stu was wrong. Stu made mistakes. He misread the whole situation. Things were going to be just fine.

Don straightened himself. He needed to make sure that Rollins knew his special area of interest. Where he stood politically on the whole matter.

"There are certain minority groups that haven't any private insurance, and are receiving inadequate care."

There. He had said it. That was what was troubling him. He had said it to the President of the hospital. Donald Gardner, son of a tie salesman, nephew of Uncle Max the butcher, was asked to help the President of the hospital. None other than Henry "Call Me Hank" Chessman recommended him for the job. Don was feeling like a great white doctor again.

Don knew Harry already knew the information about the welfare patients. Don just wanted to get it out in the open. Up front. So Harry knew what Don was planning. That's the way Don did things. No secrets. No surprises.

Don was feeling much better. He had a lot of work to do, and he was going to do a great job. With his writing background and research skills. the hospital was going to get their money's worth from his new consulting project. He reminded himself that he didn't get paid much for teaching at the hospital, and that he would not get paid much for this job either. Only full-time employees got decent money. Chessman got more than anyone else on staff because he had an administrative title. Don was glad to be given the opportunity to do something good for the hospital. It was something he'd rather be doing than "zapping" suspicious areas for dysplasia, often on wealthy women who had cancer phobias.

It was strange that this would happen now. Just when Don was beginning to have doubts about Chessman. Now Chessman came forward and did what it was Don wanted him to do. Don felt vindicated. He took a deep breath and smiled.

"Don't worry, Harry. I'll do a good job."

"We know that," said Harry. Harry wanted to make sure Don knew Harry was still the boss. "You'll eventually report back to me. Along with the other departments."

Don didn't know whether he should run and thank Chessman. Maybe he should tell his wife the good news. Maybe she wouldn't think

Dysplasia

それ

it was good news. Maybe he should call his friend Kronen. Kronen was always suspicious of Chessman. Don decided to savor the feeling. He floated around the party with a new Macallan in hand. Don got his chance to get his message across to the Mayor. Maybe it was overkill, but Don felt more secure after talking with Rollins.

The Mayor took Don aside. "Hey, thanks for seeing my daughter on emergency last week. You guys are great. Twenty-four hours. Those are the kind of hours I like for my doctors," said the Mayor, shaking Don's hand. It was important for all the partners to play up to Chessman's contacts.

The Mayor regularly went to Yankee games with Chessman. Chessman was not shy about dropping hints about the future of Yankee Stadium. Even to the Mayor. Even if he contradicted the team owner, George Steinbrenner.

Don said his "you're welcomes" graciously. "Glad we could help. That's what we're here for. I only wish the welfare patients at Morningside got the same service." Don was not pulling any punches.

"So do I," said the Mayor. "So do I." He said it with an adequate muster of sincerity while he exchanged smiles with Don.

The Mayor left with his entourage. It included one prominent sports figure, no longer in the company of his actress wife. They were on their way to yet another Christmas party. Somewhere in the core of the rotten apple. Several well-known African-American politicians smiled at the procession.

Chessman made a quick dash for the Mayor. Chessman could sense when anyone of prominence was about to leave. He always tried for a personal goodbye.

"Mayor! Don't go! The night is young," said Chessman.

"Hank. We've got three more stops. Besides, I promised my son we'd go over to Rockefeller Center and watch the ice skaters under the tree."

∞

"At least it's safe to go out at night," said Chessman. He wanted to pass on the obvious compliment to the Mayor.

"You better believe it. The lowest incidence of murders in over thirty years!" beamed the Mayor.

"And you did it!" said Chessman.

It was a political moment. Everyone smiled. Everyone acted happy.

Don thought about how the Mayor had run into problems with the homeless issue. First he was going to arrest them. Then there was something about taking away their children. It was a tough issue in New York.

Don smiled as the entourage moved past him. At that point he realized his smile was more natural than earlier in the evening. He wasn't sure if it was the malt scotch or the fact that he was being given a chance to make the hospital run better for the minorities. He checked his watch. Looked around for Linda. They had promised to run down to Little Italy to meet with Kronen. He was married a few months and Don and Linda had not seen him since the wedding.

Kronen was brilliant. But a real loner. He didn't take any crap from anyone. Don had no idea how Kronen got away with it. Kronen was brash, outspoken, albeit charming, a very independent man, something that made Don jealous. Kronen was always doing strange things. He once disappeared for almost four years. It was after his first marriage dissipated. Don and Kronen were still in their twenties. Kronen graduated from Harvard Law School a few years before, the youngest member of his graduating class. To that day when people asked Kronen what he did during those four years, he said he did extensive work for the Peace Corps. When pressed for more details, he answered teasingly. "Information of that nature is on a need-to-know basis, and you, you little protozoa are not high enough on the food chain to know."

Since that time Kronen wrote law books for the profession. Sometimes by design for famous attorneys who couldn't write themselves. Kronen's office was situated in the legal book-publishing firm of Matthew Bender. It served as a home base for his work, both academic and commercial.

Linda was through with Kronen a long time ago. The mere mention of Kronen's name produced responses from the simple, "Oh, not that idiot," to the more complicated, "I don't believe a word he says. How does she put up with him?"

Don looked around. He couldn't spot his wife anywhere. He began a search mission to locate her. He didn't want to disappoint Kronen. Lately they kept missing each other.

Don looked into one of the treatment rooms. It looked like a command post for Captain Kirk or Picard to shout out his orders. There were two overhead cameras that could either record or project images. A closed-circuit monitor was wired to the main computer. A fax machine sat across from a fetal monitor. A computer built into the wall space. Yes. They had it all. Technology was the silent partner of any successful doctor. Kronen always said to Don, "The fake is greater than the make. You white-jacketed scumbags are no different than the rest of the business world!"

Don made his way to another room where a woman was holding court from a treatment table. Her elegant Armani suit jacket hung over one of the stirrups. The half-dozen other guests were scattered around the room. Sipping cocktails, they listened intently to her pitch.

"Of course it's a crap shoot. I wouldn't invest a penny of your money in a Broadway show if I was you, but I'm not you. And that's why some of you will buy at least one unit. Hey, Freddie, what's another fifty thousand down the tubes for you? Didn't I read that you picked up that Pay and Save Drug Company at a fire sale last week?" She put her hand out as if to accept money. "And you Sheila. I heard about all your AOL stock. Nobody but me should make five hundred percent on a stock."

She had an absolutely seductive charm. People wanted to laugh at the foolishness and absurdity of her remarks. That was what she wanted. Once she had the attention, she would relentlessly pound away, eager to sell.

"Georganne, shall I write you the check now?" Fred said, playing the game and trying to keep the banter alive. Some of the group functioned only as window dressing.

"Cash is always better, darling," was Georganne's quick reply.

Georganne mockingly put one of her feet up in the stirrups and leaned back. "Or would you like to work out something right now?" she cackled.

The group was well-oiled. Big laughs came from the Barish sisters. They were always out prowling for new men. Don remembered them from years ago. They looked the same. Only Don appeared to get older.

Georganne spotted Don. She shouted as she righted herself, "Here's a playwright. Let's ask him about our show."

"Former playwright," Don apologized as he flashed his party grin.

From the corner of the room, a voice bellowed, "Once a playwright, always a playwright."

Don couldn't see who it was. Someone said, "Oh, that's profound, Chris." Don lost track over the years of who was who in New York theater.

"Did anyone see my wife?" Don asked. He was out of sync with New York's hip theater crowd.

Chris added, "Another lost wife. Try the investment bankers. They end up with all the pretty wives."

Dysplasia

"Ha, ha, ha, ha," thought Don as he excused himself.

"Enjoy the party," Don said as he left the treatment room.

"We are, darling. We are," answered Georganne as she raised her glass high, careful not to spill any on her low-cut halter top. "We know where to be properly entertained during the holidays."

About two treatment rooms down the hall, facing Central Park, Don spotted Linda. He signaled to her. He wanted to get going. He pointed at himself, then at her, and finally towards the front entrance. She just smiled at him, as if he were a stranger, perhaps flirting.

Linda was standing between two men. Both had blond hair, pin-stripe suits, and thick suspenders. Linda continued to smile and signaled for Don to come over. He didn't want to, but the two men spotted him. So Don put on his party smile and mugged his way across the room.

"Don, do you know Larry Bosler from Sanford Bernstein? And this is Lee Eastwick from Prudential." Her voice took on a formal ring.

They were either money managers or stockbrokers. Chris wasn't far off. They certainly wore the uniform of investment bankers.

Linda was in rare form when she was in WASP territory. She seemed to forget that she married a Jewish man when she was in the company of third-generation money. She could smell it. Her parents weren't rich, but lived the complete life on Long Island with all the big-moneyed WASPs. They lived on a great estate, in one of the smaller servant's houses on the main property. It wasn't so strange, not after the financial reversals in the '80s. Many classic estates were divided and sold. There were even some Jews and Italians living on old blue-blood estates. Another twist on the reversal of fortunes theme.

Don spoke immediately to Linda.

"We told the Kronens that we'd meet them in Little Italy. Remember, they're with the Scholls, who have to drive back to Colt's Neck."

"Don is so sweet about keeping up with his little friends from high school. He is such a darling. It's hard for me to say no to him," Linda informed her well-suspendered bodyguards.

"I would never say no to you either," cooed Bosler. He was trying to be a good sport.

"I'm entertaining offers. I can have a prospectus on your desk by nine A.M." Don tried to joke back. To Don, Bosler and Eastwick were just two high-salaried salesmen.

Bosler laughed in a way that limited the sound he made, keeping the laugh somewhere in the back of his throat.

Lee smiled and raised his glass, saying, "Out of Bourbon. Be right back."

"Don't rush," thought Don.

Linda gave her glass to Lee to take with him. "Get me another, too."

"What was yours?" Lee asked.

"Gin and tonic," answered Linda.

Don could see that she was a little sloshed.

"You've had enough," Don said as he grabbed the glass from Lee. This gesture was something he now did out of habit. Linda would argue for a few moments and then usually agree that one more for the road was a bad idea. Not that night.

"Don't you dare tell me what to do. You men are all trying to control women. And we're sick of it. I will drink when I want, how much I want, and if you can't live with that you can go—." She paused. "Fuck yourself," exclaimed Linda. Bosler was mortified.

This time Lee laughed. It was a friendly, full laugh deep from his belly. "Marriage is such fun," Lee chuckled as he walked off. "A Merry Christmas to you all, and to all a good night! Bosler. Let's go."

"Yes. Of course." Bosler nervously followed Lee.

Dysplasia

Don stood his ground and asked directly, "Are you coming or not?"

"Not," was Linda's answer, spoken in a slightly less hostile version from moments ago.

"Good. I'm getting a cab," Don said as he began to leave.

Linda yelled after Don to "get a car and driver". When she found out that Don's office transportation allowance, above his personal car, had been upped to four thousand a year, she insisted on it. "It's only thirty five an hour." That was without tip. Linda took a lot of chauffeured rides to Bloomingdales, Saks, and her parent's house on the Island.

Chessman's attitude was clear. "We can always give it back to the IRS if they want to take the time to prove we don't spend that much." And they did spend it. Easily. Mostly on taxis. Between the hospital, office emergencies, and meetings, they were all over town. Sometimes three or four cab rides a day. Don could live with that, but he hated the fact that his wife was willing to pay double to be picked up in a Lincoln Sedan.

As Don walked through the large waiting room, he spotted Chessman talking to Susan. Chessman smiled and touched her as he spoke. Susan was laughing and shaking her head "no" as Don walked past. Chessman took Susan by the hand and led her into the office.

"Let me show you around. You would make a very nice impression on my patients," Chessman explained. "We can always use a good receptionist."

He was trying to sell her on the idea of a job. It didn't matter what kind of job or if she was qualified. It worked in the past, and the office always did need receptionists. At least Chessman wasn't heading to the elevators. During the wild, early '80s, people were running in and out of the bathrooms snorting cocaine. Chessman used to sneak upstairs with one of his conquests during a party. He'd be back in action before anyone noticed he had left.

Don stood outside his office building. He was upset about leaving Linda. Why couldn't she have come with him? It was only once in a while. Kronen wasn't so bad.

"Doc. Where to?" It was Pierre. "Shall I get you a taxi? It may be tough at this hour. Hey. I've got my car here. I could run you where you want to go," said Pierre, pointing at what looked like an old Chevrolet. It was illegally parked in front of the building, on Fifth Avenue.

"No, thanks, Pierre," said Don. "I've got to clear my head."

"Too much Christmas already?" asked Pierre.

"Yeah," said Don.

Pierre could see that Don was angry. He dropped the subject.

"Merry Christmas, Doc," said Pierre.

"Merry Christmas, Pierre," said Don.

Don slipped his hand through the special pocket access inside his coat pocket to reach his pants pocket. He always marveled at the invention.

"Have a nice holiday," said Don; his hand slid out holding two bills. Don only kept twenties and hundreds in his pants pocket. In case he was mugged and had to give up his wallet, he always had another pocket full of cash. He handed the two bills to Pierre, not knowing the total. He always gave Pierre extra money. Pierre got a decent cash bonus from the office, but Don always gave extra.

"Thanks, Doc. God bless you," said Pierre.

As Don walked away, he thought to himself, "What a decent man, that Pierre. Always helping. Always pleasant."

CHAPTER FIVE

As Don walked east towards Madison Avenue, his mind wandered to the time he and Kronen went sailing from St. John in the Virgin Islands to the British Virgin Island Tortola. Kronen was a good sailor. A great athlete, hopping around the sloop like he was a pro. Don just took instructions, but still enjoyed the whole trip. On Tortola, they met two co-eds from Queens College, part of the City University system in New York. They were part of a travel course. After two hours of talking mostly to Kronen, they jumped ship and sailed back with Don and Kronen.

Don laughed out loud. He looked up at the dark sky and watched the little shadows of snowflakes trickle down. He was lit. He didn't feel the cold, although he felt the wind whistle around his neck.

He wanted to get some fresh air before riding downtown. He again thrust his collar high up behind him, this time wrapping the scarf tightly around his neck, making a cross-over knot in front of his treasured coat, a fashion statement that no one saw.

At Park Avenue, Don stuck up his hand high in the air and hailed a cab. A large, rickety old Checker cut over from the far left lane and made it to the curb in standard form.

Don slid into the taxi and said, "Katherine Street. In Chinatown."

Don had lied to his wife about the time they were to meet in Little Italy. If Don hurried, he could catch them finishing their Chinese meal at a little place he and Kronen always ate. Particularly when Don was in medical school at N.Y.U.

"What street is dat, man?" the driver drawled out in a dialect Don was hearing more often in the last few years.

"It's a little street. Across from Mott. Off the square," Don offered, and then changed to "Just head into Chinatown. I'll show you."

"No problem," said the driver as the cab sped along Park Avenue. Directly towards the Pan Am Building.

Don looked out the dirty, streaked window. The colored lights moved past him like blurred balloons. He liked to ride around New York City at night. When it was quiet, he could be himself. The Jewish kid from the suburbs who originally wanted to live in Greenwich Village and write plays.

Don wondered if he would stay married. They were drifting apart. It was the expression couples used, along with the old but reliable "irreconcilable differences". Don was confused about women. He tried to adjust to the feminist movement, but felt like he had been tricked into accommodating women in a new way, a way he truly didn't understand. Maybe the message wasn't clear. He really didn't know how women wanted him to behave.

"Wimp," he thought. "How they wanted him to behave. What a joke."

It wasn't his fault that his mind kept slipping back to one scene, rolling in the coats with Susan. This time Don had his mouth firmly attached to Susan's mocha breast. He reached down to his lap, and through his Aquascutum coat could feel his penis get hard under the lower palm of his hand. He moved his hand away quickly, falsely concerned that the driver might see him in the rear view mirror.

"Are you from Jamaica?" Don asked. It was idle conversation.

Dysplasia

"No, man. Haiti," the driver answered with a slight hesitation.

"There sure are a lot of Haitians in New York," Don remarked with all the accuracy of the city census taker.

"Don't know, man. Don't care," the driver said with a cheerful quality.

"I once went to the Club Med in Haiti." Don was going to be friendly, whether the driver wanted to or not.

Don was no different that a lot of New Yorkers who had no idea how to deal with the influx of people from the Caribbean. It had taken the city forty years, and several remakes of *West Side Story*, to get a grip on dealing with the Puerto Ricans. Now God had screwed with New Yorkers again, by giving them Jamaicans and Haitians. If the United Nations couldn't settle what was going on Haiti, why should Don be able to understand Haitians? It was a logical and superficial out for an intelligent man. An honest man would have to admit that the problems in Haiti couldn't be solved by anyone. Since Haiti had nothing to offer the United States any longer, nobody seemed to care very much. The news stories of problems with the police, army, and government always seemed to take a back seat to the rest of the world.

Don wasn't much of a news hound. Don got most of his news from watching CNN or MSNBC. He still read the *New York Times*, almost daily. The United States had nothing to gain by rushing in to help restore order in Haiti. Don thought maybe with Clinton in office there would have been a reversal of the Bush hands off-policy, but Clinton wavered a little by retracting his promise to let the Haitian boat people into the United States. Don read that the camps in Florida were less than humane. The country was a mess, and crime still continued at an alarming rate. The U.S. was always sending troops to Haiti. Promising to restore law and order. A stable government.

Don explained that the best time he ever had was on that trip to Haiti. After that, the driver followed Don's directions to Katherine Street.

Don tipped the driver five dollars, way above fifteen percent. He laughed to himself that this was something Chessman would never do. Chessman had a thing about cab drivers. They weren't worthy. Chessman made that clear each and every time he got into a taxi. He was always rude.

"Thank you, man," the driver said as he took the money from Don.

Don slammed the door to the cab with an unclear authority. He was usually more deliberate. He liked the sound of cab doors slamming for reasons unknown to him or anyone else. It was one of those sounds he always liked. He could even dissect it into individual parts, the whooshing of the door on its way, the clicking of the lock mechanism closing, and then the full meeting of the metal door in its place in the body of the car.

Don had fond memories of Chinatown. Don's father would take the family there for a Sunday outing. He walked briskly towards Katherine Street. The restaurant was across from a small market, beneath street level. Don walked down the mottled, concrete steps. He pulled on the thick aluminum handle to open the old-fashioned, hinged glass door. He was greeted immediately by an ancient Chinese man dressed in a starched white shirt and faded black dress slacks. The unwritten uniform of the Chinatown restaurant proprietor.

The man smiled, exposing a broken-down dentition spotted with bits of gold. He babbled incessantly in Chinese, while pointing to the corner of the room.

On one side of the room was a long coffee shop counter. Across from that were small tables for two or three diners. The rest of the restaurant had booths. Kronen sat at a corner booth which had old

Dysplasia

luncheonette-styled seating. Thick red vinyl coverings. Some were torn and repaired with black tape. One was all yellow. Kronen called it "the Happy Days décor," referring to the '50s-period sitcom.

Kronen gulped from a giant-sized beer can. When he held it up to drink, it masked his face.

A thinly built and hunched Chinese waiter cleared dishes from the table. Kronen looked good for mid-40s. He was tall, thin, and trim. He never seemed to gain weight, even though he ate incessantly and could drink like his Irish compatriots at the publishing company. He periodically didn't shave for weeks. Kronen acted like he hated everyone and everything, a character defect that seemed to work well in his profession.

Don was glad their friendship lasted into adulthood. Don had vivid memories of Kronen's mother. She always was on hand with tuna fish sandwiches and vanilla shakes. Don felt that Kronen was the closest link he had to his own family. And to his past, something he felt was slipping away.

The Scholls were nowhere in sight. Don suspected they left for their long drive to Colt's Neck. As soon as Kronen spotted Don, Kronen began his usual routine.

"Ohhhhhhh. It's the great white pussy doctor from Fifth Avenue." Kronen never spared anyone from anything. "Oh, great, white doctor, in expensive coat. Sit down and mingle with the paupers."

Don ignored Kronen. "Hi, Carrie. Sorry. Linda's not coming. She got tied up by two guys dressed like investment bankers," Don supplied smiling, realizing he had just dealt Kronen an incredible straight line.

"If you're lucky, they'll keep her. What do you think she's worth in tax-free municipal bonds? At least that's something you might have some use for when you get old. But knowing those guys, your wife will eventually show up and you'll get charged for trades you never made."

Carrie slapped Kronen hard in the shoulder.

"You lowlife, scum-sucking, bottom-feeding chauvinist."

Kronen laugh loudly. He had an incredibly loud, rumbling kind of laugh. "You could have just said 'attorney' and saved all those other words," roared Kronen.

Don leaned forward to kiss Carrie on the cheek. Carrie was a naturally good-looking woman. She used little makeup, and wore her thick, blonde hair combed back with a spike in the front. Carrie was Kronen's best critic. She met him while they both were in law school.

Don sat down. He felt relaxed for the first time that day. Kronen grabbed Don's hand across the table and shook it with two hands. Kronen beamed. He was always happy to see Don.

Carrie continued the banter. She and Kronen had a lot of "routines."

"Thanks for the kiss. That's the only sex I'll get tonight," Carrie volunteered. Kronen supplied the snare drum "da dom dom" by slapping his hands on the matching red Formica luncheonette table.

He also said "da dom dom" as he emphasized the "rim shot."

"Thank you, Shecky," Kronen concluded. He did a mediocre Ed Sullivan. "The Lennon Sisters are next, singing their medley of regurgitating love songs…how 'bout a beer, Don?" Kronen pushed an unopened beer can in Don's direction.

"No, thanks. I've had plenty already. Is there any tea in here?" asked Don as he opened the lid of the teapot.

"It's probably cold," said Carrie. "Let's get a hot one."

Kronen grabbed the teapot and forced the lid wide open. He held it up high in the air so that the waiter, who was on guard nearby, could see. The waiter jumped to replace the tea.

"So tell us, oh great white doctor. How are things up on the mountain?" Kronen asked. He hummed a chant while beating the counter drum. He intended it to be a funny parody of old movies filled with African natives. "Well, Bwana?"

Dysplasia

Don launched into a serious spilling of his guts. He included his marriage, his practice, and his new opportunity to right the wrongs at the hospital. Kronen and Carrie listened intently. They cared about Don. Kronen stopped the jokes.

Less than an hour later, the three were making their way to Little Italy. It wasn't a long walk between Chinatown and Little Italy. In recent years, the uptown population rarely ventured to Chinatown. Walks at night outside of Chinatown were a thing of the past. Kronen was fearless. He always maintained that Little Italy was the safest place in town.

"Once you fight your way through the Chinatown gangs, you're home free."

It was a trip past old, faded brick apartment buildings with little ground-floor shops. Some had big glass windows. The sights and sounds were the same as when Don was a boy. There was something nice about traveling down the same path with an old friend.

Don wished he could have more of that in his life, but he hadn't the time. Besides, Linda hated going anywhere downtown. If a chic restaurant opened in the SoHo area, all of a sudden SoHo was no longer part of downtown. It was hard for Don to admit that he had become nothing more than an adapter. He compromised willingly. Was he just trying to please his wife? He wasn't sure. He sometimes longed to go back to a simpler way of life.

Don's hands were beginning to get cold. He hated to wear gloves. He thrust his hands deep in his lined pockets. Something felt a little funny that time. He grabbed the object that startled his left hand out of his pocket. He unfolded the letter. In bold letters on top was written "Chessman, Benjamin, Gross, and Gardner, M.D., F.A.C.S., New York Obstetric and Gynecology Group." The header had fax numbers and e-mail addresses.

Below the header was a phone number. It was written in giant numbers. How did this get in here? Without giving it another thought, Don put the paper back in his pocket.

He looked over at Kronen, who was taunting Carrie with a quickly packed snowball. Kronen looked like he was ten years old. He was wearing an old powder blue, ski jacket with a black hat. The hat had a fur piece and ear patches that were pulled down and tied under his chin.

Don picked up some snow, too. The cold stung his already cold fingers. He turned and flung his snowball towards Kronen. He knew it was going to be a bull's-eye. Almost miraculously, in the final split second, Kronen casually turned his body so that the snowball whizzed past him. He looked like an action-adventure hero dodging bullets in some trashy movie.

"God. He's in such good shape. I could never do that," thought Don as he retreated up the block, dodging the onslaught of snow bombs that fell around him.

The snowball antics ended when the little pastry shop was in view. They retreated quickly for the warmth inside.

The three sat at a tiny glass table with open backed, wire framed chairs.

The pastry shop in Little Italy was a place Don and Kronen had gone to for many years. The tourists went to the glitzy Ferraro. It was the same crowd that would eat in Puglias. Don and Kronen avoided the tourist traps.

Kronen always fancied himself an elite "insider" when it came to food. He knew every little hole in the wall that served authentic food. Once the place got a positive restaurant review, Kronen would inform

Dysplasia

his friends that "we're screwed. They're going to start driving in from Long Island. We're ruined."

The place they were in survived several reviews. Because of its location, there was no place to park a new Rover or Lexus without getting a "key job" on the shiny finish. It was off limits for the Long Islanders.

Don always ordered a cannoli and cappuccino. Kronen would do his routine with any waitress willing to put up with him. That night was no exception.

"I want one of those 'cups of chino'," he would intone with all the superiority of an inebriated Italian gourmet.

"What?" was the standard answer from the waitress.

"A cup of chino. One of those cups of chino."

"You want a cappuccino?" The waitress would good-naturedly repeat for Kronen.

"That's what I said. I want a cup, of the cup of chino." Kronen would have the last word. By then the waitress was threatening to smack him. She repeated the order to Carrie; in order to get a confirmation from the sane. It was usually followed by some derogatory exchange regarding men, one that Carrie was glad to offer.

Tonight Carrie started, "Why do men think they have to be funny in restaurants?" Carrie explained it was a form of prehistoric insecurity that stayed in their genes, for perhaps a million years. Don suggested with the advent of gene splicing, they would find a way to remove Kronen's prehistoric funny gene.

Carrie falsely sympathized with Kronen by telling him that "you would have made a great hit in Bedrock. I can see Barney and Fred Flintstone loving your act. I'm not sure about Wilma." "A comedian in his own mind," was how Carrie would remind Kronen of his proper place in comedy history.

Don's cheeks hurt from laughing. He thought about the phone number in the pocket of his prized topcoat. He pictured the numbers in his mind. A thought hit him. The coat check girl? Why him? Although most everyone thought Don was good looking. Except for Don. Why would she give the number to him? Even if she found him attractive, there were so many men there. And Don saw her flirting with Chessman, the master at bedding young women, something Chessman was always glad to remind his partners. In order to put the note in his coat, she would have had to find it inside the office closet. Maybe she had it ready and stuck it in Don's pocket when he first arrived. It didn't matter. The next thought was more realistic. Maybe it wasn't Susan's number.

Kronen was on a roll. When he saw that Don was in a good mood, he abruptly changed the conversation. He wanted to make sure Don knew what he was getting into by taking the hospital assignment.

"This report thing. The report they want you to make. Does your malpractice insurance cover claims made by the hospital or by other doctors on staff?"

"Claims? What claims?" asked Don, not even thinking about what Kronen had said.

"Don. You're going to make a report on the hospital, a report that might be critical and possibly influence the hospital to make changes—"

"Yes, but that has nothing to do with my insurance."

"Oh, yes it does. You don't know what liability you'll have as a result of the report. Someone might sue. It doesn't matter anymore whether the party has a case or not. The legal fees will kill you even if you're innocent. Insurance companies are always trying to minimize their liability. That's why you should maximize yours. Look at the O.J. case. His homeowner's policy kicked out some big numbers. They smartly settled before the trial was over. They didn't want anything to do with a civil trial."

Dysplasia

"What has that got to do with me?"

"Which word don't you understand?" He drew the words one at a time. Slow and deliberate. "Does your malpractice policy cover you against claims brought by the hospital or a staff person?"

"Kronen. Don't patronize me," said Don, who took a bite out of an old-fashioned chocolate cannoli.

"He's not patronizing you in particular. You know he talks that way to everyone, particularly when it's about anything legal," said Carrie in her best get-even voice. "Robert is patronizing to the whole world."

"If you want, I can put you in touch with Murray Kest," said Kronen. "He'll give you the answer in a second. If you need it, he'll get you additional coverage. Sort of an E and O just for this report." He was referring to Errors and Omissions insurance.

"I remember that name. He was for the merger of city hospitals with private hospitals."

"That's sort of right. He was originally for the privatization of the city hospitals, but he knows the whole thing is going down the tubes if the city sells out to 'for-profit' hospitals and corporations. But let's get to the point that has to do with you. Even Kest says the system has failed. So what's knew? He always says the greatest tension comes from caring for the uninsured patient versus making a profit. The only thing you have to worry about is an old one. Is your ass covered?"

Kronen was very bright, and he liked to let everyone know it. He was one of those young men who knew everything in college before the professor spoke a word. He whizzed through law school while holding down a full-time job as a paralegal. He passed the bar on his first try, something many of the hot-shot, high-profile attorneys in New York could not accomplish when they graduated from law school.

"What did he mean by that question?" Don thought for a moment. He didn't feel that he needed any sort of insurance.

"Kronen, what are you talking about? Are all you lawyers fixed on lit-igation of some kind or another?"

"Fuckin'-A."

"Here I'm thrilled about getting involved, on improving conditions in the hospital, and all you can think of is a lawsuit."

Don wasn't going to let Kronen's extreme cynical view alter Don's eagerness to start work on his report.

"Okay, my little liberal dove. Let's go about this another way. Do you trust Chessman?" Kronen asked point blank. He was switching his operant method to convey yet another problem he foresaw.

"Chessman was the guy who recommended me," Don answered quickly.

"That's exactly what frightens me. Since you went to work for him—"

Don cut him off. "I don't work for him."

"Yes you do, and don't give me that partnership crap. The guy is a scumbag. He's a womanizer and a thief. You can be sure if he's doing any sort of a favor for you that it has to help him. That's who he is, a kind of help-himself guy."

"I don't know what you're talking about," Don replied in a hostile tone. "They need someone to do a report. For each unit. Why shouldn't it be me—to do the OB-GYN report?"

Carrie tried to change the subject. "Why don't you two boys take a break? I have five D.U.I.s sitting on my desk for review tomorrow morn-ing, and I am in no mood to see you fight over some arbitrary bullshit."

"Thank you, Carrie. Stick to criminal defense," Kronen quipped.

"I'll get the check," said Carrie as she got up. "You two have a nice time, playing with each other." Carrie waved bye-bye as she moved away.

Dysplasia

"I love that girl. She has a way with words," Kronen stated with a twisted smile on his face. "Now, Don-Don. You are the most naïve man I know."

"Kronen. It's late. Enough," Don said as he got up to go with Carrie. "Hey, Carrie. Wait up."

"Well, that leaves me all alone to play with myself. It's something I've had a lot of experience with," Kronen yelled, making sure Carrie would hear him.

After a few minutes, Kronen rose meekly from his chair, grabbed his cannoli, and joined Don and Carrie.

"Let's walk over to Houston to see if we can get a taxi," said Kronen.

It was the last part of the old routine.

CHAPTER SIX

While the banter continued at the old pastry shop in Little Italy, Chessman was standing high above New York, perched in his tower suite, overlooking Central Park. The sky had cleared and the park was brightly lit.

His jacket was off. His tie hung loose, low on his shirt. His shirt was opened down to the second button. He sipped some champagne and spoke in a low, hushed tone. A bottle of Cristal was perched in a nearby sterling ice bucket.

He sounded like the tour guide on the ferry around Manhattan. "New York is a spectacle to behold. A mix of cultures, rich and poor, all somehow intertwined, in a whirlwind-paced existence."

Chessman turned to his left to see if the eyes of the beautiful, lightly bronzed woman who stood at his side absorbed his words. It was Susan, the coat check girl. She had let her hair down. It fell well beneath her shoulders. She looked even more stunning.

She smiled at Chessman, moved to his side, and took his hand. This brought an immediate smile to his face.

"You brought me up here to try and fuck me. Correct?" She was smiling.

Chessman responded quickly. No routine or series of repartees could slow him down.

Dysplasia
∞

"Fuck you? How undignified of you to suggest that I would reduce a possible act of passion, of love, to such a base expression."

"You're an evil man. That much I can sense," stated Susan, who still smiled curiously at Chessman.

"Then evil must be attractive to you," said Chessman. He moved even closer to Susan.

"I don't know if it's the evil. But I was curious. This is quite an impressive apartment."

Chessman took her champagne from her hand and placed the glass with his own on the windowsill. He took care not to bump any of the small ivory figurines that lined the window.

"Doctor. I think I'd like to go now."

"Susan, you haven't even begun to know me. There are things I could show you, things about yourself that I'm sure you wanted to know." Chessman's voice was rising. He sounded a little angry.

Susan pulled away and walked towards the other end of the room.

"That's a Haitian primitive on the far wall." She pointed towards it.

"Yes. You have a good eye for art," Chessman offered, trying to appear less angry.

"No. I just recognize certain things. Some people even call that form by a name. Voodoo art. Correct?"

Chessman didn't answer. He moved to Susan, grabbing her firmly by both shoulders. His lips quickly moved towards hers. Susan brought both arms up. The movement dislodged Chessman's hold on her shoulder.

"Dr. Chessman. I don't want to kiss you, which would certainly discount any chance for you to get that fuck you're so desperately looking for. Have I made my position clear? At least as far as you're concerned?"

Chessman was an old pro. He smiled, not missing a beat.

"Clear. Let me show you to the elevator. The doorman will get you a taxi." Chessman gestured for her to follow him to the door.

"I really thought you were a little more complicated," said Susan as she headed for the front door of the apartment.

"I don't usually behave that way. It was your beauty and the Champagne."

"Another hot dicked gynecologist," Susan thought to herself. "This guy would hit on anyone." She extended her hand to Chessman. "Friends?"

"Friends," he answered as he shook her hand.

Susan grabbed her coat from the front hall chair. She walked with Chessman to the door. The apartment was ultra modern, despite being filled with varying forms of art, mostly in sync with the general decor, but some definitely out of place.

Something else caught her eye. Susan stopped. She looked down at a container made of chrome, the kind used as an umbrella holder. She spotted something in a collection of artifacts kept in the rectangular container.

"What are you doing with this?" Susan picked it up and held it out to look more closely. It was a decorative, spear-like object, with carvings and multiple colors. On closer examination, the multiple colors would reveal themselves to be a series of intertwined serpents.

"A friend gave it to me. Let's get going. It's late." Chessman seemed put off by the discussion.

"What kind of friend?" Susan asked.

"You wouldn't know. He's a priest."

"You mean a houngan," Susan corrected.

"That's right. A houngan. How did you know?" asked Chessman who appeared disturbed again.

"I am of mulatto descent. My father was born in Port Au Prince."

"Oh. That's very interesting," Chessman responded. With that bit of information he seemed eager to get Susan to the elevator.

He opened the door. With a tightlipped smile, he gestured for her to leave ahead of him. He followed her into the hall. Once outside the apartment, he moved towards the elevator. There were only two residences per floor. The elevator stop served Chessman and his one neighbor, an entertainment manager from California, someone Chessman never saw.

Chessman opened a chrome plate box situated next to the elevator. He clumsily grabbed a telephone from inside the box. He held the phone to his ear. It automatically dialed the downstairs concierge.

"Hello. This is Dr. Chessman. Please send one of the doormen up to escort my guest downstairs. Make sure she gets a taxi. Call one of our accounts." He wanted to be sure Susan left the building.

As he hung up the phone, Susan said politely, "Thank you, but I'm accustomed to paying my own way."

"That may be all well and good in the modern world of feminist-revisionist thinking, but you'll have to forgive me for being hopelessly old-fashioned."

Susan had trouble maintaining her composure. She found Chessman repellent.

The next few minutes were filled with tense silence. They said nothing as they waited for the elevator doors to open. Both felt the impasse. Neither cared to make small talk. Their spirits yelled silently at each other. Finally the doors opened and Susan disappeared inside, in the company of Pierre. He said nothing. Only smiled.

The hopelessly old fashioned, great white doctor of Fifth Avenue finished his champagne alone by the window. He told his wife he would not be home this evening, something she could care less about at that point in their marriage. Their children were grown. A daughter lived on

Lake Washington in Seattle. The other child, a son, lived practically around the corner from the family's Park Avenue prewar cooperative. His son never spoke with him. Chessman was on better terms with his daughter.

Chessman's wife said his daughter moved to the other end of the continent in order for her to tolerate her relationship with her father. Chessman still fancied himself an excellent parent. His son refused to go to medical school, to emulate his father. Chessman's son worked as an illustrator at the advertising offices of Norman, Craig, and Kummel. He wasn't married, and many years ago Chessman accused his son of being gay. He wasn't. Chessman continued to verbally bash his son along with other men at the advertising firm who were openly gay. Some were friends with Chessman's son. The episode was one of the final straws in an already fragile father/son dynamic. Estrangement followed quickly.

Chessman set up a trust for his kids. Unlike many of his rich friends, he did not disinherit his children when the children refused to comply with parental demands. In his mind, he succeeded as a parent because his children were good looking, well-educated, and had money.

Chessman looked out at the night view of the city. He flashed back on the day he ran out of a psychiatrist's office because the analyst agreed with his daughter. She said her father had aberrant feelings towards women. She was confused by his double standard. One for his daughter and one for other women. She felt it diminished any underlying strength in their relationship. Beyond that, his daughter simply did not trust him. He lied to her many times about plans. Things they agreed to do. He often backed out in the eleventh hour, trying to change the circumstances to fit his true desires. In the case of his son-in-law, he tried to screw him out of his share of business deals. Chessman would originally present the deals. It was a way to show his interest in his daughter's marriage.

Dysplasia

Once the deal was established he would try to change the parameters to show his power and control. He had everyone's attention. Worse, he had his son-in-law's money in hand. Chessman always explained his new position with authority, sincerity, and without hesitation. When it came to his family, he always knew what was best for them. He was always right. He had to have complete and utter control.

A quick glance at the voodoo art sent his mind drifting back to his youth. About thirty years ago, he performed abortions for an international figure who used the name Mr. Smithers. Mr. Smithers had numerous "wives". Chessman was young, aggressive, and ready to serve.

The numerous "Mrs. Smithers" were referred to the office as new patients. The nurses in the office giggled when they announced themselves with straight faces.

"Good afternoon. I'm Mrs. Smithers. I'm here to see Dr. Chessman."

The relationship between Mr. Smithers and Dr. Chessman blossomed. It was based on a very simple fact that Chessman would do anything that Mr. Smithers asked. Smithers took the eager doctor to Haiti on business trips. Smithers set up factories to make tires, a deal he would parlay into stock with companies like American Tire and Rubber. Chessman bought shares early enough in the venture to make fifty times his investment of $20,000. Chessman figured Smithers was worth over $1,000,000,000. Chessman was jealous. He regretted that he chose such a hard-working life for himself. He was only a multimillionaire. He had to continue working to keep up his life-style.

Chessman used the key on his Tiffany gold key ring to open the master bedroom door. Once inside the private room, he moved his palm over a wall plate. The large room was partially lit, affording a view of its contents. A sitting area filled one side, elevated on a built-in platform.

In the center of the platform were two large reclining chairs. Next to one of the chairs was a set of stirrups. They were similar to the ones in his office. That set of stirrups was attached to movable stanchions, the kind used at movie theaters to keep ticket holders in line. Each one of the stanchions had a tube-within-a tube arrangement. It allowed the user to raise or lower the height of the stirrups. For a moment Chessman looked at the chairs. He envisioned the beautiful Susan as his captive for the evening. She lay naked on one of the recliners. Her arms bound to the chair with rubber tube restraints. Her legs apart, inviting Chessman.

His mind flashed on the voodoo painting. Then back to the reality of his room. He opened a top drawer on one of the two matching, white-and-gold knobbed vanities. He took out a leather case.

Every time Chessman removed the case, he thought of his daughter. He bought her the same kind of case, except hers did contain an "old-fashioned" memo pad and sterling silver pen. Hers was a small portable computer. Ready for e-mail and Internet connections.

"That's what the techies carry around now," he said on his gift card, hoping his daughter found it to be humorous.

He opened an overhead cabinet by pressing on a remote control device with several buttons that looked like a garage door opener. From the same console he pushed another button, and the curtains closed simultaneously around the room. From inside the overhead cabinet, Chessman slid out a device, connected to a sliding shelf. He removed it from the shelf and placed it in the center of a desk that was built into a far wall. Once in place the image was unmistakable. It was a microscope.

The top of the microscope had a small tricolored projection device. It was a miniature version of the same device that was used for projection television.

Dysplasia

Chessman was breathing more rapidly as he opened the leather case and removed a small container made of white plastic. He opened the box with a push of his thumb. He reached inside and took out a laboratory slide. Several others filled the specially designed storage system inside the case. He fixed the slide in place on the microscope, then turned on the illumination.

Chessman disrobed as he walked to the bed. He took no care where he threw his clothing. Articles landed all over the floor or on the edge of the bed. He was humming. A kind of continuous hum, almost like a chant. By the time he reached the bed, situated on another platform across the room, he was completely naked.

Chessman sprawled out on the bed. He wasn't in bad shape, considering his age and how hard he lived. He opened the drawer to a small night table beside the bed and removed a little vial of white powder. It was cocaine, a strong hospital mix.

A wet bar stood at the wall to his left. Chessman ran to it in order to wet his fingers, quickly spreading the water from his hand to the perimeter of his mouth and then to his penis. The order mattered little to him as he quickly took the white powder and rubbed it on his mouth, gums, nipples, penis and testicles.

As his body numbed from the effects of the cocaine, he snorted a little directly from his wet fingers. He inhaled hard. Then he made the kind of sound people make when they try to clear their nostrils.

He ran back to the bed and propped himself up high with six or seven satin pillows. He had a good view of the far wall where the image from the microscope displayed a visual of the slide. He squeezed his balls hard, testing to see if the cocaine had numbed the outside of his testicles. He was an expert at self-abuse.

A flat screen on the far wall was a sea of pink/purple wavy lines. Many small black circles. A series of clouds, interspersed with pretty colored lights. Perhaps a surreal trip brought on by hallucinogens. Beauty was in the eye of the beholder.

To a histologist the slide showed the Gram Positive and Gram Negative Stains common to many tissue samples. Chessman viewed a slide of human tissue. The message carried across the synapses of his brain produced an aberrant response. To the writhing, moaning, contorting Chessman, the visual image triggered a response that gave him pleasure. It was part of the primal gratification he chased throughout his life. Chessman sought out extreme perverse forms of pleasure. He was not easily satisfied. He always wanted more. He needed more. He had to have more. Tonight would be no exception.

A chrome cabinet with marble top waited near the head of the bed. Inside were two small tanks. One green. One blue. One oxygen. The other nitrogen. A small plastic mask with a support strap for the back of the head was in Chessman's hand. It connected to clear plastic tubes which connected to the two tanks. In a flash, he pressed it up against his nose. He inhaled deeply from the oxygen and nitrogen mixture, nitrous oxide, "laughing gas". Chessman knew exactly how much would render him silly, senseless, and on the verge of total anesthesia. He learned to use it when he was a young resident. Other residents preferred to take quick hits of ethyl chloride. That wasn't for Chessman. He liked his nitrous oxide, and he liked to take his time enjoying its effects.

Chessman shook the vial and put more of the cocaine on the head of his penis. The gesture was no different than a chef on the Food Channel seasoning a pork loin.

He squeezed hard on his penis. He moaned, soft and hideously dark. He knew he couldn't come this way, but he could prolong this state of activity for almost an hour. He lay there naked in the bed. His penis lost its firmness due to the effects of the cocaine. It was just the way Chessman liked it. His system received multiple signals of pleasure. One strange electrical impulse after another. Jumping wildly over the perversely trained synaptic connections.

The evening was beginning for him. This bizarre self-abuse ritual was a warm-up. A bridge from the simplistic sexual realities of his mundane day-to-day life to some distant, tangential world of carnal pleasure, a world that Chessman made for himself after years of design.

Chessman lay on his back. His torso undulated up and down with hard, almost tearing-like movements of his hands. Sometimes he would pause and begin a rhythmic slapping.

High above the ceiling was another camera. This one was a more conventional recording device. Its red light indicator was on. Chessman was the star of the personal, self-directed effort. Chessman loved to make movies.

If someone walked into the room, they might only see a pitifully tormented man performing a sexual ritual. Others might see him more simply. A man reaching back in time and exploring the beginnings of his own sexuality. His actions were primitive and his sounds primal.

As Chessman grasped the base of his hardly discernible erection, he actually looked like a teenager exploring himself for the first time. But the expression on Chessman's face was one of a man who held the foundation of a mighty edifice in his grasp. What else could he think? A man of his power must have power in his loins. How else could he be capable of satisfying the throngs of willing women who sought him out? He could never accept that most of the women viewed his penis as an annoyance that they had to deal within the course of sexual games. Like most men, he paid an inordinate amount of attention to his own genitals during sexual activity. Something he demanded his partners treat with equal importance. Initially, women were attracted to his honest good looks and his world of power. Most exposed to his pharmacy of sexual enhancements and never-ending hunger for S & M games turned him down flat. Only a select few would keep company with a man like Chessman.

He heard all types of responses from "you must be kidding" to "you sick, mother-fucking, deluded sonofabitch. I ought to cut your balls off." But like the man at the party who asks every woman if she would like to go to bed with him, he got his "face slapped" often and occasionally got laid. Some of the takers were insecure and passive, others naturally curious. Sometimes Chessman would find a woman open to his type of perversions, much better versed than Chessman at his own games. The introduction of crack smoking had grown in popularity. Whatever the underlying motives, Chessman could always find a game-playing partner. He was the architect of his own life. He constructed it the way he liked it.

After several minutes, Chessman chemically altered his state of mind. He continued to aggressively overstimulate himself. The pleasure center in his brain was firing at an abnormally rapid clip. The messages were partially conscious. Distorted and disconnected to reality. His mind repeatedly played ritualistic chanting. All he could see were mentally created flashes of female genitalia, interspersed with the pink and blues of the slide on the wall.

CHAPTER SEVEN

After bidding the Kronens good night Don walked into the lobby of his apartment building. It was a modern high-rise, walking distance from Bloomingdales. He overpaid for it in the late '80s. Scott gave him one of his impish Woody Allen lips-together grins and said, "Boytshik. You're starting to make too much money. You need some write-offs." The market dropped and Don had to refinance. There was talk of selling or leasing. Scott talked him into paying the larger monthly payments. Fortunately, the market turned around. The unit went way up in value. Now Scott suggested he consider selling. Money was pouring in the real estate market.

Linda had her heart set on moving to Sutton Place, a short walk from where they lived. The apartment was close to Third Avenue. Don loved to walk to the restaurants, to get a newspaper, or walk the avenue. Sutton Place was more secluded and nestled closer to the East River below First Avenue. It was hard to get a taxi there. It was almost impossible, unless you called for one by telephone. Sutton Place meant nothing to Don, and it meant everything to Linda. She was pressuring Don to sell.

Don did not want to apply to another cooperative board in that area. They already tried one and were flatly turned down. Don knew it was because he was Jewish. Linda told him he was crazy, and that it was probably because they weren't rich enough or well-known enough, to have the fabled Sutton Place address.

Well-known indeed. Don had been on television several times, in fact three times on CBS with the *Doctor on Call* reporter, who was also a physician. Everyone in New York who watched the evening news was familiar with Don's lectures on "dysplasia". How to find out if you had "bad cells". Don knew that some of the women on the board were probably uncomfortable after seeing Don on television. The topic was undesirable, perhaps even bad luck to think about. They probably pictured Don in the elevator asking residents how their cells were doing. Don was sure that being "well-known" was not really an issue. Perhaps it was a hindrance.

"There is only one Jew in the building, and he goes by the name Billings," Don explained to Linda after the rejection. "I'm more well-known than half the people there."

Linda used her cold WASP approach to flatly remind Don that "this was not the kind of fame I was talking about." Perhaps if one of his plays was more successful. Maybe that might be considered the right kind of fame.

Don knew from these conversations that Linda thought less of Don. He knew he wanted a better situation, but could not bring himself to move on the concept, to get out of the marriage.

Stu Beitleman's friend was the divorce lawyer named Romano something. He had an ordinary last name and Don could never remember it. Romano told Don years ago that he should press Linda to make a postnuptial agreement to protect Don from any huge increase in assets. Don thought such agreements were undignified.

"I have two already," Stu exclaimed. They were commonplace in his world.

Dysplasia

Romano chimed in that "Stu's were all with guys." Romano was quite a character.

"Can you imagine some young stud from South Carolina or Bum Fuck Wherever going after Stu's house in the Pines? Stu would drop dead if he had to give up the Pines house. The poor bastard can't get laid in the city."

Don was so naïve in those days that he thought Romano was making typical heterosexual fun. Don was convinced that Stu's partying life in the Pines section of Fire Island was simply Stu's real life.

As Don rode up the glitzy chrome-walled elevator, he told himself not to have a fight with Linda. They had such a nice beginning that morning. Then the unfortunate exchange at the office party. He dreaded finishing the day on such a terrible note. He just wanted to kiss her good night and start in fresh tomorrow. It was holiday season. He didn't want to go through the period with a series of their routine squabbles. Maybe she would be pregnant soon and that would change their lives.

Don unlocked the modest series of three locks on their oversized door. The management insisted only two locks were necessary, but Linda felt better with a second Medeco lock. Operated from the inside.

He walked inside and quickly shed his prized Aquascutum. An antique wooden coat rack stood to receive the coat. Linda told Don a dozen times, but he couldn't remember if she said Early American or something else. Antiques mattered little to Don. He didn't understand why the same type of coat rack from the Ikea catalogue wasn't suitable at a third of the money.

Don immediately veered off to the kitchen. Late-night snacks were available in the form of leftovers from local take-out facilities. Chinese,

Japanese, Italian, and deli. One-day old was ideal for Chinese and Japanese. Italian could go two days, sometimes even three. The key was letting the sauce congeal. Deli food depended on proper wrapping. It was ultimately judged by the changing color of the meat. If the meat still had its right sheen, it was usually okay. Odors served better indicators than time. The odor test served perfectly for anything that contained mayo or milk products, like potato salad or cole slaw. Things involved with chicken broth were a personal call. A kreplach or a matzo ball had to be judged by taste. Linda called the kreplach "Jewish won tons."

Don opened the refrigerator and was greeted by six Styrofoam containers, randomly scattered about the refrigerator. Between coffee cups and food containers, Don was convinced that one day a study would appear identifying Styrofoam as the major cause of mental depression. His other theory was that Styrofoam was addictive. That's why so many companies used it to serve drinks or house food. Worse, it was just a slow poison. Someday someone would use Styrofoam consumption in a criminal defense case.

Interspersed with the Styrofoam containers were different-shaped aluminum containers with cardboard tops which often got soggy. No one in the Gardner household would replace them with aluminum foil or plastic wrap. It was unheard of to keep a neat, odorless refrigerator. The Gardners' maid cleaned on demand. Linda stood over her, pointing out each individual cleaning stroke, very much like the coxswain in a sculling event. Tidying up the refrigerator was foreign to Don and Linda. So it was unlikely that the maid would ever touch it unless instructed to do so.

Looking at the variety of designs and resultant shapes of the containers, Don wondered if the creators were the same people who originally made psychiatric tests. The kind with different textured geometric shapes. And of course, the holes. Putting away a series of Styrofoam and aluminum containers in a modern, multishelved, overcompartmentalized refrigerator was like taking one of those peg and hole tests.

Despite Don's hatred for Styrofoam, he put up with it. It was a clear winner for preserving food. The wet cardboard invited microscopic organisms to feast on their very expensive leftovers. The first container he opened was filled with sushi, two raw strips of tuna and two vegetable rolls. The small kind. Wrapped in black seaweed. It failed the odor test. Don was in no mood to play Japanese roulette with his stomach. He quickly discarded the sushi in the sink eradicator. He turned the water on full and flicked the switch that turned on the machine. The unwanted sushi was diced into oblivion, sending it down the long ride from the eighteenth floor and out of the building. A job well done. He forgot that Linda was probably asleep and quickly turned off the machine. He opened another container. Cold meat loaf and mashed potatoes. Ah, this was something that would last forever. No microorganisms champing away on cooked meat loaf. He dipped a chunk of the meat loaf in the hardened potatoes. A satisfying finger snack.

Don closed the refrigerator door. He made his way to the bedroom, munching on his snack. When he got inside the bedroom, he instantly sensed no one was there. This had happened before. The usual note sat alone over the spot where Linda slept. It was written on her pink stationery. The kind with a tiny family crest—her fictionalized connection to a Mayflower family.

Originally, Don bought the story that Linda's family was direct descendants from a Mayflower family. He wondered how come no one in her family knew anyone on a personal basis that was in the well-known family. Don learned that there were many WASPs masquerading as original blue bloods the same way there were Jews who claimed better European origins. Total assimilation with the desirable blue-blood lineage. Don resented the real hard-liners. The right clubs. Schools. Business organizations. The right to exclude. Sometimes hate.

Don thought about Linda. How she changed. He never thought his wife was one of those people. He remembered her as independent. A free thinker. An ex-hippie. She was friends with the girl that took her clothes off in *Hair*. Linda was free of all the burdensome trappings of conspicuous consumption, free of the greed and avarice that accompanied positions of power, and free to let a man lead his life independently without having to compromise his natural instincts as a man. Over time it proved wrong.

He picked up the pretty pink note only to read the same message he had read before. In the last couple of years, the notes were more frequent.

"I'll be at my mother's. We need a little time to cool down. It will be good for both of us."

It was signed, as if there was reason for substantial doubt, "I still love you, Linda."

How nice of Linda to "still love him". It angered him to read the note.

Linda knew how to make Don feel responsible. Don must be some awful person. Why else would Linda have to choose that kind of language? He must be a terrible husband for Linda to run to her mother's. Linda could be very manipulative. Don was vulnerable at times to her particular methodology. This was one of those times. Don told himself it must be the holiday season. He was suffering from holiday affective disorder. Kronen called it psychobabble mumbo-jumbo. Talk radio overdid it. Don was a person more susceptible to depression around the holidays. Linda knew this. Yet they always fought around holiday time. It seemed like Linda used the period for a more emotional leverage. Don wished he wasn't so susceptible. Sometimes he saw it for what it

Dysplasia

was, and other times he remained a victim to his own weaknesses. Whatever the underlying basis, it had happened again. A fight during the holidays. And Linda was gone.

Suddenly his mood changed. He wasn't going to sulk. He was more angry than anything else. He crumpled the paper. He reflexively walked to his topcoat. He pulled the note from inside the coat. He walked to the nearest phone on the kitchen wall. He dialed the number without letting another thought enter his conscious mind. He listened as the voicemail machine played the recorded message. He was relieved that she didn't answer. Part of him knew he would have hung up if she did. He had never done anything like this.

"Hello. This is Susan. I'm not at home, but I would like to call you back. Please leave a message at the beep tone."

Don froze. He panicked. What if she had a way to identify his number? He didn't use any of the blocking services. His home number wasn't listed.

Don was not an adulterer. He thought about the possibility of sex with women other than his wife. In his heart he just felt that he was not cut out for more than one woman at a time. He never wore a marriage band. Perhaps he should start. If he had worn a ring, this wouldn't have happened.

Why did he call back? To get even with Linda? That wasn't like him. He was angry before. It must have been the ego gratification. Susan left the number because of some uncontrollable attraction. He thought about the romantic possibilities.

Don wasn't sure that he even found black women attractive. He was brought up in a prejudiced environment where any young man from his crowd would be ostracized for dating a black woman. It was okay to be seen with a black woman providing she was the "cleaning girl's" daughter and he was giving her a ride home. If he were going to commit adultery, Susan would not be the one.

Don was saddled with the truth. The bottom line was that Don was afraid to investigate his own sexuality outside of his marriage. He didn't believe in it or he couldn't believe in it.

Then reality hit. He thought of the obvious and spoke after the beep. "Hello. This is Dr. Gardner returning your call. How can I help you? If this is a medical problem, you can reach me in my office tomorrow at 421-9500."

Then his mind played with the fantasy another time. He paused for a second, and felt his pulse increase rapidly. "My home telephone is 889-4257."

He gave no reason why he left his home telephone. He quickly hung the receiver back in its cradle. Exhaling deeply, he turned and headed for the bathroom. He was going to call it a night. He spoke to himself as he walked. "You idiot. What if she calls? You aren't going to do a thing. You never do. You're a wimp. Everyone else is out there still fucking up a storm, even with the AIDS scare. What if she calls when you're not here? You are an asshole. You can tell your wife that she's a prospective patient. Linda won't even be suspicious. Linda knows you're a wimp."

He was in the bathroom. A seriously decorated chrome-and-mirror palace. A cramped Jacuzzi tub, something he had never used. He stared at himself in the mirror over the bathroom sink. He carefully squeezed out an exacting amount of toothpaste on his brush.

"Down on the uppers and up on the lowers. Scrub a dub dub. Brush. Brush. Brush. And forget the floss." He hated to floss. He didn't think it did anything. When he told the root canal guys in the building that he didn't floss, they snickered. "It'll be more business for us." Don was willing to take his chances.

Dysplasia

He had done something he didn't understand. He laughed at himself for making such a big deal out of it. Don's last thought before he went to sleep was that Susan probably needed a doctor. He had blown the whole situation out of proportion. Very often, people hired at parties asked for medical advice, and this situation would be no different. Still, he had a hard time admitting to himself that he was curious about her. The idea that she was someone he never would have dated in the past made it all the more interesting.

As Don slept, he gulped the air with a wide-open mouth. The breaths were deep and rhythmic. He was exhausted. The annoying electronic sound of his telephone woke him easily. No matter how tired he was, he could be awakened by the slightest noise. Maybe it was Susan. He kept telling himself that the reason he left the home number was in case it was a medical emergency.

"Hello," Don said in a barely audible whisper. He felt his heart pound. What if this was Susan? Was he on his way to some forbidden life?

The voice on the other end of the line was loud. "Junior. Junior. Is that you?" The voice was frantic. It sounded like Chessman. It was a mood and tone unfamiliar to Don.

"Hank?" Don hated to call him Hank. Don reminded himself that there weren't any Jews named Hank.

Chessman repeated himself. "Junior. Answer me. Is it you?"

"Hank? What is it? I'm not on call. It's Harvey's night. He always takes the Christmas holiday."

Chessman spoke clearly without interruption. "Shut up and listen carefully. Get dressed and come to the office building. Get two security men and use your key to enter the apartment upstairs. I think I have a problem developing."

There was noise in the background.

"Hello? Hank. Hank? Are you there?"

Don heard the call disconnect. "Hank?" After a few beats the dial tone pierced the silence.

Don shook his head in an effort to shake the sleep from his body. What had he heard? He wasn't sure.

Without thinking he dialed back the apartment. No answer. He reached the voicemail. It was a voice of Cyber Secretary. "She" was programmed to track down the party you wanted, providing your name or voice had clearance on the system. Don hung up. Maybe Chessman would pick up. He dialed again.

Chessman was in some sort of distress. Chessman in distress? Impossible. This man calculated his entire existence, down to his lavatory schedule. While Don thought about a series of fantasy difficulties for Chessman, he hurriedly got dressed. Moments later he was out the door.

While he waited for the elevator to take him to the garage he thought about calling Lou. Chessman wouldn't like that. He called Don. Not Lou. There was no time to have the night doorman bring his car around to the lobby. Don brought his extra set of keys to start his car.

Don got into his metallic light blue 1996 BMW. The four door. Linda pushed for the popular auto. He had grown to love the car, never before driving a sedan that had an engine so unreasonably powerful. It was overkill to drive around Manhattan. But for nights like this, it offered speed and a false sense of security. It was a short drive to the office. Don could actually jog the distance in about the same time.

Linda's social group had forsaken the BMW for the current model Mercedes. Many stopped buying new cars altogether. That was the only reason Don was off the hook for dropping over $100,000 for a new car. Linda's hotshot friends were pouring money into art. They didn't care what the art looked like as long as they felt they were getting a good deal.

Chessman was no different. Three or four days a week at Sotheby's. On sunny days he walked straight from the office, sometimes leaving patients while he took a "break". On other days he would meet with known art dealers. First lunch downtown at the Gotham Bar and Grill, Tribecca, or Nobu. Then pop into galleries in SoHo, where the management would snap to attention after spotting "cash-and-carry" customers.

Don left his car in front of the Fifth Avenue entrance. He parked behind Pierre. He had called ahead on his car phone. Two security guards were already at the door. Pierre stood in the background. As Don entered he wondered why Chessman called him. He could have just called downstairs.

The guards escorted Don up the elevator. Don used his key to enter the apartment. One of the guards entered ahead of him. The living room area was dimly lit. Don was not going to be heroic, particularly for Chessman's sake.

"Dr. Chessman," said the guard.

There was no answer.

The second guard walked towards the kitchen area. He could see the room was empty, but checked anyway. Both guards avoided the closed bedroom door.

Once the three men were in the apartment, they heard a woman's voice singing an indiscernible melody. The door from the bedroom flung open. The men were treated to a little show as a woman danced from the bedroom. Wearing a leather thong that covered only her pubic hair, she moved swiftly towards the expansive view windows. Her large, pendulous breasts stood straight out in the air, hardly moving as she bounced to the front window of the apartment. It looked rather innocent, except for one thing. A small object glistened in her right hand. It caught some reflected light from outside the window as she twirled her body, still singing.

"Excuse me, ma'am. Are you with Dr. Chessman?" one of the security guards asked rather calmly, as if this was a daily occurrence. The security people were well-trained to avoid liability claims.

She whirled around. The object dropped to the floor. Don recognized it as a basic surgical scalpel. Don was frightened. He didn't know if the guards saw it.

"Who the fuck are you?" she demanded as she covered her breasts. She ran right past them and into the bedroom.

"Hank," she screamed. "There are some men in here!"

The guards followed her. Don trailed them.

As she entered the room, she immediately went to a figure lying on the bed. His head was covered. Don knew it was Chessman because he had a large scar on his left upper forearm. The woman removed the hood from Chessman's head and a red rubber ball from his mouth.

"Hank. What is going on here? Get rid of these people," demanded Chessman's guest.

Chessman's hands were restrained by rubber tubing attached to the posts on the bed. The woman undid the tubing as Chessman spoke.

"Junior. What the hell are you doing here?" Chessman demanded with a mock tone of anger.

The guards stood motionless.

Don began to say something, but was immediately cut off by Chessman.

"Darlene. This is so embarrassing. There's been a terrible mistake," consoled the kink master.

Dysplasia

Darlene walked to the closet and fumbled for her clothing. She grabbed them in a ball and stomped off into the connecting bathroom.

Chessman winked at Don. "Okay, Junior. Send the guys home. I can take it from here."

"Are you sure you're okay?" Don asked. He was thinking about the scalpel.

"Fine. Fine," was Chessman's answer. "Don't worry about me. Oh, and Junior?"

"What?" answered Don, eager to do his bidding.

"Not one word. You too, boys," he said as he got up from the bed.

"No problem, Doc," said the first guard. He had three stripes on his uniform. "We didn't see anything."

The other guard was already on his way out.

Chessman grabbed a maroon velour robe. He covered his body quickly. He opened the night table and removed a wad of cash. He handed a few bills to each of the guards. It looked like a few hundred, hardly bribe money for a New York scandal.

The guards took the money happily and without question.

"No problem," said one guard.

Don looked around the room. He had never seen it except when it was being cleaned. He never saw any of the special toys. He wondered if Lou or Harvey had been inside. Don saw the specially mounted camera.

Chessman took off the robe and threw on a white Fila sweatsuit that was hanging on an overnight wooden valet. Don looked around and observed the stirrups, the nitrous oxide machine, the syringes, and a dish full of cocaine. Vials and syringes sat on one of the night tables. Don leaned a little to the side and saw vials of Valium, Demerol, and a bottle of Brevatol.

Chessman was more bizarre than Don ever imagined.

Don saw the microscope. His new level of acceptance changed to unbridled curiosity. What were these slides doing there? Don didn't even think why he was doing it. He looked to see if Chessman was watching. Confident that Chessman wouldn't notice, Don took one of the slides, slipping it easily into the side pocket of his jacket.

As Don moved to leave, Darlene came out of the bathroom. She was wearing an elegant white Chanel suit. She had on fresh makeup. She looked none the worse for wear, despite the evening's activities. She looked like she had just finished an afternoon of shopping at Saks.

As she walked past Chessman, she gave him a friendly peck on the cheek.

"All's fair in love and war. No hard feelings?" she asked.

"None at all. It was all in fun, as far as I'm concerned," said Chessman, holding her hand for a moment.

"Call me sometime, when you get your nerve back." She waved goodbye.

This made Chessman laugh. He gave her a playful pat on the rear.

"Of course, darling. The doorman will get you a taxi."

"Thanks," she said, and disappeared into the hall.

"Junior. I'll speak to you tomorrow. I'm tired," was all Chessman said. Chessman's tone was clearly dismissive.

"Okay," said Don. Don really didn't want to discuss anything. He was glad to leave.

Chessman left a few minutes after Don. Within a half hour, he was home in his uptown apartment, asleep with his wife in an adjoining king bed.

Don drove home wondering why Chessman had called him. Maybe he was trying to turn things around. First the vote of confidence with the hospital situation, then the call. Chessman had the faith to call Don. He didn't call Lou or Harvey. He let Don into his private life, his inner sanctum, however bizarre. Don took it as a sign of respect. Don wanted to see it all that way, at least for the night. He wanted to feel good about the holidays, about himself. That's what holidays should be for. He didn't want to think about Linda or the fact that Chessman was a disgusting perverse man.

He couldn't go home. He wanted to treat himself to something. Don drove directly to the Carnegie Deli. He left with an oversized pastrami and corned beef sandwich. He drove home eating it and sipping a Dr. Brown's cherry soda. It made him feel good for the moment. It had been a hell of a night.

The next morning as Don drove uptown on Park Avenue, Don thought about Chessman and his kinky date. He chuckled to himself about Chessman and reminded himself that he was going to view the slide. Chessman always made a point that histology was a waste of time. Chessman rarely used the office lab microscope. If he did, it was usually to impress a patient who "wanted to see how a diagnosis was made."

Don's own curiosity was peaking. It was one thing to have his worst suspicions confirmed about Chessman's bizarre extramarital sex life. But the slide, what could that be about?

Why had Chessman called? Did he fear that woman for some reason? Playing with a scalpel could certainly be dangerous. "That was an understatement," he said out loud. If Chessman was in the situation before, and he certainly appeared to have been, why call Don? Don entertained the thought that Chessman orchestrated the whole scene to test Don, to see how he handled it. Even Darlene was in on it. That was certainly a possibility. Chessman always tested people. Darlene did seem overly relaxed. If that was the case, Don had passed with flying colors. He showed up as instructed.

Don pulled his BMW into the office garage and zigged and zagged through the lot. He came to a screeching halt in his own personal $350 per month garage space. It came off the top of the practice. Since Lou and Harvey refused to own cars, they received a credit equal to the garage cost. Years ago they tried to use the amount as a lunch credit until everyone in the practice realized that it was rare to see either one of them spend more than five bucks for lunch. If it was office business, the practice covered it anyway. Then they tried to offset the amount with travel expenses. For similar frugal reasons it didn't pan out. The decision was made to give them the cash in the form of extra salary, which suited both personalities.

Don pulled into his parking space, a black Jeep Cherokee pulled into the space beside his.

It was Dr. Jill Stover. Don liked her a lot. Don took his time getting his briefcase. He thought Jill was not only beautiful but brilliant. Don had always been attracted to Jill. What he didn't know was that Jill liked him more than he thought but repressed any further feelings years ago once Don married.

Jill was one of the few doctors in New York who had a combined degree, a DDS and an MD. She was a hospital-trained maxillofacial surgeon who also had a dental education. Jill had a clinical practice in the building where she made tons of money bailing out other specialists and general practitioners. When doctors got in trouble, they sent the patient to Jill. The root canal guys screwed up sometimes by poking into a sinus. She treated patients with rotten dental implants, some with osteomyelitis infections caused by an overzealous dentist eager to jump on the implant bandwagon. Jill bailed out all the "iatrogenic" problems, problems "caused by the operator."

If any of the dentists ever heard Jill talk about them, she would never get another referral. But she was smooth and calm and always had an air of professionalism about her. She had a way to put her less educated and clumsy colleagues at ease.

Dysplasia

Her brother was a hotshot broker with Drexel, who changed his life abruptly after the Milkin affair. After steep fines, he was able to keep over five million for himself and five million for his family. That's after giving the city town house to a charity and the ski shack in Vermont to his sister. Jill refused the gift and told him she would someday buy her own house. Each year in the city she did less and less skiing. Each year she told herself to update her skis and take time off. It never happened.

What impressed Don the most was that Jill worked for the Chief Medical Examiner. She was revered in the city for her investigative work with crimes. She would be called upon for everything from body identifications at natural disasters to DNA tests in criminal cases.

"How's that murder case going?" asked Don as soon as Jill spotted him.

"The D.A. is playing out every courtroom tactic he learned in law school. It's a joke. They've got semen all over the place. All over the body. She obviously has sex with someone, unless she accidentally dumped a vial of semen from some fertilization clinic on herself before committing suicide. They are refusing to get a DNA test on the husband."

"Is the test some kind of big deal?" Don knew the answer.

"Doctor. You should know better than that. They can do it with a cotton swab. Off the inside of his cheek."

"Any set of cheeks?"

Jill slammed the door to her car and laughed to be polite.

"Really, Don. You can do better than that. You've been hanging around Chessman too long."

Jill was all business around the office but did have a sense of humor. Don knew her from medical school and could easily elicit her playful side. Don always wanted to ask her out when they were in school, but felt he would offend her because she confessed early on that Don was one of the few male students at the school that she liked as a friend.

That made Don feel very important because he never really had a close female friend. After school was finished, he only saw her two or three times a year, usually at meetings. Since he moved into the office with Chessman, he saw her more frequently, but only for brief moments. Never asking her for a date was something Don always regretted. He secretly wished that when he was single, he found the guts to date women like Jill. He wondered if he were single today, would he take the strides necessary to qualify as Jill's type?

Jill's boyfriend was a detective named Dick Murphy, who worked for the Sex Crimes division of the District Attorney's office. Dick was nothing like Don. Aside from being older, Dick had blond hair and blue eyes.

"Maybe it's a cover-up, and the detectives spread the semen all over her, sort of like the blood in the O.J. case," said Don with a big, childish grin.

"There you go, Don. Can't you resist one sophomoric joke?"

Jill moved into second gear and swung her attaché forward, using the force as a propelling pendulum.

"Hey, wait up. I don't want to catch the next elevator." He hurried to catch up.

"No more cheek jokes?"

"Promise. Maybe one pun about the murderer losing his genes all over the victim."

"Yes. The Levi Strauss connection."

Nothing got past her. Don loved it.

The elevator was crowded. Don tried not to stare. He thought he saw Dolly Parton and Michael Caine. It wasn't unusual, but Don was always star struck. He thought about Lou. If Lou were, there he would always joke around. Don never did it alone. But Jill was there. Jill was always into shocking Don with the gory details of her work.

Dysplasia

"Did you ever find that fingerprint you were looking for? You know, the heavy duty S & M murders?" Don already knew the answer.

Jill looked mortified. She gestured with her head towards the people in back of the elevator. Then she stared straight ahead. Jill felt comfortable trying to make Don squeamish about her casework, but she would have no part of the kind of games Don and Lou played in the elevator.

After seeing Jill's reaction, he realized the game was childish. He just wanted to see if Jill would play along. He left the worst part of it for her to say. Don decided not to give the answer. Jill worked on a case where a missing fingerprint was taken from a victim after death. The fingerprint was found on about a third of a finger in the victim's colon during autopsy.

The elevator stopped on Jill's floor first. Don liked to get off the elevator and walk her to her office. He would take the stairs the rest of the way to his floor.

Jill shared the office with the most pompous man Don ever met. Manny Friedkin was a self-proclaimed guru and one of the pioneers of dental implantology. Don had never heard of him until he moved in with Chessman. Manny tested new devices on live patients. In the beginning, a lot fell out. "Sometimes the patients' jaws fell out too". That's what Lou said about Manny. Without hesitation, Manny would proselytize the newest, greatest, and most expensive implant. It was a hit and miss formula. The field was so new that watchdog groups didn't exist. Manny didn't care what anyone thought.

Manny was a different breed of salesman than Chessman. At least Manny had the surgical skill to back up his product. The funny thing about sticking around with the same procedure long enough is that it might catch on. Manny became famous as "the father of implantology."

What you saw was what you got. Manny was from the old school. No bullshit. Each spring he would whip out the same blue 10-year-old seersucker suit from Brooks Brothers. He admitted he was forced into changing the suit every ten years or so, but made it clear he donated the old suit to charity, taking a healthy tax deduction. With his fancy collection of bow ties, he was easy to find at a crowded seminar. He told you what he thought and that was the end of the conversation. He made no pretense about his failures and legendary malpractice suits. It went with the territory.

Manny was an odd but effective professional match for Jill. Jill had street smarts, like Manny. The two got along famously. Manny had someone to cover emergencies in his office. Jill had an office with a large staff and never had to go through the trouble of building a practice. Everyone in dentistry knew Manny, and the moment she hung out her shingle she was doing okay. Neither Jill nor Manny ever engaged in a conversation about money. They had no time or interest in office production or patient demographics, including breakdowns of fees. Don admired the no nonsense attitude about work, and wished he were in an office with doctors like them.

Don and Jill reached her door, and Jill asked as she did routinely. "Coming in for coffee?"

"No. I had a late night."

"Me too. I need my caffeine. I had to go to the examiner's office."

"What kind of case was it?"

Jill had a pained look on her face.

"I don't know what to call it. It should hit the afternoon editions. They fished a woman out of the East River. She had multiple stab wounds in a nicely designed geometric lattice around the perimeter of the vagina."

"Nice." Don made regurgitation sounds in his throat.

"You want nice? Our artist did a neat clitoridectomy."

"What?" Don knew the word. He wasn't expecting it.

"You heard me," she said. "He cut off the clitoris."

Dysplasia

෨

"I hope he didn't use his teeth."

"You're hopeless, Don. I'll see you later. I've got a busy morning."

"Yeah. Me too. I hope they get the guy."

"Who says it has to be a guy?"

Don knew Jill was right. Gruesome sex crimes often followed unexpected paths. New York had more than its share of the bizarre.

Don walked to the end of the hall to take the stairs. As he bolted up the steps, he flashed back to the scene in Chessman's room. Should he say anything to Chessman? He thought he should play it cool with him and not say a word. That's what Chessman would prefer. Someone who took it in stride. Don decided to play along, even though he would have much preferred to make Chessman the laughing stock of the office by sharing the news with Lou and Harvey. Lou would confide in Tina, the office manager. They shared inside jokes about Chessman.

Don thought again about why Chessman exposed his strange social life. Don was aware of the peculiar bonding rituals men used as a foundation for friendship. Sharing details about their sex lives made them think of themselves more like men. It was truly a weird "guy thing", a thing he felt Chessman understood and perhaps now expected from Don. Don had little to tell. It reminded Don of the joke Chessman told about the man who survives a plane crash with Meg Ryan. After a week on a secluded island a sexual relationship began. The man seemed unhappy. Meg suggested that he tell her what he wants her to do. He tells her to take off her clothes. "Put on my Brooks Brothers shirt. My pants. My fishing hat. My blazer. Now walk to the far end of the beach. Turn around so I can't see your face." When she was far enough away, the man shouted, "Hey, Fred! How ya doin'! Guess who I'm fucking.

Meg Ryan!" Don wondered if Chessman knew the joke was a put-down of men.

Don walked inside the office. "Good morning, Tina," he said. It was his automated hello.

Tina responded with her obligatory good-morning speech. Lou and Don nicknamed Tina "S.B." for super bitch. She was generally aloof but effective. Everyone learned to stay out of her way. Don was the most thin-skinned when it came to Tina. She knew it.

"Good morning, Doctor. The other doctors are in the conference room waiting to start the meeting. You have Mrs. Todd in room three in one hour. She's coming in early to start the fetal monitoring. The rest of the morning." She scanned to computer print-out. "Uh. Just post-ops and check-ups until eleven. Then you have Ms. Carpenter for a biopsy."

"Carpenter. She had a false positive. Didn't we run that again and get a negative?"

"Dr. Chessmen wants you to do a biopsy."

Don tried to keep his composure. The artery bulged on the side of his temple. He grit his teeth, making his thick cheek muscles flex. Tina knew that she had pissed him off. Tina's day was made early. Don was convinced she took pleasure in annoying him.

Tina usually dug into her bag of irritants before noon, when she knew Don would be eager to get out of the office either to get to the hospital or to take a two hour lunch before coming back for afternoon patients. When Don wasn't in the office, Tina had Lou or Harvey to screw with, and she was an expert with them too. Lou acted more like Tina's employee. It had gotten easy for her to get Lou to do her bidding. Because of that, Tina would tone down her actions and let him off the hook. It was almost impossible to get a rise out of Lou. Without some visible effect, Tina's efforts seemed wasted. Harvey reached the point with Tina some years ago that prompted him to ask that she be fired. At first Chessman agreed. Tina had a rough life. Her husband drank and became physically abusive. She basically supported her two little children. Tina supplied a tearful explanation of how she needed the job. Harvey didn't flinch. Tina approached Chessman for a private meeting. After the meeting, Tina emerged from the room with a smug, lips-together smile. Chessman called his partners into the room.

"Harvey. Did you ever call Tina an uppity black chick from Harlem?"

"She's from New Jersey," Harvey corrected.

"I didn't ask you that." Chessman was impatient. In situations like this, he already knew the outcome before calling a meeting. It just had to be played out.

"What did she say?" Lou chimed in. He tried to keep things rolling.

"She said a lot. Look at this." Chessman lifted up a nicely bound report of about ten pages. He handed the document to Lou.

"She wrote that?" Lou asked incredulously as he examined the document. Even as he spoke, he realized that Tina probably had it prepared by an attorney. It would not have surprised Lou to find out that Chessman helped in the preparation. It was something Lou did not want to know about.

"Did you ever tell her jokes about a ménage between a black man, a Jewish man, and a Polish man looking for a hooker?" Chessman continued.

Chessman's eyes caught Don's. Don snickered.

Harvey's face was flushed. "What the fuck is going on here? I'm not running for the Supreme Court, and she's not Anita Hill."

"Harvey told those jokes years ago," said Lou. "Am I right?"

Harvey quieted down. "Look. I stopped. But Hank. You must remember during those hearings, the jokes were flying around the office. Long Don Silver and all that."

"Don. What do you think?" Chessman asked straight out.

"Well, we don't want any lawsuits. It's not a matter anymore whether a case is defensible. It only matters that someone might bring a case."

In those days, Don was still in his supportive mode of Chessman. Inwardly, he did not want to see Tina fired because of anything that he said.

"Harvey. She said you're prejudiced. Look, I know you're not, but what's the point of firing her? She does a good job. Look at these numbers." Chessman held up the monthly flow sheets.

"She does a good job for you. She's your kiss ass. I want my own kiss ass." Everyone knew that was at the heart of the matter. Chessman was treated differently than the rest of the partners.

"So, that's easy. Hire anyone you want. Does anyone here object to Harvey hiring his own personal assistant?" He knew Harvey would never increase the office overhead.

Silence.

"Done," said Chessman as he threw the report into the wastebasket.

"Shouldn't we keep a copy of that?" Lou asked.

"Yeah. In case she changes her mind," added Don.

"Tina assured me that she desperately needs this job and will not pursue the matter if we all agree to drop the subject at this time and not refer to it in the future. Agreed?"

"Okay," said Don. He was glad to let it go.

"Okay. Great." Lou was pleased too.

"I guess so. Okay," said Harvey with a clear uncertainty. He nervously fidgeted with his hands.

Then Chessman dropped the bomb. "She's getting a raise. And we're going to put an extra bonus in a retirement account for her." Chessman stood up. "Don't say another word. Case closed. Junior. Maybe you can explain to Harvey that this is just the way the world works." Chessman left the office.

Harvey wanted to speak. He looked over at Lou. Lou shrugged.

Lou had to smooth things over. "Harvey. Let it go. In the long run it won't matter."

It was a lot for Harvey to swallow. Harvey would regret his decision every day that he had to deal with Tina in the future. They were cordial to one another, but anyone who worked in the office knew they weren't friends. Harvey ended up doing a lot of the little jobs in the office himself rather than deal with Tina. Chessman had Tina strategically placed between him and each of his partners. The era of political correctness arrived. Everyone was more careful when it came to joking with the office staff. Particularly new ones.

During the next couple of years, Tina became more manipulative with Don. She sensed that Don might eventually become the second in command. Tina functioned between Chessman and Don. Since Don was beginning to question his relationship with Chessman, it was harder to deal with Tina. Chessman always plotted everything so that he would appear innocent. Tina always supported the point of view that absolved Chessman from being the culprit, on everything from taking the extra salary checks to ordering a new type of coffee for the kitchen. Tina took the blame herself or laid it off on one of the unsuspecting staff members. It didn't matter as long as Chessman was never involved.

Don was excited about starting his hospital report. He somehow felt closer to Chessman because of last night's activities. Don strode past Tina, took a fast turn at the Jackson Pollock, and walked down a corridor filled with black-and-white framed copies of ultrasound photographs of a fetus at various months of development. He turned left at the vanity wall, the one filled with photographs of celebrities with Chessman. Dali, DiMaggio, Eisenhower, Carter, Thurmond, Clinton,

Hope, Eastwood, Pfeiffer, Marilyn, Jackie, Stone, Hanks, Giuliani, Bradley. Over one hundred photographs on the wall. Don turned left at an old photograph of Chessman and Jack Nicklaus and walked confidently into a large conference room.

The room was monstrously oversized for meetings that usually involved only the four partners. Three other physicians worked for the group part-time, with false promises of being on a path to partnership. They were used as ancillary worker bees so that an unusually wide range of services could be provided immediately and efficiently. Occasionally, a general staff meeting was called, and then the room would be filled, giving the meeting a sense of importance, parodying the board of a large corporation.

As Don approached the office, he could hear Chessman laughing. Chessman's full-blown laugh best resembled some kind of nasal chortling. Don likened it to a contented pig chowing down some corn. Lou was doing his regular acknowledgment of something funny by saying, "Funny. That's funny." He rarely laughed except when he was into the third or fourth drink later in the day. Harvey was laughing. He covered his mouth, which muffled a laugh in progress.

Chessman sat at the head of the table. He winked immediately to Don as Don entered the room.

"Listen to this." Chessmen pushed a button on one of his remote control devices. He could turn on any machine in the office from his seat in the conference room.

Don listened as a proper female voice welcomed them all to: "The TeleDoctor, brought to you as a courtesy by Dr. Stuart Beitleman."

Don smiled immediately.

The voice continued. "The TeleDoctor is always in to take your calls. TeleDoctor is your link with the latest information on your health. If

Dysplasia

you know the four-digit code of the subject you want to hear please enter that code now. If you want to hear the menu please push "two" now. If you want—"

The recording was cut off. He heard four code tones being entered.

Don was laughing in anticipation. He heard Stu Beitleman's voice. They all laughed because he was using his very straight "I'm-a-doctor" voice.

"If you've ever had an aching back, you know how debilitating back pain can be. Most people experience some type of back pain during their lives. Back pain exists in a variety of forms related to the location of the pain and the cause of the pain. The lower back is the most common site of back pain and can be caused by muscle strain or muscle tears, which in turn cause pressure on the discs in the vertebral column. Fatigue is another common cause often associated with extra pressure on the base of the spine, or the tailbone. Sciatica type of pain often travels down the buttocks and into the associated leg. There are a great number of varying causes for lower-back pain. At the first sign of any discomfort in the lower back, it is important that you consult your physician so that he or she can monitor the situation and establish a base line for the causes and symptoms. The office of Dr. Stuart Beitleman has a staff, separately trained in how to care for lower-back discomfort. On-site facilities include our new modern gymnasium and lap pool. We offer ultrasound and massage therapy by our specially trained physical therapists, who will personally tailor a routine to your needs. To get you feeling better fast. Luncheon and evening appointments can be scheduled with meals ordered from our personalized dietary suggestions."

"That asshole has it all covered," Lou stated begrudgingly. His crumb cake decorated his lower lip. He thought Stu went too far in trying to provide medical care.

"That's why the 'asshole' has got his own plane and we have to save up mileage on our credit cards to fly first class," explained Chessman.

"We shouldn't fly first class in the first place. Business class is just is good." Harvey was forever trying to scale back.

"Hank likes the private movie selection in American's first class." Lou came to Chessman's defense.

"Yeah. You can watch on your own screen." Don liked it too.

"That Beitleman is a hoot," said Chessman.

Don laughed not so much for Chessman's sake, but for the fact he found that type of new doctor advertising funny.

"Has he got any others?" Don asked.

"Any others. He's offering all types of care. Look at his booklet." Chessman sounded impressed.

Chessman displayed the phone book with codes that Beitleman gave to his patients. Don took the small leaflet from Chessman's desk and flipped through the pages. He read a few to himself quickly. "Who is an Alcoholic?; Choosing Contraception: The Condom, Diaphragm, the Pill, IUD, Vasectomy, Tubal Ligation, Spermicides and Sponges; What is Cancer?; Drug Abuse and Teens."

"Whew," said Don, as he tossed the leaflet back on Chessman's desk. "He's even into our territory."

"What about that?" Lou demanded an answer.

"That's better for us. He sends us all his good patients and the crap cases to Gaster on 57th. He put that in at my suggestion. Don't you see, he's just increasing the patient pool? Why should we advertise if we have Stu in our pocket?"

"Yeah. In our pocket," murmured Lou sarcastically. He wiped the remaining crumbs off his lip with his pinky and deposited them in his mouth, licking the end of his pinky to savor the last bit of flavor.

Dysplasia

〇

What Chessman didn't explain was that fees coming from this source would be "split" with Stu in some form that was not yet determined. It was business as usual between Chessman and Stu. Chessman knew that Stu could easily hire someone to do OB-GYN in Stu's office.

"Hey, let's get going. I've got early patients," said Harvey as he picked up his coffee cup and headed for the door. Harvey wouldn't let anyone touch his cup. It was his, only for his drinking pleasure. It was a plain, ceramic mug with a picture of a farmer standing next to a hayloft.

Harvey had his fill of frolic for the day. He was always the first to leave when patients were waiting.

Chessman turned his attention to some articles scattered on his desk. He spoke before Harvey left the room.

"Junior. I'm glad you're here. You're the only one who knows how to interpret these fucking studies."

"Yeah. Junior," Harvey said, trying to mimic Chessman. Harvey sat back down, obliging the fact that Chessman had something else to talk about. He also hoped that somehow Don would be confronted, perhaps humiliated by Chessman.

"Take a look at this study. The fucking Rand Corp isn't satisfied that Hillary Ram-Job Clinton tried to fuck up health care once and for all in this country. They're going to let this shit be published." Chessman held up the journal article.

"Let me see." Don took the article from Chessman.

"Mitch Borun. He does good work. California, right?" Don knew him as a decent researcher who did as little work as possible for manufacturing and pharmaceutical firms, although it was becoming harder and harder to ignore the massive amounts of research money funneling from the private business sector.

"What the fuck?" He drew the four-letter word into ten. "What are you talking about, good work? Read the conclusions," said Chessman, like a drill sergeant talking to a green recruit.

"I'd like to read the whole report." Don had been confronted like this before. Chessman once interrupted a review of literature session in the hospital when Don was the guest speaker.

"Fuck the whole report. Here. Give me that." Chessman grabbed the report, and threw it to Lou.

"The sonofabitch comes up with some astronomical, asshole number of 16%. He says that 16% of all hysterectomies done in those HMO deals are borscht." Now it was clear. The article could cut into business.

Lou read from the next-to-last part of the article. It usually contained a summary or discussion of the statistics, common research protocol.

"It says that over 25% are suspect." Lou sounded concerned.

"Un fucking believable. Harvey, what do you make of this?" Chessman wanted to make sure there would be no repercussions in the Chessman group.

"There are three types of lies. Lies. Damned lies, and statistics." Harvey always got a laugh with this line. It was originally attributed to Benjamin Disraeli, but easily found its way into medical research.

"Did the media pick up on this yet?" asked Lou.

"I got a call this morning from Tom Kinslet of the *Wall Street Journal*. He wanted to know if I had a comment. I won't get involved in these pissing contests anymore."

Chessman was one of the media kings of hysterectomy. He had been on every major talk show in recent years, defending doctors and their general approach to hysterectomy. It was not a popular position, especially with increasingly more powerful women's groups. When women's news shows hit the airwaves, Chessman was a popular guest. He would always be pitted against a leader of a group who felt people like Chessman shouldn't even be practicing. As the questions became more direct, Chessman came off looking like the bad guy. In many ways he was. Women's groups were onto the problem that male physicians still had with the uterus. a problem that could not be settled or reconciled easily in the minds of many women. It was a historical precedent tied to routine medical procedures that embraced a very basic and underlying disregard for the female patient.

"At least the politicians will see that these HMOs—they're so happy to toss all the business to—are turning out procedures just to make ends meet." Don had a point. The article could be spun by the media to make HMOs look bad. During the last year, the HMOs were taking a beating. Large companies lost money. Indictments were handed out to a few top-level executives in health care companies. Suspicion of stock fraud led the SEC into the structure and dealings of the top groups. Insider trading. Stock options in the form of kickbacks.

"That's right, Hank. If the *Journal* calls it the way this report is geared, the HMOs will look bad," said Lou. Nobody could be sure, and Lou knew that.

Chessman breathed a sigh of relief. "You mean it will make the HMOs look bad?"

"Of course." Don took over. "They only used HMOs for the study. It fits all the political interest in shifting business away from fee-for-service guys like us. Wait until they find out what mills those HMOs really are." Don knew that somebody in the media could easily make the jump from that article and conclude, "If the group plans are doing this, what's going on in private practice?" But the goal of these morning meetings was simple. Appease Chessman.

"What are we, a mini mill?" Harvey quipped. He looked like a comedian waiting for a laugh after delivering a killer line.

Chessman didn't like anyone but him to joke about the practice.

"Fuck you, Harvey. If it wasn't for me, you'd be working in the Bronx in some Planned Parenthood storefront, with your arm up to your elbow inside the twat of some three-hundred-pound schvartze on welfare who deliberately farts in your face."

Lou and Don broke up. It was a vulgar but funny vision. Plus it wasn't far from the truth. Without Chessman, Harvey wouldn't exist on Fifth Avenue.

This even made the sour Harvey laugh. He got up from his chair. "I have early patients. Are we through?"

He turned without saying another word and left the room, closing the door. He then opened it, turning back inside the conference room for dramatic effect. "I'm willing to bet more than half of our hysterectomies are unnecessary too." He quickly slammed the door just as a book thrown by Chessman hit squarely in the center of the door.

"The little prick had to say it," said Chessman. "At least he's predictable." Chessman looked over at Don. It was a questioning gaze. In unnerved Don for the moment.

Then Chessman gave his concluding remarks. He, too, was predictable, at least in this one area. "What is this self-loathing we've taken on? We are supposed to be doing hysterectomies. We're not fucking shoemakers! Shoemakers fix shoes. We do hysterectomies! Goddamn it. Is the whole world turning to shit, and it's only 8:15 in the morning?"

"Hank. Take it easy. We've got a busy day." Lou got up and stretched his arms as he walked towards the window overlooking the park. The sun shown brightly through the window, forcing Lou to squint. He held one hand up to cover the glare. "One article is not going to put us or anyone else out of business. We've never been sued once for doing an unnecessary hysterectomy." The reminder was clear to everyone. The bottom line was money.

"Lou. Could you leave us alone for a minute?" asked Chessman.

Dysplasia

Don grew nervous. It was about last night.

"Sure. See you at lunch." Lou was already thinking about his noonday martini. He wanted to be outside in the park, browsing the sidewalk Strand Bookstore that lined the westside of the avenue. He gladly left the room.

Don walked over to the window spot Lou vacated.

"Thanks for your help last night," said Chessman, mustering up a shred of sincerity.

"Help. Hank Chessman never needs any help." Don was playing his part perfectly.

"I did last night. It was a practical joke. It was a setup. She had a dick."

"What?" Don didn't know what else to say.

"No likey dicky," said Chessman with an enormous shit-eating grin.

Don laughed and then played the game. "A dick. Wow. What a shocker!" Don and Lou called them "chicks with dicks."

"Yeah. Not my style. Charlie Pincus thought it would be funny. What do you expect from an attorney? She was good looking, whatever he-she was, but I draw the line if they have a dick."

Don thought, "But the scalpel, was that part of his style? Whose idea was that?" Maybe she was just looking at it when everyone showed up.

Don wanted to ask about the slides. He didn't. He was going to find out himself. He would have something on Chessman, however minor, to add to this new collection of Chessman intimacies. It gave Don a tiny sense of empowerment.

Don felt he had to say something, to at least sound like one of the boys. The words came out quickly. "I didn't know you went in for all that elaborate shit."

"Let's not discuss my private life. I don't want to know about yours." Don didn't know whether to believe him or not. Why had he called Don? It was typical Chessman, impossible to read.

"What's to know?" Don thought to himself, but instead looked directly at Chessman and said, "I won't bring it up again."

"I wanted to thank you and get your assurance that you will never speak about this to anyone. Agreed?"

"Agreed." That part fit the one-of-the-boys theory.

"Hank?" Don cringed every time he called him Hank. Don felt this was a good time to talk about something else controversial.

"What?"

"Do you recall that I asked you not to order procedures on my patients without consulting me?" Don was referring to the morning news from Tina.

"Let's not get into that. I was helping you out. You still need a little help. Can't an old warrior help out a young soldier?" Chessman would ooze manipulation when confronted about anything.

If Don responded to his remarks, he would only find himself defending his own remarks. He tried to keep to the point. "Well, I'd just like to know first. Not from Tina." It wasn't his real position, but it was the most he could get out of a discussion like this from Chessman. Bottom line was Chessman would do what he wanted when he wanted.

"I'm sorry." The sincerity flowed from Chessman. "I get so damn busy. I'll try to remember to be more careful." Chessman winked. "Now get to work so we can make a few shekels."

"Oh, and Hank. Thanks for the consulting job at the hospital."

"Who else could I approve? Do you think I want some outsider coming in and telling us how to run the hospital unit?"

It didn't require an answer. Don just said, "Thanks again."

Dysplasia

"I'm really looking forward to working on that. You and I can publish quite a report. As soon as you have an outline, let's go over it." Chessman spelled out the back-story to the appointment. He was going to take credit for Don's work.

Don was stunned by the remark. It rolled off Chessman's lips as casually as "good morning".

"Uh, okay," was what Don said while he was starting to smolder. "Damn," he thought. "How could I be so stupid? He never does anything for anyone."

Chessman had done it again. Don was caught completely off-guard. "You and I." What was he talking about?

Chessman escorted Don to the door. A slap on the back was thrown in to conclude the visit.

Don smiled as he left the conference room. The entire morning, Don was troubled by this new development. His eager anticipation was gone. He was not going to share the limelight with Chessman. Chessman never wrote a word in his life. He was worse than Stu when it came to finding other people to do his work. Don was not going to cave in this time. He owed it to the patients at the hospital. He was going to help them get better care. He was tired of seeing the lower strata non private insurance patients get the fast shuffle in the operating room. Postoperative care went even faster. The patients were actually thrown out of the hospital too soon after surgeries. They were told to convalesce at home. Turnover was constantly increased. Most of the patients turned out okay, but the few that went sour suffered complications. On top of that were plain mistakes. When people were in a hurry, more mistakes happened. The wrong medicine. The wrong procedure. It happened more than people knew. It happened more with poor patients. Several OB-GYN patients died every year at Morningside due to errors that could have been avoided.

Don changed gears. He tried to concentrate on the patients he had to see that morning. He went into his private office to review his schedule, which was posted on the wall above his desk, and make his morning calls. In the corner of a desk was a computer monitor showing everyone's schedule. All his E-mails, fax numbers, and telephone numbers could be automatically dialed from the computer. As he sat down in his large, leather swivel chair, he felt something press against his thigh. It was the glass slide he took from Chessman's room. He put it in his white lab coat when he arrived. He forgot that he even had it with him. It was his intention to take a look at it in the office lab. As he reached into his pocket to get out the slide, Tina's voice boomed loudly over the telephone intercom.

"Dr. Gardner. Mrs. Gross called again about scheduling another in vitro session." Harvey's wife Karen.

He picked up the handset. "How did she sound?" He looked at the slide while he spoke. To the naked eye it looked like any other pathology slide.

"Not bad."

"Does Harvey know?"

"Yes. She said he said it was okay with him—I don't see why she needs her husband's permission—" Tina always gave her opinion.

"Tina. Thank you very much." Don didn't want to discuss his partner's wife's care with Tina.

"What do you want me to tell her?"

"I'll call her later. Tell her if it's okay with Harvey it's fine with me."

Tina made a sound that indicated her disapproval.

Without thinking Don put the slide in the desk drawer on the right side of his desk. He would look at when he had more time. He was more concerned about the practical matters of practice, particularly since

Dysplasia

Karen was growing very impatient with the negative results of her trying to get pregnant.

"Okay. And you have Rhonda Troud coming in. She's very hysterical. She's convinced she has some kind of tumor growing on her ovary."

"What did her mother tell her it was this time?" Don had been through this before.

"I don't know who told her, but she thinks her husband's dick—excuse my French, Dr. Gardner—is the culprit. So it ain't allowed inside her until you give it a pass." Tina laughed. "Sorry, Doc, but those Trouds crack me up."

They were quite a pair, but Don wasn't about to share his feelings with Tina.

"Where's Dr. Chessman?" asked Don.

"He's in twelve. He's got Liz Yout on a fetal monitor."

"Then he's probably on the phone in his office." Chessman said hello to the patients that needed monitoring and then disappeared. "Is that where he is?"

"I'm not a fortune teller. I'm just the nasty black bitch up front. Do you want me to page him?"

"No. Thanks."

Don decided to find Chessman himself. It was easier than waiting for Tina to find out where everyone was hiding from their patients. Once Tina put Don on hold, it could take a long time before she actually got Chessman or anyone else on the phone. Plus Tina had other calls on hold.

Don made his way through the halls. The young doctors that worked for the group were running in and out of offices, exhausted by the tight scheduling dictated by Chessman. No less than six nurses moved around with deliberate, yet moderate speed, amazingly bumping into no one, remaining polite, and making sure the patients got in and out without a glitch. It was an admirable style of practice, and they pulled it off everyday.

Don looked in twelve for the hell of it. There was an outside chance that Chessman might be with his patient. As Don suspected, Liz Yout was hooked up to a fetal monitor, a series of Velcro straps and hidden listening devices that spit out the information on a plotter that looked very much like a polygraph. All the high-risk patients paid over $100 extra per visit to have the baby's heart rate taken. High-risk situation babies were not to be overstressed. High risk included healthy patients past 35 years of age.

Don smiled at Liz and asked, "Would you like another juice?" A little refrigerator in the room was stocked with fresh juices. Any food or drink requests that were not available in the office were delivered. Patients with busy schedules arranged for lunch deliveries to the waiting room. Other long-standing patients made their way to the office kitchen and helped themselves from a selection that could rival most coffee shops.

"No thanks. Can I get out of here now? Every time I come here, I think I'm in some kind of Star Trek movie."

Don laughed. "I know what you mean." He was being polite, but like most doctors couldn't possibly know how a patient felt, particularly one who had cynical feelings about the frequent monitoring visits.

"I promise. It's not a Klingon baby. His father is originally from Jersey City."

"Let me take a look, Liz."

Don looked at the plotter. By that time, yards of narrow paper had spilled out from the speedy printer. He looked at the paper carefully even though he could see from across the room that everything was fine. There was little chance that anything different would happen from the preceding week.

"Looks fine. Just a few more minutes. I'll send in Dr. Chessman to say goodbye."

"Okay. Thanks."

"Cool," answered Don. His own remark surprised him. "I never say that," Don thought to himself. "Boy. Where did that come from? Why don't you move to California and practice in Encino?"

Don found Chessman in his office, sitting at his desk chatting away on the speakerphone. As soon as Chessman spotted Don through the half-open door, he gestured for Don to come inside.

"Phil. I don't give a shit what Sandy said. I gave you guys plenty in commissions over the last couple of years." It was one of Chessman's money managers. "Now, when the market has been going great, you want to charge a higher percentage. That's bullshit."

Chessman motioned with his hands for the voice on the speakerphone to hurry up.

"Hank. We are raising all our managed-account fees. It has nothing to do with the stock commissions." Phil didn't sound the least bit concerned. Chessman already had the lowest account charges of any client.

"Did I say anything when we took that hit on IBM?"

"Come on now, Hank. You bought IBM a century ago. We got you into Amazon, Yahoo and Worldcom."

"Yes. But I picked those."

"Hank. I know that. But we got you as much stock as you wanted. Look. I probably shouldn't have said anything about the dot-coms." Phil knew how to handle all these situations.

"You tell Sandy to call me. Sandy can be reasoned with. He knows how much business I've steered your way." That was the basis for the relationship. Chessman brought many wealthy clients with him. In exchange, Chessman always wanted a slightly better deal than everyone else.

"Okay, Hank. I'll tell him." That's just what Phil wanted.

The voice at the other end of the call remained polite, almost disinterested.

"Tell him if he doesn't call, I'm yanking my account and going back to Bessemer." It was an idle threat. Both men were going through the motions.

Don heard the conversation disconnect when Chessman pushed a button on his desk console.

"Junior. What's up?" asked Chessman.

"I need to talk to you about Troud, your friend's daughter."

"She's fucking nuts."

Don heard that before. He sighed. Then exhaled slowly. He inflated his cheeks with air while he exhaled. He often felt more like a psychiatrist than a gynecologist. Don always favored talking to a patient's psychiatrist if they had one. If not, he would sometimes recommend one. Chessman usually saw no need for a shrink.

Chessman's wondrous quote for the occasion was always the same, "A guy's dick is his brain, and a women's pussy is her evil alter ego."

"She wants some assurance that she can have intercourse with her husband."

"Just tell her to go ahead. It's okay."

"Let's call her shrink again," said Don.

"Didn't you say he was an old fart, from the old school of old farts?"

"So what?"

"So he doesn't give a shit about the girl. He probably thinks she's got hysteria, and her uterus is recirculating her body looking for a new location."

Chessman was referring to the fact that medical doctors in the United States once practiced that way, believing that "hysterics" was essentially a woman's problem caused by a floating uterus. Despite modern psychiatry, there were plenty of older shrinks who still had it in for women in distress.

Dysplasia

"That's cute, Hank, but I'm not helping her by telling her it's okay for her husband to have sex with her if she thinks his penis is a weapon."

"Isn't it?" Chessman never took these conversations seriously.

"Come on. Let's do another conference call with the shrink. What's his name? Blaun?"

"Yeah. Louie Blaun. He's on Park and 67th."

"I'll see if we can set it up for around eleven. This is really something for him."

"Why don't we send her to Stu? He'll put her on Prozac or Zoloft and she'll snap out of it."

"Stu is not a shrink." Don was angry.

"So what. He's got a harem of bitches on Prozac, and if it gets out of hand, he sends them to Gruber."

"Gruber is a good man." Don seemed more satisfied with this course of action. Stu was careful to handle his patients under the auspices of one of the best shrinks in the city.

"See. We agree on something. I'll tell Tina to refer her to Stu. We'll say we are not sure about something in her blood count, and we want her to see our internist."

"What about her own internist?"

"Fuck the sonofabitch. What the fuck has he done for her? The girl is walking around in a stupor."

"Okay," said Don. He didn't like stealing patients.

Despite Chessman's manner, Don knew he was right. Don turned quickly and left the office feeling satisfied.

Don went to his private office to check his messages. There were already a few on memo sheets. He flipped through them and stopped when he saw the name on one. Susan. Don read a line from Tina, who often editorialized the phone calls.

"Sounds like a new patient. Didn't want to give her last name. Said you know her."

In the security of his own office, Don felt more secure calling Susan. It was clearly professional. Don dialed the number immediately. A woman's voice answered the phone.

"Hello."

"Hello. This is Doctor Gardner."

"This is Susan. Thank you for calling."

Don wasn't certain that it was the Susan from the party.

"Do you have a last name?"

"Yes," was all she said.

Don was beginning to think she was a little kooky.

"Is this a medical problem?"

There were several beats of silence on the other end of the line.

"Don't you remember me? I would like to get to know you better."

Don was stunned. He knew that it was the Susan from the party.

"That's very sweet. But I'm happily married." ("Boy, was that a crock of shit," Don told himself.)

"I figured that. That's why I didn't call you back at home. Why did you give me your home number?" She sounded very self-assured.

"I don't know," was all Don could muster. Don found her manner intimidating.

"I knew you were married. A handsome doctor on Fifth Avenue. Of course you were nabbed up early."

"You'll have to excuse me, but I must be going." Don was nervous. He felt his palms fill up with a thin layer of perspiration.

"Can I talk to you again?" asked Susan. Her voice hinted of desperation.

Dysplasia

∞

Don didn't know what to say. This had never happened to him. What did she want? Why would she be so aggressive? He knew it was possible, but in his mind the scenario was unlikely. Perhaps she liked to stir up trouble. He certainly didn't want any trouble.

"I don't know. Why? I guess." He left the door open. "I have to get back to work."

"I will call you again then," asserted Susan.

"Goodbye." He couldn't wait to get off the phone.

"Goodbye."

Don nervously put the phone down, crumpled the message, threw it in the little trash can under his desk, reached down to retrieve it, and then uncrumpled it, placing the paper in the pocket of his white lab coat. He took a few deep breaths. His heart rate began to slow down, back to something closer to normal, but still racing as if he jogged around the park.

"Wow. What was that all about?" was his thought.

CHAPTER EIGHT

⊂⊃

That afternoon Don went to the hospital. He had a few patients he had to check on, mostly post-ops. There was another abdominal hysterectomy post-op, a Park Avenue woman who was Chessman's patient, and hence the rush to do the surgery. Don felt she definitely could have been treated more conservatively. When the pathology report came back on her case, there was only mild evidence of dysplasia on the uterine lining. She did have very small fibroids, and that was Chessman's reason for doing the procedure. The layers beneath the surface of the uterine lining were relatively normal. Naturally, Chessman embellished the verbal report to the patient by saying what most of the doctors in America tell women with a similar report. It was a very common procedure, performed routinely nowadays by most American surgical gynecologists. It probably was unnecessary a percentage of the time, but why take any chances?

After the procedure the whole process was reinforced. "It's a good thing we got in there when we did. You did have cancerous cells, but we got it all out before the dysplasia spread. Those bad cells are gone. You'll be just fine," was Chessman's standard dialogue.

After hearing that speech a woman would feel relieved despite the inherent emotional and psychological problems associated with the procedure. The Chessman speech was something Don could never recite. He wasn't part of that generation of thinking. The fact that he was educated differently than Chessman and his peers also had a lot to do with it. However, the AMA did not police its members, at least not to the point of recommending doctors cut down on a certain procedure. It was clearly impossible to control patient-doctor dialogue.

If one of Chessman's patients would ask a compromising question, Don would simply say, "That's a tough one for me. You'd better ask Dr. Chessman." That way Don stayed out of the controversy. Once the procedure was done, it didn't help anyone for Don to contradict anything.

Intuitively bright patients sometimes proved a problem for Chessman. Chessman was smart but so were a lot of his patients. Women had access to more and more information on medical procedures. The dialogue on the Internet was expansive and general medical sites were popping up all over. Quoting Dr. Koop would put Chessman on the defensive. When Chessman was confronted by a patient with a logical mind, he sought help from his partners. In cases like that, Chessman often bailed out and referred his patients to Lou, who was willing to spend an hour at a time conversing with these patients. Despite the high intellectual regard they developed for Lou, they ironically and humorously would end the meetings by saying, "Let's tell Hank what we've discussed, and get a second opinion from him." Despite their intelligence, the patients liked to hear what Hank had to say. He was their medical authority, not Lou. They used Lou like a reference book in the library, bouncing all the questions off him, but still not trusting his ultimate decision.

Don reached the hospital early. He wanted to talk to the chief of surgery, John Safer. Armed with permission to write the report, Don wanted to touch base with Safer before beginning. Dr. Safer was always on the run, something career academicians and administrators learned to do in hospitals like Morningside.

Don caught up with him in the hall outside the upper-floor surgery rooms. Dr. Safer had just spent an hour watching one of the many bypass operations performed daily. The hospital could perform two at a time. Dr. Safer rarely sat in his office. He was always checking on every-thing. Don knew Dr. Safer would be interested in Don's report.

"John. Could I see you for a minute?" asked Don as he watched the aides shut down a machine that recalculated a patient's blood during a bypass.

"A minute is about all you can get out of me." He spoke with a delib-erate Southern drawl. He made no attempt to lose his accent. to the dis-may of some of his hardened New York colleagues. Dr. Safer was from North Carolina, and liked to pose like a fish out of water in a big New York hospital.

"I'm doing a review for the administration. I'm going to spend some time looking at cases of patients who have no insurance versus patients that are high rollers." Don knew that wasn't exactly what he was sup-posed to be doing, but it was good to get the opinion of some in the upper echelon. Don knew John would give a straight answer. His take was always realistic.

"Shit, Don. You already know what the answer to that is. We're lucky to get some of these prima donnas in the O.R. at all when they find out the patient ain't got no pot o' gold tucked away up in their rectum. Sometimes the first year resident is in over his head. And you know they don't know Jack shit. I wouldn't let some of them take out my appendix. Forget about it." John said "forget about it" with his best New York accent. He said it again. "Forget about it."

John was smiling. He made Don feel at ease. He felt like he was talk-ing with a comrade.

"Come on, John. I want to let them know what's going on with these poor people. Can I count on you?"

"Hell, yes. I've written the Mayor three times myself, and asked to see him about changing the insurance coverage on these Medicaid cases. If they'll pay a few more bucks, we can get some of these doctors to spend more time in the hospital and less time paying for lap dances in the strip joint on a hundred and fourteenth."

"Great. Thanks." Don nervously took John's hand and shook it vigorously. He was happy and eager to get going with his report, albeit a little surprised at Dr. Safer's immediate support.

"Hey, Don. Let go my hand. I still do a little teaching, you know. I'll need a modicum of dexterity."

"Sorry." Don let go of his hand. "I'm just glad you understand." It was a poor choice of words. Don was far from a politician.

Don knew in advance that he wouldn't have trouble with John. His reputation was that of a fair-minded man, even-keeled administrator, and a hell of a teacher. He gave his free time readily to the residents and could be seen after hours knocking back beers with the young doctors at one of the local college bars.

Next up was Fred Childs. Also an M.D., Fred was the Vice-President For Professional Affairs at Morningside Hospital. He was an administrator and no longer practiced medicine.

Visiting Dr. Childs was a mere formality because Dr. Childs was a clear administrator, someone who gave little input into how medicine was practiced at Morningside. He was the person who carried out all administrative duties for the President of the hospital. Dr. Childs was the liaison between the civilian Board members of the hospital, the doctors, and the medical administrative staff. He was also the hatchet man for the Board and the president. He was in charge of overseeing any "conduct violations" by staff members. He basically did the dirty work for the higher-ups. Every hospital had one.

Dr. Childs appeared cold as ice, an attitude that befitted his position. Most of the hospital staff did not like him. He was the butt of countless jokes. "How's the 'child' doing?" was a popular expression. He didn't mind. He was often quoted as saying, "It's not my job to be liked. Sorry." He walked around with a perpetual scowl. When he did smile, it looked more like a sneer. Central casting could not have provided a better "actor" for the job. He had the annoying habit of drawing a little happy face on official letters, the popular circle with dots for a nose and eyes and a little upturned smile in the form of a slight curve. Sometimes he would modify the face with hair and glasses, some thought it looked like him. It didn't matter what the letters contained, which ranged from the worst kind of dismissal letters to begrudged promotions to holiday schedules. Whatever it was, Dr. Childs would use the happy face. People gave up complaining to the administration. He was the administration.

The door to the outer office was open wide. Don knocked. The secretary's desk was empty. She came and went as she saw necessary since Dr. Childs shared her with another Vice President.

"Hi, Fred. How are you?" yelled Don, leaning his head into position so that Dr. Childs could see him from inside the inner office.

"Fine. Dr. Gardner. What can I do for you?" He kept his head glued to his desk.

Dr. Childs knew why Don was there. He had to know. How could the President of the hospital okay anything without going through Dr. Childs first? Dr. Childs knew and watched everything that went on in the hospital.

"How's the family?" Don asked, looking at the pictures of Dr. Childs' children on the desk.

Dysplasia

"Fine. Benjamin is starting Columbia and 'Kath" is in her second year of film school at N.Y.U."

"That's a great film school," said Don.

"Yes. It is." Now Dr. Childs looked up.

Don got the message. "You know Harry asked me to do the review of for the OB-GYN unit."

"Review. No. Congratulations. Harry must have a lot of confidence in you."

"Fred. The whole hospital is getting one."

"Oh, yes. Of course. The consulting work."

Don spoke slowly. "I'm going to be doing some interviews with some of the Chief of Staffs. To get their take on how the OB-GYN unit melds with the rest of the services."

Don knew that wasn't exactly what Harry had in mind, but this was the best time to mention it. And the right person. Don was supposed to stick to OB-GYN, but thought the report would have little meaning without following the entire care of OB-GYN patients in other departments.

"Oh, why is that?"

"Didn't Harry Rollins tell you? I'm doing a report for the hospital." Don knew he hadn't answered directly. "To make the report as complete as possible."

"Now I remember. You think our patients without insurance aren't getting a fair shake." Boom. Dr. Childs knew everything.

Don stood as tall as possible. "What I think doesn't matter. It will be my job to find out what the present system does and does not do to our patients. Based on that, I will make recommendations."

Dr. Childs forced his weird smile. "So now you're in the recommendations business. Why don't you Fifth Avenue-hustlers stick to clinical practice?"

Don let the remark pass. "Fred. I just need your okay to proceed."

"Does Hank Chessman know about this bullshit?" Now Dr. Childs was getting to the heart of the matter. The corner of Dr. Child's mouth turned up a little, indicating a little smirk.

"Yes." Don wanted to say "fuck you."

"Well, then. We don't need to waste each other's time further. If it's okay with Hank, it's okay with me. Good luck, Dr. Gardner."

"Thank you. That's very kind coming from you, Fred."

Don turned to leave.

"You'd also better let Hank know that you're going to get comments outside of OB-GYN."

Don turned back. He was beginning to feel less in control.

"Right," said Don. He wanted to challenge Dr. Child's attitude, but he stopped himself. He hadn't met with any real resistance and didn't see any reason to butt heads with the boss.

Dr. Child's nodded. "See you," he forced out.

"Sure. See you," Don copied. He smiled his best artificial grin and left.

Dr. Alan Ronalds ran the Department of Radiology. He was a very quiet man who spent his free time fishing. He was a well-thought-of specialist who graduated from N.Y.U. who always complained about the old equipment in the hospital. He wasn't shy about stating that Morningside didn't plan far enough ahead. Don wouldn't have any problems with Dr. Ronalds as they had a friendly relationship.

Don had a clear sense of Alan. Alan became a businessman like many doctors. Consumed by his production and net. The protocol for caring for patients was left to others. Radiology was one of those automated specialties that distanced itself from the patient's care. Patients rarely met the radiologist. Technicians and nurses handled all the procedures like the popular MRI. Reports and pictures were checked by the radiologist and sent to the referring doctor. Bedside manner didn't apply. It seemed to fit Alan, not wanting a lot of contact with people.

Don caught up with Alan in the cafeteria. Alan was reading a fishing magazine while he played with a fork that was buried under what looked like the hospital's version of chop suey, a lot of rice covered by some thick foliage.

"Hey, Alan. What you got there?"

"Oh. I'm going to making lures out of this green stuff."

Alan put down the magazine.

Alan was involved in the breakup of the largest radiology practice in New York. Five partners stayed in the hospital offices and nine left to set up a competitive office a few blocks away. Medical practice could be as cutthroat as any other business. Partnerships broke out. Litigation ensued. Lives were changed.

"Are you guys finished yet?"

Alan knew what Don meant. They had talked about the case before. "Not finished! Our side has spent over $300,000 in legal fees already." Gross income from the nine partners was over $6,000,000.

"There's got to be some give and take." Don was stating the obvious.

"It's really over the accounts receivable. That's where we're stuck. Each group wants all of them. After that's settled, we have to decide what they're worth."

Don didn't want to say how ridiculous the whole thing sounded. All were making so much money. The receivables could be divided equally with each partner. Don knew what the real problem was. The minds of a lot of doctors are inextricably bound up with huge egos that make them feel like they know more than everyone else, including their partners, accountants, investment advisors, and in the worst case, their attorneys. It was common to value their own contribution to the practice at a much higher level than their partners, and there-fore always deserve more than the other guy.

"I'm sorry. I hope it works out," said Don. He meant it.

"Thanks. Life is hard and then you die," said Alan.

Don smiled. "Alan. I don't know if you know I'm doing sort of a con-sulting job for the hospital. I will have to check the procedures in radi-ology with certain OB-GYN patients." It wasn't exactly true. Don didn't have to check radiology.

"Have a good time. Go with my blessings." Alan could care less. He wasn't a hospital politician.

"Thanks. Good luck with the case."

"Yeah." Alan buried his head in the fishing magazine, lifted the fork from his plate, took a look at the mess on his fork, and dropped it back on the plate.

The Chief of Cardiothoracic Surgery, Dr. Stanley Mills, was an abrasive, arrogant son of a bitch who only spoke about two things, cardiac surgery and golf. He considered himself to be an expert on both subjects. Dr. Mills never missed the Celebrity Pro Am at the Westchester Golf Classic. When Bing Crosby was still alive, he would fly out for the annual clambake at Pebble Beach. He never name dropped any of the players, although he knew as many people as Chessman. They had different styles. Dr. Mills didn't revere other people the way Chessman did. Dr. Mills looked upon himself as the celebrity. He was as famous as Chessman. People came from all over the world to have a "valve job" from Mills. There was a major distinc-tion between Mills and Chessman. Mills was a genuine talent.

Don had to catch Dr. Mills between the two surgery rooms that Mills ran simultaneously. One patient would be prepped and the anesthesiologist would go to work, while the residents began to remove the much-needed saphenous vein from the lower leg. By the time Mills got to work, the chest was cracked open, spread with a machine that looked like a giant can opener. It had a circulating handle and pressure spreaders used for exposing the heart. Mills would get right to it. A computerized machine stood between the two rooms and could recirculate and pump two patients' blood at the same time. Mills hopped from one room to the other, as the residents worked.

"Stanley. Got a minute?" asked Don while the two stood in the doctor's locker area, a little ready room a few steps and a swinging door away from the surgery area.

Dr. Mills was putting on new surgical garb, gloves, and head covering.

"What is it Gardner?" He deliberately sounded annoyed.

"I need your permission to watch surgical procedures up here in the morning." That wasn't exactly true either. What Don meant was that he was going to be up there more frequently. Some doctors might question his presence.

"What the fuck do I care? Is that it?" Dr. Mills shook his head in disgust. He always treated Don as if Don was an idiot.

"Yes. Thanks." That's all Don needed.

Within seconds Mills was in the second room. He reached right inside the chest cavity and picked up the exposed heart for an initial close inspection.

Don left the operating arena feeling confident that he could now do a thorough job. It was something he felt should be done, and could ultimately improve the quality of care for the noninsured hospital patient. He was excited at the prospect of making such a contribution. He thought about his wife, about making love to her. He saw Susan's face for a fraction of a second. Susan's head on his wife's body. Then it was just Susan.

"Yeah, right," he thought to himself. "Mr. Faithful. Fat chance."

Over the next few weeks, Don spent a lot of his free time collecting data, reading articles, and running literature review sessions in his own department. These sessions would range from informal meetings with one or two residents to actual required classes. Some discussions included the entire OB-GYN house staff. In those sessions, discussions were held on scientific articles published in a variety of medical journals. Don normally taught a few of those sessions each semester and often volunteered to take Lou and Harvey's days as well. Harvey hated to teach. He only did it so Chessman could fill in his teaching staff with people he knew. People who also didn't need a decent salary.

When Don was a student, it took hours to find and copy the articles in the library. The library had changed. Years ago, a student found the articles by looking through thick, bound indexes with small print. Then copying the article title, journal title, journal number and page location. Following that, the student traipsed all over the library in search of the article. Heavy reference books were next lugged to a location for reading or copying the article. Usually a different book was needed for each article. It was a tedious process and took hours. The long wooden tables were often piled high with dense reference books, obscuring the worker from view. The crowded lines at the copy machines produced short tempers and frayed sensibilities.

Now Don could sit in front of a computer terminal while the computer made a detailed bibliography from the Index Medicus, commonly referred to as Medline. He could read summaries of the articles while he worked. For example, he asked the computer for all the articles in which the work "dysplasia" appeared in the title. The computer told him the number, often in the thousands. He could then modify his "search" by using the word "cervical" and then have at his disposal articles dealing with "cervical dysplasia," still in the thousands. He could look for certain authors, dates of publication, and add further modifying terms until he had a decent-sized search, one reasonably small but complete enough to scan. He could print out the abstracts immediately or ask for pull-and-copy service, whereby a library employee found and copied the original article.

The number of articles on any subject was too large for one person to read, even with a computer. Every medical school in the world regularly published articles. "Publish or perish" was real and threatening. Many articles were redundant, unnecessary, or in a small number of documented cases totally false, constructed only to attract fame and fortune for self and university. Many privately held pharmaceutical or manufacturing companies did their own research papers that conflicted with classic medical literature. Often, the seller of the drug or device was also the principle researcher. The FDA found very few cases where there was a clear conflict of interest. The system evolved permitting the outside manufacturers to control elements of medical research. Grant money came from the same outside sources.

To complicate Don's project, he was often faced with doctors who were not literature smart. They didn't read articles or journals. They relied on word of mouth between practicing physicians at meetings. Sure, they would keep up their respective board certifications and staff appointments, but most did not hunt through their mail looking for new articles. Few subscribed to more than two medical journals. Successful practitioners had "pet" researchers with whom they allied, particularly if it was financially symbiotic.

"I'll do the research and you perform the procedures."

Sometimes it was the same person. A classic example is hernia surgery, where the researcher is often the surgeon who is the major proponent of the procedure.

Don's singularly most difficult task was getting Chessman to go along with sensitive areas of his report: any area that conflicted with Chessman's present mode of clinical practice, a mode that was very acceptable by American Medical Association standards, but was geared basically towards intervention and surgery. If it would cost the hospital unit more money, then this, too, was a sensitive issue. Don quickly realized he would have problems dealing with the staff. Many saw Don's project as a threat to the status quo, which for many of them was a cushy way of existence. Don's work became slow and tedious. The early signs showed little cooperation from anyone.

Other doctors, who made their living treating patients in the hospital, had no time for Don for other reasons. This was their livelihood, their principle place of work. Many of them resented guys like Don, "Fifth Avenue guys", who used the hospital only as an adjunct. Doctors like Don had patients who could afford to get the best rooms, which often included the best nurses. Insurance didn't play a role in their hospital experience.

Don and his partners would make more money on their hospital procedures than the doctors who worked full time. It was the rumors of the perks that really ticked off the staff doctors. Didn't the Oil Minister from Qatar buy Sony Trinitron televisions for the Chessman office staff? Didn't Chessman have his own G7 Jet? Or was that Beitleman? Didn't Beitleman have a twenty-bedroom house in the Pines at Fire Island? Didn't Gardner treat that movie star from the space movie? Most of the rumors were true. Chessman once had access to a G7. The plane was actually a corporate loaner from a Hollywood studio that had several.

Dysplasia

Chessman sent the jet to pick up people anywhere, anytime. Chessman would refer to the plane as "his jet". When the studio scaled down and sold their "airline", Chessman lost his ride along with dozens of "friends", but the rumor of the "Chessman jet" still survived at the hospital.

Don met with a lot of resentment during his interviews.

"Why are you doing this?"

"What did you do, wake up and decide to become a liberal?" Despite the outward liberal appearances, most of the doctors were right of center.

"I don't have time for this shit." The remark was followed by a sour expression. Then a turned shoulder and a hasty exit.

"What are you trying to do, fuck it up for those of us who make a living here?" Some doctors followed those remarks with implied threats.

CHAPTER NINE

Linda called the office and didn't ask to speak to Don. This always infuriated Don because it isolated him further from his wife. Linda knew it made him uncomfortable for Tina to leave personal messages.

"Be home later today," was all the little memo slip said. She stayed at her mother's for a full week. She never did that before.

It was stuck on the desk between several other phone calls, the lab, the hospital, Robert Kronen, and Vivian Lefrak, an annoying stockbroker who called incessantly looking for business. Don told her several times the new issues market was of no concern to him. He wasn't risking any of the retirement money he kept in a tax-deferred account. She kept sending him the skyrocketing dot-com stock information. She neglected to send the ones that were selling at twenty dollars a share after going over one hundred the first day of trading.

Seeing Vivian's name made him think about money. He had enough, at least to start over somewhere else. He fantasized about leaving New York, living a more simplified life. He had saved enough to live a modest existence in a more suburban area. Like many doctors, who rat-raced in big cities, Don deluded himself by saying he would be better off by packing it in someday and moving to the boonies. It was that type of condescension, looking down at the rest of the country, which kept most of the city doctors firmly in place. They were sociological city prisoners.

Don was glad his wife was coming home. He left the office as soon as possible. On the way home, his first eight or nine thoughts were all sexually related. He eventually entertained, but for a brief moment, that he was tiring of the game she played by going to her mother's whenever Don and she had problems. He made his mind up to leave it alone. He didn't want to stir up things in his marriage. Not then. Things in the office were going well. He was determined to keep working on the hospital report.

Don got home before Linda. He stood in the doorway of his building. He watched Linda as she left the passenger side of a black 600 SEL Mercedes that was double-parked in front of the building. The woman driving the vehicle was Linda's mother, who Don described as having a "black belt in aloofness," a state-of-the-art socialite. When Don first started dating Linda, she represented her mother the same way. As time went on, Don learned that Linda's rebelliousness was transient. He would eventually hear the same calculated language from two socialites instead of one. At least Linda didn't always mimic her mother. Once they were together, they played the same song, never giving Don a break. After seeing her mother, Linda would speak the same way for at least a day. When Linda was angry she became her mother.

Linda smiled at Don as she walked to the door. Don was glad to see her. He put his arms out to hug her. Linda maneuvered inside the arms in such a way that she could plant a cold-as-ice kiss on his cheek without even touching his body. "A true WASP talent," he thought.

"I'm glad you're back. We have a lot to talk over." Don wanted to make amends for the holiday incident. He was drinking. Perhaps he made too much of it.

"Don. You're right. But I've made a few choices."

"Choices? What choices? What are you talking about?"

He looked back at the car and could see Linda's mother smiling. That was not a good sign.

"Don. We're growing apart." It sounded rehearsed.

"Not that again. I hate when you start using those paperback chapter headings."

"Don. We are different people." She stood face to face to confront him.

"There. There you go. Another quote from Oprah."

The doorman was getting an earful, although he was pretending not to hear.

Linda grew impatient. "Do you mind if I come in? I do own half of this place." They had been through the routine before. It was almost the same conversation as the last time.

Don held back his anger. He hated the fact that the two of them kept going 'round and 'round. The repetition was painful. He walked ahead of Linda and opened the door like the doorman. He gestured for Linda to go inside. She looked great. As she walked past him, he stared hard at the firm, sculptured muscles that rounded down below her bikini pantyline. He loved when she wore short tight skirts, and that day was no exception.

Linda knew Don was watching and spared little in the rock-and-roll movements she practiced since age thirteen. Linda still wanted to be with Don. This was her way to communicate it.

Once inside the apartment, Don felt a familiar hardness against the inseam of his zipper. He slipped his hand inside his pants to point his penis in the downward direction, so the head wouldn't press against the back of the metal.

Linda pretended to not see. She walked into the kitchen. Once inside she quickly opened the refrigerator. Don followed her like a dog in heat.

"I'm thirsty." She took out a plastic bottle of designer water and gulped it straight from the bottle.

She deliberately let some water trickle from her mouth, collecting in droplets on her neck. "Want some?" She offered the bottle to Don, who took a large gulp.

Linda grabbed the bottle and took another drink, this time letting the water cascade over her lower ruby lip and onto her cotton blouse. The water quickly found its way to her nipples, a pair easily excited by the cool water, immediately showing their response by jutting out hard against the wet cotton. "Oh. I rushed when I was getting ready to leave Mother's. I didn't have time to put on a bra." She knew it drove Don wild. The issue of a bra or no bra dated Don's misogynist generation.

Linda helped embellish the visual from the Playboy Channel by running her hands down over her breasts, making sure they were saturated with water.

"Oh, look what a mess I've made," said Linda, lowering her voice to her purr level.

She knew it wasn't a mess to Don or any other man who had any interest in tits. This wet-nipple look had become part of the American model of sexuality, and for obvious reasons.

Don was breathing faster and irregularly.

Linda moved quickly to seize the moment. She opened her blouse and pulled the fabric aside. "I'd better put on a dry blouse." She stopped after a few buttons. "I'd better get this off."

She moved towards Don as if to move past him. Now she made sure her perky, creamy white breasts were fully exposed. The red nipples were jutting out like little rocks straight up in the air.

Don grabbed her as she tried to move past him.

"Hey, Don. We just came upstairs."

She wanted him on the spot, but could never reveal her own sexual premeditation. He would have to fight for it. It was part of their regular game.

"Linda. I missed you."

He didn't mean to say that, but that's what came out. He always wanted to say things like, "get on your knees, you bitch, and suck my rod until I tell you to stop." If she refused, Don would take her across his knee, pull down her jeans and spank her bare bottom until the juices from her pussy absorbed onto his trousers. So much for fantasy.

Linda shook loose from Don's grasp. She ran to the bedroom.

Don chased Linda into the bedroom and then played cat and mouse. He would hold her for a series of deep kisses. She would push away. Then a little more clothing was removed, interrupted by classic, vocal nonsequiturs like "Don. Stop. Please. No."

Don thought of the old, Please-Don't-Stop jokes about women, and was convinced that for some, the reputation of cock teasing was well-deserved. He was married to a professional. They both liked it.

Don pulled his own pants below his knees. That's as far as he could get them. Linda, upon seeing his penis pointed almost straight up to the ceiling, made her common error of shouting, "Oh, my God. You're huge." Before a beat could go by, her mouth covered three quarters of the "huge" monster. Don was shocked by her action. He couldn't remember the last time she did that. After her head bopped several times in a nice, neat rhythm, Don screamed as he ejaculated with a tremendous force into Linda's mouth. As soon as the semen hit her palate, her head jerked back from the bobbing position, her mouth wide open, as she simultaneously gagged and gasped for air. A combination of saliva and semen oozed out the side of her mouth, like bad special effects in a cheap horror flick.

Dysplasia

∽

Now that sex pervaded the atmosphere, Don's penis became his dick, leaving the medical anatomy behind. Don grasped his dick hard and continued to pump it to get out the remainder of the semen. He was the only one left to do it.

"Honey. Let me do it." Linda pushed Don's hands away and with a two-handed approach, pumped his dick like she was operating a jackhammer. To Don, she really was more equipped to handle sailors in port, looking for some heavy duty S & M, although hers was unintentional.

"Too hard," he moaned.

"Sorry." She tried another approach.

It was too late. The excitement had diminished, and Don felt uncomfortable from the heavy manipulation. Linda never learned how to probably handle his dick.

"Honey. I wanted you in me," said Linda. She was thinking about getting pregnant.

Don realized the same thing. "Give me a minute." He knew it was wishful thinking, but at his age he could still get a second erection, especially if he didn't fully ejaculate.

"Okay."

Linda stood up and curled at his side. She took her hand and began to stroke Don's thigh, and then grabbed his dick once again. Don took her hand away and used his own hand.

Don joked as if he were talking about a superhero. "Let's see if little Mr. Rubber Fella can turn into big Mr. Steel Rod." It was to no avail. He kept trying.

"It's okay, honey," she said.

The remark made him feel inadequate.

Linda moved to the bed. She lied down. Don moved to her side. After a few minutes he finally got it up and in. They spent a few minutes in each other's arms, exchanging long kisses. Don hardly ejaculated. Linda was happy that they tried. Having a child seemed to be their only singular common interest.

All of the activity made them both feel secure that things were back to their level of normalcy.

Don felt guilty that Linda didn't have an orgasm. It was almost as if Linda didn't care about her own orgasm. It was a rare event to let Don go down on her. She used to let him, but insisted that "men didn't like doing that." Eventually Don became disenchanted because Linda put such a damper on the activity. He thought she might have had an orgasm during intercourse, but couldn't be sure. When they were dating, Linda used to scream and dig her nails into his back. Was that an act? It was so long ago. Don gave up wondering.

Both adjourned to the kitchen and feasted on leftovers and white wine.

Just before she fell asleep, Linda made a very clear speech about what she expected of Don. It wasn't what he was expecting.

"You know, Don, there is a way to write the hospital report so that everyone comes out a winner."

She held up her finger and pressed it against Don's lips to prevent him from speaking. He was tired. He wasn't looking for a confrontation. He listened as Linda continued her speech. She always chose the moments after lovemaking to express her opinions on sensitive subjects.

"Don. You must face the reality that we are in business. Medicine is a business. In business, you do not become a whistle blower if you want to succeed. Yes. Say you want to help the poor but you really don't have to follow through on it. Make some suggestions. Let Hank have his name on the paper. Give everyone what they want. Get in. Get out. Take the positive credit, and let someone else dish the real dirt."

Dysplasia

Don had a sick feeling in his stomach. He could not fathom how little Linda really knew about him. How he felt. Or maybe she did, and felt he was so weak that he would go along. He had up to now. It didn't matter. Part of Don knew that Linda was right. She was doing what anybody else would do in the same situation. Cover your own behind. Don't rock the boat. She had every right to be worried.

His thoughts trailed off in visions and sounds of Simon and Garfunkel in Central Park. Don lying on top of Linda, on the grass, near the lake in the park. It was a pleasant memory. His mind wandered. He was a child again, swimming in the public pool. He saw the nine-year-old Don cry when the swimming coach bullied him. His mother soothed him by saying, "Don. You don't have to do it if you don't want to." Maybe she coddled him too much. Maybe Linda saw him as a pain in the ass to get along with. Maybe Linda was right.

Don flashed on Susan, helping him off with his prized Aquascutum the night of the Christmas party. He saw right through her blouse, and stared at her beautiful, sculptured mocha breasts.

He was almost asleep. He told himself the silly punch line of a joke. "Dysfunction is as good as dat one." That was his life. Clearly dysfunctional.

He started a dream he would never remember.

Linda drifted off hearing her father scold her for not using the proper response in front of the neighbors.

She said, "I'm glad to meet you." Her father slapped her hard across the face, and said, "You are never 'glad' to meet anyone. You say either "I'm pleased to meet you or it is nice to make your acquaintance. There are no 'glads'. How many times do I have to repeat myself? My daughter is never going to sound stupid."

He was a brutal alcoholic. She was secretly "glad" when his liver gave in to cirrhosis. She thought about her stepfather, a classic Long Island Blueblood, the type of man her mother wished she married in the first place. She wished Linda married the same kind of man. Stepfather was an alcoholic of a different breed. He was the sweetest, kindest man she ever knew. She envisioned him in one of the local watering holes near Brookville, Long Island, surrounded by green blazers and green Madras slacks. He liked to stay "on the island. Those bluebloods in the city mix with everyone." She swirled the image in her mind, making a pleasing, hypnotic kaleidoscope of images, a view much more comfortable than any other reality she had known as an adult. She had regrets about marrying Don. She knew how Don felt. It hurt her to know that Don was disappointed. Linda was disappointed too. Before she fell asleep, she envisioned herself at the country club in Brookville, smiling, happy, sipping martinis.

Linda was up early. She sat at the dinette table in the kitchen sipping coffee, courtesy of her computerized Krups coffee machine. Every night she set the coffee on a different time, a time that would be convenient for her the next morning. She never asked Don what time he would like coffee. She knew that Don got up to go to work at the same time every day, and if he happened to get up before her, which was the case ninety percent of the time, he could turn the machine on manually. It would keep the coffee warm for two hours. But sometimes Don had several cups and would have to refill it for Linda.

"Pretty tricky," Don would tease. "You've made me your coffee maker by default."

Linda wished Don would get up. She wanted to have some of the usual banter. To reinforce that they were back in the regular routine. She sat quietly, huddled at one end of the table, dressed in a red tartan robe. A copy of *The New York Observer* was on the breakfast table. Linda opted to flip through the pages of *People* magazine. She didn't like to read periodicals that "were so critical of people, people who are really nice." There was also a copy of the *New York Post* alongside the *New York Times*, two that Linda occasionally read. The office had these papers and the *Wall Street Journal*. No sense getting them at home.

Don was already dressed for work when he vaulted into the kitchen. He picked up a piece of toasted bagel from a counter that connected to the dinette area. Instant dislike shown on his face.

"Linda. Where did you get these?" He knew the answer.

"I don't know. I called to have a delivery yesterday. From my mother's. I think I got them with the food delivery."

"What do you mean, you think?" Don was back to being himself. Rather than appreciate that Linda made an effort to stock up, he was determined to complain.

"Don't give me that shit. These are the Jewish bagels. The guy's name is Leder or Lederer or something. His name is on the bagel, and he's a Jew. I saw him advertise the damn things on television." She knew that Don always wanted the New York-styled bagel, which Linda called the Jewish bagel.

Don started a slow burn. He realized he was wasting his time, but decided to go over it slowly. He knew he was torturing himself by even trying to explain it again. As they spoke, he stared out over Linda's head. He could see a limited view of the New York skyline, looking west.

"I like freshly baked bagels. There are over one thousand bagel stores in New York that sell freshly baked bagels. Three are within walking distance from our building. All are open early. I think two deliver."

He seemed to be staring out at those three bagel bakeries, almost smelling the freshly baked bagels as he spoke.

Linda wanted to say something in her defense, but Don signaled with his hand for her to refrain from speaking. Don's carotid pulse started to push his white-collared shirt against his jacket. It convinced Linda to wait. She wasn't interested in fighting. He was usually anxious before he got to the office. Don ground his teeth for a moment, sending the thick masseter muscles on his cheeks into a twitching, spasmodic movement that resembled a stroke.

"I don't like these white-bread bagels. It's not a Jewish-Gentile thing. It's a personal taste thing. What's worse is you bought these frozen. In New York City, you buy frozen bagels. People in Des Moines are eating fresh bagels, and all I've got is fucking frozen bagels."

"Don. You know I don't like the 'f' word." When Linda was drinking, she let the "f" word slip out once in a while.

Don didn't use it as much as he heard it, usually when he was very upset or angry. For some New Yorkers, it was woven into the fabric of daily speech.

"Linda. Please. You know what I like." He said it calmly.

"But after you toast them, what's the difference?"

Don pulled himself up to his full height and walked slowly out of the kitchen. He turned for dramatic effect and whispered loudly across the kitchen, much the same as Clint Eastwood.

"I don't like toast."

"Oh, yeah. Right. Sorry. I forgot. Don't make such a big deal out of it. Where's your sense of humor?"

Don was out of earshot and humor by the time Linda uttered the last line. She shook her head as she heard the outer door to the apartment slam shut.

Linda took another sip of coffee. She reached for the *New York Post*. The headline read:

Dysplasia

MODEL MUTILATED IN WEIRD SEX RITUAL.

This was the kind of juicy story Linda liked to read. The model's name was being withheld until her family could be notified. Linda read the beginning of the article. When she reached the end of the first-page column, she quickly turned to the inside pages to continue.

When she got to the section that said the model had her genitals mutilated, Linda stopped reading. It was too gruesome. She threw the *Post* aside and switched her attention back to the new issue of *People*.

CHAPTER TEN

As Don rode up the elevator, he looked to his left and saw the usual one or two celebrities. He thought one of the men was Johnny Cash, dressed all in black, staring straight ahead. Don replayed the image he remembered of Johnny at Folsom Prison, about the last time Don had heard any of his music.

The elevator was empty by the time Don got off on his floor. As he walked down the hall to his office, he tried to remember how many times Linda had walked out on him, come back, tried to seduce him, and always succeeded. The less-than-satisfying sexual encounter always accompanied the reunions. The worst part was that the very next day Linda would be back to her WASPY, upwardly mobile mode. Don felt he deserved a better marriage. Linda too. He believed that everyone had problems in their marriages. Were they doing the best they could? He had to concentrate on his patients. At least they got his full attention.

Don entered his office. He walked past Tina and gave the cursory "hello", to which she responded with "Hi, Doc". She didn't look up from her desk. There was time before his first patient. Don went to the kitchen, grabbed a cup, and poured himself coffee from the Starbucks thermos. There were fresh bagels next to the coffee machine, the kind he liked. He grabbed one, not caring what kind it was, and took his coffee and bagel with him.

Don overheard laughter from Chessman's office, so he poked his head inside. He was treated to one of the lowest versions of the office "boys-will-be-boys" activity.

"Lou. Is that where you're dumping your bad surgeries?"

Lou laughed heartily at Chessman's patter. Chessman was on a roll.

"Did you fuck her before she was dead, after she was dead, or after you sliced the pussy up? Sort of adding to the lubrication?" Chessman was holding up the *Post* article.

"Lou's a K-Y man," chimed in Don. "At least that was his reputation in school, but he usually used it on himself."

"Look who's here. Mr. Welfare Reformer," needled Harvey.

"Good morning, Harvey," said Don. He sprinkled some poppy seeds on Harvey.

Harvey reacted as if it were acid.

"Don. Come to think of it, Don. Would you have fucked her while she was alive and just slightly mutilated? What's your preference?" Chessman was doing his usual gross-out routine.

"I'm definitely a live-and-mutilated kind of guy. What are you guys talking about?" asked Don. Then Don remembered his conversation earlier in the week with Jill.

"What did he do to her?" asked Lou.

"It doesn't say," answered Chessman, checking the article again. He handed the paper to Lou.

"He did a clitoridectomy," supplied Don.

"So you were there," said Harvey.

"Where did you get that information, from your sexy friend downstairs?" asked Chessman.

"Yeah. Jill said she was a mess," answered Don.

"Can I eat my Danish now?" asked Harvey. "I've been waiting until you guys get your ya-yas out of the way."

"Sure, but go eat in your office. You and Lou are always messing up my carpet. Don. Here are the new path guidelines on dysplastic cell descriptions. They're using new grids to do the counting," said Chessman.

"I've got mine already," said Lou as he got up. He took a few papers in hand. "I'm going to make a living. Excuse me." He left the room, trying in earnest not to spill any crumbs.

"Ditto." Harvey left the room, deliberately trailing crumbs as he bit down hard into his Danish.

"No doubt we're going to be using stricter interpretations of dysplasia," said Don, anticipating that the guidelines were anti surgery. If the new guidelines suggested there had to be a higher incidence of "bad" cells in the biopsy, there would naturally be less surgery. The public didn't know the nuances of how doctors decided what was cancer and what was not. There were a lot of steps in between. The pathology reports were detailed in descriptions, but by the time the information reached the patient, it was either "yes" or "no".

"Hey. You want to fuck with liability? If they have any form of dysplasia, it's our job to make it all better. Here. Read these." Chessman kept to his usual stance.

Don took the papers. He began to read them as he left the room. He didn't want to get into an argument with Chessman, who obviously set him up by telling him the new guidelines called for them to do more surgery instead of less.

"Don?"

"Yes, Hank?" Don clutched his bagel.

"Are things okay at home?" asked Chessman.

"Yeah. Fine." Don was surprised but didn't show it.

Dysplasia

Don wasn't interested in any matrimonial advice, especially from Chessman. Not after seeing him blitzed out of his mind with a transsexual brandishing a scalpel. Just then Don remembered the slide. He made a mental note to look at it under a microscope.

It was another routine day in the office.

CHAPTER ELEVEN

Later that week, Don had a Review of Literature session scheduled with Chessman and the first-year and second-year residents. Chessman made periodic appearances to show the students that he was an attentive educator. A few would catch on that it was far from the truth. Most accepted Chessman in that role, particularly when Don was present. It was clear from these sessions that Chessman was biased, always stirring some form of a debate. It was generally a good educative process. But when Chessman was present, the core group of residents was far from rebellious. They wanted the ticket to make the big bucks. The specialty certification, the pass to get into medical Disneyland for the rest of their lives. They acted for Chessman.

The mechanics of the class were to review scientific publications, new and old, in an effort to make each of the would-be specialists fluent in the jargon and controversies of the day. They were exposed to every possible point of view. There wasn't a single method for doing a procedure. Nor was diagnosis and treatment a constant in any specialty.

Joe McFarland was a working-class kid from suburban Jersey. He was smarter than the rest, and rarely showed it. He had no respect for Chessman, but never let on.

Arnie Baer was a typical Brooklyn boy who wanted to be a specialist so he could get into a higher tax bracket. He was the only resident who wore shirts made in the Custom Shop, a place where pseudo custom work got you your initials on your sleeve and/or pocket. Arnie was already competing in an area of medical practice rarely discussed by the public: How do I train so I can get to be a great white doctor with the matching practice? This included wearing the right ties, shirts, suits, and being able to rattle off the right cars, places to live, and recent unique vacations. It also helped to be able to claim intimate social relations with a few famous people. Arnie was training hard, particularly with his shirts, and was naturally envious of Don because he wore expensive shirts like Chessman. One of Arnie's goals was to have his own Turnbull and Asser shirts made to order, just like Chessman. This goal ranked higher than being the best read in obstetric and gynecological literature. It was no contest since Arnie didn't have goals when it came to learning what he called "background information". He wanted to be shown the "how to" of everything, and wasn't the least bit curious as to how techniques were derived or who did the original research.

Chessman made fun of Arnie whenever possible, probably because he saw a little of himself in Arnie and probably because Arnie was such a young caricature of a great white doctor.

The other members of the class were Mohammed Faroud, Gloria Chin, Miles Cohen, and Steve Boron. Mohammed was already a doctor in Iran, and, like thousands of families, was forced out after the Shah was gone. He was probably in his late 40s, had a family with lots of kids and tried his damnedest to be Americanized, but with that name, his dark oily skin, and the already prejudiced hospital staff, he aged a lot in his first two years at Morningside. Despite all, he stuck it out, desperate in his attempt to get his specialty training. He recently changed his name to Mike, a very common choice among Iranians who practiced in mostly white, affluent American neighborhoods. Mike wanted very much to move to Beverly Hills where there was a

Brad Lewis

large Iranian population, where many of the physicians had names like Kevin Bakshandeh, Mickey Karamooz, Fred Nikaktar, and Alan Tzadik.

Gloria was a whiz who knew and read everything. Don knew that she was the only one who actually read all the articles. The others would assign articles to each other and then make a synopsis which they would share. Each week there was a designated reader. It was a great system, except when someone's life depended on you having read the whole article. It was wise to assume that the patient under the knife wished you read the whole article.

No way. No how. Students were always looking for shortcuts, even at the postdoctoral level of study. By the time students left medical school, they were exposed to every type of shortcut, some cheating, some not, that was devised and passed down from over a century of medical training.

It was easy to find out what was important and unimportant. Clinical procedure was important if you expected to make any sort of decent money. You needed to quote "how to" and not "what if." The "what ifs" were eggheads who ended up teaching or doing straight research. The "how-to" group drove new Mercedes. Like any other type of learning, there was an understanding among students that ninety percent of what they had to do was bullshit, and reading articles of intellectual and scientific controversy was probably the highest level of bullshit available.

Chessman loved to wait until someone gave an opinion, then watch while the opinion was seconded by either of the residents. He preferred if it was Don. Chessman proceeded to explain why the article was incorrect, as well as everyone else foolish enough to give an opinion. Chessman favored his opinion over that of any researcher, no matter how famous, no matter how well-established. The residents didn't take

- 189 -

Dysplasia

୭ଚ

Chessman too seriously except when it came to how to run a practice. They really didn't need him to know how to be competent doctors. They basically wanted to pick Chessman's brain about business. The biggest exception to this was Joe, who wanted to know the best way to do things. Gloria was unlikely to go into competition in Manhattan and therefore had little interest in Chessman's business life. She was catered to about the same way the United States was catering to China. Polite and at a distance. Miles and Steve were both playboys, whose interest lay more in getting time off during the summer to disco all night in Westhampton. During the winter they would call in sick so they could go on long ski weekends. They were a familiar pair on one-night junkets to Atlantic City, often traveling with their hospital scrub shirts still on, laden down with various popular pharmaceuticals for the girls, who they knew from the casinos. Chessman liked them a lot. He encouraged their antics.

The first article was from Harvard Medical School.

"Mohammed, why don't you start us off." Don still called him by his given name. Don liked to get him out of the way early. It was tough going.

The accent was thick. In order to compensate, the diction was clear and deliberate. He was boring but understandable. Everyone was used to it by now.

"Adenocarcinoma in situ of the uterine cervix. Do you want me to give the objective?" He read directly from the prepared cards.

"Yes. That is what we do here," answered Don.

Mohammed continued. "Yes. Of course. The study wanted to assess the diagnostic accuracy of cervical conization in women with adenocarcinoma in situ, and to determine whether a select group of women could be managed by conization alone without hysterectomy."

That's all Chessman had to hear. Put off hysterectomy? No way. He couldn't control himself. He didn't wait for any opinions.

"That's another of those bullshit studies. Most of them should have hysterectomies."

Don wasn't going to let Chessman disrupt the session so early. "Gloria. Will you please give us the methods," Don continued, ignoring Chessman's remarks.

In a petite, polite, squeaky voice, Gloria read from her prepared card just as Mohammed did. "Forty cases of cervical adenocarcinoma in situ diagnosed on cervical conization. A review was made of the cases."

The study involved women who had a type of cancer that was possibly only local to the uterus and could possibly be managed without doing surgery.

"Continue with the results please," said Don.

Gloria continued. "Cervical conization revealed adenocarcinoma in situ alone in fifteen of the women. Twenty five had the adenoCA in situ coexisting with squamous dysplasia. Microinvasive squamous cell carcinoma, just two."

"That's fine. Joe, do you want to take it from here?" asked Don.

Joe barely glanced at his cards. "Sure. After cone biopsy, twenty-two women underwent hysterectomy. The specimen showed that only one of twelve women with the adenoCA actually had a full adenoCA, as shown by the fact that there was no involvement in the cone margins."

"What about the cases with involved margins?" asked Don. Follow-up questions were wasted on the others.

"I'm getting to that, Don. Let's see." He checked his own handwritten notes. "Yeah. Seven of ten with involved margins. And two of the seven also had foci of invasive adenoCA in the hysterectomy specimen."

"Anything to add, Miles?" asked Don. It was an inside joke.

"No. He's doing a fine job. He could operate on me anytime, that is if I was a woman."

Dysplasia

Chessman smiled.

"Steve?" asked Don. He tried to include all the residents.

Steve grabbed a card from Arnie Baer's pile. "Yes. Conization was the only treatment for eighteen women with adenoCA in situ and uninvolved margins. All were relapse free after a median interval of three years. From one point five to five."

"Thank you, Steve, or should I say Dr. Baer?" asked Don.

"My mother had the flu. I had to take her some chicken soup," said Steve. "Do you know how long it takes to drive from the Carnegie Deli to Brooklyn?"

That got a laugh from everyone in the room, including Don. Steve was likeable despite being lazy.

"I had to loan him my car," said Miles. "Twenty bucks and I threw in unlimited mileage."

"What happened to the Corvette?" asked Arnie. He sounded very concerned.

"I don't know. It conks out a lot in the winter," answered Steve. "I'm going to trade it for a Porsche."

Chessman nodded in approval.

"Okay. Okay. This isn't the auto show. So, who wants to give us the conclusions?" asked Don.

"I will," volunteered Arnie, grabbing back his card.

"Women with cervical adenocarcinoma in situ diagnosed by conization who have positive margins are at high risk of residual adenocarcinoma in situ and moderate risk of occult invasive adenocarcinoma; expectant management is not warranted. However, a cone biopsy with uninvolved margins can reliably guide subsequent therapy. Selected young women who desire preservation of fertility and have uninvolved margins probably can be managed by conization alone, but further study is required to establish the safety of this approach."

This somewhat supported Chessman's point of view. "Like I said. You do the hysterectomy. Play it safe so you don't have to do two procedures."

"Thank you Dr. Chessman," thought Don. Still ignoring Chessman, Don commented on Arnie's report. "Well done. That was the best verbatim reading from Medline we've had all morning."

This also got a laugh from the group because it was well-known that Arnie Baer was totally dependent on the computerized abstracts of articles. He didn't even care to hide the fact. He shamelessly read them word for word. This was his contribution to the class. If Arnie had been around in Don's class, Arnie might have been forced to find another specialty. Things changed.

"I wouldn't put too much faith in this study. When a patient comes in, you want to do the best job possible, and if a patient comes in with a possible adenoCA report, you'd better go in there and cut it out," volunteered Chessman.

Don had to address the subject. Chessman would not let up.

"I think we have to look at each situation. Know the patient, their life situation, their family needs, and then make the best decision based on what we know about the reliability of cervical conization techniques before complete hysterectomy." It was Don's obligation to be even-handed.

This opened up the discussion to patient population. Don cleverly led them into one of the other articles assigned for this session. It unfortunately gave more credence to Chessman's aggressive stance, at least for poor hospital patients.

"Miles. Why don't you start off the next article."

Dysplasia

∞

"Sure." Miles was a slow reader. What he lacked in basic intelligence he made up in good looks, charm, and negotiations. He was clearly Chessman's personal favorite.

"You got 'Compliance with therapy for cervical dysplasia among women of low socioeconomic status'. South Med. Bowman Gray School of Medicine." Miles read the last line with a Southern drawl, eliciting instantaneous laughter, particularly from Chessman.

Miles kept a little of the accent and adjusted his already borderline grammar to an even lower level.

"You got a project designed to look at compliance with referral for follow-up treatment of cervical dysplasia. Let's cut to the chase. If they is poor, you've got a one-third chance they is not comin' back, regardless of diagnosis. It's like the opposite of Schwarzenegger's 'I'll be back.' They won't be back."

"So do what you can while you've got them in the hospital," added Chessman.

Chessman was correct in his recommendations for hospital care. But his attitude, along with many other doctors on staff, was patients with no insurance needed to be treated fast. It was right there in the literature.

It was a fair trade for hospital residents and the local patient pool. The only way the residents could learn was by doing cases. The locals relied on the hospital teaching program for their medical care. The hospital residents got the experience, and the patients got the work done. This was precisely what Don wanted to emphasize in his own report for the hospital. Sometimes the work done created a "trade imbalance". The work was shoddy and a lot of poor people died unnecessarily.

The article collected data by chart review, parity/gravity, education, previous papillomavirus infections, method of payment, and previous Pap smear results. It was sad to know that one-third of those referred for treatment of dysplasia were noncompliant with referral. This was a problem that Don and any other doctor could not correct. Patient education had to be developed over a long period of time. Perhaps they didn't trust doctors, perhaps if they were feeling okay they thought they were okay, or perhaps they didn't understand the severity to which their diagnosis could change.

Before the session was over, Don was sure to throw in an article entitled "Management of the mildly abnormal Pap smear: a conservative approach." Don liked it because it was done on an Army base and showed very high percentages of a return to normalcy with conservative treatment. Information like this was in direct conflict to the money-making office zapper. The article showed that it wasn't necessary to immediately jump in and get rid of any hint of bad cells.

They ended the session with "Management of Intraepithelial Neoplasia of the Uterine Cervix in the Black Population." Articles like this had to be read, particularly since Morningside Hospital catered to blacks.

Arnie read part of a summary. "Because of the effectiveness of outpatient management in cervical preinvasive lesions, health providers should make every attempt to motivate people, particularly those at high risk, i.e., black women, to undertake preventive measures."

"Nice reading again, Arnie," said Don. This time the group was spent and only a quiet murmur was heard instead of laughter. It was time to call it a day. There was only so much attention available for Lit Review.

While Don suffered through the review of the literature session at the hospital, Jill listened with attention to the staff at the medical examiner's office. The discussion centered around the DNA gene typing that was now being accepted as admissible evidence. Jill was sitting next to Dick Murphy, the man she dated.

Dysplasia

It was a joint meeting between the Chief Medical Examiner's office and the Sex Crime Division of the District Attorney's office. When someone was fished out of the East River, these two groups had to work together. Evidence gathering before the autopsy was of paramount importance in any suspected murder situation. The autopsy report often became important evidence, requiring one of the staff to testify in trials. One of the former chiefs in New York testified that one person did not commit the Simpson murders. Evidence wasn't always clear-cut. Interpretation played a large role.

The lecturer that day was a laboratory owner whose company had the contract with the city for doing DNA testing. His background was in pathology before opening up a laboratory that did only DNA work. His name was Perry Bauer and his company was upstate New York.

"Forensic casework frequently contains a mixture of genotypes. The more biological material recovered at the crime scene, the higher the trace amounts from the person committing the crime. The conventional typing and multilocus DNA fingerprinting methods have not worked well. Especially when we have only one minute vaginal swab stain. It helps if there is blood in the sample, both from the murder victim and the subject. If we have enough material, we can use the amplification system of the HLA DQA1 locus. Once we separate alleles of individuals in a sample with mixed genotypes, we can make positive I.D.s. The allele-specific enzymatic amplifications or polymerase chain reaction seems to work well."

"Yeah, but that doesn't change our path to get evidence admitted in court," said one young attorney.

His question brought many of the sleeping members in the room to momentary alertness. It was a welcome question because the answer contained one of the major points Perry wanted to get across to his less-than-attentive audience.

"At least the evidence is there," continued Perry. "You're right. I can't get the evidence admitted. I wish I could. Perhaps you should be taking a course by Barry Scheck or Peter Neufeld." This got a laugh.

The attorney smiled. Everyone knew Scheck even if he wasn't in the murder-defense business. A lot of people were giving the credit to Scheck for being the driving force in the not-guilty verdict for Simpson. It was a symbol that times had changed. DNA experts were running the show.

Jill took notes as the lecture continued.

Perry went on. "You better get the boys or girls who arrive at the crime scene first to get in the habit of tagging everything. You can't overlook anything anymore. And be careful. The stories going around border on silly. Take that case in Cape May County, the Negersmith case. The guys show up on the scene and they're staring down at a piece of bloodstained cardboard. I'm talking out in the open, right there, clearly visible on the victim's legs. Now how does this happen? It was never tagged as evidence. So there is no blood from the cardboard at the autopsy. Can you believe that? It wasn't tagged. I have no idea what the criminalist could have been thinking. It's more likely that whoever got to the scene first wasn't thinking at all. You saw the ridiculous testimony at the O.J. case. The criminalists were over the place like ants on a Hershey bar. The bottom line is simple. If your people don't see that the evidence gets tagged, you'll end up looking like idiots in court. In the Negersmith case, they went to the trouble to collect pubic hair. But nobody tested it. What do you suppose they were saving the pubic hair for?"

An uncomfortable series of laughs filled the room.

"To review about the only point I want to make. I can't help you unless you tag the evidence. And make sure each item tagged is admitted for testing. Otherwise, kids, you're on your own. How about the case where they admitted a pair of bloodstained pants for evidence? The guys did a nice job. Brought it in. Got it admitted. But nobody ever looked in the damn pockets. During the trial one of the jurors found a note from the accused. This was a note from the accused to the dead man, the man he was claiming he "never met." They had to throw out the case because the jury is not allowed to find evidence. God. Was that embarrassing for the D.A's office or what? Remember. Tag all the evidence, all the time, and don't forget to look in the pockets."

Perry knew his field cold. The hard part, as the nation observed in the Simpson case, was getting the police, criminalists, the D.A.'s office, and the Medical Examiner's office to work together in a logical, irrefutable manner. Otherwise it was tough to make a convincing case. It was a transition period. It would take time for the system to absorb the new technology available. Only through education and cooperation could the judicial system work smoothly with outside companies.

Don came home later than usual. He was easily seduced to have a few beers with his residents at a local ratskeller near Columbia University. He was completely disoriented after the session in the hospital. It was the pressure of dealing with Chessman. The apathetic approach by most of the residents to the review of literature program. On top of that, the residents freely aired their complaints to Don. Because he was closer in age to most of them, he was an automatic ally. It was a role he liked, but it took its toll on him. The residents mostly complained about the verbal abuse from some of the higher-ups. They also complained about the insurance handouts that were routinely distributed to the house staff. Despite the complaints, the residents took it in stride. Don thought about the difficulties for his students.

Some older doctors were merciless in their approach to residents. "How could the residents take it so lightly?" Don thought. "Doctors training to become specialists should be treated better." In one instance, Dr. Childs publicly humiliated Arnie Baer in front of the house staff.

Don suggested Arnie write a letter to the hospital board. "Are you nuts? I'll get my balls handed to me on a platter."

The constant issue was the need for residents to learn about clinical practice outside the hospital. The residents knew as much about insurance as they knew or cared to know about the current controversies in clinical procedure. Like Arnie Baer was fond of saying, "Let's learn the bread and butter and get the hell out of here." It was the extreme point of view, but Don had to admit it was practical under the circumstances. The practice of medicine was still trying to keep track with the general evolution in world markets. Money was the center of everything.

Don went straight to the refrigerator. He made a leftover sandwich out of sweet-and-sour pork pieces and a slice of fresh tomato. He was still stuck with the frozen bagels. He forgot to pick up the bagels he liked on the way home. He made due by microwaving the whole concoction in one glorious heap, topping it off in the final seconds of cooking with a piece of American cheese.

Don wondered how old the Chinese was? "When was that?" he thought. Two days. Five days. Or was this the container from last week? What was the difference? The pork was cooked and killed any "worms" that were living in it. He remembered that from college. "Animals Without Backbones" by Buchsbaum, a basic primer in invertebrate zoology, a book that would keep anyone from eating steak tartare. It only took one picture of worms boring holes in a human brain to cure an addiction to rare meat.

Don found a third-full bottle of twelve-year-old Macallan near the wine bottles on the kitchen counter. That's what he was in the mood for. Don impulsively took a gulp right out of the bottle. He never did that. He took a second shot. He felt the scotch warm his body on the way down.

Dysplasia

He grabbed a light beer from the refrigerator. Coors was close to the front but he also spotted some Beck's Light. The Coors went down more like water. Don would sometimes have four or five while he bounced from his bed to the kitchen. Tonight was no exception. He precariously carried the Macallan, Coors, and sandwich to the bedroom.

Once plopped on the bed, he turned on CNN and watched the weather lady. He was convinced in his fantasy world that in order to get the weather jobs on CNN, the applicant had to sleep with Ted Turner. He loved to see what she was wearing, since the ladies seemed to have the most eclectic wardrobes on television.

On the bedside table was an unsigned note from Linda.
Gone shopping. See you later.

Don channel surfed until his sandwich was gone. He finished his beer quickly and had about two shots of the scotch left. He still felt hungry.

Don's second sandwich of the night was creamy Gorgonzola cheese with kosher salami. Linda hated his eating habits, citing them as being uncouth. She never complained when they were younger. Then, he was creative, inventive, and rebellious. Now he was a gas-producing menace that could strike at any hour of the night or day.

After another hour of culinary debauchery, Don was satiated. He sat up in bed reading articles for his hospital report. One was about the cost-effectiveness of obstetric services in hospitals. After awhile the articles appeared to run together. Most were written in a style that was big on cramming in facts and light on entertainment. But these were not intended to tickle the reader, merely get across the results of the study. The articles that were entertaining would often prove in the long run to be on the wrong track. The researcher's job was basically to state the facts, not editorialize and not overstate the results.

Don took a break. He checked his voicemail.

"Hello, you have three messages," said the friendly computer voice that lived somewhere in the "minds" of the computer chips. "Cyberspace Lane" was the address Don gave the voice.

"Hi, Dr. Gardner. Dr. Gross is on call. Have a good night." The friendly, feminine voice of the service operator was a fixture in Don's life. She was at least human.

"Hey, butt face. When are we going for some chink?" It was Kronen.

"Hi, Linda. It's Larry. Please call." A man's voice. At first Don thought he had the wrong number. He played it again. He did say "Linda".

Who? Larry. Don wrote down the name on a piece of scrap paper by the bed, the one with the artificial Mayflower crest.

Don looked at the clock on the bedside table. It was almost 11. Sometimes Linda went out for a couple of drinks with her friends after shopping or attending a lecture or show. He didn't remember where she went. Don tried to read a few more articles. It was harder to read, the later it got, but he continued.

Don fell asleep with the light on. Linda slipped into the bedroom somewhere about 1 AM. She tried not to wake up Don, but when she finally entered the bed area, dressed in a scanty silk teddy, Don rolled over and moaned. "Hey. Want to play with Mr. Little Overachiever?"

"You look like you're half dead," Linda said as she rolled to her side of the bed.

"Call it necrophilia." He moved towards her. He grabbed his stomach. "Wow. I think I ate too much."

"Go to sleep." She seemed serious.

"Some guy named Larry called," said Don as he rolled back to his place.

Dysplasia

Without missing a beat Linda said, "Oh, Larry, he's the new travel agent my mother wanted me to talk to. He's supposed to be great for cruises."

Don mumbled something about hating cruises. He moaned. "Cruises. We never go on any cruises." It was incoherent. He was fast asleep in a second.

Don dreamed about flying. He took a high turn and was over Central Park. He zoomed over the top of his office building, then pulled up to the residential side. He looked inside Dolly's window. She was dressing. She walked to the window and slapped Don's face through the glass. It was a windy night, so he pulled the collar of his Aquascutum coat high up over his head. It completely covered his head. He looked down at his body and realized he was only wearing his topcoat. His testicles were cold. He hoped no one from his building saw him as he turned to go east towards the river. Perhaps he would go spy on Harvey Gross. He increased his speed and it made a large whooshing sound.

Linda turned quickly around to her other side and faced the wall as Don treated her to a raucous bugle of gas. Linda referred to the behavior as Don's "problem". At those moments Linda saw Don as a most repellent character. She couldn't stand to be near him. She got up from the bed, got her robe from the closet, and went to the kitchen to read. She had never heard her father or stepfather behave like Don. Linda thought if Don changed his diet that he wouldn't have the "problem". She asked him to speak to their internist. Don thought it absurd. Another area of incompatibility.

Chapter Twelve

The next morning Linda was reading the *Post* as Don rushed into the kitchen. He was behind schedule. There was no hot morning coffee left. He didn't even think of stopping, but poked his head into the breakfast area to say goodbye.

"Hi. Bye. Big day. Lot of patients."

"Don. Can't you ask Stu Beitleman if there is something you can take for your stomach?" Linda meant it.

"There's nothing wrong with my stomach," answered Don.

"Then there must be something wrong with your nose." She sounded angry.

"That's very funny. I've got to get going." He started to leave.

Linda held up the newspaper. "They found out who that girl was. Her name is Melinda Foster. She's an actress. It says she used to work on *The Guiding Light*, like me."

"That name sounds familiar. What else does it say?" asked Don.

"Not much. The usual garbage. Except that she was badly mutilated."

"Yeah. I heard. He cut her up pretty bad."

"Your snot-nosed friend Jill tell you?"

"Okay. I'm late. Bye."

Dysplasia

⌒

Linda turned her nose up in the air. Don didn't deserve a goodbye that morning.

At the office things were bustling at their usual pace. About half way through the morning, while in the middle of a biopsy, Don noticed the lights above the surgical area blink in the programmed colored sequence. The code meant that Chessman wanted to see him.

"Intercom," said Don.

The nurse nearest the wall console pushed a button and Tina's voice pervaded the operating area.

"Yes. Dr. Gardner?" asked Tina.

"Tell Dr. Chessman I'll be done in ten minutes." Don continued to work.

"Is that all?" Tina was making sure.

"Yes."

"Will do." Tina was very professional, particularly if patients could hear her.

Don washed his hands in one of the many stainless steel hall sinks. He made his way to Chessman's office.

"Junior. Do you remember Melinda Foster?" asked Chessman the moment he saw Don.

"The murdered girl?" Don was intrigued.

"You know?"

"My wife reads the *Post* to me in the morning. She doesn't think I'd understand it on my own."

The joke fell flat. "Sit down. This is serious." Chessman pointed to the chair directly across from his desk. Don sat in one of the soft, plush leather chairs patients used for consultations.

Don thought of the worst-case scenario. "Did you date her?" asked Don, realizing it might be taken as a joke. His mind was thinking something more horrific.

"Thank God no. But she was a patient in our office. About four years ago. We will have to answer some questions. Tina has been instructed to let the detective speak to each one of us on the same day."

"Why would they want to talk to us?" asked Don.

"It seems there was some suturing done after she was carved up. The wounds were done with a surgical instrument, and the suture work looked professional."

"That wasn't in the paper," thought Don. Maybe Jill told Manny and he told Chessman. Chessman always got the details. "What kind of questions?"

"How the fuck should I know? These guys dream up all kinds of theories so they can go out and kill time before they find the drug-addicted psycho who would do such a horrible thing."

"Drug-addicted psycho." Don thought that might be a good description of Chessman. "Sure. Have Tina put him on my schedule. I'll talk to him."

"These guys love to come over to Fifth Avenue and see how the upper crust make a living. Humor the guy. We'll take him to lunch if we have to." The tone in Chessman's voice signaled the end of the meeting.

"Yeah." Don left the office wondering how Chessman knew so much so soon about the case. He realized one call to the Medical Examiner's office and they would fill him in quickly. After all, he was so well-connected.

When Don stopped at his desk, there was a pink memo sitting on his stack of charts. It said simply "Susan called." Don crumpled the paper and threw it in the wastebasket. Don wondered why she didn't leave her number. Maybe Tina didn't put it down. That was paranoid, even for Don. He wondered if he had kept Susan's number. Where did he put it? He couldn't remember. He wasn't going to call anyway. He opened the first chart of colorful patient records.

That night Don sat up in bed. He had a few drinks. His mind wandered. He always envisioned the worst. He wondered if Chessman was a bad-enough man to commit murder. He wondered if Lou or Harvey could kill anyone. The police obviously thought the killer was someone who knew how to use a scalpel and do decent suturing. Don thought about the night in Chessman's apartment. The scalpel. "Don't be stupid," thought Don. "Over a million people in the city had legal access to a scalpel."

His mind was wandering so much he couldn't concentrate on the articles. He bought a box of Pepto Bismol tablets at Stu Beitleman's suggestion after Linda phoned Stu and volunteered her unhappiness with Don's stomach, and subsequent gas production. He munched on two tablets and fell asleep watching Jay Leno. He thought Jay was okay, but sometimes boring, perhaps too ordinary. Don longed for the thrill of watching Johnny Carson in the days when there were only three networks. Don felt old.

Don woke sometime later and mechanically found his way to the bathroom. While he was urinating, he looked at the little Tiffany clock on his wife's vanity. It was after two in the morning and Don did not recall seeing his wife in bed. He thought he'd better look around for a note. When he was finished in the bathroom, he walked back into the bedroom and realized Linda was still out. She never stayed out that late. He went through a series of irrational and somewhat horrific outcomes before settling on the notion that his wife was bright, self-sufficient, and probably went back to a friend's place, talked too much, drank too much, and decided to stay over. But she always called. Don realized he hadn't checked the voicemail. He walked to the machine and pushed the "new messages" button.

"Hi. This is Larry. I have that information about the cruises." Cruises. Don hated cruises. What was with all this cruise stuff? Maybe Linda was planning a trip with her mother. Linda had done that twice since marrying Don. Once to Bermuda and once through the Panama Canal, flying back from Los Angeles.

"Hey, Don. It's Harvey. Want to enter the Corporate Challenge 10K next month?" Last year, Chessman, Lou, Harvey, and Don ran as a team. Lou never finished. Chessman cheated by cutting across the park. Harvey gloated all year that he beat Don by a full two minutes.

"Don. Hi. It's me, Linda. I'm over at Sue Lundergreen's and the time just flew. I'll stay over. Don't call. You'll wake her baby. Love you. See you tomorrow."

Don pushed the erase button. He fell back into bed, anxious to get back to sleep. Everything was okay. He worried unnecessarily.

Don thought about the note and phone call. He was still sensitive to the details. "At least she didn't say, 'I still love you.'" It was a long time since either of them used the term "love" in a sentence. Anytime Linda said or wrote the word "love", it was usually preceded by the word "still". Then he thought Sue must have been listening when Linda left the voice mail message. That's why Linda didn't say "still". Then Don told himself he was crazy for overanalyzing everything.

CHAPTER THIRTEEN

The next day, Chessman called for an unscheduled office meeting during lunch. It was important. Something had just come up and had to be dealt with that day, on the spot. Chessman loved to hold court in restaurants, particularly if it was business related.

The old Copacabana space had been redone a few years back and turned into a decent room for lunch, at least decent by Chessman's standards. It was perfect if they had to talk business because it was unlikely Chessman would run into any of his hotshot friends. They could talk uninterrupted for as long as they wanted. It was no Mortimer's or '21', but it was fine for business purposes. Chessman nearly cried when the patriarch from Mortimer's died.

Big red booths lined the perimeter of the room. They were made to look like one giant Carmen Miranda hat, complete with giant fruit and trees.

Once all arrived, they knew it was serious. Thomas Burns, one of their attorneys, a huge man who rivaled Orson Welles in girth and verbal sparring was already into his second martini.

Lou and Harvey sat at the outside of the semicircle. Don and Chessman sat inside, on each side of Burns, their backs to the huge mirrored wall. When it was business, Chessman obnoxiously ordered for everyone, the proud parent, feeding his dependent flock.

"Junior will have a club sandwich with blue cheese dressing on the side. Give my brother Lou a club with Russian. And Harvey wants something to graze on. Maybe you can go to the park and get him a few well-fertilized twigs."

"I'll have a plain spinach salad," supplied Harvey for the uneasy waiter.

"And give us another round of martinis. Junior, you want one of your malted deals?"

"Yes," was Don's answer. He didn't know why he said it. But he felt he wanted a drink. He was on edge. A little scotch could not hurt him. He had a light afternoon. No surgery.

Chessman and Lou thought nothing of a two-martini lunch followed by a lengthy surgical procedure.

"I'll have a light beer," volunteered Harvey.

Lou always drank whatever Chessman had.

The waiter left to fill the orders.

"Let me get right to it. Burns called me early this morning. You know that's no good."

Thomas Burns had the dubious distinction of being the attorney assigned to all claims against the office. Since the mid-'80s, Burns was on retainer due to the increased number of claims.

"Who is it this time?" asked Lou nervously. He had just gone through a series of three separate cases, three days of interrogatories. It was ironic because Lou was one of the best in town. The patients often mistook his passive nature as meaning he was not so sure of himself. If anything problematic occurred, they sued, led on by the bloodsuckers eager to get a new case started, and thereby increasing the probability for a big payday for everyone. Even though Lou did nothing close to malpractice, the insurance carrier settled the three cases in favor of the patient.

Dysplasia

Burns said that the three cases totaled $172,000, plus legal fees. And these were absolutely bullshit cases.

A woman claimed that Lou delayed her conjugal relations with her husband by not letting her know precisely when she could begin having sexual relations again. Lou said in a week or two, perhaps even three. The woman waited three weeks to be sure. A friend that had the same procedure reported that she only had to wait a week. The couple wanted to be compensated for the delay. Two weeks of unwanted celibacy seemed to be worth something, perhaps only in America. The other cases dealt with complications, problems with healing, and in one case having to repeat a procedure. To an outsider the complaints read as if the patient was tortured. To a doctor in practice, they were all possible outcomes, albeit undesirable and sometimes painful.

"It's Junior this time," said Burns, mimicking Chessman and enjoying the opportunity.

"It's about time," said Harvey. Harvey resented the fact that Don had never been sued.

"Who sued?" Don asked. He was clearly upset.

"Mrs. Workman," said Burns.

"Mrs. Workman was your patient," Don remembered, looking at Chessman. Don smelled something fishy.

"She loves Hank. How could she sue him?" Burns said while he was laughing.

"Don't you remember examining her for me before the holidays?" asked Chessman. He could see that Don was fuming.

"Yeah, so what?" Don could feel the setup coming.

"Well, she had a lot of bleeding the next day," said Chessman.

"But I had nothing to do with that. You were the one trying to control the bleeding," Don blurted out.

Chessman raised his voice. "Junior. Shut the fuck up and listen. She had a big flow one night at a black tie. It was the next night after you saw her. She ruined a new Donna Karan outfit, and was humiliated at the table because she bled down her legs. She is convinced that it was you who caused this."

"You know that's bullshit!' Don screamed.

"Hank, let me answer this," said Burns.

"Be my guest," said Chessman as he continued to sip his drink. "Waiter. Can I have a few more onions?"

"Right away, Dr. Chessman," said the young waiter.

"I may know that. You may know that. Every fucking OB-GYN in the United States may know that, but we are a country of over 800,000 attorneys. They have to make a living and Mrs. Workman is helping them. I spoke with her. The number was too high to pay her off. So I called Hank, and he agreed to let me work a deal with the insurance carrier. It's a fait accompli. The complaint will be filed, but the numbers they'll ask for are bull. It's already settled. I spoke to Workman's attorney who knows us from a previous case where we testified to help him. It's better for you to take the hit. You've never had a formal malpractice suit. The office rates will be essentially unaffected. It's a good deal all the way around."

Burns was pleased with his presentation. His already flushed face reddened even more as he forced a smile, making him look like a ripe watermelon.

"Am I supposed to be happy?" asked Don. He wasn't asking anyone in particular. It was more a statement. He was livid.

Chessman raised his hand, indicating he would take care of this. He cleared his throat and rubbed a toothpick on the inside of his mouth. Then he bit down on the end of it, not enough to break it.

"Junior. Goddamn you. You take everything so damned personally."

Don thought, "It's about me. How else am I supposed to take it?"

Dysplasia

❧

Chessman continued. He played the role of annoyed friend. "I took care of this for you and you didn't even have to do one fucking thing. If you weren't in this office, they would have tied your ass up for months. Who knows? It might have leaked out and everyone around town would know about it. So shut up. Yes. You should be happy it's a done deal. No harm, no foul."

The waiter finished placing the drinks. In the process, he delivered what appeared to be a whole jar of onions on little toothpick skewers. It was enough for four drinks.

Don grabbed his scotch and took a few fast sips. He felt the warmth as it flowed down his esophagus to his stomach. At that moment, he really hated Chessman. Chessman did all the things Don hated. The worst was acting on Don's behalf.

The rest of lunch was uneventful. Chessman and Burns name dropped for about a half hour.

Burns told the old joke about the second-rate musician who went to heaven. "St. Peter told him he could have whatever he wanted," said Burns. "I always wanted my own band," responded the musician. "No problem. How's Buddy Rich, Benny Goodman, Satchmo, and say, Glenn Miller? St. Peter did have a nice group. "You're kidding?" responded the musician. "Boy. This really is heaven." "We can get the Gershwins to write a few things for you," added St. Peter. "If you want to go more modern, we have Buddy Holly and John Lennon." "This is unbeliev-able." The musician was beaming. "We only ask one thing in return," said St. Peter. "What's that?" asked the new arrival. "God has been going with this chick singer..." It was an old joke. Someone always had a wife or girlfriend who wanted to sing.

All of Burn's jokes were antiwomen, just like Chessman's.

After any meal, Chessman made some type of pronouncement, usu-ally meant to put down someone in the group. He would discuss how the food there was just okay, indicating it was good enough for his partners, perhaps an insult to Burns. It was as if Chessman was doing everyone a favor by lowering himself to have lunch in an ordinary restaurant. For Lou it was a step up. Lou was happy to eat in any of the local coffee shops, Greek Gyro stands, the hot dog vendor in Central Park, or any of the dozens of cheap noodle shops that had opened in recent years. For Lou the lunch tab was more than he wanted to spend. Harvey put up with the cost of lunch since most of the time business was discussed. When he first joined the practice, Don was envious of Chessman's lunch outings. Chessman must have sensed that Don was anxious to be invited to one of the lunches at '21.' Chessman never invited Don. That day, as if to add insult to injury, Chessman launched into an update on '21.' Don could see it coming. Chessman kept a mental history of all the legendary restaurants in Manhattan.

"It was bought by the same company that owns the Orient Express. They put in a new chef and redid the place. I think it will be as good as when Jack Kriendler and Charlie Berns still had it. I think Cogan fucked it up a little. He had two chefs, and one was that chick, Anne Rosenweig. They put that French shit on the menu. The regulars don't eat that French shit. Who wants chicken hash and steak tartare? At least the new people kept Harry and Walter. I hear they paid 21 million for the building." Chessman paused. He knew Lou would speak.

"That's a lot of C-sections," said Lou. He always described money in terms of his own work.

"The guy that worked for Cogan, Aretsky, opened his own joint. I think it's called Patroon. Everyone's trying it. It's like '21'. I used to know Aretsky when he was trying to get the Eastside singles crowd. I think the place was called Oren and Aretsky. What a flesh joint that was. And he ends up at '21'. Only in America."

"Was that the same guy?" asked Don. Nobody was sure. Nobody cared to answer. Don just asked to show that he was listening.

Dysplasia

Burns always tried to be part of Chessman's scene. "I hear Aretsky and some of his people got in trouble for selling Cubans." Burns was referring to the big cigar boom in the city.

The conversation was comical to Don. He had heard it before.

"Do they still charge twenty-seven dollars for a hamburger?" asked Lou.

"What do you think?" was Chessman's challenging reply.

"Isn't Erik Blauberg there now?" asked Harvey. He never went but read the newspapers.

"Right. He was at Bouley and American Renaissance." Chessman was on top of his '21' facts.

Chessman continued with an update on ownership changes.

It was a boring after-lunch monologue. Don didn't listen anymore. He had more important things to think about. That was the first time he was sued. He felt violated in a strange way. It was a rude awakening for any doctor, the fact that any patient could sue. With the advent of more law schools with larger classes, a glut of lawyers emerged in the '80s and '90s. It was easy to find an attorney who would sue, regardless of the merits of the case. Medical malpractice in some ways followed the ambulance-chasing style associated with automobile accidents. It no longer mattered if a patient was actually harmed. What mattered was that a case was filed. Settlements were fast, providing the legal firm was experienced in dealing with the insurance companies.

In a perfect world, Don didn't see any reason why he would ever be sued. Granted, he couldn't do every case perfectly. Nobody could, but even Don's absolute worst effort, brought on by complications or lack of patient compliance, turned out better than average. Even Don's worst surgeries were way above the norm. He had no reason to expect a patient to sue. His medical school education left him totally unprepared to deal with lawyers, paralegal staffs, lengthy written interrogatories, and sometimes courtroom appearances. Don knew sooner or later in the real world he would get sued, but he didn't envision that it would be at the suggestion of one of his own partners.

Back at the office Harvey took Don aside. Harvey was saving something for when Don was down. It was gang-up-on-Don day.

"Look, Don. This is none of my business." Then why did Harvey sound so happy?

"What is none of your business?" ask Don. It was evident Harvey was up to something weird.

"One of the guys at the club, you know the squash guys, made some remark. I didn't want to say anything."

"Harvey. Spit it out. You obviously want to say it."

"He said something about Larry Bosler."

"Who the fuck is Larry Bosler?"

"That money guy. He was at our Christmas party."

Don remembered him. "So?"

"So. He said Larry and your wife were. You know. I'm sorry." There wasn't a shred of remorse in his voice.

"That's ridiculous." Don said it, but didn't mean it. He knew at that very moment that Larry the travel agent was Larry the guy from the Christmas party.

Don realized that his wife was brazen enough to let Larry call her at home. Or was it that she thought Don was so stupid. He would never catch on. Don told himself he would never have caught it if Harvey hadn't told him.

Don's carotid was pulsing and his cheek was twitching. It scared Harvey.

"Okay. Okay. I didn't mean anything. I just wanted to tell you. If it were reversed, I'd want you to tell me. Take it easy." Harvey thought Don was going to hit him.

Dysplasia

"Fat chance of your wife having an affair," Don thought. "She's a nervous wreck."

"Okay," said Don. "No problem."

"Sorry." Harvey left the office, almost tripping on his way out the doorway.

Don knew Harvey deliberately told him about Linda because of the meeting with Burns. Harvey was saving it up, waiting for an ugly moment to present itself so Harvey could add insult to injury. That was Harvey's style. He was sneaky and always a little malicious. It bothered Don almost as much as the news about Linda.

Don shook his head. He felt sorry for himself. He slammed his fist on his desk in disgust. Don knew Harvey was a little prick. He repeated to himself a statement from college that was taking on real meaning in his life, "once a prick, always a prick."

That night in bed, Don was about half-way through another thick series of articles, mostly on abortion policy in hospitals, when Linda came to bed. He had more than enough scotch, hoping the effects might dampen the pain he felt. Even if it was a rumor, even if Harvey made the whole thing up, even if his marriage was so bad that Linda felt she had no choice but to have an affair, it still stunk. There weren't enough "even ifs" to make Don feel any better.

"Good night, honey," she said.

"Linda?"

"What?"

"What's that Larry guy's last name?"

"What Larry guy?" asked Linda as she made herself comfortable, pulling up a green down comforter that was kept only on her side of the bed. It was too heavy for Don.

"What do you mean 'what Larry guy'?"

"Don. What are you talking about?"

"Larry. The travel agent. What's his last name?"

"What is so important about his last name?"

"Can't you just tell me?"

"No. I can't. I mean. I won't. Because of your attitude."

At this moment Don was convinced that what Harvey told him was true.

"Larry Bosler, isn't it?"

"Don. You are being ridiculous. Larry Bosler is not a travel agent."

"There is no travel agent, or do you know two Larrys?"

"Don. What is wrong with you?"

"Have you been sleeping with Larry Bosler?"

Linda got up slowly from the bed and walked to the open door. She turned back to face Don and make what she thought was a passionate speech.

"How dare you speak to me this way. I would never question where you go and what you do. I feel there has been a total breakdown of trust. I would never treat you this way. How would you like me accusing you of sleeping with your patients? Don. I am very disappointed. Very disappointed."

Linda walked to the closet. She began to pull out articles of clothing.

"Linda. Don't go to your mother's. This is getting boring." Don accepted that he made a mistake.

What Don didn't realize was if Linda left to go to her mother's, she could see Larry more easily, an activity that Linda's mother fully endorsed.

"Larry is more the long-term, stable type. He comes from the proper kind of family," Linda's mother often said, approving of the affair with Larry.

Sadly, at this point in her life, Linda was totally back in the confines of her repressed upbringing. It wasn't her fault entirely. She tried to get away, but never quite made it far enough. Don would never know how

Dysplasia

frightened she was of her mother, how being under her mother's control made her somehow content while simultaneously allowing her
mother to totally dominate her. It was what the paperback shrinks grew
to call "codependents". Linda's mother needed to control and abuse her.
Linda couldn't break away from her upbringing. It was a perverse
match. It was a match made in codependent hell or heaven, depending
upon the observer.

Linda began to sob gently, quietly, but loud enough to be noticed as
she slid back into the bed, pulling the comforter high up over her head.

Don found the words leaving his mouth, but was disappointed in
what he heard himself say.

"Linda. I'm sorry. Please. I'm sorry." He felt that's what most men say
when a crying spouse confronts them. Even if the spouse is guilty of
something, of anything, the man is supposed to apologize for upsetting
the wife. Don wished he could be more direct and say what he was
thinking, that he thought she'd be happier with someone else. They had
made a mistake and he didn't see why they had to keep pretending they
were going to make everything right by having a child. A child was the
furthest thing from his mind.

"Donald." She was very upset. "Donald." Once more for emphasis. "I
don't know how long I can go on like this if you don't trust me."

"There. The cliché of all clichés," thought Don. He remained silent.

They called it a night without another word.

CHAPTER FOURTEEN

Don was in the office early. He sat in his private office, wading through charts.

"A lady named Susan on line one," said Tina. "She said you'd know her."

"Okay," said Don. He took the call. He thought fate was pointing him into some sort of trouble. Perhaps it would be sexual trouble. Who was he kidding? That wasn't his style. He was confused.

"Hello. This is Dr. Gardner."

"Listen. When I originally gave you my number, it was because I thought you were a nice man. I need to see you about something more important. It is about your Dr. Chessman."

"I don't understand." That was an understatement.

"Please. Meet me."

Don was intrigued. Maybe she had juicy gossip about Chessman. He didn't care what it was. Maybe that was just an excuse. He never did anything like that. Since he was married, Don had never even met alone with a woman. Plenty of his friends had. According to Kronen Don was a social-intercourse virgin.

"Okay. Where?" Don asked, wanting to sound cool about the matter.

"Do you know the White Horse Tavern downtown?"

Dysplasia

֍

"I think so."

"Can you meet me later today?" she asked with a distinct sound of urgency in her voice.

"Okay. I can be there at 5:30."

Don already knew Linda wasn't going to be home. She left a "shopping" note near the coffee that morning.

"Fine. Good. Thank you." Susan hung up.

Don thought about the White Horse. God. He hadn't been there since he was in medical school. It was known as a watering hole for the likes of Dylan Thomas. Actors, artists, and revolutionaries would hang out there, along with future schoolteachers who went to N.Y.U.

In the taxi on the way downtown, Don wondered what he was doing. He placated himself by saying he was just going to hear what she had to say, find out what it was about Chessman and call it an early evening. He was married, and as far as he was concerned, this meeting had nothing to do with romance. She had made it clear in the telephone conversation that this was strictly business. Yet that wasn't the tone of their earlier conversations.

When Don came in, he spotted Susan sitting at a corner table. She was striking, even more beautiful than Don remembered. He was taken by her beauty and in a flash envisioned himself on a date. It made his heart race as onlookers watched him follow a path to her table.

She was wearing a multicolored sweater, a plain white blouse, with the collar up in the back. The outfit contrasted nicely with her light brown skin. Her shapely breasts were clearly discernable through the tight sweater.

"Dr. Gardner. Please sit down. Can I buy you a drink?" she asked, smiling.

"Maybe in a minute. I'm a little uncomfortable about meeting you." He was shocked at his own honesty.

"Don't you worry. I will not violate you while we sit here at the bar." She laughed.

She had a wonderful diction, with an accent he could not place. Now that he heard her voice again in person, he remembered thinking about it during their first meeting.

"Where are you from?" he asked.

"Jamaica," she answered proudly. "Let me get you that drink. You'll feel better."

Don thought of the girl in the wet T-shirt that did the old ads for the Jamaican Tourism Board.

"I love your accent," he stated. He was far from an expert, so he didn't pursue it. Besides, he thought it rude to comment on someone's manner of speaking.

"Thank you. But I don't think of it as an accent."

"That's right. I must sound like I have an accent to you."

"Particularly the New Yorkers." She drew out the words and sounded like she was from the Bronx. This made Don laugh.

The waiter stopped by the table.

"Can I get you anything?" he asked.

"Yes. I'd like another rum and Coca-Cola. Have you changed your mind?" asked Susan.

"Sure. Do you have any malt—never mind. Scotch and soda." Don held back his request for two reasons. He didn't want to seem pretentious by getting into a long discussion about malt scotch. Don told himself that even a scotch snob had to make allowances. He was beginning to second-guess his own taste in scotch. "Did you really like it or was it another affectation?" he asked himself.

Dysplasia

❧

"So. What did you want to tell me about Chessman?" Don decided to get right to it.

Don was anticipating a problem she or a friend had with Chessman. Occasionally a patient would try to rectify a situation if they could leverage one of the partners. People were always looking to get money back or reduce their bills, claiming some form of dissatisfaction. Susan didn't seem the type, but maybe someone asked her to intercede.

"How long do you know your partner, Dr. Chessman?"

Don was thinking that he might be wrong about Susan.

"I don't know. What's the problem?"

"Did you know he brought me to his apartment after the party?"

Don pictured her cavorting in the bedroom.

"No. How would I?"

"You know how men talk."

The waiter put the drinks down on the little wooden circular table.

She must have seen the look on Don's face. He was growing steadily more uncomfortable.

"No. I didn't fuck with your Dr. Chessman, if that's what you were thinking."

Whew. Don was relieved, but he wasn't sure why.

"What is it then? I don't understand. Did he attack you or something? What's wrong?"

"I can't tell you. I mean I don't know exactly. He had some things in his apartment."

"You mean in the bedroom." That room could scare anyone.

"No. I would not set foot in a bedroom with this kind of man. If you insult me again, I will leave."

Don found this funny that she was threatening to leave. She was extremely charming and her blunt language was completely disarming. Her demeanor intrigued Don. He had never met anyone quite like this.

"Sorry. Go on."

"His type of art. He had things he shouldn't."

"Okay. Susan. You've lost me. I have no clue what you are talking about. You're saying he stole some art?"

"I'm sorry. Maybe I shouldn't have called you."

"Maybe." Don agreed. The whole situation sounded like trouble. He thought Susan was being evasive.

"Do you mind walking me to my place on Bank Street. I live across the street from my studio. I'm studying acting there with Uta Hagen and Bill Hickey."

Now Don was back on his sexual-interest kick. A black actress from Jamaica was inviting him back to her place near her studio. The thing about Chessman was designed just to lure him into her trap. Trap? Why did she want him?

"Sure. You want to be an actress?" It sounded like a dumb question to Don.

"In my country I was very successful, but now I am here and I am starting over."

"It's a tough business."

"So is yours."

Susan refused to let Don pay for the drinks. She paid for them in cash and left a ten-dollar bill on the center of the table for the waiter.

They walked west on Bank Street after turning from Hudson. It was a beautiful block of neatly arranged attached buildings, some with brightly painted shutters. It evoked an era gone by, an era that New York will never see or feel again. He remembered seeing the block in a popular low-budget movie, the *Brothers McMullen*. The writer, who was also one of the leads, stood outside HB Studio for one of the scenes.

"Those two buildings there. That's where I study." Susan pointed to the freshly painted old buildings.

Don looked across the street and saw a sign that said "HB STUDIO."

Dysplasia

"How often do you study?" he asked.

"Everyday. I do something everyday. It is like playing a musical instrument. Somedays you just do the scales, somedays you improvise, and somedays you learn new material. The process never stops."

"I used to write plays." He knew Susan would like that.

"Plays? My God, you're a playwright. Good for you."

"I don't know what's so good about it."

"Are you still writing?"

"I haven't for several years. I got involved with my practice."

"You shouldn't stop writing. It's a gift."

Don was sorry he brought up the subject.

"I am writing. Sort of. I am doing a study for the hospital, to improve the conditions, particularly for those patients who do not have insurance."

"I read in the paper that your President's wife, this Hillary Rodman woman, the one who wants to be our New York Senator, wanted to give everyone free health insurance, but it never worked out."

"Something like that. Who knows what she could have accomplished."

"This woman does not like doctors."

"I don't know if it's that."

"I think she doesn't like men either."

"Really?" asked Don, totally incredulous.

Susan could see that she was embarrassing Don and changed the subject abruptly.

"Here is my building. Thank you for your time, Dr. Gardner."

She extended her hand and gave Don a firm businesslike handshake.

"Please. Call me Don." "Why had he said that?" he thought. What was the difference? They would probably never see each other again.

"Okay. Thanks, Don."

"Bye." Don turned to walk back to Hudson. He would get a taxi to drive uptown.

"Don?"

"Yes," he answered as he turned back to face Susan.

"You must be thinking I am some kind of crazy woman. I am not. I want to assure you of that. Please forgive me for taking your time. I am sorry."

She turned a key quickly in the large wrought-iron gate. Don heard the bolt snap open and she hurried inside the little courtyard in front of her building.

As Don walked to Hudson he challenged himself. What was he doing down there? Damn. She was a beautiful woman, but she was worlds away from Don's life, and he felt he should stay far away from that kind of temptation. His tie was bothering him, so he undid it with an annoyed, frenzied kind of a motion, rolling it up carelessly and stuffing it in his pocket. He apologized out loud to his father.

"I'm sorry. I never really cared that much for ties, but I never let you know. I didn't want to hurt your feelings."

Once inside his apartment, he immediately went into the bathroom. He reached for a jar of Vaseline and opened his trousers. He began a soft, stroking motion on his penis. Now it was a penis. Perhaps it would become his dick if he lost himself in fantasy and substituted pure slang for anatomical labels. He hadn't watched himself masturbate since he was dating in college.

He played out a fantasy. He could have gone upstairs with Susan. They would sit across from each other on Susan's leather sofa. It had to be black leather. She would sit back so her square shoulders thrust her breasts up and out.

Dysplasia

❦

"Why do you keep staring at my breasts? All you American men have a problem with breasts. Here. Do you want to see them?" She didn't wait for Don's answer.

Susan pulled up her sweater. Don saw her nipples standing out firmly against her blouse. Yes. It was exactly where he thought they would protrude through her sweaters. God. He loved nipples. Before Don could say a word, her blouse was open and two exquisitely proportioned light-brown breasts were staring across at him.

Don lunged across the room and buried his head between her breasts. The weight of his body pushed her down on the sofa. His hands fumbled to hike up her skirt. He felt the bulge in his pants press firmly up against her pubic bone. He bit her neck firmly and she moaned, an appreciative series of responses, while her lower body started to find a rhythmic center with Don's.

Don was losing control. His lack of confidence crept inside his fantasy.

"Oh. Oh. Oh, my God."

Don ejaculated in his pants.

"I'm sorry. God. I'm sorry."

"You American men." Susan tried to cover her mouth to hide her laughter.

Don removed his clothes. He turned on the shower, rinsed off his sticky hands in the sink, and then got under the flow. He thought of how ridiculous men looked when they masturbated. No wonder people found it such an unpopular subject. They either laughed or tried to ignore the subject completely. Don thought it must be partly due to the peculiar images people associate with autoerotic acts. Don laughed at how ridiculous he appeared in the mirror, his face twisted by the frenzy of his actions. From the waist up, it could have been the close-up in a torrid sex scene made for television. If it was an X-rated movie, the next line in the script would have read: "CUT TO: CU: THE HAND. NO.

THE OTHER HAND. THE ONE ON THE PENIS." When Don ran out of self-amusements, he realized that masturbating wasn't as erotic or satisfying as he would have liked.

The rest of the month was business as usual at Chessman, Benjamin, Gross, and Gardner, M.D. P.C., F.A.C.S., etc.

Linda ended up at her mother's again until they could "work things out." Her departure, unlike the others, wasn't stimulated by anything in particular. She left quietly, without incident, on a rainy Sunday morning. The night before, Don and Linda had a three-hour dinner at Daniel.

"We have to go to the new Daniel," she said. It moved to the Mayfair Hotel on Park Avenue and 65th Street. Daniel Boulud was quite famous.

They began with champagne. Don didn't know it was a goodbye toast. They overordered: asparagus wrapped in prosciutto and phyllo dough, a Parmesan crisp with goat cheese, a slice of foie gras terrine on toast, and finally a small plate of thinly sliced raw tuna with matsutake mushrooms. Dinner at the "in" New York spots could be very complicated.

Don let Jean Luc, Daniel's sommelier, order the wine. Don didn't know an Alsatian from a Vouvray from an Hermitage from Chapoutier. Few people did.

Dinner began with cold soups, cream soup with caviar, cold lobster with tomato. The food kept coming, seafood salad with Spanish mackerel, onion confit, shrimp on a mousse of corn purée, deep-fried zucchini flower stuffed with crab meat, roasted tilefish and lobster, medallions of lobster, veal chop.

The desserts dwarfed the meal, poached pineapple, coconut meringue, chocolate ice cream, chocolate mousse and citrus cream cake, hazelnut chocolate mousse cake. Of course, a dessert wine. Don couldn't remember one letter from the wine's name.

Dysplasia

When all was said and done Don's strongest memory was the price of the meal. Almost $300.

When they got home, they made love with a forgotten heated passion, no doubt brought on by the intoxication of the meal. In retrospect, Don thought it was because Linda planned to leave.

When Don woke up on Sunday morning, Linda was already up and about. He staggered from the bedroom into the hall to the front door. He had a colossal hangover and in no mood for an argument. He could see Linda. She was already dressed. He watched as she removed an already packed suitcase from the hall closet. It was tucked inside the small closet near the front door. The suitcase was slightly larger than the one she usually took with her. He didn't know why he said it, but he was glad, in a strange way, to see them take a break. He felt a sense of relief when he figured out what was going on.

"If you think it's best, then go," he said.

Linda was solemn. "Just for a few days," said Linda.

They didn't kiss goodbye.

The days became a week. Then two. It was a difficult time for Don. He thought about seeing someone. Perhaps Gruber, the shrink he liked. Over cocktails Don would mention something, casually. Don put it off, throwing himself into the hospital project with new fervor.

Don wrote dozens of article summaries for his report, despite managing to drink two or three neat scotches every night. It was the only way he could sleep.

CHAPTER FIFTEEN

Chessman left the next Thursday for the coast, a publisher's party for Stu was being held at Jimmy's II just outside Beverly Hills. Those parties were filled with celebrities and celebrities in training. Chessman asked Don if he wanted to go. Chessman was feeling sorry for him.

"Come on, Junior. You've been moping around ever since your wife left. You'll have fun. I can hook us up with a few young actresses." It was about as sincere as Chessman got.

When they first met, Don jumped at those opportunities, minus the offer of dates. Things were different. The thought of spending that much social time with Chessman was repellent.

"Junior. Come on. Loosen up. Just because you're separated you don't have to act like you're married. That's why they call it separated. Get it?"

"Hank. I'd rather stay here and work. Okay?"

"Hey, it's your dick. Do what you want."

Jimmy's II restaurant in Century City, Los Angeles was a center of activity for the mainstream glitz and old money. It was an odd pairing of social groups that somehow always managed to get along. Not unlike the unwritten liaison between Washington and Tinsel Town, there seemed to be an attraction between the powerful in business and the powerful in show business. In Jimmy's II, they dined together with an expected regularity.

Stu's public relations firm was no stranger to Hollywood. Stu hired the best. Stu paid dearly so he could mingle over champagne with the "right" Hollywood people. It was the same with his literary agent. He wanted the best. Scott Meredith previously represented him. When Scott died, he went with the newly formed Scovil, Chichak, and Galen, three of the luminaries from the Meredith agency. Stu dealt with Jack Scovil directly.

Beverly Hills was a second home to Chessman. Chessman loved the old days when he would sit in La Famiglia in Beverly Hills. Dean, Frank, Sammy, Joey, and Peter would show up. The young Chessman loved to kiss their asses. He was the great white doctor for many of their wives and girlfriends. Up until this trip, Chessman always stopped by to say hello to Joe Patti, the owner of the restaurant. With Dean gone, and the younger celebrities avoiding the Beverly Hills crowd, Joe packed up and moved to Palm Desert, disappearing like so many "in-crowd" people. Chessman used to sit with Dean for hours, swapping stories and being ogled by the dentists, doctors, accountants, and attorneys who came to "dine with Dean".

On the day of the book party, Sammy Kingsley, a well-known real estate developer, took Chessman to lunch. Sammy was a former child actor who traded shamelessly on his fame. Chessman was particularly fond of this connection because Sammy was once as famous as Freddie Bartholomew, Spanky, and Jackie Cooper. Everyone Chessman's age grew up envying Sammy. Sammy had it all, the Hollywood connection and a thriving business. Sammy floated in and out of either world, knowing when he could camp it up and when he should play cool.

Sammy picked up Chessman at the Four Seasons Hotel. It was located on Doheny, a palm-tree-lined drive that lived up to all of the expectations of Hollywoodland. Sammy drove a black Corniche convertible with the top down. Who could see them with the roof up?

The ride to town was short. Sammy pointed out that the old Chasen's building was becoming an upscale grocery. He showed Chessman the location of the new Chasen's in Beverly Hills proper. No tour would be complete without pointing out the new Spago location.

The valet parked the car at the Armani Collection, a flagship store for the world-famous designer. This store also boasted a restaurant, with all the trappings Beverly Hills had to offer.

Once seated, Sammy updated Chessman on their mutual investment deals.

"We got skunked on the Ritz Carlton in Palm Springs, but the new Costa Mesa shopping center just got a long-term lease from Nike. They want to put in a superstore. That's the ticket now. We're better off with Nike than a Barney's, Bloomingdales, or Macys. Once Nike is signed, they'll come on board, anyway, but Nike is the leader. We're negotiating to get Planet Hollywood right next to the Nike store. Can you imagine, right next door? The foot traffic generated by these two will be astronomical!" Sammy knew what he was talking about. Even the City of Beverly Hills succumbed to Nike and Planet Hollywood, to the chagrin of many of the older residents.

They interrupted their conversations several times to be sociable. The place was jammed with familiar faces that needed hellos.

First came Olin and his father Monte, the shortest and richest people at Sammy's tennis club. Chessman knew Olin very well from previous trips. They had a lot in common. Debauchery was the cornerstone.

An older couple, known jokingly as Mr. and Mrs. Save-A-Buck, waved hello from another table. They made a fortune in discount stores

Dysplasia

known for their cheap prices, dirty floors, and "fast food", long before the era of giant discount houses and fast-food chains. They even had little pharmacies in the store.

Chessman got up to go to their table. Mr. Save-A-Buck loved to tell the story. "The chicken lunches put us over the top. We took a loss on the chicken, but we only needed them to buy a box of Band-Aids or aspirin on the way out, and we were ahead. Way ahead. When we got bigger, we had the best iron-clad lease in the business. As the shopping centers grew, so did we. It was a slam crunch!"

Everyone knew he meant "slam dunk", but nobody wanted to interrupt his rags-to-riches marketing saga.

Last year Walter Matthau stopped at Chessman's table and explained to Chessman how corned beef is metabolized in the body. Walter knew Chessman hadn't a clue what he was talking about, so he made up some of the process as he went along. Walter educated himself on dietary matters, and when he came across a doctor who knew less than he did, a little fun at the doctor's expense was not out of place. After Walter passed away, Chessman began to tell people "I told him he wasn't looking well."

Olin came to the table wearing one of his specially constructed Mafia-white suits. When Olin crossed the room, everyone took note. They had to. He was always terribly overdressed: white patent-leather boots and a black-and-white print tie with an overlay of red circles.

"Dr. Chessman. When did you blow in?" asked the beaming, cherub-faced Olin.

"Yesterday."

"Sammy, my boy," said Olin.

"Hi, Olin. Would you like to join us?" asked Sammy, politely. He didn't mean it.

Before Sammy could say "us", Olin was squeezed in the booth between Sammy and Chessman. Olin's legs and body were so small he was able to squeeze past Chessman, using his lap as a brace.

"See those two over there?" asked Olin, his head a clear foot lower than the two men.

Olin gestured with his head to a table at the right. Seated against a mirror were scantily clad Carol-Ann and Crystal, hidden behind their respective sunglasses. Their twenty-something tan legs stretched out forever. Both wore scant summer cotton dresses, supporting what appeared to be jutting braless figures. They were laughing, telling jokes. They gave each other "high-fives" as they laughed, making sure every-one in the room knew they were there.

"How could I not?" answered Chessman.

"Would you like me to bring them over?" asked Olin, smiling as if he was the devil's personal representative.

"Olin, I'm married," lamented Sammy, who really wanted no part of it. Olin and Chessman were married in a similar manner, unlike Sammy, who in public always behaved in the best possible way. Olin was always trying to get Sammy to commit to something scandalous. Sammy never obliged. Not even with verbal hints. It frustrated the hell out of Olin, who could only relate to men through scatological humor and tales of adultery.

Chessman smiled. He had his eye on Carol-Ann.

"Should I invite them to your hotel for drinks later?" continued Olin, trying to feel out Chessman, still hoping to get a rise from Sammy.

"No. Don't do that," said Chessman, actually concerned. He wasn't on his own turf.

Dysplasia

"What? I've got to invite them somewhere," said Olin, like a little boy who arrives too late and is stuck staring at the "closed" sign in the candy store window.

Olin always wanted to impress men with his "power" over women. Chessman knew by this point that Olin probably knew the girls. In fact, it wouldn't have surprised Chessman if Olin had already given the women a cash advance or a bottle of Dom Perignon to play along.

"They aren't prostitutes," Olin loved to say. "Just women who like money, and knew how to get their hands on it."

"There's a book-signing party at Jimmy's tonight," said Chessman.

"Say no more," answered Olin, again smiling broadly.

In a flash Olin was at the girls' table, gesticulating and laughing loudly. He eventually spilled red wine on his white suit. The incident took center stage in the crowded restaurant. Olin was in his glory.

Carol-Ann McIntire had been in town for about two years. She led a common life for attractive women who made their way to Los Angeles. The combination of good weather and hearing the heartbeat of the entertainment business drew thousands of new faces every year.

At nineteen, Carol-Ann was married for a few years to a man who was caught flying a plane of drugs from Miami to Los Angeles. She was not implicated in the scheme after testifying against him, and was given probation for a lessor crime. She decided to stay in Los Angeles. Arthur Laurens, her well-known criminal attorney, introduced her to a lot of people. She made many new friends and enough money to get by. Her best-paying odd job was carrying attaché cases from one city to another. Carol-Ann liked a lot of money and began accepting "gifts" for a night of partying, particularly if it included smoking "coke." She and her friend, Crystal Krise, made the rounds at night, and slept most of the day, getting up "early" on somedays around noon in order to get to Rodeo Drive for lunch.

That night in the star-studded private room at Jimmy's II, Chessman sipped his glass of Perrier-Jouet, a bottle he ordered especially for him. He stood near a wine bucket that held his chilled beverage. He was disappointed with the selection for the party and asked to have the Perriet Jouet added at his expense. He naturally charged the extra expense to his New York office.

Stu was in the center of the room near a table of presigned books. Outside the room, a small table was set up for on-the-spot sales.

Carol-Ann spotted Chessman the moment she entered the room. She wasn't shy. She took a direct line to Chessman. Crystal took another route. She thought she spotted Warren Beatty across the room, and had always wanted to find out if any of the stories about him were true, particularly the ones having to do with the size of his genitals. Crystal thought of the old joke about the actress who sneaked into Warren Beatty's trailer. She suggested that she give him a blow job. The response was, "Okay. But what's in it for me?"

Chessman watched intently as Carol-Ann crossed the room. She was wearing a crème-colored silk blouse with matching pants. Her hair was up and braided in swirls behind her head. Several of the women let the daggers shoot from their eyes as Carol-Ann walked the room. Chessman liked that scene a lot.

"I've been waiting for you," cooed Chessman.

"How do you do. I'm Carol-Ann McIntire," she said, extending her hand.

"I'm Henry Chessman. Call me Hank."

"Okay, Hank. You going to drink that bottle of champagne yourself or what?"

"No. I was going to "or what." Chessman picked up a glass from a nearby bar. He poured Carol-Ann some champagne.

Dysplasia

Carol-Ann didn't get the joke, but smiled anyway. She accepted her freshly poured glass of champagne.

They spoke about the artificial life in Los Angeles and how most people were only interested in power, money, and sex, not necessarily in that order.

"Which do you prefer?" asked Carol-Ann, not expecting a direct answer.

"With the proper woman, there can be no finer joy than a night of playful adventure."

Carol-Ann thought that was a colossal crock of shit, but continued to smile as she took notice of Chessman's solid gold bracelet watch, onyx cuff links, and what she figured to be at least a $200 shirt. She didn't think much of his taste in shirts. There were plenty of guys in town who wore $200 shirts. She figured Chessman's watch and ruby pinky ring were worth about twenty-five grand, minimum. His suit looked like a Zegna, but she couldn't be sure. Maybe two or three grand for the suit. That was more comforting to her.

"You know, a good Versace silk shirt could run ya two grand," she thought. "At least when Johnny was alive." But she already knew that this new guy was a doctor, and two hundred for a shirt was a ton of money for a man in a health profession. The collar bar looked like real gold. His nails were manicured and neatly polished. She was ready to play. She needed a new friend in New York anyway. It was always good to have another source for airline tickets. "He'll be my own personal Priceline.com." Carol-Ann moved into play mode. She was thinking of the new Internet service that offered tickets to customers "who named their own price."

"When are you going back?" she asked, with all the formality of a travel agent.

"Tomorrow."

"That's funny. So am I." She was lying but felt the trip to New York might be worth it. She could see the eager look in Chessman's eyes. Even if he didn't offer a ticket, she had plenty of frequent flyer coupons to use. She knew better than to appear like a hooker, hoping to have her tab paid up front. She was smarter than that and knew from experience that she was making a well-calculated investment. The worst thing that could happen was that she would end up shopping in New York and visiting a lot of her new L.A. friends, some who kept apartments on the Upper Westside of the city or downtown in SoHo.

"Where are you staying?" asked Chessman.

"At a friend's apartment at Lincoln Center." She felt that would sound convenient to Chessman.

"Well, then we must have dinner."

"What about tomorrow?" Carol-Ann wanted to firm up this arrangement.

Even Chessman had to pause for a moment.

"Yes. Why not? Here's my office number," he said, producing the office card. "I'll have Tina my office manager make a dinner reservation at Lutece."

Chessman was now in his full play mode.

"Wonderful. I'm looking forward to it."

Carol-Ann extended her hand and gave Chessman a little kiss on the cheek, the kind a daughter might give her father on his birthday.

"Looking forward to it too," she said as she turned, looking back only once to make eye contact and smile.

Carol-Ann found Crystal preying on a soap actor who was being very polite and professional.

Chessman went over to Stu, who was talking up his book with a group of local doctors, Gene Barry, Zsa Zsa, and Mr. Blackwell. These parties got strange mixes of Hollywood people.

Dysplasia

Chessman picked up Carol-Ann in a chauffeured black Lincoln sedan. Chessman rented the cars for the entire evening. On the way over, Chessman gave Carol-Ann a brief history of Lutece.

"Andre Soltner is no longer there. He sold out to someone named Weinstein, who had popular restaurants, but nothing like Lutece. Andre stayed on in the beginning to introduce the Lutece crowd, trying to make the transition as painless as possible. It's not easy taking over a legendary restaurant like Lutece." Chessman poured it on. Carol-Ann feigned interest. She expected to go to the best restaurants. At least Chessman was polite. The conceit was nothing for her to handle.

Once inside the vestibule of the elegantly styled Midtown townhouse, Chessman indicated he wanted some privacy by using a recognizable gesture with his head while pointing his index finger. Lutece was one of Chessman's "legendary" restaurants. A tourist could easily mistake the treatment at the front door as rude. The same could be said of some of the waiters. Regulars called it professional.

Chessman and Carol-Ann were led into one of the smaller private rooms. Carol-Ann looked striking. She was disappointed that Chessman didn't want to show her off. It was part of his routine. He knew people who frequented this restaurant that were acquaintances of his wife. He tried to remain courteous, to publicly keep up the pretense of their marriage.

There were two other tables set up in the room. Chessman knew how to enjoy his life. At least it seemed so on the outside. He was articulate, even funny. Carol-Ann found him entertaining in the way an adult might find a precocious child who liked to show off what he learned in school.

A visitor broke the monotony. One of the chefs who wrote for the *New York Times*, Francois, recognized Chessman on his way in. Francois was directed to the little dining room. Francois spotted Chessman's table as soon as he poked his head into the room. He smiled as he walked towards them.

"Doctor Chessman. It ez zo good to ze you."

The last time Chessman saw Francois was on a week-long cruise featuring famous chefs. Hardly anyone onboard cared about the ports of call, just the food and wine.

"Francois. I'm glad you're finally cooking with those flavored vodkas. You got that from me!" Chessman really believed it.

"Sure. When I need to call you for advice ez when I finish for good!" It was hard to tell if Chessman was joking. Francois had to treat it as humor, but part of him knew Chessman was serious. "Who ez dez beautiful woman?"

"Carol-Ann McIntre, meet my friend Francois."

"How do you do?" said Carol-Ann, very politely through her boredom. Famous chefs were not important to her.

"It is always a pleazure to meet a woman of your beauty." He took her hand in his.

"Thank you very much."

"I will leave you two alone. Zorry to intrude." Francois wanted to continue his tablehopping.

"If you need any more help call me," said Chessman with his lips pressed together in an idiotic smirk.

Francois smiled and waved goodbye. He didn't know what to make of Chessman. Francois knew thousands of people in all types of businesses. Many overachievers, A-type personalities, who thought they were also great chefs. It went with the territory. Chessman did take himself more seriously on average.

Chessman ordered mostly classic dishes like snails and wild mushrooms in phyllo dough and Dover sole with brown butter. Dessert was a flourless chocolate cake with ginger ice cream. After the gourmet's dream, overseen by the new chef Eberhard Mueller, Carol-Ann slipped her hand over Chessman's thigh. To her it was a signal that she was comfortable. His interpretation was she couldn't resist him.

During an after-dinner wine, Carol-Ann felt she could be herself. "How can you eat the brains of an animal?" she asked. Carol-Ann had passed on some of the food.

"The sweetbreads are the thymus and pancreas," answered Chessman. "Not the brains."

"Double yuch!"

They shared a laugh. Hers was real. His was accommodating.

Chessman placed his hand very gently over hers and said, "Shall we go have an after-dinner drink at my place?"

"Where's your place?" she asked.

"On Fifth. Across from the park. A little place. 799 Fifth. I have other obligations in town."

Carol-Ann liked the way he said that. She knew the building. It was full of high rollers. She wasn't sure how Chessman lived. A lot of men in Chessman's world used hotels. Carol-Ann was beginning to have a better time.

"Okay. Sounds like fun," she said. Carol-Ann was game. She was naturally a little curious. She always reminded herself that "some of these guys turn out to be good fucks." That was a rare bonus. Chessman looked in pretty good shape to her. Olin had told her that Chessman was "into art." She liked men who were "into art."

Chessman swirled his fork in the colorful cream surrounding the second dessert. The cream began as a mosaic of intertwined colors, but now Chessman had used his fork to rearrange the swirls and patterns. It looked something like one of the slides he liked to project on the wall in his private bedroom.

He ran his fork up and down, using two of the thongs to create his masterpiece. In his mind he made the peaks and valleys of squamous epithelial tissue, the microscopic view of human skin. He needed more pink to complete his pathologic vision, and took a petal from the flower arrangement on the table.

"Oooo. That's pretty," said Carol-Ann as she leaned over to look at the art of the moment, courtesy of her talented date who was "into art." Little did she know that to Chessman the masterpiece was a biopsy of vaginal epithelium. That's what Chessman liked to look at from a supine position in his bed, human skin.

Carol-Ann smiled at Chessman as the pair passed the white-gloved doormen in front of 799 Fifth. At least three "Hello, Dr. Chessmans" would follow them to the elevator. Pierre followed them to the elevator. He pushed the button for them, making it clear he was at Chessman's beck and call.

"Dr. Chessman, will you be needing anything else this evening?" asked Pierre, knowing full well he was putting on the full show to impress Chessman's date. Act or no act, it was what Carol-Ann liked. Olin had come through.

The lights were already on in the apartment, and the view from the living area window was spectacular.

Carol-Ann moved quickly to the window. "Gawd. I love your view."

"Thank you. What can I get you?" Chessman walked to an open bar.

"Do you have Sambucca?" she asked. "If not I'll take a vodka. Straight."

"I think we have Sambucca."

Chessman began to prepare her drink.

Carol-Ann turned from the window. "Where is the little girl's room?" asked Carol-Ann.

"First door on the left. Where we came in." He didn't want her to go to the bathroom inside the bedroom. Besides, it was still locked.

Dysplasia

"Be right back, Hanky-Panky." Every other step was a skip, like a happy little girl playing as she walked.

Chessman waited until he heard the powder room lock from the inside.

Chessman reached for his keys. He walked quickly to the bedroom door and unlocked it, opening the door to look inside. Everything was prepared to his satisfaction. He closed the door. Once back at the bar, he finished preparing the drink. He poured himself the same drink.

Chessman waited by the window for Carol-Ann. He stared at a painting on the wall. His body was beginning to tingle. He didn't wait for her to return before gulping down his drink. He stared at the painting again. His body's pulse became a rhythmic pattern until he actually heard chanting.

"Here I am," sang Carol-Ann as she walked from the bathroom.

Carol-Ann danced over to the window. Chessman handed Carol-Ann her drink. "Thanks." She sipped it several times. "Mmmm. I love Sambucca."

She looked around the room. She didn't see one art object she fancied. The art looked like a child did it.

"So. What do you think?" asked Chessman, following her eyes around the room.

"Your taste is very unique." There. That was safe.

"That's why I'm with you."

"What a crock," she thought, but allowed Chessman to put his arm around her back, followed by a soft kiss on the mouth. She let her mouth fall open wide, her lower jaw hanging on its hinge.

Chessman put down his drink. He placed his other hand on her shoulder. He squeezed her firmly and ran his tongue over her lower lip. She liked that but pulled back.

"Hey, Hanky. I'm not quite ready for this."

"What's the matter?" he asked.

"I'm a little too straight."

"Do you want something to relax you?"

"You probably have everything, don't you? Are you one of those kinky doctors?"

"You'll have to find out."

Chessman walked toward the bedroom. "Be right back."

"No. I want to see your stash."

"Okay." Chessman took her hand and they walked into the bedroom. Chessman used a dimmer to raise the lights only slightly. It was enough light to see the restraints, the nitrous oxide mask, and the audiovisual paraphernalia.

Carol-Ann didn't flinch. She could have just entered a public library.

"So where's your stash?" she asked.

"In the bedside table." Chessman walked to the table. Chessman opened the drawer and took out several vials followed by a syringe.

"You are a toy freak, aren't you?"

Chessman laughed and said, "How about a little Valium?"

"Don't you have any pills?" She was hoping to smoke crack, but didn't want to ask. Chessman seemed to have plenty of goodies.

"This is much better. You won't even feel it."

Chessman reached for her arm and pulled her towards the bed. Carol-Ann sat on the edge.

"Sit and relax."

She sat and watched as Chessman quickly prepared a syringe with Valium. He took out a piece of tan rubber tubing and tied it around Carol-Ann's arm. He waited a few seconds for the vein to protrude in the cuboidal fossa.

"I can't believe I'm letting you do this. I can't get sick or anything, can I?" Carol-Ann was good at feigning amateur status. She was a great actress. She wasn't fond of needles but had tried heroin a few times.

Dysplasia

∞

When she had her third molars extracted, she always insisted on intra-venous Valium. She knew one dentist in Marina Del Rey who gave her intravenous Valium to get her teeth cleaned. She knew exactly what to expect from the Valium injection.

"No. Don't be silly," answered Chessman. He rubbed the area on her arm with an alcohol swab.

Chessman gave Carol-Ann the injection. The scene was no different than two junkies in a tenement uptown near Morningside Hospital.

Carol-Ann lied back on the bed. There were several satin pillows piled high behind her.

"How about some music?" she asked.

Chessman was putting the syringe and its contents into a bag that would be disposed of with the office waste. "There's a remote control beside you in that sleeve on the wall." Carol-Ann found it and took a moment to decide whether to turn on the cassette, CD or radio. She pushed for the CD player. It was Bobby Short singing Cole Porter tunes.

"Cool" she thought as the Valium circulated her bloodstream on its way to her brain to depress the central nervous system.

Chessman poured some cocaine from another vial onto a small rec-tangular glass slab. He snorted some through a hollow glass tube.

"Going in the other direction?" she asked.

"Sort of. Just for the moment."

"I'll have a little if it's okay," said Carol-Ann.

Chessman passed the glass slab and straw to Carol-Ann.

Chessman put his face into the nitrous oxide mask. He turned on the machine and took some deep breaths.

This frightened Carol-Ann for a second. "Gaawd. You look so creepy." She thought of a movie where a man sucking gas from a mask abused a woman. Something with "Velvet" in the title.

"It's just laughing gas."

Chessman took off the mask and offered it to her. He was smiling. Carol-Ann forgot her momentary fear. She took several deep breaths.

Chessman lay next to her while he lectured for several minutes about Bobby Short's talent. He liked him as much as Sinatra and Bennett or even Mel Torme.

Carol-Ann was not interested in listening to the differences in singing style and vocal ranges. The combination of drugs had taken her to a relaxed high she rather liked. She didn't want to waste it on some bullshit conversation. She began to massage her breasts.

Chessman watched for a few seconds. Then he pulled himself closer to her. Chessman and Carol-Ann went through several minutes of what might be classified as conventional lovemaking. It was a little rough by most standards, and after Carol-Ann tried a little cocaine she got very aggressive. She insisted on doing a series of Hustler magazine poses while Chessman undressed and played with himself, an activity that did little to visibly excite the great white doctor.

Chessman loaded up another syringe that Carol-Ann incorrectly assumed was more Valium. Chessman also mixed in Demorol and Brevitol with the Valium. It was a classic mix that in higher doses could be used as a form of anesthesia. It could render a patient unconscious and pain free, fit to have surgery performed.

Chessman guessed her body weight to be no more than one hundred and ten, maybe twenty at the most. He was careful to give her enough solution for plane one of anesthesia, described also as conscious sedation. With a little nitrous oxide, she might slip in and out of planes one and two, two being a deeper anesthesia, but he knew that she would not reach the surgical plane, plane three. Four would be close to death. In the wrong hands it would be easy to make a fatal mistake. It happened sometimes in hospitals.

Dysplasia

After a few minutes, the second injection rendered Carol-Ann almost motionless. She was in a semiconscious state. Her movements were slow and deliberate. Her speech was slurred like a bad drunk's.

Chessman slowly removed the rest of her clothing, a bustier and thong panties. It was the same pair she used earlier to pose and play peek-a-boo. By this point she breathed in a slow, rhythmic beat, signaling Chessman that he had her exactly where he wanted her.

He put restraints on her hands and attached them to rings that were cleverly hidden, recessed into the frame of the bed. By opening a little compartment similar to those systems used to hide recessed batteries, he could lift out the rings.

He turned off all the lights except for a small spotlight, the kind that would showcase a painting or a sculpture. Chessman walked to his slide box.

When he had one projected on the wall, Carol-Ann moaned. "Hey, that's real pretty."

Chessman took off his clothing. He stood over Carol-Ann, slowly massaging parts of her body. He started with her breasts, pausing to squeeze her nipples hard. She was somehow getting more and more aroused, despite her sedation. He reached down and ran his hand over her moist labia. Carefully, skillfully, and with deliberate style, he opened the folds of her vagina in a pattern, continuing to rub her clitoris after pulling up the little hood styled tissue that sometimes covered over one third of the bulb. He would insert fingers with the intention and mindset of a sixteen-year-old boy in the back of Dad's old Chevy wagon, not knowing how many to use or how far to place them or how often to repeat the act. He would rediscover sex all over again, a reacquainting ritual that pleased him.

Chessman moved away from Carol-Ann. He took a black leather case from a drawer. A clean pair of surgical gloves was removed from the case, ready to be pulled over his hands. He took a small gauze pad already wet with alcohol and wiped it quickly over Carol-Ann's vagina and pubic hair, as if he was sterilizing the surgical field before a case. He followed this with a few drops of betadine on a Q-tip, this time only on the inner labia.

From the case he took a shiny device made of stainless steel, which he inserted across the outside of her vagina. It could be turned in the center and the motion of turning would spread open the tissue, making the canal all the more accessible.

Carol-Ann felt the cold steel on her pussy. She wasn't quite sure what he was doing. She would guess later that it was some kind of dildo. She liked it. "I want you to fuck me," she announced.

And fuck her he would, but in his own way, a way that could not have been more perverted, twisted, warped, and beyond the scope of even the wildest human comprehension. To Chessman this was a way to pleasure.

For about twenty minutes Chessman had one hand inside Carol-Ann, feeling, groping, pushing, at speeds of gentle caressing up to hard thump-like activity, sometimes with as much of his fist as he could fit inside her. With his other hand he held hard on his penis, staring at the slide and listening to the sounds inside his head, which resembled no brain activity that could be measured by science.

When he tired of that, he took out a giant vibrator. Wide at the top and bulbous. By that time he had Carol-Ann stretched so wide he was able to place the top third of the device inside her vagina.

"Fuck that pussy," Carol-Ann would murmur, deep from what looked like a sexual hypnotic trance.

When Chessman turned on the machine, her previous moaning turned to screaming. Chessman was thrashing his body up and down on hers while holding fast to the electronic pleasure tool. Their bodies dripped in perspiration. The uncontrollable undulating made the entire bed platform vibrate.

After that activity dissipated, they paused to take several hits from a pipe. Chessman did have Carol-Ann's favorite. Chessman learned how to smoke "coke" or crack from Arnie Baer, one of the straightest and therefore unlikely sources for drug information. Very few people knew that Arnie was heavily into drugs all through medical school. Arnie thought it hip to smoke crack, especially with some of the "chic" contacts he was making in the city.

Carol-Ann was beyond being able to enjoy the coke she inhaled.

After a few hits, Chessman reached into the leather case and took out a small instrument that looked like a tiny scalpel. He had left the vibrator inside Carol-Ann, so he slowly pulled it out to facilitate his next step.

Chessman performed this next step quickly, and what he thought would be painlessly, given the amount of sedation. It didn't. It hurt her to the point of transient awareness, indicated by the change in expression on her face. She grimaced. Chessman was finished. The device was stained with blood and had a tiny piece of tissue attached to it as he removed it.

Chessman reached for one of his medicaments, the same he used in his office to control bleeding. He quickly wiped around the inside of her vagina.

Within seconds he had taken the little scalpel and reached down into Carol-Ann's inner labia and snipped off a tiny piece of tissue, almost indiscernible. Carol-Ann felt nothing after the initial discomfort. A clear stream of blood oozed out of her vagina and onto the slightly elevated curvature of her rear.

It took a few moments to control the bleeding. Chessman wiped the scalpel on a blank slide, leaving a sample of tissue, which would have to be sectioned and stained further, securing another centerfold for his personally erotic slide collection. When he did this, his penis became fully erect for the first time, and he spontaneously ejaculated over Carol-Ann's limp lower body.

Carol-Ann fell asleep. Chessman cleaned her as if he had finished a surgery. No more bleeding. The spot where he had taken the tissue sample was less than one centimeter, hardly noticeable. He undid her restraints, let her sleep and went into his bathroom to shower.

The telephone rang around noon in Carol-Ann's apartment, the one she had access to in Lincoln Center Tower. Carol-Ann was wrapped in the elegant sheets. She didn't budge. A small brown stain shown through the sheet in the area of her pelvis.

The telephone kept ringing.

Carol-Ann groaned. She finally turned over to answer the telephone. "Hello?"

"Carol-Ann? It's Crystal."

"Crystal. What the fuck are you doing up so early?"

"I set my alarm. I wanted to get you before you went out. How was your date?"

"Okay. He's a kinkmeister."

"You'll have to tell me all about it."

"I don't remember that much except I think I came a zillion times."

"Those old farts in training sure know what to do."

"God. He was working on me for hours. My pussy is really sore." Carol-Ann looked under the sheet.

"Maybe he's got a friend and we can double date."

"I don't know. He said he'd call me. My pussy feels really raw. I'm going to take a bath. What a fucking animal."

"Did he give you anything?" asked Crystal.

"That's right," thought Carol-Ann. "There was something."

Dysplasia

Carol-Ann looked around. It only took a second to recall what she was thinking.

Next to Carol-Ann's pillow on the bedside table was a velvet rectangular box. She picked it up.

"Uh-huh. A Tiffany gold tennis bracelet," she reported to her eager friend.

"All right!" Crystal shouted. "That's a start."

"Listen. My pussy is killing me. This guy is a real butcher. Let me go take my bath."

"Okay. Speak to you later."

"See ya."

"Kiss. Kiss. Kiss."

"Love you."

Carol-Ann placed the receiver in the cradle. She walked naked to the bathroom and turned on the bath faucets. She walked back to the window. She opened the shades by operating a small remote control. She watched the huge furrowed banana-colored monsters open in sync.

The sun lit the room brightly. Carol-Ann smiled. She made a new friend in New York. She might see him again. She made a mental note to send Chessman a proper thank you note for the gift.

CHAPTER SIXTEEN

∞

A few days later Susan called Don at the office. She left her telephone number. Don was more than curious. He called right back.

"Hello?"

"Hello, Susan. This is Don Gardner. How are you?" He was no longer Dr. Gardner.

"I am very sorry to bother you. Look. I might as well tell you the truth. I was very attracted to you. I wanted to meet you. Okay? I'm sorry for making it so complicated. If you want nothing to do with me, I will understand."

Don paused for a beat. This tact conflicted with what she had said last, at least as he remembered. He told himself to stop being so analytical. If he wanted to see her, she was giving him an opening.

"No. That's okay. I'm flattered."

"Can you meet me at the White Horse tonight? I have an improvisation class with my acting teacher Bill Hickey. It ends at ten."

"I guess I can."

"I would like you to meet Bill. He is my friend."

"Sure."

Don replaced the telephone receiver. He remembered a dinner date he had with Kronen at Smith and Wollensky's, a steak house in the 50s.

Dysplasia

Kronen read through Don's hospital report. They were to meet so that Kronen could tell him what he thought of Don's effort to date. Don figured he could easily make it downtown after dinner.

Don thought about Susan as he finished his patients that afternoon. He really should go through with it, if that's what he wanted. Linda wasn't living with him. Who would fault him? Just himself, he thought. He knew it wasn't going to be easy, but he was going to follow through.

Don ordered his dinner while sipping his first scotch.

"I'll have an end cut of prime rib. Well done. Can you char the other side."

"What other side?" The waiter in the white coat had been serving for about forty years, and always gave Don a hard time with that request.

Kronen smiled.

"The other side that you didn't char last time." Don was persistent.

"I don't know. You know the chef is Italian. I don't want to mess with no Italians." The waiter was stringing Don along.

"Burn his fucking meat, Gus," added Kronen. "And whatever he leaves over, sell it to the shoe shine guy for heel patches."

"And what about you, Mr. Kronen."

"I'll have a steak, still bleeding."

"Creamed spinach?"

"You bet," answered Kronen.

"For the table?" The waiter looked over at Don.

"Yes," said Don.

"Fries?" he asked, never missing a beat, and like most experienced New York waiters never writing down a thing.

"Yeah. Bring everything," concluded Kronen.

Kronen came there frequently for lunch with attorneys and clients. He leaned back, flashing his bright red suspenders. They hardly supported his drooping trousers.

"Listen to me. This black bitch is up to no good. She either wants your money or free medical care." Kronen was on his second Bloody Mary.

"What about my dick?" asked Don.

"Those days are over. When you reach our age, you are not exactly looked at as some fucking sex machine. Worse is they're right. How many times do you think you can come in one night?"

"I don't know and I don't want to talk about it."

"Okay. But remember that Kronen warned you." Kronen took a few quick gulps from his drink. He buttered the fresh bread with two tabs and began to chomp away.

"You love those cholesterol sandwiches, don't you?" asked Don.

Kronen disliked when anyone spoke about food while he was eating, particularly if it was a comment about health. "I am going to die happy, something you ought to start thinking about. First you medical dickheads tell us that cholesterol is bad, then that only some of it is bad, and then it comes down to a very objective reality. Madison Avenue made billions for the food industry with the hype they put on this shit. It's all bull. Either you are a cholesterol former or you ain't. I ain't. So I ain't at risk. Even if I was, only a few percent of the guys that give up living and switch to no fat, no meat, no nothin' that tastes any good ever benefit from the changes. You know the bullshit routine, lifestyle garbage. Just a small amount of these scared, shitless assholes actually benefit from becoming food monks. It's a bunch of shit. And I ain't buying into it."

"That's a very nice speech," said Don.

"Well, it's true. Isn't it?"

Don was afraid that it was, but didn't want to give Kronen the satisfaction.

Dysplasia

"I don't know. There's a lot of conflicting research."

"Conflicting research. Kiss my ass. Stick to the pussy. That's all you know. One guy knows pimples. One guy knows the pussy. One guy snakes out your ass. What's the matter with you guys, can't any of you do two things?"

"Shush!"

Two women at a nearby table were staring at Kronen.

"Oh, fuck them," he mumbled under his breath. He took a huge bite of his butter sandwich and downed the rest of his drink.

"Waiter. Another Bloody Mary. And buy my two darlings a round of drinks." He pointed to the two women.

One was a blonde, well-dressed, probably in her 40s.

"Thank you very much. I overheard what you said, and I think you're absolutely right," said the woman.

"Thank you," answered Kronen, as he slowly developed a wide, shit-eating grin directed at Don.

They had a brief conversation with the women before they left. They liked Bill Bradley better than Al Gore, and McCain better than Bush. Kronen couldn't have been happier.

During the main course, Kronen let out a long, not-too-loud, slow belch. He pushed himself away from the table.

"That's my signal to stop," said Kronen.

"I think it's a good idea since there's nothing left to eat except the bone and the bread basket," said Don. "The basket would make good roughage."

Kronen smiled and then laughed, acknowledging his incredible appetite.

"Don. I read over what you asked me to. I don't think you have any liability problems beyond what your normal insurance would cover. Most of what you're saying is based on fact, and as long as you don't accuse any individuals in the hospital of actual criminal impropriety, I don't have any problem with your paper. However, I don't think Spielberg will be knocking down your door to buy the movie rights to it. You docs write such boring shit."

"Thanks. I really appreciate you taking a look at it, almost as much as I appreciate your editorial comments."

"I think you're bucking the wrong boys. Hank Chessman does not appear to me to be a great innovator. Correct me if I'm wrong." Kronen knew he was right.

"I told you. He wants his name on the paper. That's it."

"Just watch the sonofabitch. He's a complicated sonofabitch." Kronen didn't trust anyone's motives, least of all Chessman.

"Thank you for your concern."

Kronen lowered his voice. "Don. I know what you're trying to do, but remember, we're not college kids anymore. You're playing with the big boys. Be careful. Everyone is sue happy, and doctors as a group are running scared ever since the government started trying to reform HMOs."

Don knew Kronen was always looking out for him. It made him feel close to Kronen. Even though Kronen was fond of saying that he had no friends, both knew otherwise.

"I heard you. Do you want dessert?" asked Don.

Kronen slid back in, closer to the table.

"Why not?" answered Kronen. "I've had a long-enough break."

After desert Kronen waited until Don got into a taxi. Kronen headed back to his office to finish some work. He always made his own hours, paying little attention to the time.

Dysplasia

Don entered the White Horse tavern right on time. At that time of the night the place was jammed. Don spotted Susan sitting between an older man who looked to be in his 70s and a middle-aged man wearing a jogging suit and running shoes.

Susan was wearing a red, hooded sweatshirt with matching sweatpants. She looked beautiful. Don had to tell himself not to stare.

"Hi," said Don as he walked up to the crowded corner.

"Dr. Gardner. Please say hello to Ike Horvin and Bill Hickey."

"Hello," said Don as he shook hands with the younger Ike.

"Pleased to meet you. Susan tells me you write plays also," said the well-known playwright.

"Not anymore," answered Don.

Don extended his hand to Bill. "Hi. Don Gardner."

"Bill. He wants to shake your hand," said Susan. "Bill can't see out of that side," volunteered Susan.

"I'm sorry, Doctor," Bill apologized.

They shook hands.

"He's so handsome," said Bill.

"Bill, please behave," said Susan.

"What? I can't say that your doctor is handsome. My God. How many handsome doctors do you know? My old doctor in Brooklyn, the one who gave me the pills for my epilepsy, he wasn't so bad looking, but who cared? Now, Buckey's veterinarian, he was a good looker, but I think he only loved animals, and I really don't blame him. Can you?"

"No. I guess I can't," said Don. He meant it.

"Bill. We have to go over my one-act play. Can you two excuse us?" asked Ike.

"Yes. Will you two love birds have a nice time?" added Bill, as Ike prompted him to get up by putting his arm under Bill's.

"Bill, please," said Susan.

"Now, Susan. You may be a great actress, but I'm the expert around here on love."

Ike took Bill by the arm and practically lifted the frail man off the ground.

"It was very nice to meet you, doctor," said Bill.

"Same here, Bill," answered Don. "Nice to meet you, Ike. Good luck with the play."

"Thanks," said Ike.

Susan got up and kissed Bill on the cheek. "Love you," she said.

"Love you," he answered.

Ike and Bill walked off arm in arm.

They heard Bill say, "Will you let go of me? People will get the wrong idea. If you were Tom Cruise, we could talk."

"Don. I'm so glad you made it," said Susan.

"Me too."

"Would you like a scotch and soda?"

"Yes, I would."

Don liked the idea that she remembered his drink.

"I'm on a date," he thought.

He smiled across the table, and Susan smiled back.

Not much was said over drinks, as if they were meeting for the first time. Susan didn't say one word about Chessman. Don felt it necessary to tell Susan that he was separated from his wife. Kronen would have advised him against it. She appeared sympathetic.

Susan took Don's hand as they walked slowly along Bank Street.

"Would you like to come to my place?" The words popped out of his mouth. These were words he hadn't said for years. He was having a great time. The fact that he had four drinks helped a great deal.

Dysplasia

"Sure. Do you have any wine or should we get some?" she asked.

"I have plenty," answered Don.

"I'm hungry. Let's pick up a pizza."

"Great idea," answered Don even though he was still full from dinner. He pictured himself getting up in the middle of the night, turning for a moment to see Susan's naked body sprawled on the sheets next to him. He tiptoed into the kitchen and nibbled on the cold pizza.

They stopped on the way uptown at Ray's Pizza, one of the six or seven Ray's that claimed relations to the original. It was one of those things indigenous to New Yorkers, knowing which Ray's had the best pie. New Yorkers still argued over which one was the original.

While they stood inside the brightly lit store, Don described his first experience with Ray's pizza. He must have overdramatized his passion because Susan started to laugh.

"Do you always get this excited over pizza?" she asked.

"Isn't there a food like pizza in Jamaica that everyone eats?"

Susan looked puzzled. She quickly changed the subject.

On the way to Don's apartment his mood changed. He was bringing a strange woman home. He must be crazy. He fought hard against his feelings. He was going through with it.

Once inside, they took the pizza into the living room and ate it on the floor. Don opened a bottle of inexpensive Valpollicella wine, which he announced would be perfect for the pizza.

Susan insisted on drinking the wine from the bottle and they passed the wine back and forth. Don thought back to his college days when he would booze it up with dates, rarely "scoring" as his friends called it, rarely forcing himself on women like his friends. It was the usual method, waiting for your date to get intoxicated. He could never do it. Tonight, he kept telling himself he would become aggressive. Why not? He couldn't spend the rest of his life trapped in his disappointing sex life.

He lay next to Susan on the floor. He couldn't help staring at her breasts. As he stared he got an erection.

Susan stared directly at his penis.

"You American men have no control, do you?" she asked.

"Huh? What did you say?" Don was intimidated.

The erection disappeared, slapped down by her words.

"You want to fuck every woman you meet. Isn't that how you do it? You meet a woman, and you want to fuck her. Am I right?"

Don didn't like this side of Susan. It's as if she changed personalities in a second. Don was ready. Don was going to hold his ground. Don was going to act like a jerk.

"Let me see your tits," he murmured as he moved closer. He never said anything like that before. He was drunk, and confused about his own sexuality. Perhaps if he stayed aggressive.

"Doctor. Come on. You are not serious?" she laughed.

Don moved his hands across her breasts, lingering with one hand.

She laughed again. It wasn't malicious. It was a fun laugh, a playful laugh. Don was back in business.

Don's erection came back in full swing.

He reached under her sweatshirt and pulled it up so that it fell on the upper part of her breasts.

He buried his head in her breasts. She was still laughing. Don was so aroused he lost control of where he was, who he was, and what he was doing. He pulled her under him on the floor, his mouth still trying to kiss her breasts. His heart pounded fiercely as he tried to move his head up to her mouth. By the time it got there, it was too late.

Dysplasia

∽

"Oh, oh. Ohhhhhh." Don had ejaculated in his pants.

Susan laughed as Don rolled over to one side.

"Oh my God. I'm sorry. I've never done that before." He thought of what a weird, self-fulfilling prophecy he brought on himself. Like in his fantasy, he lost control.

"What is that you have never done before? Letting your seed out too early, or trying to rape a woman in your own home?"

Don felt embarrassed. Humiliated.

"Could you excuse me for a minute?" he asked.

"Sure. Don't worry. It happens."

Don headed for the bathroom.

Once he was out of sight, Susan got up and began to look around the apartment. She was looking for something. She moved quickly and walked down the hall to the bedroom. She listened for the sound of the bathroom door opening. Hearing nothing, she proceeded into the bedroom.

Don nervously blotted his groin with a towel. He abandoned the procedure and moved to the toilet to urinate. It had been so long since he had an orgasm in his pants he had no idea how to clean it off.

There were a lot of papers strewn around the bedroom. Susan picked up one, read a little, and put it down. She looked at another and realized that was not what she was looking for. She moved across the bedroom and into the hall that led to the kitchen. In the hall, she heard Don's voice.

"What are you doing in here?" Don was at the doorway to the bedroom, behind Susan.

"I wanted to see what the bedroom was like."

"It's a bedroom."

"I see. Maybe I should go?" asked Susan, pretending to be uncomfortable, trying to take attention away from her trip to the bedroom.

"No. Please stay."

Don was feeling like a child. He wanted her to stay and was hoping he would get another chance.

Susan revealed yet another side of her personality.

"Do you have any coffee? I like plain American coffee," she said.

"Sure," said Don, as he walked a little ahead of her. They continued on towards the kitchen.

They sat across from one another on the breakfast chairs, much the same as Don did with Linda.

"In my country we do not promote this idea of a woman being all things to all men. A man and woman can be all things to each other, at least in spirit, and we make the best of the rest of it."

That was a disappointment. Make the best with the rest of it. What did she mean?

"I'm very sorry for what happened. I haven't been on a date in a long time." Don started babbling. "My wife and I are recently separated. It's not really a separation, just that we're not together, although my partner, Dr. Chessman, he calls it a separation." Don stopped himself. He thought he sounded like a first-class jerk. "I find you very attractive."

"I think you are attractive, too. I find people attractive. Men. Women. I like to touch women. There is something very serene about touching a woman."

"Are you telling me you're a lesbian?"

Susan laughed. She was beginning to like Don, but in a way that would have offended his masculinity.

"I'm sorry. But again, I have to tell you that I find you American men so amusing. You like these categories. Categories. You like to put it all in a category. The maker did not sit one day and pretend that life was full of categories. Sexuality is within everyone. The potential is there. You must use it, the way it is comfortable for you. Lesbian? I don't know if I like that category. I do like men. Haven't you ever thought about men beyond your American macho image of Monday Night Football? You know, those football players can't all fit into your classic American stereotype.

"I'm sorry. I'm a little drunk. I never did anything like that before."

"Donald. You keep harping on you, on what you did, on what you could have done. Did you ever consider that a woman is interested too, worried too, wanting things, like a man?"

"I'm not sure what you mean." He didn't mean to say that. He felt even more like a jerk.

"Look. I don't want to hurt your feelings. But I do not 'fuck around', as you people are so fond of saying. I am interested in sex after time, and we have not put in the time."

"That I understand. Not on the first date."

"Perhaps it is best to say it that way."

Don's trousers were getting a little uncomfortable. "Can you give me a minute to change my pants?"

"Take your time."

As soon as Don disappeared, Susan got up and began to look through the drawers on the armoire in the dining room. What she didn't know was that Don had become suspicious after finding her in the bedroom. He remembered what Kronen said. In his drunken state, perhaps he was a little more paranoid than he should have been, but he kept hearing Kronen's voice warning him.

He closed the door to his bedroom loudly, although he remained in the hallway. He walked silently back to the living room and peered inside to see Susan going through his things piled on a coffee table next to a big, leather sofa.

"That's it," said Don loudly. He snapped out of his confused puppy love state and realized he was in his home with a stranger who was rifling through his things. He worried that she might have a weapon. He controlled the thought and pretended not to be afraid.

Susan turned around, startled.

Don was next to her and grabbed her by the hands. "You are full of shit," he said. "What do you want?"

"Let go of me."

"I will when you are out of here."

"Take your hands off me. You are crazy!" she yelled.

"What did you think you were doing?"

"Nothing. Let go of me."

"You were looking for something to steal."

"I am not a thief."

Don grabbed Susan more tightly as she struggled to release her hands. One slipped free and she tried to hit Don. Don ducked and caught a glancing blow on the side of his head. He let her go and she backed up quickly, opening the front door Medeco lock while keeping her head facing Don.

"Damn. What did you do that for?" Don backed up. He lost his balance and fell back on the sofa.

"I'm sorry." She sounded legitimately sympathetic.

"Tell me what you're doing if you're not a thief."

"I can't." Susan struggled to unbolt the locks. By the time Don got there, the door was open and Susan ran down the hall towards the stairs.

Don didn't know what to think except what Kronen had said. But in his heart his instincts told him that Susan was afraid of something. He could see it in her eyes. "But what did he know about eyes?" he thought. He thought she wanted to go to bed with him.

Don didn't pursue her. Don locked the door behind him. His head hurt. He felt dizzy.

Dysplasia

‿

"What a night. You are some fucking Romeo," he spoke out loud. "You could have been killed." He thought about what his parents would have said, or worse old Uncle Max, if he told them he brought a black woman to his home and found her trying to rob him. Don really didn't think she was a thief. But what else was going on?

Don took his last bottle of malt scotch to bed with him. He felt he was making a mess out of everything. Before he fell asleep, he thought back to Susan's first conversation about Chessman. Maybe it did have something to do with him. Within seconds, rational thought would cease. Don passed out.

He woke up a few hours later. His head throbbed. He felt miserable. He hardly remembered the details of anything that happened, just one joke in the White Horse, a few bites of pizza, his sexual faux pas, and then the fight.

CHAPTER SEVENTEEN

Weeks passed quickly. Linda made up her mind to stay at her mother's. Don suggested they go for counseling to see if they could reconcile their differences. Linda refused. In the back of his mind, Don felt Linda might have lied to him about the "Larry" episode. Kronen suggested that Don hire one of the detective agencies that specialized in that kind of research. Don procrastinated. He couldn't believe his marriage was falling apart. He decided to concentrate on what he felt was a positive step, trying to help the hospital offer better care to its indigent patients.

Now that Don had clearance from Kronen on liability, he set up a meeting to challenge Chessman with some additional information he was going to include in his report, information that was more controversial.

They would meet at the Hotel Pierre after office hours. Chessman preferred it to any of the lessor places. It had to be the most elegant "happy hour" in the city. "They have great appetizers during happy hour," Chessman pronounced to anyone who listened. It was an expression that was never used at the Pierre.

Free appetizers from five to seven. Salmon on black bread, caviar on miniature scooped-out potatoes, and a colorful tray of fresh vegetables. Crudités.

Dysplasia

Don waited for Chessman at the bar. When Chessman arrived, it took him twenty minutes to work his way down to the other end of the bar where Don sat. Don recognized one of the men at the bar as a news reporter from CBS. He couldn't remember his name. Shiffer or Schaeffer. The other man was Jill's office mate, Dr. Manny Friedkin.

Chessman eventually reached Don. Chessman always carried the *Wall Street Journal* with him and used it to cover other papers he was carrying. He put the WSJ on the bar next to him.

"Give Junior some of that 'malted' scotch he likes." That was a repeat from his regular Don routine.

"I'll have another Macallan, with a tiny drop of ice please." Don acted like Chessman said nothing. Don kept up appearances. He didn't want Chessman to know that the verbal abuse was annoying.

"Do you want the twelve or the eighteen-year-old this time?" the bartender asked.

"Give Junior the eighteen," said Chessman.

"Fine. That's good stuff," volunteered the bartender.

Chessman didn't care about the cost of a drink. It came off the top of the office gross. Chessman wanted to appear like he was buying. He wasn't above impressing the bartender or anyone within earshot.

Chessman ordered his "martini" with a side of onions. It still made Don laugh.

Chessman fractured his pronunciation of certain words. If he got a laugh, he played along as if he wanted to get a laugh in the first place.

It reminded Don of his father who had the same problem with new words, particularly when Americans began to embrace French culture. Don's own father would get angry if anyone laughed at his pronunciations.

Chessman made it into a positive. He had a regular routine. "Pass me some of those "crew-dee-dees."

Don laughed as the bartender obliged. Chessman did have some comedic ability.

Manny came over to continue his talk with Chessman. Don was forced to make small talk until Manny said his goodbyes. Don waited until Chessman was well into his second drink. Once Don had Chessman's full attention, he began what he knew would be a tough sell.

"The Finkler article from '91, focuses on what I've been saying all along. The hospital has to zero in on practice patterns in relation to outcome."

"Come again, Junior. You want to talk about outcome. My unit is one of the best."

Don read from his notes. "If the hospital wants to run the unit more efficiently, all they've got to do is look at staff levels and mix rather than just on how we practice. The guy looked at eight city hospitals. Care management should focus on practice patterns in relation to outcome."

"Okay. Next." Chessman was patronizing Don.

"If we want to improve our follow-up care, we have to do something with transportation."

"Fine. You could use the office limo company."

"We need personal follow-ups and slide-tape type programs if we want to get them back in."

"Who says we want them back?" as Chessman forced one of his hideous nasal chortles.

Don ignored Chessman and pressed on, carefully following his high-lighted and single-sentence notes, knowing how short Chessman's attention span was when it came to those kind of realities.

"I came across several articles on loop electrosurgery."

"We don't do a lot of that in the hospital," Chessman stated with authority.

Dysplasia

∞

"It's about how we should utilize it in the office." Don planned all along to sneak in an article about the office procedure.

"The LEP thing?"

"Yes."

"Yeah. I want you to get me more involved in that. That LEP thing is a money maker." Chessman was glad Don mentioned it.

"It's LEEP, loop electrosurgical excisional procedure."

"Let's see if you can say that three times fast." Chessman was feeling his drinks.

"It may replace cryotherapy, or laser treatment for cervical neoplasias."

"It's a one-visit deal, right?" That was the key issue for Chessman. Time was money. A one-visit procedure could be billed as a full in office surgery.

"Yes."

"Let's look into increasing our office volume. Let our referral sources know we're leaders in the field. What's the name of the guy who wrote the article?"

"Mayeaux," said Don.

"Get him on the phone tomorrow. Maybe we'll give him a weekend in town. Book him in the Regency. No. The Plaza. They love that shit." Chessman always suggested that without having any idea who the doctor was, where he lived, or if he was the slightest bit interested.

Don arranged these trips dozens of times, utilizing the computerized office accounts. Chessman would have the doctor's attention all weekend and milk his brain for every last piece of information. There were very few men who weren't impressed by dinner at Lutece, a new Broadway musical, and a party or two with a few famous hypochondriacs who loved to be around doctors.

Don launched into another subject entirely. "Okay. What about this article that says we don't have to do a cervical biopsy for KC atypia unless we get two consecutive smears that are positive?"

"Junior. That's why I love you. You keep trying. Listen to me. If there is any hint of underlying dysplasia, I want to run the full gamut on my patients. If you want to practice otherwise, fine. But watch your ass. Burns will have his hands full defending you."

Don saw that Chessman's eyes were altered from his alcoholic intake. Don was wondering what other drugs Chessman had taken before having his drinks. A Valium? Zanax? Ever since that night in the apartment, he saw Chessman in a much worse light than he previously imagined. Don could see that Chessman was already getting bored. What kind of perverse games was he planning for later that night?

"I have to be going. Here." Chessman was through. He reached for his newspaper and unfolded it, revealing a set of papers. He dropped them on the bar.

"What's this?" asked Don.

"It's from Burns. You're being sued again."

"What the fuck are you talking about?"

"I'm sorry. Stu tried to stop her."

"Stu?"

"Stu told her that he didn't think it was malpractice."

"Who? And why was she talking to him about malpractice?"

"Junior. Shut up. I am getting tired of trying to save your ass and having you act ungrateful."

"Okay. Who was it?"

"Tracy Zacharia."

"But she had her baby without any problems."

"She's suing you because you did a Caesarean."

"She can't sue for that."

"You know she healed very slowly and the scar is pretty thick."

Dysplasia

"I can't believe I'm being sued again."

"She claims you knew that she was a swimsuit model, and claims that you have ruined her modeling career."

"And Stu discussed malpractice. This is bullshit."

"This is real, and you'd better call Burns. You have to sit through a series of oral interrogatories. Call Burns."

Chessman got up from the stool. "Good night, Junior. Sorry. We did what we could."

"Yeah." Don wanted to say "fuck you," but decided that it wasn't worth it.

Don finished his drink. Chessman kept a running tab at the Pierre. He didn't need to settle up. Don headed out the Fifth Avenue exit a few minutes after Chessman. He was fuming at the fact that Stu talked about malpractice with Tracy. Nobody thought of telling Don.

"Stu and his fucking beautiful people," thought Don as he walked to the office garage to get his car.

CHAPTER EIGHTEEN

The next day, Detective Dick Murphy was scheduled to meet with Don. Tina booked him in between patients. It was about the dead model, Melinda Foster. Don reminded himself that he still had a responsibility to the office and would not do anything to jeopardize his relationship to it. He had bad instincts about Chessman. What if Chessman once dated Melinda? It was Don's best guess that it was possible. But it still shouldn't be brought up unless asked directly. Don could say that he didn't know about it, which was true. No matter what he was asked, Don would not say anything about Chessman's social life. If Don alluded to the fact that Chessman was a "player," it would complicate the investigation as far as the office was concerned.

Dick Murphy had been on the force for twenty-five years. He had a rugged, ruddy complexion from years of stakeouts in the worst kind of weather (freezing to super humid). He was a career cop, whose father and grandfather were New York City cops. Dick was well-known, albeit with some mixed reviews in the popularity category. He was one of the cops who helped the Knapp Commission, a city-appointed group that went after their own police, judges, and city officials. Dick was involved in a few other investigations that shook up the entire city. He was young and rebellious then, like the young attorneys who worked tirelessly for the city in the hope to indict the bad guys. There were still plenty of politicians around who wanted nothing to do with Dick. That went for a shitload of cops as well. To that day Dick rarely called for backup unless he thought it was absolutely needed. One of two things usually happened when he called for backup, the cops were slow getting there or were uncooperative when they arrived.

Dick worked for one of the brightest minds in the complicated legal system that kept the city afloat, Letty Farmer. Farmer was only forty-five years old, and she had headed up the sex crime unit in the D.A.'s office since 1990. The office handled as many as 700 cases a year, ranging from rape to a wide variety of sexual abuses. They had a nice team of fourteen full-time assistant district attorneys, young men and women who recently graduated from law school and went to work for the city. It was a great education. A few would stay on and make careers, hoping to follow in the footsteps of their boss, Farmer, or District Attorney Robert M. Morgenthau. Letty would go into court with the best of them. She wasn't afraid of anyone. She was a striking redhead who could attract attention easily. She rose to fame prosecuting Harold Robert Hamrept, the "preppie murderer". Aside from the fourteen lawyers, two paralegals, and a secretary, she had one full-time detective at her disposal, Dick Murphy.

It bothered Dick a little that Farmer was friends with Jill. Jill knew Farmer before she met Dick. He was in disfavor with the department before Farmer hired him. He grew so unpopular because of his work for the Knapp Commission that he was thinking his career in police work was over. After a stint at the United Nations doing some work for Amnesty International, Dick finally got back into homicide where he had started his police career. Farmer hired him immediately when she heard he was available. "He's talented, honest, and perseveres. Not a bad combination." On occasion, Letty, Dick and Jill would go out for Chinese dinners. It was Jill and Dick's favorite night out.

Dick was asked to wait in Don's private office until Don was available.

When Don walked into the room, Dick was admiring the awards and plaques displayed on the wall behind his desk. Dick was embarrassed when Don entered the office. Don decided to act very formal.

"Hi, Dr. Gardner. Dick Murphy." He put out his hand. He seemed almost shy.

"Hi, Dick. How are you today?" responded Don.

They shook hands.

"I've already spoken to your partners, and they've filled me in on most of what I need to know." He was very soft spoken.

"Fine. Then this won't take long."

"You're Jill's friend, aren't you?"

"Yes. We went to school together."

"She likes you. She thinks most of the guys she meets in your business are major assholes." That was cordial for Dick.

"That's nice to hear," said Don, keeping his formality intact.

"So. Did you actually work on this Melinda girl?"

Don was surprised that Dick referred to her so informally. "No. I spoke to her a few times—when I was on call."

"Did she ever complain to you about any personal problems? You know, something strange?"

"I don't know what you mean."

"Did she ever come in with her pussy beat up?" He said it in the same polite tone as everything else. Dick was a master at finding out what he wanted. He studied Don's reaction, hoping to get his answer even before Don spoke.

Don stuttered. "Dick. What? Hey. Come on. First of all, if that were the case, we couldn't talk about it. You know that it's part of her medical records and you can't read that without a subpoena."

"Can I sit down?" asked Dick.

Dysplasia

"I'm sorry." Don pointed to a high-backed leather office chair. Don sat and swiveled to face Dick. "Look. I'm sure none of my partners commented on Ms. Foster's medical records."

"Take it easy. All you doctors get so nervous about the truth. I've already read your office records. We subpoenaed them. But this kind of stuff you guys rarely write down anyway, particularly if the girl is a piece of ass."

"Look, Dick. She wasn't even my patient. Did you ask Dr. Chessman?"

"Yes. I spoke to Slick. He's a piece of work, isn't he?"

Don was getting very uncomfortable. He didn't like what he was thinking, that Chessman possibly treated Melinda for ailments caused by physical abuse. He didn't want to know anymore.

"Dick. Are we through?" Don stood up.

"Sure. We're through. Thank you very much for your time."

"Do you think someone in the medical profession killed her?" asked Don, wanting to know the extent of Dick's suspicions.

"Why, you know someone who likes to do that sort of thing?"

"No."

"Well, I don't either, but I'm going to find out who does. Thank you again."

Don was worried. Did Dick actually think a doctor could commit a murder like that? Then Don thought, "Of course that's what Dick was thinking." It was a perfectly obvious assumption.

Dick left the room ahead of Don.

"I know my way out."

Don followed him to the center hall and turned into an adjacent corridor. Don wanted to tell Dick what he really thought at that moment. If Chessman were so kinky, maybe his friends were, too. Maybe Chessman introduced Melinda to one of his buddies. Maybe they were all dating Melinda. Don didn't speak. It was his imagination, spurred on by his dislike for Chessman. Part of Don wanted to get Chessman into any kind of trouble to get even for the malpractice cases.

Don knew if he spoke up he would seem ridiculous. What if it got back to Chessman that Don had suggested such a thing? It was pure supposition. Don knew that doctors covered up for special patients. But these were generalities. The only thing Don witnessed was the recent night when Chessman called him. Even Chessman had a right to his own privacy. Don grabbed the chart for his next patient from one of the nurses who automatically tailed him once he was out of his office. He decided to concentrate on his work.

The nurse spoke. "Judy Conway is in three. She's been on the fetal monitor for about twenty minutes."

"Normal?" he asked.

"Normal," she answered.

A quick $100 crossed Don's mind. He had made the money while talking to Dick. Don didn't like the thought anymore. He used to get excited about efficiency in the office, how it was set up to be a money machine. Now he was beginning to think that they were just ripping off a lot of the patients. Don felt like he needed some time off. Perhaps some help. Maybe he would call Gruber to talk. Nothing professional. Just as a friend.

Dick was stalled in traffic on the 59th Street Bridge. He thought he could make it to Shea Stadium in time for the end of the first quarter. The security guard at the box level always let Dick inside for free. When the Jets were hot, this proved a problem since Dick had to stand in the back near the concessions. Not a great problem. Dick was used to being on his feet most of the day anyway. This season the Jets were playing poorly. They had become a joke source for New Yorkers. Dick always found a seat by the end of the half.

Dysplasia

Dick liked to tell one of the knock-knock jokes about the Jets. There were plenty of jokes floating around the last few years.

"Knock-knock."

"Who's there?"

"Owen Jets."

"Owen Jets who?"

"O and nine Jets. That's who."

Dick's old boss Ira Parker, a certified football nut who almost played for the old Polo Ground Giants, kept insisting that the quarterback for the Jets could have won ten games with a better team.

Ira and Dick liked to joke about how they were sports racists. To them, football was the only sport that didn't utilize the talented pool of black players. That's how they perceived sports.

Ira described basketball simply. "You get the best blacks in your city and we'll get the best ones in ours. If you don't got 'em, then buy the best ones you can get, and then we'll play ball."

After Larry Bird of the Celtics retired, Dick couldn't think of a white man in basketball who had any super talent. It wasn't like they were available and the basketball teams were keeping them off the court.

The reverse situation was true in football. Dick didn't understand how the NFL got away with so few black quarterbacks. This made even Pop Warner coaches for kids encourage the black kids to play wide receiver, running back, or linebacker. In his heart, Dick knew that the NFL was more racist than he was and didn't want to end up with black leaders on all the teams.

Jill would get into heated arguments at dinner. "Dick. There are plenty of great white athletes in sports."

"Name one," he would reply half seriously.

"David Duval and Pete Sampras. How much time do you have? I'm just starting my list."

"Golf and tennis are no sports."

"Are not sports," she corrected.

"Whatever. Look what happens when one black guy gets to play golf? He wins two tournaments right off the bat, and finishes in the top part of the money list. Three years later he's the king of golf. Won something like five or six tournaments in a row. Go figure that one. He's got the other guys knocking themselves out all year to beat him. Imagine what would happen if golf opened up to the black athlete."

"If you're referring to Tiger Woods, I agree he's remarkable, but it has nothing to do with the fact that he's black."

"We'll see. Wait until they start recruiting blacks to play golf when they're kids. You'll see. Did you ever see Michael Jordan hit a golf ball, and it's not even his sport?"

"Dick. There is no sense arguing with you once you've made up your mind," was all Jill could conclude. Jill knew Dick's habits and he knew hers.

Dick finally got off the Bridge. He decided to head for Michael's Pub in Astoria, a well-known cop bar. Ironically, two Irish brothers named Moran, who were known to make a little book on the side, ran the pub. Their grandfather started it, a hard-working immigrant who used to settle fights himself, occasionally landing in jail for the extra shot on the head he would give the culprit with an oak walking stick. Most policemen didn't consider bookmaking at the local level such a big deal. They rationalized that it was a local mom-and-pop operation, hardly noticeable, compared to a few of the regional and national networks. Some even used the Internet.

Dick pulled up outside the bar, parked in an illegal zone the cops had set up for themselves, and hurried to get inside the bar. He felt thirsty as he walked from his car. He was looking forward to a few cool pops of beer.

The bar was a magical transition from the day-to-day grind in the city. It typified what New York was and could still be. Cops had been coming there for three generations. The pub was a second home, a place of refuge, and sometimes even confession.

Dick sat down next to Irv Schacter, a career warrant officer for the District Attorney's office in Queens. Irv was a giant compared to other men from his generation. He was about six foot five inches. Irv was no stranger to fighting. He refused to tolerate even friendly humor about the Jews.

Irv would easily volunteer his point of view. "All jokes are hostile at the core of the thing, and if you are using a Jew in your joke, then you are as big an anti-Semite as that black S.O.B. Farrakhan."

Moran always followed that type of statement with, "New York is the melting pot of racism. Why should the jokes be any different?"

Next to Irv was Jerry Shaunessey, a third generation cop who pounded a beat on Ditmas Boulevard not far from the bar. Jerry was a roly-poly guy who swore he could beat anyone in a race around the block. "When I made all city linebacker..." was how he started his athletic challenge. Nobody ever took him up on the race.

As soon as Dick was spotted, the usual banter started.

"Well, if it ain't that Irish aristocrat from the city," said the bartender. John Moran was a giant of a man like his grandfather. He had a dark shock of black hair that he wore long, like the mane on a stallion.

"Hey, city boy," was Irv's greeting for Dick.

"I thought you Jewish cops were getting some kind of special minority status so you could retire early," said Dick matter-of-fact.

Irv stared Dick down. Irv knew Dick loved to provoke him. Years ago he would have swung already. That day he just moved his beer to the other end of the bar. He mumbled something about "uncouth patrons" as he slid his beer down the long mahogany bar.

"Let me have a draft," said Dick, laughing at Irv's poor acting skills.

"Come on back," said Moran.

"Let him sulk," said Jerry.

Moran obliged the order for a draft within seconds.

"Dickey, what's the scoop on those cut-up broads?" asked Jerry. "They say they was carved by an expert slicer." Jerry knew Dick might have inside information on the homicides.

"I heard the second broad was no broad. Lost his dick in the battle. They should award 'em the purple 'heart-on,' shouted Irv from the end of the bar.

That got a big laugh from the boys.

"They thought it was a sex crime, but now they think it might even be two separate slicers," said Dick. The news of the second body traveled fast. The press release only went out that morning. The autopsy was finished late last night.

"That's a lot of bullshit," said Jerry. "This is a one-slicer deal. I don't buy any of that psychology shit. The slicer here is an equal-opportunity kind of guy. One night he likes pussy, and the next night he wants to play hide the Kilbasi."

"You mean one night he likes to slice up pussy and the other night a nice set of garbanzos," said Irv, trying to top Jerry. Irv moved back to his original spot at the bar.

"I knew you boys could relate," said Dick.

"I heard the first broad's doctor practices with your girl," said Irv. He threw it in subtly as an afterthought, but the dig was strong.

"That's bullshit. She don't know the guy," said Dick, not wanting to hear any shit about Jill.

"Same building, ain't it?" asked Irv.

"I heard it was his office," said Jerry.

Dysplasia

Since the newspapers didn't carry the information yet, Dick knew that Irv and Jerry must have talked to someone in the D.A.'s office or in Sex Crimes Division.

The press release didn't contain any information about suspects. The D.A. was being very careful with that type of information. Everyone in the country was reticent about naming suspects, particularly after what happened in the Atlanta bombing. NBC forked over about a half a million, way over nuisance value, for the case because Tom Brokaw incriminated the suspect on the air prematurely. Eventually the FBI had to back down.

"What if it was? What's your fucking point?" Dick had enough.

He took his beer and slid down to the other far end of the bar, the furthest from anyone in the room. He took a quarter from his bar change and walked over to the old-fashioned Captain Fantastic Bally pinball machine. One of the Moran boys bought it for a few hundred years ago, and now it had turned into a collectible. It had a big picture of Elton John on the glass, decked out in bell-bottoms, with one of his long-haired wigs. Bally had no idea it would become so valuable.

Dick put his beer on the pinball glass top.

"What's his fucking problem? Overpaid?" asked Irv.

"Irv, get off him. It's the weather," suggested Jerry.

It was unseasonably hot as the weather was pressing for an early spring. Everyone was overdressed. Most of the bar patrons peeled down to their sleeves or T-shirts.

"Too hot to eat," said Irv.

"Too hot to fuck," added Jerry.

"Never too hot to drink," said John, as he set up a round of beers. "On the house, boys. Drink up." John knew how to handle the boys. Today was a mild interchange.

- 280 -

Dick thought about Jill, whether she would continue to stay with him. He told her she was too smart for him. She assured him that she thought he was smart. He realized now that those were not the issues; he simply couldn't get any closer to her. He kept his distance, something Jill complained about. The past few months were beginning to show the wear of a relationship that was on the skids.

His mind switched to the murder. He didn't think a doctor did it. Doctors don't do that, or do they? He reconsidered and then lost himself in the travels of the metal ball, bumper to bumper, chute to chute, a flip saving the ball's demise, only to ricochet and be lost in a dark hole. Wasn't pinball a little like his own life? He gulped his beer and listened to the ball reset into position for another ride. It was a lonely life and Jill was the only spark in it. He drank a few more beers that afternoon, letting his mind find its own dark hole devoid of the pains of his career.

Dick left the bar about the time the Jets were in the last quarter. "To hell with the game," he thought. He had to be back in the city for a meeting with Farmer and two of the shrinks tied to the medical examiner's office. He hated these meetings, and only went if he was a little loaded.

At the meeting, Dr. Marvin Mayer, a criminal academician, was giving the boys the scoop on who killed Melissa, at least from a shrink's point of view.

"There is no doubt that high levels of plasma testosterone are associated with these types of sexual violence," said Marvin, with the conviction that he could locate the killer based on testosterone levels.

"What are we supposed to do, run around town and give all the suspects a yank to see if they have a stiff rod?" Dick mumbled.

Dysplasia

~

Farmer was quick to keep the mood serious. She didn't look at Dick but he knew it was for him. "Dr. Mayer is an expert on psychiatry and the dangerous sexual offender. If any of you boys want to take a pass on this meeting, please be my guest. But you'll need to supply me with a twenty page report on Dr. Mayer's research."

Farmer smiled as she looked around the room, to see if anyone was leaving.

A few throats were cleared before Dr. Mayer continued.

"The most frequent forms of psychopathology shown by these patients are antisocial attitudes, depression, somatization and cognitive disorders. What's odd is that as you interview your suspects, they will vehemently deny that they have had any type of treatment in the past, and completely deny the possibility that they would harm anyone. In fact, most of them are damned polite. They go as far as to say things like, "I certainly would never treat a lady in any way accept as a lady. I never so much as said a harsh word to a lady." I took that quote from the transcript of a man accused of killing sixteen prostitutes, mutilating their faces, and cutting out their eyes. His aunt was a taxidermist. He had great hands, could have been a surgeon."

Farmer added, "Just because we see a neat surgical job on our victims it doesn't mean the guy we're looking for went to medical school."

"I would hope not, but anything is possible," added Dr. Mayer.

Dick thought this was a waste of time. The television and movies carried as much information as the shrinks had. After *Silence of the Lambs* everyone jumped into the mutilation business. Shows like *Hard Copy* were featuring serial killers as their featured subject. As far as Dick was concerned, there were some very sick motherfuckers out there, so sick that there is no way any of these shrinks could ever figure them out.

Dick dozed off. He was dreaming of lying on a beach in the Caribbean with Jill. As he was about to roll over onto Jill's topless body, he heard the voice of Dr. Mayer give his concluding remarks.

"The Hucker article points out that people who commit sexual violence, necrophilia, and asphyxiophilia may be treated in the same manner since they have an underlying psychological connection. This overlap can only be established with more empirical data, both clinically and in the laboratory."

"Thank you, Dr. Mayer. Okay, boys, go out and find the doc a subject," said Farmer.

Dick exhaled a sigh of relief. He moved to Dr. Mayer. "Hi. Dick Murphy. We met last year at that trial for the guy from the island."

"Oh, yeah. Sure. The landscaper."

"He cut lawns," said Dick, trying to keep the conversation in his own realistic world.

"Okay. He cut lawns. How are you?" Dr. Mayer was a polite, sociable man who happened to make a career out of a horrible subject.

"Since they fished out this other girl—I don't know—the guy. The trans whatever. Don't these guys stick to the same deal? You know. Why would he be after both sides of the sex thing?"

Dr. Mayer knew that Dick's thinking was right on target. "That's an interesting question. I don't have the answer. For a long time we thought that, but a fellow named Abel just published a study that says we really don't know their boundaries. They might cross over. Basically, their main problem is that they lose control."

Dick didn't like the answer. He always had trouble with shrinks. They danced too much around the obvious. "Could it be a lot simpler, that this guy was so pissed off when he saw that the girl had a dick, he went berserk because he was disappointed?"

Dr. Mayer found this funny and he laughed. That gave Dick one more reason to hate shrinks. They found places to laugh that made Dick uncomfortable. Dr. Mayer turned beet red, and smiled.

"I said something funny, Doc?" The antagonism showed in his voice.

Dysplasia

Dr. Mayer cleared his throat. "Well, I think it's possible that the same man or woman committed both crimes."

"A woman?" Dick never considered it. Not for a second.

"Why not?"

"I don't know of any cases like this where a woman was involved, do you?" Dick's instincts told him it wasn't a woman. If it was two different people, one of them might have been a woman.

"Not offhand, but I'm always learning. Hey, I've got to get going. Look at the time." Dr. Mayer was one of those guys that made the statement and then looked at his watch.

This little exchange reminded Dick that he still hadn't interviewed some doctor who Melinda listed in her address book as her shrink. They subpoenaed the guy's records, but he scribbled a lot, and most of what he sent was illegible. Dick decided to visit the shrink.

Dr. Barry Gruber was the psychiatrist of record for Melinda. Dr. Gruber was well-known in New York for his straightforward, no-nonsense attitude. He was not a model's shrink. He was a shrink's shrink. More than half his practice was made up of social workers, psychologists, and psychiatrists. When all the psychobabble was reduced to its lowest common denominator, a lot of professionals preferred Barry's style to the more established practitioners of New York "shrinkdom."

Barry was from the southeast corner of Queens, a little-known town called Rosedale. He grew up surrounded by lower-middle-class Italians and Jews. Nobody was rich in his neighborhood and basically nobody seemed to care. That lack of pretension stayed with Barry his whole life. He still wore jeans at local psychiatric meetings, and refused to close his top collar button for anyone under any circumstances. When the smokers sneaked outside for a few drags, Barry thought nothing of lighting up a joint.

The telephone rang in Barry's office. A freckled hand reached out from behind a pile of files and picked up an old-fashioned black rotary telephone. He didn't wear a watch, drive a car, or watch much television. He had an old Philco black and white television. He did hook it up to the cable so he could see the news more frequently. That was enough technology for him.

"Hello?" The voice was connected to a man well over six feet tall. He wasn't great looking but tried to keep himself well-groomed, pulling back the bushy sides of his salt-and-pepper hair into a little ponytail, held together with a rubber band.

"You Dr. Gruber," said Dick, almost annoyed.

"Yeah, 'I' Dr. Gruber," answered Barry, mimicking the sound and diction of the caller. "Who dis?"

"I just didn't expect you to answer your own phone."

"Why? It's my phone. Why shouldn't I answer my own phone?"

Dick realized that guy could pull him way off track.

"I'm Detective Murphy with the District Attorney's Office. I am assigned to the Sex Crimes division. I understand you were Melinda Foster's doctor?"

"Yes. That's right. I already have a request for medical records on my desk. It's at the top of my file. "

"You already sent them."

"I did? I'll have to take your word on that."

Barry's desk looked like a wind blew in and had a party reorganizing his papers. As Barry spoke, he kept sifting through the mounds of paper garbage on his desk.

"Could I speak to you in person?" asked Dick.

Dysplasia

"Sure. I'm on my way downtown to a place to hear some jazz. It's called Bradley's." There was no hesitation in his answer. He sounded like he would enjoy the company. Just two guys out to hear music.

"I was hoping to come to your office." Dick was not prepared for Barry's direct response.

"Office. Sure. Hold on a second." He fumbled through his calendar. "How's next Thursday. Wait. No. Haircut. Uh. How's Uhm. Uhm. How's a week from Tuesday. In the morning. Ten. No. In the afternoon. Four. No. Three. Yes, three. But I'll only have fifteen minutes."

There was silence at the other end of the telephone line.

"I know where Bradley's is. I'll see you there in about an hour," said Dick.

"In an hour."

"Fine." After he hung up Dick smiled and murmured to himself. "Another nut-job shrink."

Barry laughed as he grabbed his shabby blue blazer from the mottled antique coat rack. "How easily the police can be manipulated."

At Bradley's, Barry was situated in the corner at the bar.

When Dick entered he looked around. Too many guys in the bar to pick out Gruber.

Dick asked the bartender for help. "Hi. You know a Dr. Gruber?"

The bartender turned without making a sound and gestured with his whole body towards the other end of the bar. Barry raised his bottle of beer up high as a signal, almost as if he were greeting with a toast.

Dick slipped between the patrons, who were two deep at the bar.

Barry got up from his stool as Dick approached.

"Here. You sit. I've been flat on my ass all day."

"Are you Dr. Barry Gruber?"

"That's me."

Dick sat down with his back to the bar. The bartender asked him, "Do you want something?"

"Beefeater martini. Real dry."

"Right." The bartender went to work preparing the drink.

Dick looked over at the bass player playing a solo. "Nice place." He meant it.

"Yeah."

Dick started right in. "How well did you know the girl?"

"Not well at all. When I got the notice she had been murdered, I had to look up her records."

"But you were her psychiatrist."

"I'm a lot of people's psychiatrist. And I don't know them well."

"Doc. I'm a simple guy. Could you please answer the questions? I mean. How well did you know her?"

"Not well."

"That's what you just said." Dick thought Barry was being deliberately difficult.

"That's what you just asked." Barry thought Dick was an idiot.

The tone of the conversation was taking a turn for the worse.

The bartender brought over Dick's drink. Dick turned around to take it. He turned back to Barry and slowly put his lips over the glass, taking a big gulp, keeping his eyes fixed on Barry as he peered out over the glass.

Dick put his drink on the bar. "Did she ever talk about her sex life with you?"

"Probably."

"Do you remember much about her at all?"

"Not much."

"But you were her doctor."

Dysplasia

∞

"Detective. Sorry. I forgot your last name."

"Dick. Call me Dick."

"Detective Dick. That has a nice ring to it." He said it to be obnoxious.

"Doc. Are you pulling my pud here?"

"I don't believe so."

"Why do I feel like you're pulling my pud?"

"I don't know." Barry was getting uncomfortable. He wanted to curtail the conversation, but knew if he did that the police would only come after him again with more dumb questions. He found the whole matter annoying. He thought if he spoke to Dick it would be over.

"Did she ever mention any men that she was having trouble with?"

"She was having trouble with all the men she knew. That's why she was referred to me."

"Did she ever tell you that she thought anyone was trying to harm her?" Dick could tell by the look on Barry's face that he was not a happy camper. Maybe he was hiding something. It was just a hunch.

"Look. Dick. First of all, I don't have to discuss anything about this woman's life. Second. I don't remember very much. This was not one of my most remarkable cases. And thirdly. I don't like you. So. Piss off." Barry was showing his true personality.

"Dr. Gruber. You know the process. Over time we can subpoena you for your records, phone calls, and we can subpoena you to testify. I can become a real pain in the ass." Dick didn't like the style, but Barry asked for it.

"I'm sure you've had a lot of experience in that regard." Barry was not backing down.

"I'd hate to think you left out something important."

"There is a question of patient-doctor privilege. And since you do not suspect Ms. Foster murdered herself and then dumped herself in the East River, I have a feeling her personal life may be safe with me."

"Don't you want to see her murderer caught?"

"Frankly, I hadn't given it much thought. Okay. Yes. Yes. I'd like to see him caught. You see, Detective Dick, I'm really a model citizen." Barry didn't care how irritating he became.

"You said 'him.'"

"That's right."

"Why?"

"I don't know."

"What the fuck is your problem, Doc?"

"You. You are my problem. Are we through?"

Dick picked up his beer and gulped it down. "Yes. No. The papers didn't give all the details of how she was mutilated."

"I don't read papers that describe mutilation anyway."

"The medical examiner says that her clitoris was cut off while she was still alive."

"Thank you. I think I'll order my dinner now."

"I thought you might want to know what we're dealing with here."

Barry was breathing rapidly. He was visibly shaken.

Dick stopped abruptly. He felt he already went outside the bounds of "detective protocol." "Okay. Okay. We're done. Here's my card. Call me if you think of anything."

Barry took the card and slipped it into his pocket. "A pleasure." Barry extended his hand and when Dick took it he squeezed hard and pulled Dick off the barstool, a physical antagonism that could incite almost anyone.

Dick laughed and shook his head as he walked away. "You're some piece of work, Doc."

Barry raised his beer bottle in the same fashion as when they met earlier. He had a familiar feeling, a feeling that he was trying to remember something, but he couldn't quite jumpstart his brain to make the right connections. A cloudy series of electrical starts, appearing only in his conscious mind as little broken thoughts, scattered to bathe in the alcohol that was further dulling his senses. Damn. What was that thought? Clitoris. Scalpel. He flashed on the counterman in the Carnegie Deli.

"Lean as if you cut it with a scalpel." That's how they would tease Barry at the Carnegie. They knew he was a doctor, but didn't know he was a shrink, a usually scalpel-less profession.

Another thought. Barry gorging himself on a hot pastrami rye in the early hours of the morning. His office. Darkness. A voice. Cut it. Who? When? His mind fought to remember. He had totally blocked out the memory.

The bass barged in first. Then the sax, bum-bum bum, do-what, do-what, do-what. Bum-bum. Do-what. The thoughts were lost in a sea of disorganized neurological transmissions linked together by the sound of a saxophone. The sound of the saxophone pleased Barry, and soon he was just feeling pleasure. His life did not afford him many of these moments since his mother died. He tried not to think about her, but her memory overshadowed these moments, as if she wouldn't let him enjoy himself.

CHAPTER NINETEEN

Don walked to his office early, figuring the walk would get some of the cobwebs out of his brain. He hadn't done any exercise for a few weeks and was distraught over the growing fear that he was losing his grip on everything. The hospital report was keeping him going. He felt good about the fact that he was following his conscience.

From his view outside his building, across the street from Central Park, he saw the light on in Jill's office. He was coming from the Viand Coffee Shop, a great local Greek place where Don had great New York breakfasts instead of jogging. Four cups of coffee, two eggs over easy, bacon, home-fried potatoes with onions, and plain white toast drenched in real butter. Many New Yorkers had their fill of the healthy eating craze. The coffee shops were jammed with requests for standard fare, and new restaurants were cropping up everywhere, featuring barely consumable portions of meat and potatoes.

Don wore his jogging clothes to breakfast, half-jogging half-walking to the Viand. He hurried upstairs, showered, and dressed. He wanted to see Jill. They hadn't spoken for some time, and he hoped spending a few minutes with her before work would make the transition to work more comfortable. It was unusual for Manny to come in early. It wasn't his

Dysplasia

∞

style. Manny worked hard when he was in the office, and he played hard when he was away from it.

Don knocked on the locked door, hoping Jill would be there. Maybe they could have coffee. Those days Don was drinking coffee all day. He felt he needed the caffeine.

He heard someone walking towards the door. Little steps, but they weren't Jill's. The door opened. It was Manny.

"Hi, Donald," said Manny.

Don's first thought was that he was seeing an emergency. Otherwise what would Manny be doing there? His second thought was that Manny was having an affair with Jill. Then Don told himself he was being a jerk. Manny couldn't possibly interest Jill sexually. Even Manny would have to catch up on paperwork sooner or later.

"Hi, Manny. Is Jill here?" Don asked.

Manny smiled. "Of course. She's here every morning early. If I'm not careful she'll be taking over everything," Manny said in a mocking tone necessary to express how much better his practice actually was than Jill's. Some men were threatened by women, and Manny was no exception. It was a competition, even though Jill was not a threat to Manny's practice.

They walked towards Jill's private office. Manny veered off towards a little kitchenette.

"There's fresh coffee up. Help yourself."

"Thanks."

Don walked into the kitchenette behind Manny. Don poured himself a cup. No personal cups in this office, only the disposable plastic kind with little reusable holders.

Manny sipped his coffee. "You know, Don. It takes a lot of guts to do what you're doing."

"I'm sorry?" Don wasn't expecting anything from Manny.

"The hospital thing. A lot of guys would never do that, particularly if Hank were their partner and chief in the hospital. A lot of guts. I think you should be commended."

"Thanks." Don didn't want to talk about it.

Don took his cup in hand and headed for Jill's office.

Don paid little attention at that point to anyone's comments on the hospital. By that time, he was the talk of all the units, not just OB-GYN. Don ignored the remarks, like he did that morning, with some polite response.

Don knocked on the open door to Jill's office. She could see Don once she looked up from her desk. She had a cup to her right. The desk in front of her was filled with charts. A radiograph lighted box behind her displayed a series of black-and-white X-rays. To its left were colorful MRIs of a patient's head.

"Don Gardner, magical baby deliverer," she said.

"Good morning."

"How are you?"

"Do you want the long version or the short version?" Don sat on an ominous brown leather chair facing the desk.

"Any version will do."

"Aside from waking up each morning thinking this is the day my entire life will fragment around me, I'm fine."

"Join the club. That's normal for anyone that practices on Fifth." Jill took a sip of her coffee.

"Any news on the Melinda Foster case?" Don asked. The interaction with Dick was still bothering him.

"Not yet, but there's been another floater fished out."

"A serial killer?"

"Dick doubts it." Jill started to laugh. "I know I shouldn't be laughing because there is nothing funny about this at all."

Dysplasia

"What is it?" Now Don wanted to know.

"It looked like the same kind of mutilation sex crime except this time it wasn't a woman."

"I don't get it."

"Neither do I, except the fact that this was a transsexual who had his penis cut off."

The word "transsexual" did not register with Don. "Neat," Don said, trying to show that Jill couldn't shock him. He exhaled slowly after the word left his lips. Then the thought hit Don. The transsexual in Chessman's bedroom. The scalpel. "Forget it", he told himself.

"This should give Farmer's staff a run for their money," said Jill.

"Do they think it was the same guy?" Like most people, Don automatically thought it was a man.

"Who knows. Dick says it's just coincidence."

"What if the DNA matches from the semen of both?"

"There was no semen on the transsexual. Like Dick said, it could be totally unrelated."

"Or the guy could have gotten so upset when he found out the girl was a guy—." Don stopped in midsentence. He thought again about that night with Chessman. "Holy shit," Don thought. "That is probably what happened with Chessman. Chessman got angry when he found out his date was a transsexual. That's when he called Don; instead of making a scene, he used Don as the out. It bothered Don that Chessman's date was playing with a scalpel. "It should bother anyone," he thought to himself.

"Don. What is it?" Jill could see that Don was upset.

"I know I shouldn't tell you this, but..." Don told the entire story of the night at Chessman's. Too many things happened recently. He had to tell someone. He couldn't tell Lou or Harvey. Particularly after Dick had interviewed them about Melinda.

Jill's reaction was logical and intelligent. "Don. I know you don't like the guy. But do you really think Hank Chessman is that unbalanced?"

That is the same question Don had been asking himself.

Jill could see that Don was not himself. He looked distraught. She could see signs of stress in what he said and how he behaved. His hand visibly shook when he lifted his cup. She didn't remember Don having any sort of tremor. It didn't happen every time. Just enough to notice. She also noticed that his tie was not perfectly centered. It usually was. He also missed some spots shaving. It made his face look dirty. Plus, a slight weakness in his voice came through when he told the Chessman story.

"Jill. Aren't the police thinking that a doctor or someone in a medical field did this because of the suturing?"

"Dick thinks it could be a doctor, but probably not. I don't think so. I've been doing some reading." Jill reached behind her desk and removed a file from the top of a waist-high bookshelf.

"Take a look at these if you want," she said, opening the Velcro fastener.

"What is it?" asked Don, as he reached inside the envelope, and slid out a few papers.

"It was Manny's idea, and I think he's right. He suggested I take a look at the research on clitoridectomy. It basically points away from doctors. Most doctors in this country either don't know how to do it or won't do it. There is a copy of the Melinda Foster autopsy report in there."

Don flipped through some of the article abstracts.

"I'll get us some more coffee," said Jill. She took the cups and left the office to get refills.

Jill had the abstracts well-organized and highlighted in yellow, with blue ink notes alongside. It was easy for Don to follow. It took a few seconds for each one.

Dysplasia

∽

The Swedish kept tabs on Somalian women who had clitoridectomy procedures. Most of them were operated on at home.

Any kind of female genital mutilation (FGM) was banned in Canada. Obstetricians and gynecologists in Canada saw a lot more FGM because of immigration patterns to Canada.

Most FGM was performed in Africa, the Middle East, Muslim parts of Indonesia and Malaysia, was around age 7.

The ritual female genital operation was done in varying degrees, from clitoridectomy and removal of the labia to removal of the clitoral prepuce. The Bedouin women in Northern Israel report that the practice was considered normative in several tribes.

A procedure called deinfibulation enabled a surgeon to restore the external genitalia and vagina.

The French laws were very strict. Immigrants who allowed mutilation procedures were jailed.

Don knew very little about FGM. Within seconds of reading the article he thought Melinda's killer could be anyone.

Don paused when he read a startling statistic. In 1981, it was estimated that more than 74 million women and female children had this procedure done in Africa alone.

Don was taken by the amount of information on the subject. He was educated in one of the best American medical schools, and completed a surgical OB-GYN residency that put his education in the 99th percentile of all worldwide programs, or at least that was the hype given by American medical educators.

He read on. There were three general categories for "female circumcision," another term describing the same procedure: Pharaonic, Intermediate, and Sunna.

Women with these procedures suffered from various uncomfortable physical symptoms like urinary tract infection and chronic pelvic infection. Often, a woman would appear in a doctor's office in the United States, reporting only that she had difficulty urinating. Once the nurses saw the patient's post-operative vagina, they called the doctor in a panic. It was rare to see anything like that in the United States.

The psychological, emotional, and physical damage to those women was not measurable. Fortunately the times were changing, but slowly. Social workers in the United States tried their best to discourage the procedures. When they failed and the child's parents couldn't find a doctor to do it, they would often go to a nonmedically trained "surgeon" to do the procedure.

As recently as 1995, a Muslim perspective on female circumcision appeared in "Women Health" (1995) 23 (1): 1-7: "Muslim communities should not become dependent on and indentured to Western agencies and their own nation-states to solve the problems they face, including the tragic consequences of widely practiced infibulation and clitoridectomy; instead, we need to apply our own traditional practices and to support an indigenous Islamic legal discourse."

"Islamic legal discourse," Don repeated to himself.

Jill came back with refills.

"So. What did you think?" she asked as she placed the refills on the table.

"But nobody is sure. I mean. It could still have been done by anyone with basic surgical skills," he said. He was fixed on the murders.

Jill expected Don to comment on the subject matter, not the homicide. She brought the subject back to what she wanted, but didn't mind letting Don know what she thought about the murders.

"I guess so, but I don't think so. A lot of people in this country want to have clitoridectomies done on their daughters. Some of the people here must know how to do it. It's passed down, generation to generation."

Dysplasia

✑

"But aren't most of the people having them done abroad?" asked Don.

"I've got plenty of newspaper articles that report that it's still being done here in the United States. Doctors are afraid to report it, even when they see a patient they are treating."

Don looked at his watch. He wasn't absorbing what Jill was saying.

"I'd better get going. I have a full schedule," said Don.

Don left his coffee on the table. He was preoccupied with thoughts about Chessman. He kept telling himself that it was absurd, but he thought about some of O.J.'s friends, how they even thought in the beginning that he didn't do it.

Jill stared at Don as she walked him to the outer door of her office. She was worried about him. It bothered her that he was distraught. She was afraid he was going to say something stupid, something that would embarrass him and jeopardize his relationship with Chessman. Jill was not a Chessman fan, but she understood the basic principles of commerce, marketing, and the fact that business was not based on loving one's partner, but tolerating him.

"Don. Don't tell anyone else what you told me about Chessman. You do know that it's just a coincidence." Jill was beginning to think about it like Don. Anything was possible, but this was very far-fetched.

"I guess so." He wanted to believe that it was true. He was so down on Chessman lately.

"Don. You need a vacation," said Jill.

For reasons unknown to him he flirted with Jill. "Want to go with me?" he asked in jest.

"Great. My life's ambition, to be rebound material."

"You'd be great rebound material."

Jill slugged Don in the arm playfully. "You're still married. Now get out of here."

Don got a sense from Jill's voice that she might have given his joke serious consideration, if only for a moment. He didn't know how he mustered the remark, but he said it without hesitation.

"How are things with Dick?" Don asked, trying to sound legitimately concerned.

"Don. This is not the time and the place," said Jill.

"Sorry. I didn't mean anything by it."

"I know," she answered. "Go on. Get out of here."

"Okay," said Don, playing the role of sheepish sophomore.

Perhaps having hit close to rock bottom gave him a better perspective. Maybe his self-esteem would improve. He couldn't believe that he flirted. He didn't know what was going on. The interchange with Jill made him momentarily happy.

Don ran down the hall, waving wildly to the surveillance camera as he headed for the stairwell.

When the police got the complete story together, they made a statement to the media. The tabloids had a field day with the second murder. He was also a dancer in a review in Atlantic City and his own employer supposedly did know that she was a he. The family initially asked to keep his real name out of the papers. The papers gladly obliged, since his actual name sounded so ordinary, hardly the makings of good copy. Misty Waters was dead. The privacy didn't last more than a second.

Shows like *Hard Copy* were on the story. Misty, a.k.a. Gary Walters, was from a small town in Indiana, majored in Communications at Northwestern, and got fed up putting on shows at college. He quit to begin a career in show business.

Hard Copy paid off some of the townspeople, and soon Misty's baby pictures and high-school yearbook shot was all over the television.

Dysplasia

When the show finally aired, including footage at his parent's house, the viewers were treated to a clip of his father hitting the *Hard Copy* reporter across the mouth, a blow that a lot of the viewers shared with Misty's father.

CHAPTER TWENTY

Don was up late working on the hospital report. He went to the kitchen for a snack. The daily papers sat unread on the dinette table. Don read that the victim was a transsexual.

After reading about the second murder, Don thought back to the night he saved Chessman from the uncomfortable sexual encounter. He was still fixed on Chessman. Don thought that Chessman only objected to the genital nature of his playmate, not the activities that even included a scalpel. Don tried hard to remember if the face in the newspaper was the same person in Chessman's bedroom that night, but in the excitement Don did not take such a clear look. He was, in fact, like the two security guards, staring at her massive breasts.

They did look alike. Could it be? Could Don's creative mind be playing games with him? Don realized that he totally forgot about the slide. After the momentary sense of power associated with the theft passed Don dismissed the slide taking as foolish. He mentioned it to Kronen, who agreed. But something in his muddled thought process pushed him to satisfy some curiosity, even if it was only something created from his wildest fantasies. Don decided to go to the office late that night.

He turned on the main light switch, which illuminated the entire office. He was still somewhat afraid of the dark, and the bright light made him more comfortable since he was in the office by himself. He went to his desk drawer, found the slide, and proceeded to the laboratory situated strategically in the center of the office complex.

Don sat at one of the high stools that overlooked the lab counter, in front of one of three microscopes situated at different counters that lined the walls. There was also a full kitchen in the lab with scaled-down appliances, with the exception of the standard dishwasher. Don flicked the switch on an automatic coffee machine that dripped into action immediately. He unzipped his lined, powder-blue Polo spring jacket. He sat in his sweater, wondering for what seemed like a long time if he was going to be too warm. He decided not to alter the office temperature.

He placed the slide under the scope and for a moment could not look at it. He felt silly going through this process. What did he expect to find on a laboratory slide? But why did Chessman have it at home? He realized that his mind was playing tricks on him. It was probably some old slide that Chessman used to impress his dates, to illustrate his great scientific interest.

Don missed Linda. He called her yesterday. She was cordial but kept emphasizing that they needed more time apart. Don walked to the window. He unlocked it and slid it open with a quick jerk. He breathed the fresh air. He looked down on Fifth Avenue and saw Pierre, who Don was sure looked up at him, but instead of waving Pierre ducked quickly back into the vestibule, out of sight. The lobby phone had probably rung. Don took in a few deep breaths of night air. He made a mental note that the decision to keep on his sweater and open the window was a good one. No sense turning up the heat when it was warm outside.

Don looked through the ocular piece. He adjusted the focus by rotating one of the two bilateral circular knobs on each side of the scope. Don was dumbfounded by what he saw. It was a slide of epithelial tissue. The hills and valleys of skin, stained in shades of pink and violet, the violet being the more external layers, which contained epithelial cells. But this slide looked familiar. Could these be vaginal epithelial cells? Don was shocked. He knew what it was, but it was hard to fathom. Why would Chessman have a slide of vaginal epithelium in his bedroom?

Chessman screamed with laughter when he poked fun at how much time is spent looking at "Rhesus vaginatus", the source for research and education slides. "Damned idiots would have us stare at monkey cunt for hours. Histology was such a fucking waste of time." Why would a doctor who thought it a joke have a slide of vaginal epithelium?

"Ridiculous," Don told himself in an effort to make some sense out of it. Chessman didn't even know what was on the slide. That's what he always said. But this did not look like a slide that came from the pathology lab, that did the biopsies for the office and hospital.

Don looked at it more closely. The little cover slip on the sample was placed on sloppily. There was a great deal of moisture under the cover slip. Don put the slide back under the scope and moved it to another section. Don stared at a lot of red blood cells. That was not the work of a pathologist, but someone in a hurry to make a slide, someone that didn't care if the sample had blood on it, someone who maybe wanted to see the blood.

"Don. You're being ridiculous." Don took the slide and placed it in a plastic carrying-case box designed to carry glass slides. He closed the window, grabbed his Polo jacket and left the laboratory. Instead of leaving the office he walked into Chessman's private office and reflexively walked to a cabinet, designed to hold VCR tapes, recessed in the desk. Don knew it was locked, but tried to open it anyway. In the cabinet were videos of office procedures. Years ago, Chessman encouraged the office to install the video system, one they could turn on and off easily, to keep a living record of procedures, particularly conversations with patients.

"The best defense is a good offense," quoted Chessman, as Burns stood at his side, agreeing that having this kind of record keeping would keep their malpractice claims at a minimum and provide a solid defense.

Don was thinking that maybe Chessman kept his porn tapes there, too. Lou alluded to the fact that Chessman "liked his movies." Don didn't know what to think. He was looking for any avenue that would incriminate Chessman in any way.

"Will you go home?" Don convinced himself to leave. He had to rest, to think things over.

Pierre was on the phone downstairs. His side of the conversation resembled someone beholden to the caller. It wasn't a surprising tone, since that was Pierre's job, and he was good at it.

"Yeah. He went upstairs and was there about a half-hour. Right. Will do. Good night." He was probably talking to his security boss who kept tabs on night visitors.

Pierre hung up the telephone and walked back outside to the street. A few moments later Don exited, and said good night to Pierre.

"Pierre. See ya," said Don.

"Hey, Doc. You have a nice evening. Okay?"

"Okay."

Don had trouble sleeping that night. Something kept telling him that Chessman was somehow involved in the murders. He started to sip malt scotch. First a little at a time and then big gulps from the bottle. It was about two thirds full when he started. Maybe Chessman knew who did it. Chessman was always getting his friends dates. Melinda Foster could easily have been one of those dates. Don thought about the transsexual in Chessman's room. The slide was weird.

Don told himself that he was hallucinating. Maybe the slide wasn't vaginal tissue. Squamous epithelium was tricky. Perhaps it was just a piece of skin.

"Who knows, maybe Chessman cut himself," he thought. But why make a slide? Don knew there was no easy answer. It was too weird to comprehend. His mind was making little sense out of the information. He told himself he was too eager to find out dirt on Chessman. Everything might have a reasonable explanation.

Don was upset about so many things he didn't know which to concentrate on. His research for the hospital was coming along fine, even with Chessman's interference. But this was more important. Chessman linked to murder? What if he killed one of them? Chessman would have no reason to kill them. Except if Chessman was crazy, crazy in a way that slips through society under the label of what two consenting adults do in privacy until one of them goes too far, beyond the boundaries of safety, and into a territory few people ever come to know. Perhaps Chessman stepped over into that world, maybe by accident, and was forced to horrible extremes.

Don thought he was being too judgmental. Maybe he was jealous of Chessman's kinky sex life. After all, Don was no sexual maestro. But this was just too much.

Don tried to think about something else. He finally fixed on Jill, sliding his hand to his groin. He was exhausted and fell asleep within seconds, after taking his last swig from an almost empty bottle.

CHAPTER TWENTY-ONE

The next day, Don asked Chessman to spend a couple of hours with him after work in the bar of the Pierre Hotel. Even if he didn't want to talk to Don, he never passed up the Pierre. Chessman went through the entire regular routine.

About half way into their drinks, Chessman informed Don that he had some plans later that evening. The information was accompanied by one of his peculiar smirks, signaling he was up to no good. It was followed by that snorting chortle.

Now that Don knew of Chessman's salacious escapades, his stomach gurgled at the thought of Chessman romping in his bedroom. He asked the bartender if he had any Pepto Bismol. The bartender came up with an Alka Seltzer and a side of bitters and soda, letting Don have his choice.

"You only have to walk across the street. What's the rush?" asked Don.

"Not tonight, Junior. It's a road trip." Don knew at that moment that he would follow Chessman. He wanted to know more about his after hours activity.

Don opened his portfolio. He took out one of the articles he was using for his paper, "Clinical usefulness of computerized colposcopy: image analysis and conservative management of mild dysplasia." Three doctors at Albert Einstein College of Medicine, a well-known facility in the Bronx, wrote it. The study investigated the use of computerized colposcopy to examine and record colposcopic changes associated with cervical dysplasia. It would eliminate or reduce the need to make subjective evaluations about the severity of precancerous lesions. It could reduce the need for surgery or even intervention with freezing, or as Chessman called it, "the zapper." Don knew this was going to be a hard sell since it went directly against how Chessman liked to run the practice.

"Did you see the article in the Journal of Obstetrics and Gynecology?" Don thought that was a safe start. The only way Chessman would know anything was if Lou spoke to him about it.

"It's bullshit. Pass me a salmon thing."

Don passed Chessman the appetizer tray. Chessman took three of the "salmon things."

"Hank. They avoided active therapy in 66% of the cases and repeat biopsy was avoided in 94.1%. And all of the patients had progressive or regressive cervical dysplasia." Those were persuasive facts.

"Fuck the statistics. Fuck the article and fuck your attitude. Are you trying to fuck up my evening or what? Is that it?"

"Hank. Calm down. I have to recommend that the hospital try to include this along with histological and cytologic. It's well-documented." Don knew if the suggestion for the office didn't go over that he could at least include the information in his hospital report.

"Junior. Listen to me and listen carefully. You go ahead and recommend that the hospital spring for the device. Okay?" Chessman sounded as if he didn't care.

Dysplasia

"Okay." Don knew if he said anything else about the office, there was going to be a fight. He hoped it was over. It wasn't.

"But if you bring this article up at any of the office meetings, you can start thinking of places where I am going to hide your balls after I excise them neatly from inside your scrotum. It will be like hunting for Easter eggs."

In Don's present state of mind, it sounded like a very real scenario. "Okay. Okay. Take it easy. Here. Have some more salmon." Don's voice must have reflected his anger. He tried to mask his feelings and ended up sounding sarcastic.

Chessman reserved his "thin-skinned" response for moments like that. He spoke slowly, savoring every word. "Don't ever patronize me, minimize me, diminish me, or even think you can use that tone on me. I don't want any more salmon."

With that, Chessman got up from his barstool, instructed the bartender to put it on the office tab and "take twenty percent for yourself." He floated down the side of the bar smiling at patrons, whether he knew them or not.

Chessman paused, wheeled around, and walked back to Don.

"I've read parts of the hospital study. When you've got it all together, I'll finish it. You know I'm a good editor. I'll edit it when you're done. Some of the parts go too far. We don't want to offend any of our referral sources who also work in the hospital. Junior. I've told you this before. You can't say whatever you want. That's not the way things work."

Chessman didn't wait for a response. There wasn't any forthcoming. Don was furious. Chessman could see it in his eyes.

Don waited until Chessman was out the door to get up. Don was going to follow him. Don had mixed thoughts on what he was about to do. He wasn't sure why he was going to do it. His thoughts encompassed the extremes, from an overly juvenile fantasy to being on the trail of a murderer, the same man he once liked. Whatever the reason, his mind was made up.

Chessman hated to go into the garage. He always asked Pierre to call downstairs to have his car brought up. Chessman stood in front of the building, next to the building's main entrance. He puffed on a cigar while he waited for his car.

Don went out the side door to the Pierre Hotel on 61st. From his vantage point, he could see Chessman standing on the corner talking with Pierre. Chessman was facing Fifth Avenue and couldn't see Don slip across the street and down the ramp to get his BMW.

Don's car was positioned further in the back of the garage than Chessman's car. He passed Chessman's new four-door, black Mercedes Sedan, the one with the big V12 engine. Chessman's car was kept in front with the Bentleys, Rolls Royces, and Ferraris. The garage attendant still had to move two other cars in order to get to Chessman's since his was third in a three-deep line. Since they had the incident in the garage, the cars that cost over $100,000 were kept in the front area where the security guard spent most of his time.

Don began to jog in order to make sure he had time to get into his car and drive out of the garage before Chessman got his delivered on the corner.

Don opened the door to his car. He noticed that Jill's car was still in the lot.

"God. She's always working late. Why isn't she with Dick?"

Don was feeling sorry for himself because his romantic life was stifled. He didn't know how he could follow up on his conversation with Jill, not until he knew what was going to happen with Linda. Jill probably thought he was an idiot, and was only humoring him because he appeared to be such a wreck. Then he thought about the flip side, that he could recover from his depressive state, and things could be better. He could start dating. It didn't have to be with Jill. That was an extreme thought.

As soon as the car engine turned over, he dismissed further thought about his social life. He put the car in gear and drove along the oil-slicked ramps until he was at the front ramp. He waved to one of the garage security guys in the office, who was watching a black-and-white portable television while munching on some of the Colonel's best chicken. Two huge KFC containers partially blocked the guard's view. The guard raised his hand and waved. It was a limp wave, a gratuitous gesture to appear attached to the moment and justify his presence in his own mind.

Chessman's car was gone from its spot, so Don accelerated as he drove up the ramp. He turned quickly onto 61st Street by making the sharp right out the driveway, the only way he could legally turn. He did not see Chessman's car at the corner. Chessman must have arrived at a green light and taken off.

A voice in Don's head told him to "floor the German mother", which still had plenty of power. He could catch Chessman even though Chessman loved to speed down Fifth Avenue at night. Don knew his "poor-man's Mercedes" was every bit as good as the real thing.

Don decided to run the red light on the corner, making a sharp left, narrowly avoiding a cab that was taking off from the curb on Fifth Avenue. As soon as he turned the corner, he spotted the Mercedes weaving in and out of traffic as it moved to pass the huge traffic circle in front of the Plaza Hotel.

Chessman was no more than two blocks away, having just crossed 60th Street after waiting for the light to change in front of the Sherry Netherland Hotel. Chessman didn't mind waiting at that light because he could flirt with any women walking into the elite Cipriani Restaurant that replaced the once-active bar.

Chessman loved the old bar at the Sherry Netherland. It was a hotel familiar to many commuters who wanted to relax for a few hours before getting on the trains to the suburbs. For the price of a few drinks plus a negotiated $200 to $1000, a tryst could be arranged before heading home. The transients there were the high-priced crème de la crème of the "pros" in Manhattan.

Chessman turned left to head East crosstown. Don followed him as they crossed Madison and Park Avenues.

As Chessman passed the Black Hair Is Salon, he wondered if a white man could get his hair cut there. As he crossed Lexington, Chessman looked to the right at the newer residential Trump Building. The Trumps used to live in one of the apartments, a few floors above Chessman's, years before the divorce.

Don had trouble keeping up with all the things Trump named after himself.

It was a typical ride through Manhattan's streets, a series of stores, buildings, pedestrians, vendors leaving late, all types of vehicles, and a general visual and acoustic stimulation not found anywhere else in the world.

Don slowed as he passed three fire engines flashing in full regalia. He passed the corner of Second Avenue, moving slowly through the increasing traffic. Don thought Chessman must be headed for the entrance to FDR Drive so that he could drive downtown on the only thing close to a highway in Manhattan. Perhaps he was headed to SoHo or Tribeca to look at art or eat dinner. Chessman knew Nobu, the owner of the restaurant with the same name.

Don watched as Chessman flicked the ashes from an oversized Cuban, Montecristo cigar out the window. Chessman loved to smoke a cigar while he drove. Even Lou went along with the ban, no smoking anywhere inside. Chessman didn't like to smoke in the office. It wasn't the right environment for him. He let his partners think he was adhering to the ban.

Don stayed back about three car lengths so he would not be noticed.

It was very unlikely that Chessman would notice anyone following him. His mind was in another world. All he could hear was the methodical rhythm of chants from that other world, his private world. His thoughts turned to his twisted, perverse desires.

After making a left on York, and a right on Third Chessman made his way onto 63rd Street, pointing his car straight into a messy construction site.

Once they circled the loop entrance onto the Drive, the traffic backed up for blocks. Unfortunately the left lane was closed past the East 53rd Street exit for no apparent reason.

Don thought they were probably better off going slow on the Drive. Giant potholes sprang up all along the route. Occasionally, a car's wheel would be swallowed up in one of the potholes, resulting in a flat tire or a lost rim. Those holes were to a New York City driver what the bunkers at the British Open were to a golfer. Drivers considered themselves professional, having learned to drive in some of the worst conditions in the world, a close second to Rome.

To the left was the obtuse Citibank building in Queens, the only high-rise of its kind that faced Manhattan. People never adjusted to that kind of skyline facing away from New York.

The yellow arrows blinked, signaling them to move to the right lanes. One of the many overpaid construction workers held another sign signaling the same thing in case anyone thought the lane without any pavement was meant for driving.

Three lanes finally opened up as they passed the United Nations. Now they were going top speed. Fifty-five miles per hour was fast for that highway. Don carefully watched the road for potholes as he bravely saw the speedometer inch over 60 mph.

The murky, dark East River loomed on the left. It was a little choppy. Don thought about the murdered victims whose water-bloated bodies were found floating near the shore. Melinda was found alongside the elegant Water Club, an exclusive New York restaurant on the River. Misty surfaced near Gracie Mansion, the Mayor's residence. A morning jogger who spotted her phoned it in after he completed his exercise routine.

They drove past Waterside Plaza where Don's friend Bradley, an enterprising, young, self-made socialite, hosted many parties during medical school. It reminded Don of his single days. Don reminisced on his missed opportunities. He turned on the radio and searched for a station that played '60s music to remind him of a time when his life was less complicated.

NYU Medical Center was across the Drive on the right side. The newer Rivergate Apartments were deliberately constructed to obscure the big Con Ed plant that occupied the area for years.

Behind them, a police car with its siren blaring appeared out of nowhere. The traffic in any other part of the world might have slowed down, but not in New York. Speeding tickets were almost nonexistent on the Drive.

The police car sped past and turned into the exit lane for East 23rd Street, not far from the 34th Street heliport, a quick route to any New York area airports.

Dysplasia

∞

Near the heliport was the only gas station on the dock. Another confidant of Chessman and his pals gave them a break on the price of gas for their yachts and seaplanes that had to refuel on East 23rd Street. This was the jumping-off point for those adventurous enough to take the seaplane to the Hamptons or Fire Island.

Further along was the East Houston exit, the gateway to the homeless who stood there all day, offering to wash windshields in exchange for cash. Don remembered when he was a child the homeless were called "Bowery Bums." But now the numbers were huge and hoards roamed the streets downtown. It was no longer a matter of a few dozen men who were mostly chronic alcoholics. Like everything else in Manhattan, the homeless grew more complicated with a large percentage of the men and women in need of psychiatric help accompanied by the proper form of medication. It was a big political issue, something that appeared too complicated to handle.

As they drove farther downtown on FDR Drive, it occurred to Don that Chessman was on his way to Peter Luger's in Brooklyn, one of the oldest steak houses in New York. Chessman often went there for dinner without his wife. It wasn't posh enough for her. What a strange twist. Chessman the restaurant snob would go anywhere for a good steak. On top of that, she didn't eat meat anymore and insisted that Chessman do the same. He played along when she made him attend obligatory dinners at their home, filled with guests who typified different variations of meat haters.

Both slowed as they approached the Williamsburg Bridge. Chessman signaled to exit. Don was disappointed. It looked like they were headed for Peter Luger's. The talk in the bar had been typical Chessman talk.

As they neared the exit Chessman accelerated and moved even farther downtown. He changed his mind. Maybe he made a mistake.

As he was about to exit, it appeared that he changed his mind again. His Mercedes accelerated and pulled sharply to the left and sped ahead into the center lane, still doing around 60 mph.

In one of the many city public parks, a twilight softball game was breaking up to the right next to a series of antiquated buildings. Some of the buildings near FDR Drive could be traced back to the turn of the century. There weren't many left.

They passed the Manhattan and Brooklyn Bridges. Chessman seemed fixed on staying in the middle lane although there was hardly any traffic. They reached 65 mph on a clean stretch of pavement. It was rare for that twisting, decaying type of highway as there were no prolonged straight sections. The driver had to be alert in case there was a jagged stretch of road around the bend or a freshly dug out crater from the ugly, wet winter.

Downtown was clearly a possibility, but Don couldn't imagine what Chessman might be doing much further downtown. Despite his pretensions, Chessman had no special interest in anything that went on below 57th Street, except the occasional trip to a SoHo art gallery. He didn't go to any of the fancy restaurants unless he was showing off.

Don was hit with the ridiculousness of his own actions and shook his head in disgust. But part of Don was enjoying this. It was a false sense of power. Don was following Chessman and Chessman had no idea. Don compiled a list of fantasy theories that made Chessman out to be the murderer.

Then under the old, decaying Brooklyn Bridge. The South Street Seaport was on their left; a tourist trap built in the early '80s. Not far from there was the old Fulton Fish Market, the present target of the Mayor's drive to control organized crime and restore lower fish prices to the city's zillion restaurants. Rumor had it a lot of fish were being caught and sold "untagged" from the taboo waters around the city.

Dysplasia

The signs for West Street came up on them quickly. Chessman exited into a short horseshoe tunnel that looped around the Battery, the very tip of the city, the southern-most point of Manhattan Island.

"Hello darkness, my old friend." The lyrics from the Simon and Garfunkel song permeated the car. "I've come to talk with you again." Don increased the volume on the radio as he veered off the same exit, following six car lengths behind Chessman. Don struggled to hold back his tears as the lyrics from the song stroked his soul. He remembered the innocence of his youth, his college days of continuous study, and an uncomplicated social life. He had no idea that men like Chessman were part of the real world.

They were near the tunnel entrance on West Street. A right lead to the Battery Tunnel. Chessman drove past the tunnel entrance. It was clear they were not going to Brooklyn. Chessman's car approached Battery Park City. Chessman must have met someone who lived in the new complex.

The excitement diminished. The song was over and Don was back to feeling stupid for following Chessman. Don thought about turning around to stop at Tribeca's, the hip restaurant in a complex owned by Robert DeNiro. Don could have a few drinks and mingle with the crowd. Maybe he would actually meet someone to take his mind off Linda, the office, the hospital study, and his growing depression. Don realized he and Linda were speaking less and less. He left messages with her mother or on voicemail. Maybe Linda didn't get all the messages. Maybe it was better that they didn't communicate for a while at all.

Battery Park City was a city within a city. It was on the left, occupying what once was a large empty space. This architectural monster now blocked the view of the Hudson River.

Chessman made a right turn onto Rector Street and then a left onto Washington. Don thought this was very strange. They were close to the World Trade Center.

Chessman pulled over to the curb on the corner of Carlyle and Washington and parked at the Carlyle Parking Corp. It was after hours. All the offices had to be closed. Maybe someone was waiting for some kind of clandestine meeting with Chessman.

Don parked across the street. He waited for Chessman to come out of the garage. After about two minutes Don realized Chessman was not exiting. Chessman must have taken a route directly inside the building.

Don was parked in one of the multitude of hard-to-understand parking zones. It would take Don too long to read all the ambiguous signs. He couldn't leave his car, figuring his chances were pretty good that it would be towed. He pulled the car further up the street and quickly turned into a flat lot parking area across from the World Trade Center. He got out of the car quickly and shouted back to the attendant, "I don't know. Two or three hours." If he couldn't find Chessman, Don thought he would have that dinner by himself. He envisioned himself at the bar, suddenly whisked to the table by his friend Paul, an actor who introduced Don to Tribeca. Don sat with Paul at Tribeca and watched a parade of sharkskin suits and pinky rings march in and out of the offices behind and upstairs from the restaurant. Don would later learn that they were casting the movie *A Bronx Tale*, which needed "Mafia" types. That was what they got.

Inside Don didn't see Chessman in the lobby. Facing Don were a series of stores across from a subway entrance. Chessman wouldn't be caught dead in the subway, so Don first walked towards the stores. After a few minutes, Don realized he had lost him. He left the building and went back to his car.

He felt stupid. Chessman probably went upstairs to the office of a stockbroker or an attorney, signed some papers, and then was on his way.

Don abandoned the idea of the hip restaurant; Chinatown was more his style. He was never comfortable walking into a fashionable restaurant by himself.

Sitting alone in the Chinese restaurant on Katherine Street made Don sadder about his own life. He felt he was prolonging his stay in a bad marriage. He no longer wanted to practice with Chessman.

Don thought about the hospital report. He knew that if Chessman had the final word, the article would be nothing but compromise. It could become a giant waste of time, like the rest of his life.

Don decided no matter what Chessman said, he was going to print what he thought was the truth. It was the only part of his life that was in his control. He would do the best he could for the hospital patients. That's what he set out to do, and that's the job he was going to complete. Don felt Chessman was using and manipulating him, and developed an even stronger hatred for the man he once envied.

Before Don left the Chinese restaurant, one eerie thought returned. Chessman was a murderer.

CHAPTER TWENTY-TWO

Don quit exercising, not even the fake jogs to the Viand. He gorged himself on big breakfasts and midnight "snacks". He drank scotch every day. His face looked puffy. It didn't matter what kind of scotch. He would sometimes stop his car at any Eastside restaurant, run inside and have a few on his way home. He felt lonely, a type of loneliness he experienced before he was married. He hoped his marriage would afford him the kind of love and nurturing he read about. He thought about calling Linda, suggesting they try to get back together, to work things out. He rationalized that perhaps his marriage "was as good as it gets." His marriage had peaked. He didn't know anyone who claimed to have a great marriage, especially people who lived in the city. It was one big compromise.

Friday night Don reluctantly met with Chessman to talk about the hospital report. Don was practically finished. Don fell into a pattern of letting Chessman begin his recent additions. When he read the article, he butchered the copy with red ink, inserting his comments wherever he chose. Don was weakening.

Before the meeting, Don completely changed his mind about the hospital study. He was going to cave in completely. He was going to let Chessman have his way. He made up his mind to say "yes" to whatever Chessman wanted. Chessman did his usual routine of glad-handing all the big shots in the Pierre, making sure to embarrass "Junior" whenever possible.

As Chessman spoke, Don was separating from the man, the situation, and felt a sudden calm. After the hospital study was published, Don was going to quit the practice. Maybe even leave the city. He had not worked out any details of the idea, just that he could no longer stomach working with or around Chessman. That would be the first step. Maybe he could fix his marriage. "Ha," he answered himself. "Linda would hate that."

Chessman had more to drink than usual. He made his sophomoric sexual remarks about what great plans he had later that evening and included Don as his sexual confidant.

Chessman told one of his off-color jokes. He waited until the bar was crowded, and three female stockbrokers from Merrill Lynch were part of the crowd.

"Little Billy came home from school all confused. His father asked what the problem was. Little Billy asked his father 'What's the difference between a vagina and a cunt?' His father smiled and answered, 'Son. That's an easy one. The vagina is the sexual organ for a woman. The cunt is everything else that is attached to the vagina.'"

One of the women smiled at Chessman. "You are a complete asshole," she said and walked away.

Don followed Chessman downtown again. The colored lights became one continuous blur as Don retraced his previous trip on FDR Drive. He kept his window open and listened to the hypnotic sounds of the cars. Don knew his own behavior bordered on pathological and he thought about getting help. He had a lot of apprehensions. He kept telling himself that things would change. He could handle it. At least his mind was made up to quit the practice.

Brad Lewis

Chessman drove into the same garage underneath the building.

Don parked his car as soon as they reached the World Trade Center. He planned to beat Chessman inside the building. Don parked on Liberty Street, near the corner of Church Street. Don slipped into the lobby of the World Trade Center and went directly inside the Buy-Rite Liquor store near the entrance. It occurred to Don since the first trip here that Chessman may have walked past the stores and into the famous towers. Don still kept his eye on the other stores. The possibility existed that Don was making more out of Chessman than was necessary.

Don scanned the stores, an Alexander's department store, closed due to bankruptcy, a jeweler, a Fanny Farmer chocolate store, and a Florsheim shoe store. Chessman wouldn't have been caught dead in Alexander's: a department store for the "third-world shoppers. I'm glad they went out of business." The jewelry store was a possibility because Chessman would go anywhere if he knew he could do some horse-trading. Forget Florsheim shoes, their most expensive shoes were "only three hundred. How good could they be?" Don thought his old Florsheim Broughams were as good if not better than Chessman's thin-leathered Italian shoes that looked like slippers. Don realized that he hadn't shopped in Florsheim since he met Chessman.

Chessman walked quickly into the lobby. He continued with a deliberate pace directly to the men's room. Don bought a bottle of cheap scotch to keep in the car. He didn't wait. He began to take sips from the brown bag. Don kept his eyes glued on the men's room door. He looked past the stores, ahead to the entrance to the Commodity Exchange at 5 World Trade Center. Maybe that was it.

Dysplasia

Of course. Chessman was doing some night trades, something illegal or close to it. That's why he came in person. The Twin Towers were to the left, exactly where the bomb went off a few years ago. Don even fantasized that Chessman was involved in that. Boy. He really wanted to get him. Anything. His vendetta.

Chessman exited the men's room rapidly. He had changed clothes. He was wearing khaki pants, a safari jacket and a cap with an elliptical brim. His other clothes were wrapped in a bundle, tied with string. Chessman made an immediate right. He was headed straight for the subway. Wherever he was going, he didn't want anyone to know.

Don left the alcove of the liquor store and hurried along behind Chessman.

Don hated the subway, too. It was dirty and damp. He was afraid of all the people. His mother frightened him at an early age, warning him of the dangers that lurked beneath the city. There were more than enough real stories to fuel Don's fears.

Chessman boarded a BMT train. The train was about half full. Don entered the car behind Chessman's, careful not to be seen. Don stood at the glass window by the door that led to the next car. He could see Chessman standing, holding onto a strap. Don sipped slowly out of the bottle. He blended in nicely with the strangest mix of people found anywhere in the world. Businessmen, shopping-bag ladies, Rastas, and gangs. All colors, shapes, and sizes.

After a few stops, Chessman moved towards the automatic doors, getting ready to exit at the next stop. Don followed. The train doors opened after the classic annoying screech. Steam wafted up everywhere from under the train.

As soon as Chessman left the train, he marched to a stairway. It was a path to make another train connection. The sign overhead indicated that the "F" train was their destination, in the Borough of Brooklyn.

Chessman's gait picked up. He took long, uncharacteristically long strides, as if walking outdoors in a field.

Don stayed out of sight, still on the steps leading to the F Train platform as Chessman stood on the nearly empty platform waiting for the train. He talked out loud to himself.

People moved away from him, taking him for one of the many nuts found roving the subway. The train pulled in and Don ran towards the platform, again taking his position in a different car so he wouldn't be seen. The connecting door's glass window was dirty. It was hard to see into Chessman's car. At each stop Don would have to hold the exit door open in his car, peer out to see if Chessman was getting off, and then let the door go if he didn't see him.

Chessman finally got off at Church Avenue in Brooklyn. It was dark by the time they hit the streets, and Chessman was moving very fast. Don was scared. He was about a block behind Chessman. Where could he possibly be going?

Even in the dark, the old buildings were lit enough to show their profiles. It appeared to be one of the quaint sections of the densely populated borough.

There were a few black faces on the streets. Don could hear their voices as he passed them. They were speaking English, but with a sound Don could only identify as somewhere south of Miami, perhaps a Caribbean Island, perhaps Central America.

Storefronts lined the ground floors of many of the buildings. Don glided by a meat market, a check cashing service, and a laundry. It put him at ease, the thought that life here was no different than anywhere else. His prejudiced upbringing was simply wrong.

Don stopped walking near an area where he lost sight of Chessman. Don heard murmuring from inside a building, the kind that reminded Don of a synagogue during a prayer. The building looked vacant.

The door was clearly locked with a bolt and large padlock. The front windows were boarded up, the exterior sprayed with requisite graffiti.

Don leaned closer. The murmur was definitely coming from the vacant building.

Don walked to the adjacent old building which had a framed glass door. Don could see inside to the first floor: a staircase and a few apartment doors painted in drab, pale green. Chessman could have entered that building. Who would he visit?

Don decided to walk back to the vacant building. The murmuring got louder. It had a rhythm of chanting. That was it. A chant of some kind. Don's mind envisioned the first Tarzan movie he ever saw, with Johnny Weismueller, waiting for Cheetah, his pet monkey, to help him escape the unruly natives. Don's first impulse was to turn back.

Don had come this far. He was feeling his scotch, which made him more secure. He went to the large metal door and tried to open the door. It was clearly bolted shut, and the padlock was firmly in place.

Don slid between the buildings into the alley; his heart began to pound.

A faint light reflected on a huge window, divided into four panes by its wooden frame. It was several feet over Don's head. He had to take a look. His mind and heart told him "no, get out of here. Go home."

He walked back to the end of the alley, enduring a series of foul odors. He kept hitting small objects with his feet. He bent down to touch one. His hand felt feathers. He knew immediately he had touched a dead animal: the smell of rotting flesh. He pulled his hand back in disgust.

He walked a few steps into an even darker area and stubbed his toe on a metal garbage can from which the stench was unbearable. He turned the can upside down and dumped the contents. Don thought he saw the head of a big bird, maybe a chicken or a rooster. He told himself this was probably food that was thrown away and left to rot.

He had heard about animal sacrifice, but what would Chessman have to do with sacrificed animals? It made no sense. Perhaps he had picked up a piece of decayed meat. He wasn't far from the butcher shop. Don told himself to forget the whole thing and head for home. That's where he should be, at home, trying to make sense out of his own rotting existence. But not before looking in that window.

He placed the can upside down under the window and hoisted his body over it. He leaned against the side of the building, placing his palms on the bricks for support.

It was hard to see what was going on. His eye level was just even with the wooden frame that divided the panes. He had to get on his toes in order to see clearly.

Thirty blacks were inside. He couldn't tell if any women were present. The group was arranged in a circle. The perimeter of the room was filled with drums and what looked like jars and little dolls. From Don's angle, they looked like children's toys.

All were in a great deal of motion. Was that a bone in one man's hand? He looked around. Some people held marbles, perhaps rocks.

In the center of the activity was a large pole painted with multicolored designs. A light hit the pole. He could see it for a few seconds. Don thought the designs looked like serpents. Don rubbed his eyes—more bones? He wasn't sure. A tall man in the center held a goat. He had his back to Don. The goat's body was covered with blood. "Holy shit," thought Don.

Don was getting dizzy. He had seen enough. The tall man turned towards the window. Chessman! Don jumped above the wooden window frame to see more clearly. He lost his footing on the garbage can and went down hard, falling in the pile of rotting garbage.

The fall made a loud noise. Don felt like he twisted his ankle.

Scared, he got up and tried to run. He couldn't. He limped out of the alley into the street. He looked back over his shoulder. No one followed him. He limped back to the subway station and sat alone, waiting for the train. He left his scotch on the ground in the alley. He wished he had some. He needed a drink.

Don was convinced that either he was delirious or he had seen Dr. Henry "Call Me Hank" Chessman conducting some sort of sacrifice on Church Avenue in Brooklyn. He thought of Susan. Maybe this is what she meant. He would have to find out.

Don woke up with a start. He felt the pain in his ankle and knew he had not been dreaming. It was Saturday. He wasn't on call that morning and made up his mind to go back to Church Avenue. He couldn't drive because he wouldn't know how to get there. He would have to take a taxi.

When he got into the taxi and said he wanted to go to Church Avenue in Brooklyn, he lucked out. The driver turned back and stared at him. "Where on Church Avenue? You know dat is a big avenue." It was that same accent he heard on the street the previous night.

"There were a lot of stores. The stores were new. A meat market. A laundry. A store to cash checks."

"Dat is where my sister has taken up with her lazy husband she met here in the States."

It was going to be easy. The charming driver was one of many immigrants that settled in or near that part of Brooklyn. Don made small talk while he relaxed in the back seat.

Don got the grand tour of Church Avenue, west of Flatbush Avenue, the commercial heart of a very thriving neighborhood where Haitian Creole and other Caribbean English lived together. People named Ho and Yong ran the shops, but the clientele was mostly black, from the Islands.

The driver gave Don a more-than-adequate education. His descriptions sounded familiar. Don had read local newspaper articles about the area. It put Don's mind at ease. He felt like he was driving into a nice neighborhood, not some God-forsaken place. In the light of day, the area was bustling with people in colorful clothes and endless streams of children.

"That's it. Stop," said Don, as they approached the block.

The driver stopped the cab. Don got out, asking the driver to wait. He ran into the alley. No dead animals. No decayed meat. The garbage can was gone, so he couldn't look into the window.

The cab driver was standing outside the cab when Don returned. "What are you looking for?" he asked with a huge smile.

"I don't know."

"Doctor Gardner?"

Don looked around and spotted a very well-dressed man crossing the street, wearing jeans, a blue blazer, and a Panama straw hat.

"Hey, Doc. What the hell brings you to Brooklyn?"

Don turned. Pierre ran towards Don.

"Pierre?" asked Don in sheer amazement.

"Yes. It is I. Pierre. I live in dat building dere." He pointed to the building next to the vacant building.

Dysplasia

Don paid little attention to where Pierre pointed. He was still shocked.

"I am security on Saturday for the store owners. I make good money and I can go home for lunch. What are you doing here?" Pierre asked. He was the one who should have been more amazed.

Don made up the first thing that came to his mind. "One of my patients in the hospital didn't come back for a very important checkup. I thought she lived here." It sounded reasonable.

"What is the name? Maybe I can help you?"

"That's okay. I realize my mistake. She is on Church Street. Not Church Avenue. We have to go back to Manhattan." His own quick thinking surprised him. He knew it might make him appear stupid. It was a possible mistake.

Don also knew how unlikely it must seem to Pierre that a doctor would travel to check up on a poor hospital patient. But that was all he could think of, and why did it matter anyway? Pierre was his doorman.

After a few pleasantries, Don got into the taxi and instructed the driver to take him back to Manhattan.

The first thing Don did when he got home was call Susan. After her voicemail finished its outgoing directive, he left a simple, brief message.

"Susan. This is Donald Gardner. Please call me. I would like to talk with you. It's about Dr. Chessman." He left his home number in case Susan discarded it.

Don sat doodling at his desk at home. He drank from a tall plastic tumbler filled with scotch. He tried to draw some of the things he saw: the pole, a bone. Then he made notes. He couldn't make any sense out of what he was thinking. The murders. The bizarre night on Church Avenue. His mind was racing. It was the booze.

Brad Lewis

He reached for the telephone. He dialed Linda. Maybe he could tell her. At least she might put his fears to rest. As he dialed, he realized he was better off not mentioning anything to Linda. He admitted to himself that he just wanted to hear her voice.

"Hello?" It was his mother-in-law, someone he didn't want to speak to.

"It's Don. Is Linda there?"

After a pause Linda's mother said, "No, but I have a message for you."

Linda was standing next to her mother in her mother's dingy city apartment, overlooking the West Side of Central Park, one of those buildings near the Dakota. Linda's stepfather kept it for the weekends in the city. The call was forwarded from the house.

"What's the message?" Don asked.

"She said to tell you that she's hiring a lawyer." Don's mother-in-law took no pleasure in the statement.

Don exhaled slowly. He was numb and would never remember what he said after that moment.

"A lawyer. What for?"

"Don. You know what for. She asked me to ask you if you were going to use your friend Robert Kleinberg." Linda's mother made up her own Jewish-sounding last names.

Don's marriage had completely slipped away. It was his entire fault. How did he let it get this far?

"Yeah. Tell her to have her attorney call Kronen." Don hung up and breathed an unexpected sigh of relief. For a moment he was glad that his wife wanted a divorce while simultaneously feeling totally rejected.

His personal brow beating was interrupted by the building intercom. He walked to the front of the apartment and pushed a button that allowed him to speak to the doorman.

- 329 -

Dysplasia

∾

"There's a Ms. Susan here to see you. Shall I send her up?" asked the doorman.

He paused and then said, "Yes." Don should have expected this type of aggressive move from Susan. He did say he wanted to see her.

Don opened the door and Susan held her hand up signaling Don not to speak.

"I am not from Jamaica. I am from Haiti. My family works with people who want to see the Reverend Jean-Bertrand Aristide stay in power in my country. I have been spying on Chessman for my father. Dr. Chessman was a friend of Duvalier."

"Whoa. Hold on here." Don closed the door after Susan walked into the vestibule. "Who did you say?"

"Duvalier. From Haiti."

"Baby Doc, the guy in France?" Don asked.

"No. Papa Doc. You know that Papa Doc was licensed to practice medicine in the United States."

"Okay. Hold on here," said Don. His head was spinning. Haiti. Chessman. Chessman had a place in Haiti. "Please sit down. Would you like a glass of wine?"

"No. Thank you," Susan said. She sat down on the sofa, and leaned forward. "Your Dr. Chessman and Papa Doc were associated through medicine, at least in the beginning. Did you know that?"

"No. I didn't. What has this got to do with—?" Don stopped himself in midsentence. It was beginning to have more to do with everything. "How close was Chessman with Papa Doc?" Don asked.

"This I don't know. But Papa Doc had many friends who were doctors. Your Dr. Chessman. He is something different. I think he is houngan."

"A what?" Don was trying to absorb everything.

"A houngan. In your country you might call him a white witch doctor."

Don laughed, then he suddenly stopped. "Wait a minute. I need a drink. You sure you don't want one?"

"I will try your drink," she said.

Don pulled Susan by her hand and led her into the kitchen. He poured two scotches into paper cups kept in a pile for handy use near the refrigerator.

"Is this the new minimalist look?" she asked. Susan was bright. She seemed to know more about what was going on in Manhattan than Don.

The kitchen was a mess. Don told the maid not to come back anymore since he thought she was spying on him for Linda. After the phone call with Linda's mother, he was sure the maid was reporting in regularly to Linda.

"Okay. What are you telling me?" asked Don. "Let's go over this slowly. Please."

They stood in the kitchen with their backs pressed against the gray-and-white speckled counters.

"A houngan spends his time healing. They are the doctors for the Haitian people. They make the medicine from herbs, and use magic to help make people better."

"Magic? Chessman?"

"Yes. If I am right, and I think I am, Chessman learned everything about our culture."

"Why would Chessman want to be one of these houngies?"

"Houngan. Because it is a great honor. Particularly if he was the personal houngan to Papa Doc. But that I don't know."

Don was fighting it but it sounded right. "The other night I followed Chessman to Church Avenue and I thought I saw him standing in the middle of a circus. Is that possible? It was a whole lot of people. There were poles. Some sort of chanting." Don was breathing rapidly.

Dysplasia

"It is possible. The Church Avenue area is filled with Haitian families, some boat people, but many part of our wealthier middle class. In New York they are all still poor, but make a go of it driving taxis, working as janitors, going to your American schools to learn new trades. Many of them still cling to tradition. Outside of Haiti, things aren't much different than fifty years ago. Ritual is very important. It is as much as what is good in Haiti as what is wrong." She stopped herself, as her voice rose. "I am very proud of my people. It is a very sad thing, what goes on in Haiti. Very sad. The Haitian people are a good people."

"I'm sorry," said Don. It seemed like the right thing to say. "You're saying I might have seen some kind of ritual?"

"Yes. It was possible. For the ceremony, the houngan makes his ride down the poteau-mitan, a pole of painted serpents. If it is a woman, she does the same and is called a mambo. They leap out to possess the worshiper, to possess the spirit. Is that what you saw?"

"Holy shit. The room was filled with all sorts of stuff. I think I saw bones."

"Yes. You saw the houmfor, the chapel. You saw the magic."

"Do you believe in this, too?"

Susan did not answer and avoided his stare. "What I believe is unimportant. My father thinks Dr. Chessman is an evil man who has done bad things in our country. We don't have the FBI or CIA to track down people we think are bad. We only have the rich and our own personal contacts and security."

"Susan. Are you telling me Chessman could have been doing this mumbo-jumbo ritual stuff in Brooklyn?"

"It is called voodoo. You must have heard of voodoo."

"This is crazy. What's next? Zombies?"

Susan stared at Don with a blank expression.

"Come on. This is bullshit. I'm taking you home," he said. Don downed his scotch and walked Susan to the door.

"I know how strange it sounds to you, an American. That's why I couldn't tell you when I met you."

"You could have told me," said Don, trying to appear a liberal thinker.

She yanked his hand. "Would you have believed me if I told you this the first night I met you?"

Don thought for a second. "I guess not." He still wondered what she was trying to find in his apartment. It didn't matter. Don had a lot of other information to digest.

They took the elevator directly to the garage and walked towards Don's BMW. It looked like someone was sitting in the front seat of the car.

Susan took a few more steps, stopped and screamed.

"You have been cursed!"

"What? What are you talking about?" Don walked to the car. Susan held her ground.

Inside was a chicken, plucked and painted blue, propped up near the steering wheel.

Don opened the door, grabbed the chicken and threw it to the ground.

"Did you do this? Is this your idea of a joke?"

Susan shook her head "no." She was visibly distressed.

Don slammed the door to the car and walked to Susan. He took her hand in his. "You do believe in this stuff, don't you?"

"No. It just scares me, okay?"

"Okay."

"The people that do this can be very violent."

"But you won't go in the car. Right?"

Dysplasia

∞

"I am a little superstitious. I am more worried about you. These are bad men who would curse you."

Don realized they were standing in the garage. He looked around. It was quiet. He thought they'd better get out of there as soon as possible.

"I'll get you a taxi."

They walked over to the elevator, and he pushed the up button. Don decided to retrieve the chicken in order to throw it away. He didn't want any trouble with the people in his building.

"Where are you going?" asked Susan, clearly not wanting to stand alone.

"To get the chicken," said Don, in his brave voice.

"I'll go with you," she said.

"Okay," said Don. He took her by the hand.

Don wrapped the chicken in the *Wall Street Journal*, a three-day old copy that was sitting in the front seat. He hadn't read a paper for a few weeks now. He was pleased to put the *Journal* to such good use.

During the ride downtown to Susan's apartment, Don wanted to tell Susan what he knew about Chessman, what he thought about the possibility that Chessman knew something about Melinda's death. Don finally found a way to mention the fact that she was a former patient of Chessman's.

Susan didn't blink after hearing what Don had to say.

Don went further. He told Susan about the slide. "I know this sounds gross and ridiculous," said Don.

"No. It doesn't," said Susan.

Don didn't know if Susan was trying to cover up her squeamishness or perhaps he wasn't describing things in a way that characterized his worst fears.

He told Susan about the transsexual, the second murder, and the hospital report.

"I see," was all Susan would say.

"Didn't you hear me? I said these murders were done with surgical instruments. They cut off parts of their genitals."

Susan stared across at Don. "I have heard this all too many times before," said Susan.

Don was stunned. Susan was acting as if Don had told her reasonably, relevant scenarios.

Don didn't say another word until they reached the front of her building. "Will you be all right?" Don asked Susan as she exited the taxi.

"It is I who should be asking that of you. You be careful. If you want to talk more, call me."

Don watched as Susan got inside.

He asked the driver to let him off a few blocks from his building. He walked slowly through the almost-deserted streets, trying to rethink everything, to construct it into terms that he could understand. The only thing he could come up with for certain was to tell Kronen and perhaps Jill. Kronen would call him an idiot so he decided to tell everything he knew to Jill. Jill was bright, logical, and would be able to tell him if he was crazy, irrational, too stressed out to make sense of anything. Even if he was, what about what Susan said? They both couldn't be insane.

CHAPTER TWENTY-THREE

The open plaza of the IBM building was ideal for a planned rendezvous with Jill. There were a few open wire chairs scattered around the slightly stark, but nonetheless private meeting place, where two people could be easily ignored.

Don seated himself at a table between a homeless man who was finishing the remains of a sandwich left generously by two young German speaking girls. Several tables away, on the other side of the plaza, were two young men in security uniforms, obviously on a coffee break.

Don sat almost motionless and stared at the sky, which looked surprisingly blue for a New York City skyline. He thought back to how he lay awake in the middle of the night. It was happening more often. The sweat poured off his chest, a small physical reminder that accompanied the now-familiar panic in his mind. He remembered leaving a message for Kronen, making sure he knew what was going on with Linda. That's all he could remember.

Don looked at the moist ground. It must have rained recently, which is why the sky looked so blue. He felt momentarily content, that he had made that simple deduction and remembered the rain. Any logical deduction made him feel better, however simple, however trite. Don loved the rain. He recalled how he loved to watch the rain from the living room window when no more than eight. He had a favorite part of the concrete where the water would collect and the raindrops would perform an aquatic ballet, his own private ballet, a ballet that let his mind drift into the idyllic wonder of childhood fantasy. He longed for a fraction of that moment.

His hangovers were starting to bother him big time, clouding his thinking during the day. In the beginning, Advil, Tylenol, or aspirin worked. Now he just accepted the headache, even with 600mg of Advil four times a day. He was worried what the Advil might be doing to his system. His liver was being overworked from the alcohol. It was a terrible combination, worse with the Tylenol.

Jill moved quickly into the plaza. She was wearing a plain beige raincoat over her white doctor's blazer. She looked great, her wavy auburn hair just reaching the collar of her raincoat.

Jill spotted Don and headed towards the table, signaling in her best sign language that she was first going to get coffee from the vendor stationed across the plaza. Don nodded "yes" to Jill's pointed finger, which quickly changed to two fingers accompanied by a smile. She mouthed the words "two coffees" as she still held up the two fingers and headed for the vendor.

Don felt an even stronger desire for Jill and fantasized about lifting her raincoat while they lay in bed, finding nothing but a smooth, bare bottom. He wondered if Jill had any sexist thoughts about him.

"Doctor, where are your clothes?" would be Don's cute line uttered in a hushed, seductive voice, a voice he never used in real life.

Jill would answer, "How else can I get a full exam?"

"What a dumb line. You idiot." Don scolded himself. "You can't even have a good fantasy. Damn. That's trite. You are one low life typical male."

Don abandoned the idea of trying another fantasy as his mind flipped back to the horrific scene he encountered in Brooklyn, a scene he ran over and over in his mind since Susan told him what she knew about Chessman. Jill interrupted Don, back with the coffees.

"You drink it black. Right? I don't know how you do it. Your stomach must be lined with Maalox or Pepto Bismol," she said.

"I don't digest milk all that well."

"Is it lactose intolerance?"

"I don't think so."

"Doctor. We are scientists," Jill said in a strained, sarcastic voice. "We must empiricise everything. Logic is our savior."

"I don't think 'empiricise' is a word."

"It is now," said Jill, her lips curling into a silly smirk.

Don laughed out loud, different from the way he laughed with his wife. It was a freer response, one he remembered from childhood. Jill made him feel like the child he wanted to become again, the child that most men learn to hide.

"Don?" Jill was very serious now.

"Yes?"

"I know you've been very upset, but I have to warn you that you could get in a lot of trouble."

Don blurted out his immediate thoughts. "Chessman has something to do with those girls. I know it. I just know it."

"I spoke to Dick."

"Who's he?" asked Don, trying to keep the conversation light.

"Don. Cut it out. We can trust him."

"I know you trust him. He thinks a doctor killed Melinda, doesn't he?"

"Yes."

"Do you agree with him?

"No," said Jill. "But I trust him." Jill blushed.

At that moment Don was feeling jealous of Dick.

"Something wrong?" asked Jill, puzzled by Don's glazed look.

"No. I have more news about Chessman. That's why I called you."

"Why couldn't we meet in the office?" asked Jill.

"I don't know. Manny is always running around somewhere."

"And you think he's part of a conspiracy or something?" She was teasing.

"No," said Don, smiling.

Jill looked directly into Don's eyes and realized that Don was jealous. She tried to convince herself that she never thought about Don in any other light except that he was colleague who went to the same medical school, someone she always thought of as just a professional man. She repressed any feelings she had for anyone connected with medicine a long time ago. She thought it would be unhealthy to have a doctor-doctor relationship. Now she was at least willing to entertain the idea. She had never been in demand by men, particularly in college. She was busy studying. They all knew it, and she made a big point of the fact that she didn't have any time. After the usual first semester flirtation rush, she was left alone.

She liked the idea that Don was jealous. She admitted to herself that she had other feelings for Don she could not have had in medical school, feelings that a woman has for a man, feelings that Jill felt were beginning to materialize. It occurred to her that she had actually repressed her attraction for Don, chalking it off as brotherly love. God. She liked Don more than she previously thought! The fact that he was running around so vulnerable made him more human. She realized that she knew Don as well as anyone. Even Dick.

"Say something," she told herself. "You tell me yours first, and then I'll tell you what Dick said."

"Okay, but you're not going to believe this."

As Don leaned back, Jill studied him. He took a deep breath, raised his eyebrows, moved his lips as if he were going to speak, but no words came out. He trembled slightly and shook his head, as if to clear out the cobwebs.

Don took the pocket square from his jacket pocket. He moved it over his brow, much the same way a garage mechanic might hurriedly wipe off grease. Jill was reminded of how Don mopped his brow the same way when they stood over the cadavers in Gross Anatomy, the very first course in medical school.

Jill had a bad time in medical school, fighting off the overt sexist bastards who would abuse her at a moment's notice. On top of that, the majority of the doctors pretended to be politically correct (a virtually unknown expression then) by acknowledging how nice it was to have more women doctors in the profession, a token verbal gesture that came off patronizing and nauseating. Jill never faulted them since she was aware that the women's movement had thrown some men off their masculine centers. But Don was different. She didn't know exactly what it was about him. He always put her at ease. She guessed that's why they remained friends. Don treated her the same way he treated anyone else in the class. She stopped her thoughts. How could she be thinking about Don this way? Don was still married. She laughed to herself. She already had those thoughts and considerations. It was too late to pretend that she wasn't attracted to Don.

Don started to speak slowly, with a deliberate speech pattern, one that indicated fear. "The other night I followed Chessman around town. You know. He has those nights where he gets in a rented limo or Town Car and makes the rounds."

"Yes. Your office is the only one I know of that picks up patients in chauffeured cars."

"Some of our patients from out of town expect the service," said Don, surprised at his own defense of the service.

"That's one of the things that cracks me up. You would think you could find enough people in New York to treat, but 'noooo'." She drew the "no" out for comic emphasis. Jill was deliberately trying to distract Don, almost as if she didn't want to hear what Don had to say.

"Come on, Jill. It's not such a big deal."

"Not such a big deal. You guys have to fly them in from every corner of the globe. Who was that guy who came with an armed surveillance truck, you know, the one that had its own satellite dish on top. I remember the morning I went upstairs. This guy in the elevator had an Uzi sticking out of the bottom of his jacket. He scared the hell out of me!"

"Some big shot from Manila. His wife or girlfriend or someone saw Chessman. Let me finish."

"I was changing the subject deliberately," Jill confessed. "Are you sure you want to tell me this? Shouldn't it be kept between you and Chessman?"

"This is serious. It goes beyond anything I could ever have thought about Chessman."

Don looked scared. It frightened Jill. She avoided his glare. "Don. What's happening to you? Are you okay?"

"Of course I'm not okay," said Don. His hand trembled as he took a sip of coffee.

Jill reflexively copied Don and sipped her coffee. The last thing she wanted to do was to agitate Don further.

"Did you ever talk to anyone?" asked Jill.

"No," answered Don sheepishly, like he had just confessed to a minor crime.

"Look. I know you don't believe in shrinks, but you might. I don't know." She was legitimately worried about Don.

"Jill. Let's get back to that night. That night he didn't call the car service. He drove himself."

Dysplasia

⌒

"Let's switch. I'll tell you mine first. You may not want to tell me anything after that. Dick is convinced that the murderer had medical training."

"Chessman," said Don.

"Dick said I shouldn't talk to you about the case."

"Oh. Come off it, Jill."

"And if you tell me any stuff I could be in some kind of trouble, so I don't want to know." It was a poor presentation, but Dick did tell her not to talk about the case with Don or any of his partners.

"Jill. Chessman is much more scummy than you think."

"We've known that for some time."

"What if Chessman is the murderer?"

"He's not. You're way off here. Don. You can't blame Chessman. There's absolutely no evidence.".

"You just said Dick is convinced that a doctor did it."

"I'm still not," said Jill. "He's not totally convinced. Don, we've been over this."

"Listen to me. I saw Chessman at a voodoo ceremony," Don blurted out.

Don then took the slide out of his pocket. "And I found this slide in Chessman's bedroom. It is a sample of epithelial tissue, and appears in section just like vaginal epithelium."

"Don. Did you say a voodoo ceremony?" She spoke calmly.

"Uh-huh."

"How do you know it was?"

"That's what it looked liked. Someone verified it for me. They essentially described the things I saw."

"Are you sure you saw Chessman there? Where was this?"

"Brooklyn. Church Avenue. In a predominantly Haitian section. That's where we ended up the night I followed him."

"Are you cracking up on me?"

"I don't think so. If I am, it's a hell of a story anyway."

Jill smiled. "Okay. You say you saw Hank at this soiree in Brooklyn."

"Right. It was dark, but I'm pretty sure it was him."

"Don. Please. Uhm. This is really something."

"Will you help me?" asked Don.

"Give me the slide."

"Why?"

"Don't get paranoid."

"I am already paranoid."

"I'm going to see if any of the cellular tissue matches that of any of the deceased. That's what you want, isn't it?"

"Jill, the story is true. If I told you anymore you'd think I was absolutely nuts."

"Try me."

"I found a blue chicken in my car," he said laughing.

"I don't want to talk about his anymore."

Something in Don's voice scared Jill. Maybe he was pathological, suffering from paranoid delusions. Jill was also frightened. Maybe because she disliked Chessman enough to believe that he could be a heinous murderer, or maybe it was that she knew Don wasn't the type of man that would lie.

Don asked meekly, "Are you taking it?" Don took the slide out of the side pocket of his sports coat. It was in a small plastic box.

"Yes." Jill took the box and placed it into her purse. "Don, don't discuss this with anyone."

"I already have."

"Who?" Jill was startled.

"Susan."

"Tell this Susan that you were kidding or something before she calls the police and has you committed."

Don laughed. "I don't think she thinks I'm crazy. She knew about why the chicken was in my car, and she knows about Hank. There's a lot more to this."

"Just get some rest. Let me check the slide for you. Okay?"

"Okay. But maybe I'm not explaining it right. The whole thing seems to fit together. There were other slides in the bedroom. I think he's taking these samples from women he dates. I think—"

Jill cut him off in midsentence. "I mean it. I don't want to hear anymore. No more theories. Let's stick to facts. Don. It couldn't hurt if you spoke to Barry Gruber. Maybe he can settle you down."

Don shrugged his shoulders and smiled. "Jill?"

"Yes?"

"Thanks."

She nodded.

CHAPTER TWENTY-FOUR

Jill's head popped up from the floor and looked out the window. For a brief moment when her head was in the up position of the exercise, she could see across the street from her upper Westside apartment. There wasn't much activity on that section of Columbus Avenue that early in the morning. Years ago, most of the ground-floor stores were converted to restaurants. At night the street was jammed with people.

Jill's arms extended around her head. Her hands clasped tightly behind the notch on the back of the skull, an area she knew to be just above the foramen magnum, the area where the spinal cord entered the brain stem. She continued her sit-ups. Ever since college she stayed in shape. Her running skills got her a brief stint on the lacrosse team.

She thought about her apartment. It wasn't a bad apartment, but each time she looked outside at the dull view of the city it reminded her that she would rather be in Vermont looking out at snow-covered woods. It wasn't easy being a career woman in a profession that initially was cool to women.

Staying in Manhattan was a trade-off. She could easily be the chief medical examiner in one of the small cities in Vermont, but felt an obligation to stay in New York. Her parents were alive and refused to live anywhere except Valley Stream, a town on Long Island where they owned a candy store and soda fountain since the day Jill was born. It was the kind of store they had in the Bronx but the neighborhood changed. Most of the storekeepers moved out, many of them ending up on Long Island. The Stovers accepted small gifts from their rich and somewhat dishonest son, but refused his offers to help them move.

"I'll get you a nice condo in Boca," he would repeat, hoping he could show his parents what a good son with a lot of money could do, buy them a condominium in one of Florida's upscale retirement communities.

They liked it where they were. Jill was saving a lot of her own money, and planned to go shopping next year for her own little "ski chalet" in Vermont. Nothing fancy. Just a good, solid house near Stowe where Jill could get her share of skiing and not run into the crowd that "was only skiing East this week because the airport was down in Aspen or Park City."

Her head popped back down as she continued to do very slow repetitions. At least in New York Jill was seeing a variety of cases in a short period of time. She would be overqualified when she moved, and could have her pick of areas to work. If there were no openings in the medical examiner's offices, she could always continue her oral surgery practice, an idea that did not please her as much.

The buzzer rang. Jill got up quickly and ran to the door. She was wearing tight-fitting panties which exposed the gluteus maximus muscles in fine definition, the way she would like to describe them, rather than succumb to Dick's description of a plain "tight ass". She pushed the button that allowed her to be heard through the intercom.

"Dick?" she asked, anticipating his arrival.

"Yeah. Should I come up?" was the somewhat muffled reply.

"I don't think so. It has to be an early night."

"Okay. I'm parked across the street."

"In the no-parking zone?"

"Where else? I'm a cop."

"Be right down."

Jill walked into her bedroom. Her entire apartment was about 1,300 square feet, a decent size for one person in Manhattan.

She pulled her jeans off a wooden rocking chair near the bed and slipped them on quickly. The room was mostly American woods, with a large mahogany chest at the foot of the bed. The bed had a canopy and would probably not be the choice of most of Jill's women patients. It took Jill years of collecting to decorate this room. Jill opened her closet and pulled out a three-quarter denim jacket and a pair of soft, brushed suede boots with fur lining. She looked at herself in the mirror as she slipped on the boots and hurriedly threw on her jacket. She did not look like anyone's image of a doctor, something that she liked as much as she disliked. What woman doesn't want good looks? But in her profession, it has always been the source of unwanted comments, accompanied by a harder set of standards. She was damned proud of herself because she had shown them all that she was a good doctor. As good as any of her colleagues.

There were dozens of restaurants to choose from on Columbus Avenue. When Jill was a resident, there were only a few, but Columbus had a long run as a haven for Yuppie couples who had new-found cash in the '80s. The '90s were no exception. All the restaurants were packed during the millennium celebration.

Dick and Jill stopped in front of a Chinese restaurant they frequented since they began dating.

"Chinese again?" Dick asked.

"Sure. It's always good. The owner likes us," Jill answered. Jill used the same place for take-out dinners when alone.

They stepped inside. A few heads looked up to see who arrived.

Dick was a handsome man about fifty. Even through his clothing, it was apparent he was in great shape, trim as any man his age. His sandy hair receded just enough to show his age; otherwise, he might be taken for a much younger man.

Dick met Jill inside the Museum of Modern Art at a function for sponsors, people who shelled out $300 for membership so that they were advised of upcoming events and were able to participate in special museum activities. It impressed Jill, who at those events was used to meeting investment bankers, art dealers, and the general smattering of nouveau-rich people who felt they were getting a great deal, since the real "sponsors" were patrons who shelled out a lot more but attended the same functions. When Jill found out that Dick was a detective, one who spent time on sex crimes, she almost said "no" when he asked her out. She wanted nothing to do socially with anyone who knew anything about her activities. Her psychiatrist friend Barry Gruber was always telling her that she went overboard with her obsession to not date doctors. Jill admitted to Barry that the only doctor she liked was Don, and he was married. That eliminated any other possibilities in medicine.

The owner recognized Jill and greeted her quickly. "Two, Doctor?" he asked, beckoning them towards an empty table.

"Yes. Thank you," Jill answered.

Dick didn't mind going to places where Jill was thought of as the significant leader of the couple. In fact that's what he liked most about Jill. She was independent. Dick was turned on by the fact that Jill loved to order dinner for them. When she ordered she would look over with a twinkle in her eye for some acknowledgment that Dick's testosterone level was undergoing positive alterations.

The owner showed them to a little table in the corner away from the aquarium, filled with edible fish. Jill made it clear on a previous trip that she did not want to watch her dinner swim before eating it.

The food came out in a drove as the efficient staff raced to fill the table. The meal was fast and furious.

Dick put his napkin up to his lips. "God. I am stuffed. I don't think we needed four pancakes for the Moo Shu Pork." Dick took a few more gulps of tea.

"If you keep drinking tea at that pace, you'll be hungry again in two hours."

"I know, Doctor. You 'splained' it to me. The 'tan man acid' or somethin' does it. I got it. So I'll have a salami on rye with mayo later."

Jill took the teasing well. "You're such a typical Irishman."

"I have to keep up the standard."

"Do you want this last piece of fish?" Jill held the head of the fish on the end of a chopstick.

Dick took it and placed it aside. "You are such a child."

"And what are you?" Jill demanded.

"My twenty-one-year-old daughter is more serious than you when she's out."

"That's because she's afraid of you." Jill knew that would get a rise out of Dick. Jill told Dick on many occasions that he intimidated his daughter.

Dick picked up the fish head and tossed it across to Jill. It hit her plate and sent sauce splashing upward. She quickly grabbed her napkin and laughed uncontrollably.

"You can be such an asshole," she said, as she thought about some appropriate retaliation.

Dick laughed too. He stopped for a second as a dumpling landed in his hair. He reached up and grabbed the dumpling. He ate it as if to gesture that he was getting the best of the deal. He slapped his fingers across his mouth when he was done and smacked his lips before letting out a huge belch.

Dysplasia

"Pig," said Jill, giggling like a high school sophomore.

"Pig's lover."

"Truce?" asked Jill, formally extending her hand.

"Truce."

Dick pulled out a personal Palm Pilot, the kind that could supply the time on the moon or leap year in the next millennium.

"I went over everything you told me. It's still nothing. There is no motive. Your guy is Mr. Clean. Tell whoever it is to forget about it." Dick knew who it was.

"But those slides in the bedroom?"

"You have one slide, not slides," said Dick.

"It did check out. It was a sample of vaginal epithelium. It was a 'homemade' slide. Where do you think he got the sample?" Jill was just trying to satisfy Don's curiosity. She couldn't believe that such a bizarre connection to Chessman existed.

"The doc is in the business. Can't he look at slides? A lot of guys look at slides. It's his business. So he wants to study in the bedroom." Dick was taking the approach of a defense attorney. There wasn't a shred of evidence.

"But the slide Don gave me was a slide of normal tissue. Wouldn't he have slides of tissue that were abnormal? If he were studying it, and I want to impress upon you that Hank Chessman is not your basic book worm."

"I don't get what you mean."

"A doctor like Dr.—"

"X," said Dick as he looked around uncomfortably. "I don't want no law suit thrown at me for slandering the guy. I shouldn't even be talking to you about this."

"Yeah, yeah. Dr. X. He would look at abnormal slides. He has no reason to look at normal slides."

"I'm confused. Some biopsies are normal, right?" Jill wasn't making any sense.

"Okay. Listen to it this way. That's not the area of the vagina where he would take a biopsy. What if he's taking these from women he sleeps with?"

Dick looked at Jill with an expression that said, "Are you crazy or what?"

"That's what my friend thinks," said Jill.

"You mean Don," said Dick.

"What happened to getting sued?" asked Jill.

"I hate to play pretend. It's not like I don't know how you got the slide. It had to be from one of his partners. What's the difference?"

"No difference," said Jill. Her expression indicated she wanted a more detailed answer from Dick.

Dick thought for a moment. "Wow. Okay. Let's say you're right. Let's say he is doing this. There's a big difference between murder and kinky. Nobody's complained that he does this. We interviewed dozens of people. This guy is Mr. Clean."

"Dick. I want you to see if you can get Farmer's office to approve a DNA check on the Foster woman. The first one who was pulled out of the river. I want you to check her DNA against the DNA on this slide."

"Okay. I'll play for another minute. This is only one person on the slide, right?"

"Right."

"Odds are slim that he's going to leave a piece of one of his victims in his own bedroom. Let's say he's the sick, deluded motherfucker you say he is. Then he's got a lot of slides. Are we supposed to subpoena this guy and get a search warrant and go through the whole mess because Don found a slide in the bedroom?"

Dysplasia

∽

"Come on, Dick. Just ask for it. I promised Don I would do what I could," said Jill.

"It would take a long time. Say my boss says okay. The D.A. might not be able to use the evidence at all. Some judges don't rush to admit this kind of stuff."

"Why not?"

"They all play games. You saw the Simpson case. That was the biggest piece of DNA trashing I've ever seen. It's now part of the game. How to get the proper evidence admitted. The system sucks sometimes."

"Thanks for trying."

"Did I say I would try? I guess I did. Okay, but tell this friend of yours, Donnie boy, to stop playing cop. Ninety-nine point nine says this whole idea is bullshit."

"That dead woman was his partner's patient."

"I know. Come on. Let's get the check."

"I'll get it," Jill said as she removed a small slide case from her purse and handed it to Dick. Then she took out cash. She counted out the money and placed it under the corner of a dish.

"I love when you pay for me. It makes me feel like the cheap whore I really am." He put the slide case in his pocket as they got up from the table to leave.

"I'll meet you outside. This tea goes right through me," said Dick, who looked for the path to the men's room.

Jill went ahead to the front door. It was a nice night. She walked next door to look inside the window of an antique store. The store had a 19th century poster bed she had her eye on for a few months. It wasn't selling at the asking price. She dreamed of having two bedrooms in Vermont, with the bed in the window in her new house.

"Bonjour, Madam," said a voice out of nowhere.

She turned to see two well-dressed black men in dark suits. One was wearing sunglasses, even though it was dark.

"Yes?"

"Give us the slide and we go quickly."

Jill moved away from the glass window, the two men right next to her. An elderly man was near them on the sidewalk.

"Help," Jill yelled as she ran away from the pursuing men.

The old man hastened his step in the other direction, clearly avoiding trouble.

Jill suddenly stopped. She turned back to run towards the restaurant, feeling she could easily run past them on the wide sidewalk. There were enough people who could run "interference."

By then several people were staring at the scene from across the street.

Dick walked out of the restaurant, picking his teeth with a toothpick.

Jill managed to slip around one man, but the other caught her around the shoulders. The two went down in a heap.

The first man fled down the street. He got inside a black Lincoln sedan double-parked on the corner.

Jill got to her feet first and stood between Dick and the man on the ground. Jill began to kick the man in the side.

Just as Dick got close the man on the ground jumped to his feet swinging. He decked Dick with a roundhouse. Dick never saw the punch coming. The man ran into the street. The Lincoln accelerated backwards and screeched to a halt. The man was in the car and the car was gone in seconds.

"Oh, Dick," said Jill. "I'm sorry."

Jill yelled to the owner of the restaurant, who stood in the doorway.

Dysplasia

"Call the police. Get some ice."

"I am the police. Just get the ice," mumbled Dick, his hand clutching the side of his forehead. "Motherfuckers. Did they get anything?"

"Are you okay?" asked Jill. "That's what they ask in the movies."

"I think so," he answered as he pulled his hand away from his forehead. It revealed a nice-sized welt, well on its way to a larger size.

"They wanted the slide. They knew about the slide," said Jill.

"What?"

"They knew about the slide, Dick."

"Okay. I'm convinced something is going on. But it's not what you think it is. When you steal property, people sometimes want it back." Dick's voice showed a great deal of anger.

"Hey. I didn't take it," said Jill.

The owner brought out ice in a towel. Jill applied it to Dick's head.

"Oww! What happened to bedside manner?"

"Come on. Let's walk to my place," suggested Jill. "Maybe you should get an MRI."

"I'd prefer a drink," said Dick, as he got to his feet. "I'd better call this in."

CHAPTER TWENTY-FIVE

That same night Barry Gruber was trying to sort hundreds of his mother's hats. They were strewn all over the apartment in old-fashioned hatboxes. He had a very hard time disposing of any of his mother's things. They lived together most of Barry's adult life. He moved out briefly, two blocks away. When she had her first stroke, Barry moved back. The doctors didn't think there would be much of a recovery. They were wrong. She lived eight more years, and two more strokes later, finally succumbed the week she felt well enough to see the Statue of Liberty a last time, one of her favorite ferry trips. They had hot dogs and Cokes like when he was in elementary school. They bought another miniature Statue to keep company with the collection of almost fifty old-timers.

The door buzzer rang, followed by a few knocks.

Barry walked out of the bedroom, trying not to trip on the hatboxes. His black cat slept in one. He crossed through the living room, filled with puffy old sofas and chairs. Many were covered with clear plastic. Through the peephole he recognized the person in the hall and opened the locks. There were four, including two Medeco locks. It took a few seconds. He pulled the door open wide.

It was Don. "Hi, Barry. Thanks for letting me come over."

Dysplasia

∾

"Hey. No problem. You're busy. I'm busy. Why bother with the office? Come on. We'll talk in the bedroom. You should see some of these wild hats."

Don looked around. It was an apartment from another New York era, a time when people could walk on the streets at all hours of the night, and taxi drivers said "please" and "thank you." The furnishings looked a lot like the kind Don's parents had, except it was apparent that Barry Gruber's mother was wealthier than Don's parents. There were dozens of knickknacks, clocks, silver trays, and walls saturated with oil paintings. Don recognized a Chagall. It couldn't be real, he thought. As he passed it he read a little Lucite tag underneath the painting. Authentic.

"Sit down. Sit down," said Barry. He pointed to the large yellow Formica breakfast table. Don hadn't seen one of those for thirty years.

Don sat on one of the old, straight-back wooden chairs. He instantly began to talk about why he called. Barry could put anyone at ease.

Barry made coffee while Don spoke. He used an old percolator. It took him a few minutes to find the device for the coffee.

Don spoke at length about how he thought his marriage was over and how he felt responsible. Barry reassured him that, from the things he had mentioned over the years in casual conversation, the marriage seemed like it was doomed.

"What do you want to do?" asked Barry. He turned on the gas flame under the percolator.

"When things calm down, I guess I'll go through with the divorce."

Don changed the subject to business and kept the discussion limited to the fact that he felt his relationship with Chessman couldn't continue and after the hospital report was done, he was thinking about leaving the practice.

"I'm glad you made a decision."

"I've been having that dream again. Do you remember? I told you about it last year. You said something like I should call you if I really thought I wanted to go over it. But I didn't call."

"I know," said Barry, serving the coffee. He then walked out of the kitchen.

"Where are you going?" asked Don.

"Let's get it on tape. Okay?"

"Sure."

Don waited for Barry to return a few moments later carrying a large black box.

Barry fiddled with his old Sony reel-to-reel tape machine set up on a table in the kitchen. It was a monster. It took a long time to get it ready for operation. His colleagues often criticized him for not getting something smaller and modern. His answer was typical. "I like to see the words go on the tape."

While Barry took out a large reel of magnetic tape, he waved his arm towards the cutting board.

"There's some fresh veggies. I just got them. Help yourself."

"Thanks."

Don wasn't hungry, but he was very nervous about talking to Barry in such detail about his life. They had a casual, ongoing dialogue since Don was a resident.

Some of the carrots were already cut into thin slivers. The small stainless steel blade of a surgical scalpel lay next to the vegetables.

"I like your Ginsu knife," joked Don.

"It's the original scalpel from Gross Anatomy. I put the whole kit in the kitchen after graduation. You can do dozens of things with it. Skinning chicken is a snap." Barry sounded proud.

"Don't tell me you worry about cholesterol? The skin is the best part."

Dysplasia

"I'm not French. Only the French can get away with eating fried skin."

Don made a conscious decision not to tell Barry about the murders, the voodoo, or anything else that seemed too far-fetched. He talked mostly about the fact that he could no longer stand Chessman. He thought if he told Barry everything, Barry might label him more fucked up and demand that he go on medication or, in the worst-case scenario, he might call the police. A doctor in Beverly Hills who knew that his patients were planning a murder lost his license for not turning them in before the crime.

When Don left he felt more confident about his decision to leave the office. Barry told him to come back anytime.

Chapter Twenty-six

∞

Don picked up Susan early on his next Saturday off. They had a quick breakfast of bagels and coffee in the car.

Don had set up a meeting between Jill and Susan. When Susan first heard about it, she was apprehensive. Don insisted they could trust Jill, that she was an old friend and had an open mind. Don's only hope was to get Jill to understand and accept what Susan knew about Chessman. He didn't know how much she knew, but she certainly had him convinced that Chessman was twisted.

Don also spent a lot of time trying to convince Jill to meet Susan. Jill was initially reluctant, but was persuaded by Don's insistence and her own newfound curiosity. She felt if this proved to be a folly, perhaps Don would stop dwelling on the subject. On the other hand, if Susan turned out to be legitimate, the news might prove unbelievable.

Susan had a rally to go to at the U.N. and suggested that Don escort her so they could leave from there.

Don parked a few blocks from the U. N., and they walked along First Avenue.

Don was surprised to see so many people standing outside the U.N.

Dysplasia

The reporters were interviewing a member of the black Caucus, Ron Jones, the New York Democrat.

"He is a good man, your Jones," said Susan.

"If these boat people coming from Haiti were white, the rules would be changed. You would not be treating them this way. Look how differently you treat the Cuban boat people. Look what you did for that one poor boy," pronounced Jones.

"What's the current status on the military in Haiti?" Asked one reporter. "What good did our military do there?"

"Do you think the return of Aristide made any difference in the long run?" asked another reporter.

"The Haitian police said they are in control. Two hundred human rights monitors are still in Haiti. We have asked for another five hundred international police to be deployed there." answered Congressman Jones.

"Will they get it?" shouted another reporter.

"It certainly would be a step towards a stable future," answered Jones as he waved goodbye. He walked with his entourage towards waiting vehicles.

Susan smiled and pulled Don by the hand.

"Where are we going?"

"Congressman!" shouted Susan.

Congressman Jones stopped. He smiled at Susan. "Susan. How are you? I spoke to your father yesterday."

"Fine. I'm fine. Meet my friend Dr. Gardner."

Don and Congressman Jones shook hands. When the Congressman's eyes met Don there was a glint of recognition.

"Hi. How are you today, Congressman?" said Don.

"Where's your office, on Fifth?"

"Yeah."

"The Chessman office," said Jones.

"Right," said Don.

Congressman Jones was all smiles. "Hey, you guys throw a hell of a party. Say hello to Hank for me?"

"You bet."

"Nice to see both of you." The Congressman got into his car.

"He will get the power back into the hands of the right people."

"I hope you get what you want," said Don.

"Come on."

Susan pulled Don in the direction of another speaker. They stayed about an hour, and then walked to Don's car. It was a short drive crosstown to meet Jill.

Jill was waiting at the IBM Plaza when Susan and Don arrived. Jill was stirring her coffee without even thinking, staring at the metal sculpture. Don and Susan sat down quickly.

"Dr. Jill Stover. This is Susan Drouin."

"Please. Call me Jill."

"Thank you."

"Do you want some coffee?" asked Jill.

"We've had plenty earlier," answered Susan. "With a New York bagel. It is the best."

"Jill is the genius I told you about," said Don.

"I don't know about that."

"Don't be modest. Someone has to set the standard," said Don.

"Why don't we tell each other what we know or what we think we know? Will that work for you?" asked Jill.

"Okay," said Susan.

"Let me go first since mine is factual," said Jill.

This resulted in a playful smirk from Susan.

Dysplasia

"Both dead models were mutilated with surgical tools. There was suturing on the first."

"So it was probably done by someone in the medical profession," said Don.

"Not necessarily," said Susan.

"I agree," said Jill. "The clitoridectomy skills can be learned by lay people."

"Absolutely true," said Susan.

Jill smiled, as if to say "I don't need your approval."

"I have to look at the suture work in more detail. I'm doing it today. We didn't pay that much attention to it when she first came in. But because of Don I am going to look at it again."

"Jill, what about the DNA and the slide?" asked Don. "Any progress?"

"I wasn't sure if Susan knew about that." Jill was uncomfortable.

Don nodded in the affirmative. Now Jill was sure that Susan was involved in her attack outside the Chinese restaurant.

"Okay. We're checking to see if the slide that Chessman had in his possession was a sample of tissue taken from the dead models, which by the way is something I personally think is ridiculous," said Jill.

"If Chessman is a houngan, probably not. But Chessman may be a bocor, and then who knows?" stated Susan with purpose and authority. "That's what my father thinks. He thinks somewhere along the way Dr. Chessman became a bocor."

Even Don raised his eyebrows. This was new.

"What?" said Jill.

"Susan thinks Chessman is a Haitian priest."

"I see."

"But he may be a very evil man, a bocor, and then we can't tell for sure what he is doing."

Susan rose to her feet and took Jill by the hand. She held and stroked it gently with the upper part of her own hand.

"I feel something bad here. I have no bad feeling for either of you. I only want to help my people and if that means I can help you and Don, too, then this is a good thing for me."

Jill pulled her hand back.

"Maybe this meeting wasn't a good idea," suggested Don.

"Excuse me," said Jill. "It was nice to meet you. I am sorry if I hurt your feelings."

"No. You have not hurt my feelings. Let me make a dinner for you and Don tonight. It will make it all better."

"That's not possible." Jill was very uncomfortable. "Don, I'll be in my office."

"Okay, bye," said Don, not knowing what to say or do. He was upset that the meeting failed.

As Jill walked off, Susan laughed.

"What is so funny?" he asked.

"There is only one thing more difficult for me to understand than American men." Don laughed as he and Susan said, "American women." "This is a good woman. And she is pretty. How come you and she are not together? She was acting like a jealous woman," said Susan.

Don was embarrassed at Susan's frankness. "I don't know. Come on. I'll take you home."

They walked from the IBM Plaza. It was a cool afternoon and it looked like rain.

In the car on the way home, Susan pictured the three of them eating dinner on the floor of her living room. She would direct them into a seductive evening of love and lust. Susan knew the taboos of most Americans, and never pressed an issue that made people uncomfortable. Susan saw Don and Jill as very unlikely partners for her desires, but indulged the fantasy for a brief moment.

CHAPTER TWENTY-SEVEN

Before Jill and Dick went out to meet Farmer in their favorite Chinese restaurant they spoke about Susan.

"She might be the one who sent the two guys, but you don't really know that," said Dick. "If she did, what's the motive?"

Jill didn't want to tell Dick everything Susan said. It was a lot to accept, especially for Dick. "She thinks Chessman is a real bad guy."

"He might be, along with a million other guys in New York." Dick was impatient. "Maybe he sent the two guys to get his property back. That makes the most sense to me. Maybe he knows that Don took it."

"Maybe he arranged for Don to take it," said Jill.

Dick shook his head for a few moments. "Forget being a detective. You're good, but not great."

Jill was a little annoyed. "Okay. Let's go to dinner. You do think it's safe to go back to the Chinese place."

Dick laughed. "As long as you stick with me and promise not to try to beat up anyone without me." Dick thought there was little if any chance Jill would be threatened again.

There was more talking than eating with Farmer present. They hadn't consumed nearly half of what they normally would. Large plates of food were only half-eaten.

The owner walked over to the table. "Something wrong? You no like something. I take back. Make fresh. Please."

"No. Nothing. We had big lunches," said Jill. The truth had more to do with the subject matter of the meeting. It wasn't exactly an appetite stimulator.

"I put in doggie bags for you." He began to remove the platters.

"Thank you."

The owner walked away carrying two platters. He signaled for a waiter to help him. Another waiter cleared the table as they talked. Dick lashed into Jill as the waiter cleared the rest of the table.

His voice showed a clear frustration. "Look. Every type of sexual trauma has to do with the taboos of our society. If the sexual what-do-you-call-them, mores include not slicing up the genitals, then some deviant sick fuck is going to find a way to slice them up. That's the way it goes."

"What if the murderer is not from this country?" asked Jill. "My research shows that dozens of countries practice procedures related to what was done to Melinda Foster. They also train nonmedical people to do the same procedures."

"Look. Some sick motherfucker did this, and I'm sure he knew how to use a scalpel and sutures. One of the guys at the M.E.'s office said it looks like a pro job."

"Dick, that's pure speculation," said Jill.

"So is yours," Dick whined.

Farmer interjected. "I've listened to you two fight all night. We went over this. The mutilation was considered to be professional. The suspect was not some part-time Sunday-morning butcher. He knew what he was doing. But on close examination, there was conflicting information. Jill, you were the first one to point out that the suture job was amateur night in Dixie. What did you say?"

"I said that a third-year dental student could do a better job."

"And that most of them can't suture to save their lives," added Farmer. "I read your report."

"Maybe I shouldn't have put that part in my report," said Jill, embarrassed that her dislike for dentists' surgical skills found its way into a report for the Medical Examiner. She knew it would get back to her. There were several oral surgeons on staff who went to dental school followed by hospital residency programs. She didn't have it in for them, but she realized they would still get a lot of mileage out of her remarks.

"Let me finish my point," said Farmer, throwing her napkin aside. "You two are fighting in a vacuum. This may not be a professional job. Plus that ridiculous notion about some slide somebody found that was supposed to be vaginal tissue from the first victim. Give me a break!"

"The slide was not a match?" asked Jill. It was the first time she heard about it. She didn't know Dick was going to let Farmer know about the slide. Jill told herself that she was now acting paranoid like Don.

"No. I told Dick to tell you."

"Sorry. I forgot," said Dick. "I was going to tell you." He didn't think it was a big deal one way or the other.

Jill disregarded her growing anger and pressed on. "There might be other evidence."

"What evidence?" said Farmer.

"I gave Dick a sample of Dr. Chessman's epithelial tissue to check against the DNA found on the two murdered victims," said Jill, lying in an effort to keep Farmer's interest. Jill didn't believe Don's friend Susan, but didn't want to give up. Somehow she owed it to Don. At least in the end she could look Don in the eye and say she gave it her best shot.

Brad Lewis

Dick shook his head to Farmer, indicating that he wasn't playing along, that there were no skin samples, not even after appearing to owe Jill one.

Jill slumped down in her chair. Busted by Dick.

Farmer was direct. "Jill, I don't mind if you want to help, but Dr. Chessman is not a suspect. We can't afford to keep sending tissue samples upstate for DNA analyses. Besides, it won't be admissible under these circumstances."

"We already sent for it," advised Jill. Jill knew she was being ridiculous, but she did not want to see Chessman dismissed as a suspect. Maybe it was because Farmer was so sure. Jill had problems with people that were always certain, a rebellious streak that went all the way back to her childhood.

Dick's eyes told Farmer that it wasn't so. Dick did not want to be a part of Jill's scheming. He didn't like getting between his boss and his girlfriend.

"What about frequenting the places where the two victims socialized?" asked Jill. "I offered to do it myself."

"Yes. Dick mentioned you wanted to do that. It sounds like you think all the people attached to the M.E.'s office should behave like Quincy." Farmer could see that her remark fell flat on Jill. Farmer continued. "I have no problem with that so long as you report anything you think or find directly to Dick." Farmer was getting bored. "It's not normal police procedure but if you want to spend your time hanging out late in the city, that's your business. If anything goes down, I never said 'yes.'"

Jill nodded "yes," and seemed pleased.

"I don't want you to think I'm a loony toon or anything," said Jill. "But…"

"What are you going to say now?" cautioned Dick.

Dysplasia

"You know how Don is convinced that his partner is mixed up in all this stuff."

"Is that guy still all wound up? What is it with him? Why can't he stick to pulling babies out on time?" Dick was totally disgusted.

"Don is okay. Trust me." Jill was going far out on a limb for Don.

"Don is okay. Trust you?" Dick mimicked the words.

"You know what I mean."

"No. I don't. Please tell me. You said 'Don is okay. Trust me.' You know this guy that well that you want me to trust you about him? Maybe you and Don should solve this thing. Maybe you and Don should go out for Chinese on Columbus. Maybe you and Don should go back to your place. Maybe he won't rotate." Dick regretted the words as soon as he said them. It was too late.

"That's it. I can't believe you said that. I'm not going to sit here and listen to you do a second-rate DeNiro. You're acting like some deviant macho reject from a movie of the week. For God's sake, I'm not sleeping with Don. Is that your problem? You think I've been to bed with him, don't you?"

The owner of the restaurant dropped the food bags at the table without saying one word. He didn't want to interfere.

Farmer got to her feet and cleared her throat. "You don't mind if I leave." She was already on her way out.

They didn't answer and Farmer walked away from the table, looking back and smiling as she left. Neither Dick nor Jill realized that she was actually leaving.

"Jill. No. I'm sorry. I've been working a lot. It was a dumb-shit thing to do. I'm sorry." Dick got up to leave. "I'd better go. I'm sorry. Where did Farmer go?"

"I guess the ladies room," answered Jill. "Call me tomorrow."

"Do you still want me to?"

"Yes. You know I don't hold grudges over stuff like that, but don't ever try that abusive behavior on me again. In public or otherwise." Jill knew they had reached a point of no return. Dick showed a side that Jill could never tolerate.

"I said I was sorry," said Dick. He turned away in a huff.

"Okay. Right. Yeah. Try and get a good night's sleep. Do you want the food?" Jill held up the bags of Chinese food.

Dick was out of earshot.

Jill was almost glad the conversation got hostile. It gave her a good excuse to think about what Don had said. She was beginning to believe that there was a remote possibility that Chessman did know something about these crimes, even if he didn't do it.

"What if he did? No. That's too bizarre," she reminded herself. She also reminded herself that her affection for Don might be clouding her judgment.

Jill thought about how she could get a tissue sample from Chessman to check the DNA. It could be done easily. Jill pictured Don, Jill, and Chessman at lunch at the Pierre.

"What would be the reason for the lunch?" she asked herself. Jill would ask Don if Chessman could introduce her to some of his "special" patients. She knew that would peak his interest. There would be some kind of cross referral, a trade-off, if Chessman helped Jill expand her practice in a different direction. Jill would explain how she wanted to expand her business and let more of the "upper echelons" know who she was. Chessman loved this type of meeting where people would kiss his ass and act beholden to him for the rest of their lives.

During lunch Jill would pick up her napkin and move towards Chessman's face.

"Oh, Doctor Chessman. You have a little something on the corner of your mouth."

Dysplasia

Chessman would move to brush away the foreign object that was part of a twenty-five-dollar-per-person lunch plate, the Pierre Hotel's equivalent of a blue-plate special.

"Oh, you missed it. Let me get it."

Jill would move her napkin very gently over the corner of his mouth. Inside her napkin would be a neatly concealed Q-Tip. With her surgical skills, Jill would easily brush the cotton tip over the external epithelium, and with a slight rotation get a little swipe of the cells on the inside of the lips. Dead cells would be loose inside the cheek. After wiping, she would remove the Q-Tip from the napkin under the table and pass it to Don. Don would place the Q-Tip in a sterile tube and they could send it to be analyzed that day. Jill would have Dick check the DNA results against the cells analyzed from Melinda Foster and Misty Waters. They would know if Chessman was involved. That way was certain.

Seconds later, Jill was already onto another less-intrusive idea, since the legal ramifications of such information might be compromised by the method of discovery. Jill was going to suggest that Don talk to Chessman. Actually ask him about it. Don could observe his reaction. She doubted if Don would go for it. Chessman was too smooth.

Jill grabbed the check. She left soon, her head filled with thoughts of her next day's office surgeries.

As she walked along in a self-involved daze, a tall figure followed a few steps behind.

"Let's see. Four impactions, a blocked salivary gland, two implants," she thought. God, she hated implants. Maybe Manny would do those cases, but that's all he did all day, and they were referred to Jill. "A biopsy of clinical-appearing leukoplakia." She was sure about the leukoplakia since the patient was a heavy smoker. The only worry was if there were other kinds of dysplasia mixed in. The biopsy would tell her if it were just leukoplakia. She would surgically remove the area. It could be peeled off, without taking too much tissue.

"Jill. What is with you? Can't you just relax?" she asked herself. She forced herself to hum a few bars from *Phantom of the Opera* as she walked along Columbus Avenue.

"What the hell are you going to do about Don?" The thought once again startled her brain. As she spoke, she got a sense of the man walking behind her. He was only a few feet away. She walked faster. So did he.

Jill knew that the odds were slim that anyone would be out to do her harm, right there on Columbus, a path she walked thousand of times. Dick said it was unlikely the men who were after the slide would try again. But then again, this was New York City, where anything could happen to anyone at anytime, a fact she could attest to personally. The recent experience left her more on guard. A little fear made New Yorkers more cautious.

She was approaching a darker section, where three restaurants on the same block went out of business. Jill thought to retrace her steps and then cross to the other side of Columbus. Yes. Jill turned to walk back in the other direction. As she did, the man put his head down and stared at the sidewalk. He moved quickly as they passed each other. She glanced at him for a moment, checking for an imagined weapon. He had none. She knew him. Better not to look back again.

Jill went back to the corner of the restaurant where she ate and crossed over to the other side of Columbus. When she reached the block of her building, she slowed down. She heard footsteps behind her again. Now she was very scared. She turned; it was the same man. His head was up and she could see his face.

"Hi, Jill."

Dysplasia

"Barry Gruber. You scared me. What are you doing following me around at night?"

"I didn't know you lived in the area. I just wanted to say hello. I'm across the street. Been here forever."

"That's funny." Jill was certain Barry knew approximately where she lived. He was absent-minded.

"That we never saw each other?"

"Yeah. Well, you know the city. You sometimes never meet your next-door neighbor," said Jill.

Silence. It was an awkward pause. Barry stared at Jill. He was smiling ever so faintly. Jill avoided his eye contact. Barry realized she was uncomfortable, so he spoke first, hoping to call it a night.

"Well. I'm sorry. I don't want to bother people. I'd better go."

"Good night."

"Good night."

Barry walked to the corner. He waited for the light to change. Jill was already in her building when he crossed the street.

Jill was on edge. Why should she be frightened of Barry Gruber? Everyone liked Barry. It was funny how some very successful shrinks were such flops in their own social lives. Barry's behavior on the street was like an amateur stalker. If Jill didn't know Barry, she would have thought that he was following her, not because he knew her but because he was just following an anonymous woman. Maybe Barry didn't know it was Jill until she turned around and walked towards him. At that moment, he must have been embarrassed too. That's why he didn't say anything.

Barry went upstairs, got into his pajamas, and made himself a hot chocolate, the kind that came in a mix with little tiny marshmallows.

Over the years, he had tried to make his own hot chocolate from scratch, a tedious and messy process at best. He gave up to the little packet, realizing that technology did have some benefits.

He fell asleep thinking about Jill and what an idiot he was. Damn. Why couldn't he be more relaxed around women?

That night Barry had a very disturbing dream, that he was sailing in the East River on the boat with his mother, the same boat they sailed from Huntington Harbor. It was a Hinckley Sloop, a boat to be envied. His father was a Captain Bly; and if not for his mother, Barry would have jumped ship. After his father died they sold the boat he so hated, but Barry always dreamed that he and his mother would sail together. Tonight there was another guest on board.

The dead model Melinda was pulling in the jib. She turned and Barry saw the area where she was mutilated.

"Mother. Don't look. She's a nasty girl." Barry always protected his mother.

"Barry, why did you do this to me?" asked Melinda, pointing to her surgical wounds.

"I didn't do that to you. Women like you do that to yourselves. Isn't that right mother?"

"Barry. Don't be so hard on her. She seems like a nice girl." His mother smiled, and changed her hat from a floppy straw sun hat to a New York Mets baseball cap.

In his dream Barry made note of his mother's encouragement which somehow backfired in his own life.

"We've got to come about," shouted Barry.

In the bow of the vessel, Jill was shaving her legs. She stopped as she reached her pubic area, and yelled across the vessel to Barry. "Do you want the clit or should I throw it overboard?"

Dysplasia

Barry screamed himself awake. He sat up in bed, his forehead filled with dots of perspiration. His mouth was wide open and he breathed heavily for a few minutes, not knowing what he uncovered in his dream.

He moved towards his night table where he had a yellow legal pad and pen. He forced himself to make notes.

Chapter Twenty-eight

The plan was set. They were going to get Chessman's cheek cell. Once Jill told Don what she had said to Dick and Farmer, Don prodded Jill to go through with it. If Chessman's DNA was a match, it wouldn't be conclusive but it would show that Chessman was in contact with either one or both of them close to the time they were murdered.

Early that morning in Jill's office, she admitted to Don that she thought there might be a small chance that Chessman knew something about the murders.

"Why did you change your mind?" asked Don.

"I've known you too long to discard something you believe in, even if I think this stuff Susan is telling you is a bit much."

"I think Chessman might have done it," Don said.

"Don, there's no evidence. That part is all in your mind." Jill kept trying to keep her thoughts rational and logical. Ever since she met Susan, it became more difficult.

"Don't you think what I've told you makes him crazy enough?"

"Look at the O.J. thing. How would anyone have predicted it?"

"What do you mean?" Don was not following Jill's thinking.

"All of the guys who commit these kinds of crimes have forms of antisocial attitudes." She thought it better to stick with science.

"Like what?"

Dysplasia

൭

"Depression, somatization, and cognitive disorganization."

"You don't think Chessman is screwed up enough?"

"I'm not an expert. Chessman comes off in public as a perfectly normal egomaniac. What he does in the privacy of his own bedroom may be things you and I wouldn't do, but that does not make him the murderer. If everything we know about him is true, we can say he is a sick, disgusting, deluded person who needs help. But murder is excluded."

"What if?" was all Don kept asking. He refused to let go of the idea.

Don set up the lunch under the guise that Jill wanted to get some business coming in from Kuwait and Qatar. Naturally, Chessman suggested the Copa space over the Pierre. He didn't want to be seen in the Pierre with such low-powered lunch company.

Jill sat at the same table usually occupied by Chessman, Benjamin, Gross, Gardner, and sometimes Burns. The table conversation was boring. Lou was almost asleep. Harvey was trying some unsophisticated flirting with Jill. Don never told him how pathetic Harvey appeared to her. Chessman held court.

"How's a single doctor doing in the social scene these days?" asked Harvey.

"Not bad. Not good." Jill didn't know what to answer. She didn't care what she said to Harvey.

"You go with that cop, don't you?" asked Lou, pretending to be involved.

"He's a detective," added Don to be protective.

"Yes. I find detectives have a better sense at probing than ordinary policemen," said Jill, hoping to strike the first lewd chord, and perhaps put an end to the subject. She spent years in "boys-will-be-boys" environments.

"Ha. Ha. That's great. I didn't know you were funny," laughed Chessman. "Did I ever tell you the one about what happened when Dolly Parton and Princess Di are competing to get into heaven?"

"Princess Di is already there," Lou cautioned. Chessman had been telling the joke for years.

Don cringed as Chessman told the joke anyway. Jill placated Chessman's need to drag it out.

"Dolly sticks out her tits and says 'This is why I should get to heaven', which certainly seemed like good credentials. Princess Di holds up her hand and says, 'Hey wait a minute. I've just taken a shower, including a douche' which was her explanation as why she should go ahead of Dolly to get into heaven. Well, God thinks for a moment and signals Di to go ahead."

"I don't get it," said Jill, accidentally playing the straight man for Chessman. Aside from offensive, she thought the joke was plain dumb.

"A royal flush beats two of a kind anytime." Chessman let out one of his nasal chortles.

Harvey actually thought the joke was funny.

Don gave his obligatory smile.

Jill chuckled to herself thinking, "My god. You are really pathetic, now aren't you?"

During the meal, Don and Jill looked over at each other wondering how they were going to get the sample. They previously discussed the way Jill originally imagined, but decided that it would be too clumsy. They thought they might get a large-enough sample from Chessman's lunch napkin. Plenty of cells would get trapped in the fabric. All they'd have to do was steal the napkin after everybody left. There were also other possibilities like the fork or his drink glass.

Chessman began fingering his toothpick, the one that held his onions. He started to massage his gums with the toothpick. He placed the toothpick between his teeth and twirled it around.

Dysplasia

Jill smiled at Don. They had the cells.

As they left the table, Jill fumbled with her purse, giving her the extra few seconds at the table. When everyone had his back to her, Jill picked up the dry end of the toothpick. Once outside the dining area, she slipped it into a little tube in her purse. She would give the tube to Dick, and Dick would see to it that the DNA test was performed.

At one of the last meetings before the hospital report was going to be submitted, Chessman finally agreed to leave out some of the changes he had put into Don's paper. Don was surprised, but could only think that Chessman showed the work to someone else he respected, and that person told Chessman the changes didn't belong. That's how Chessman operated.

Everything seemed to go okay after that last meeting, and it appeared that Don was going to present the information at the hospital. Don was very proud that he completed the research. He felt gratified that he was finally doing something for the welfare patients. Besides, his recommendations would help the overall care in the hospital, too.

CHAPTER TWENTY-NINE

It was two weeks away from the summer office party and the place would be packed. It was one of those pre-Hampton kick-off parties. The Chessman office never had one before. After the summer got into full swing, very few parties were held in the city. Beitleman had no plans for that week in early June, except his seasonally early trip to his house in the Pines on Fire Island where, as he put it, "I don't have to talk straight for one fucking second. It's a real pleasure."

The party was going to be a huge bash. They expected a larger turnout than the Christmas party.

Don arrived early that Monday to go over the plans. Harvey was munching on a bagel while Lou was fiddling with his wig. Chessman sat at his desk looking over the party memo as Lou read from his copy. It sounded like Joan Chessman had vetoed all of Harvey's ideas. Plus the last two quarters were the most money the office ever made. Harvey was stymied.

"We have the appetizer period from the new caterer. That will run from noon until four for the people who can't make a night deal. The caterer from the Pierre Hotel will set up twelve little sit-down tables throughout the office, four at a table. They measured the lab tables and think they can do their entire hot-and-cold dinner service out of the lab. They do a summer theme with all of the crap the goyum do for

Dysplasia

summer. Beach balls, you know, Beach Blanket Bingo stuff. Of course the band and—." Harvey cut him off.

"Can't we cut the jazz guys down to three? We only need a bass, sax, and drummer," pleaded Harvey.

"I want all the players and that's that," said Chessman.

"I don't even want the damn party. We had a Christmas party. Why do we have to do this?" pleaded Harvey.

"You won't take your wife out for a good dinner. Jesus, Harvey. You can't even knock her up. The least you could do is buy her a meal other than pizza or deli," said Chessman, meaning to hurt Harvey's feelings, the easiest way to shut him up.

Harvey's face flushed. He jumped to his feet.

"Harvey. We all know your sperm count wasn't the problem," Lou volunteered as if that would make Harvey feel better. Nothing would. The office was spending money and this was against every principle he had.

"Yeah, but they didn't say anything about the size of his dick," added Don, who looked over at Chessman to get his approval. Don cared little about Harvey's feelings, not after how he broke the news about Larry Bosler.

Chessman roared. He picked up the memo from the top of his desk. "Come on. Next year everyone will copy us and then I'll have to invent something else for the lemmings to copy. Fifteen grand tops. And that includes the air tickets for those bastards from The University of Philadelphia who want to change the way we practice. We'll feed them, get them drunk, make them our friends, and send them back home to sit in front of the computers and rewrite their point of view so it matches ours."

Harvey wouldn't give up. "Fifteen thousand dollars is a ridiculous amount of money to spend for one night for a party. We're not in the entertainment business, you know."

Chessman had enough of Harvey. "Harvey, that's where you're wrong. We are in the entertainment business and I'm the CEO of this fucking business. Look, if you don't want the party don't come, but the office is paying for it."

Harvey turned in order to throw his bagel up against the wall. It ricocheted off the wall and barely missed Chessman's head. Harvey marched out of the office like an angry boy on the verge of tears.

"I wish he didn't work so hard, because I'd love to throw him the hell out of this office. The asshole couldn't produce a referral standing in a village of pregnant Chinese women," said Chessman.

Don and Lou got the larger message, loud and clear. There was going to be a huge presummer bash.

Chapter Thirty

Don called Kronen. He decided it was time to get his take on the situation with Chessman. Don also needed to review what was going on with his divorce. He mentioned his last conversation with Susan and the meeting with Jill. Don didn't think Kronen was paying much attention.

The day before the party, Don met Kronen at the restaurant on Katherine Street in Chinatown. Kronen sat alone in one of the booths drinking a beer. A second bottle was near at hand.

As Don walked down the steps, he heard Kronen yell, "An occidental. This must be an occident."

"Kronen. Where's your bride?" said Don as he took his seat in the booth.

"She's taking some course about mysticism and the woman of the new millennium. You should see the group. Some angry faces. Looks like a dyke-of-the-month party."

"You're cruel."

"Realistic." Kronen paused and picked up a bottle of beer. "Here. Have one of these Chink Town beers. You don't look so good."

"That's Tsing-Tao." Don gulped from the bottle.

A waiter brought over a large platter of food. "Ah, mis seafood and pah fry noodle," he said as he delivered the tray.

"I figured you wanted to dig in as soon as you got here."

"Thanks, Kronen. You're more considerate than Linda."

Kronen let the remark pass. Under his gruff demeanor was a level of civil sensitivity. He wasn't going to start in on Don about his marriage, at least until Don had something to eat first.

They took their portions from the center plate as more dishes arrived.

"Bean cur an musroom, sal an peppa squid, mis fry rice, an chicken and brockley."

"Thank you," said Kronen.

Waiting until the waiter was out of earshot, "Now take your ugly, broken-down, stained teeth to the other side of the room so I can eat. What is with these people? Don't they believe in dentistry?"

"They do, Kronen, but not like Americans," said Don.

"Gosh. You are so fucking smart. It's unbelievable how you knew that off the top of your head. Here. Have some more noodles."

"You ordered too much," said Don, holding up his hand to signal "stop."

"Yes, I did. Now how is your considerate wife Linda?"

"Still at her mother's."

"I never got any papers. I spoke to her attorney twice."

"How long does something like this take?" asked Don.

"Maybe she's reconsidering," said Kronen. "There is no special time frame."

"She thinks I'm a complete asshole, doesn't she?"

Kronen smiled, as if to say, "Isn't that correct?" "Let's not draw any conclusions until we see it in writing."

Don changed his mind and nervously scooped up a pile of noodles, dropping it sloppily on his plate. He continued to talk while he ate, although he really wasn't hungry.

Dysplasia

"I know. I know. But she thinks I'm a fool for going ahead with this hospital thing. She's wrong. Everyone understands what it is. Even Chessman has come around."

"The murderer likes it?" asked Kronen.

"Don't say that so loud," said Don, looking around.

"What? You think these people give a fuck what some great white doctor from Fifth Avenue does? They have values, a little peculiar and a little different than ours, but they have them. They like to keep murder in the family, you know, in the neighborhood."

"Tomorrow is our first summer party." Don conveniently changed the subject. He knew Kronen would make fun of him if he told him anything more about Chessman.

"No chance. Count me out."

"There'll be a lot of food."

"You're like some of the famous attorneys I write books for. They start thinking that they have a brain, that they are in fact persuasive, and that they can influence people. But you know what?"

"What?" Don was laughing, causing him to choke on his food.

"They don't have a brain, they have a tiny little mouse that runs around in a circle to produce a single current of electricity that gives their alcoholic faces a bright red glow so when they go on Oprah or Geraldo or that bald black guy's show—what's his name?"

"Montel Williams."

"Yeah. 'Monte' Williams. When they're on television and saying, 'Yeah, I remember the one juror in that case, a petite woman who said she believed in God but not Satan' spouting words of no meaning, a bullshiter's bullshit chopped up and spit out by me in print, me, the voice behind the genius attorney writers, at that one moment their face lights up and the camera gets a good shot, because that's all the fuck there is left of them, a snapshot of a bullshitter spouting his macerated bullshit out into nothingness. That's all they've got, except what their

God-given genetic make-up gave them, hoping they would at least look good behind the trail of shit that just left their mouths."

"You don't like the guys you write for, do you?" asked Don.

This made Kronen laugh at himself, with a positively childlike charm. "One word of advice on your hospital deal. I've seen plenty of whistle blowers end up with their balls inside the lotto machine, you know, the one with the ping pong balls."

"I'm not a whistle blower. I'm a hired consultant."

"Don't take the money." Kronen was referring to a stipend that went with the work.

"Why not?"

"Because a whole lot of shit is involved if they pay you. Do it as a volunteer. I'm sure it's only peanuts anyway."

Kronen was right. The lowest bid was some ridiculous figure. After Don asked Rollins' secretary for the amount, he found out he was only going to get a percentage. The low bid was for a team."

"What about my expenses?" asked Don. "Can I ask for those?"

"What, like the computer time? Forget it," said Kronen.

"Forget it," Don repeated.

"My best advice is do it for free. Okay?"

"Okay, but I don't see why?"

"Don, my boy, you are still as naïve as the day I took you over to Ellen Green's house to go bubble bathing. These guys at the hospital are not looking to spend any money unless it's to their benefit. No matter what they tell you, I'm telling you not to take the money. Did you sign a contract?"

"Yes. Well, no. It's been on my desk. I never signed it."

"Why didn't you tell me they gave you a contract? Now I'm convinced. You don't sign it and you don't take a nickel. Got it?"

"Got it."

Dysplasia

"I don't want to see you get hurt."

"Don't worry about me."

"Didn't Custer say that?"

"Eat your bean cur and fry rice."

"Eat this!"

"In your dreams."

They were the last customers to leave that night. They walked out to the cheery goodbyes of the workers.

"You cum ba soon. Tank you berry mus. Tank you berry mus."

At the top of the stairs, Kronen broke into a full run. Don smiled and took off after him, zigzagging around the puddles on the narrow Chinatown street. This was something they hadn't done for years. They would run to the Chinatown arcade and play pinball, and in later years, Atari Pong and Space Invaders. That stopped about the time Nintendo started. It was the place that had the famous abused chicken that played tic-tac-toe. Every year some local station would do a story about chicken abuse. It detracted from the gang-style murders that took place in Chinatown.

They would play the new games that night since Don wasn't on call and didn't have a wife to go home to. Carrie never gave Kronen a curfew. Her verbal threats kept him in line. She never worried about any extracurricular interests.

"Why should I worry when he's out with you, Don?" she would ask, intending to show that Kronen was "safe" as long he was with Don. "If he wants to get laid, he doesn't have to pretend to be having dinner with you. He can get laid whenever he wants, but then he could also be dead soon thereafter."

As they played one of the newer Mario games, Don thought of what Susan told Don about Chessman and whether he should confide in Kronen. Don decided to tell him everything, including what she said recently about Chessman being a bocor. Then Don explained about the slides, the kinky episode in Chessman's bedroom. Everything Don could think of to support his idea that Chessman was involved in the murders.

Kronen didn't make any judgments. He listened carefully. When he absorbed the information, he became dead serious. It wasn't what Don expected from Kronen. The information struck Kronen. "Don. Make sure you have all my telephone numbers with you at all times," said Kronen.

"Okay," said Don.

"Do you have my cell phone?" he asked.

"Yes. I think so," said Don.

"Don't think so. Here's a card with all my numbers. Add this new one." Kronen told Don the number. He wrote it on the card. "There is also a pager."

Kronen didn't have to say much. He knew there was a problem. His instincts told him that it wasn't something that was going to go away by itself. He could see how it was eating at Don, that Don knew, too, but couldn't put it all together so that it made sense.

CHAPTER THIRTY-ONE

The summer party was in full swing. There wasn't anything particularly remarkable about it except for the fact that a young group of college students from Columbia was invited, probably by one of the doctors on staff at the school.

The students were all questions about getting into medical school and cornered doctors anywhere they could find them. The rest were about money and private practice. "Aren't we just as well off day trading technology stocks?" For some the answer was "yes."

Chessman was talking to a beautiful young black woman. This surprised no one in the room. When Don arrived and saw Chessman doing his act, he had to leave the area, paying little attention to Chessman's antics, a sight that now revolted Don.

Chessman started drinking heavily. He was on automatic pilot. He introduced the young woman to his cronies. She seemed to like the attention, having one of the hosts show her around personally. It was rather harmless.

Don was worried about his upcoming meeting at the hospital. It was scheduled for the following Monday. The hospital officials would decide on his recommendations. He was getting mixed comments from people who had read it. He was to make an oral presentation, and then comments would follow.

Don went right to the bar and had a double shot of Macallan. Little did anyone know that Don was no longer a scotch snob. At least at his office party he could pretend.

He felt a hand on his shoulder. "Junior."

Don turned around. "What's up, Hank?" asked Don, hoping that the interaction would be brief.

"I've read over your final report. It's good. Damned good. You know, I was leaking out bits and pieces as we went along—"

"You did?" Don was shocked. Then he told himself, "Of course."

"Junior. It's good. The boys like it. I've taken the liberty of taking my name off the report."

"You don't want your name on the paper anymore?" Don couldn't believe it.

"It's not what I want. It's what's right. You did the work. It's your deal."

Don downed his drink. This was a strange twist. Could it be possible that Chessman's friends told him to butt out, that Don did a good job and Chessman had no right to take credit?

"Okay. Thanks," said Don.

Chessman smiled and walked back to the pretty young black woman.

Don was on call at the hospital later that night. He wasn't enjoying the party so he decided to drive uptown earlier and amuse himself by talking with Arnie Baer. Arnie could tell him the cost of new equipment and which regional suppliers were running good deals. Arnie was an expert about that kind of small talk. It was another way he could ingratiate himself with the house staff.

Don slipped out of the party and walked around the block. He knew he had crossed Chessman by including in the report what Chessman was against it, even after Chessman tried to accommodate some of the material. Don rewrote seven of the pages before handing in the final copy. Don left the pages the same way he wrote them originally. He didn't care. He knew his relationship with Chessman was winding down. Don figured he only had a few months to half a year left at best. Chessman was playing it cool, so cool it was beginning to upset Don.

As he drove uptown, he realized that he was losing a grip on his life. He was separated from his wife, trying unsuccessfully to link his own partner to a murder, and becoming a career alcoholic. He would get past the hospital meeting and then have a face-to-face talk with Chessman. He would leave the practice. Anyone would tell him he should make his new plans first and then tell Chessman. Don would start over. He thought about Jill and how he would take the step that could make them lovers.

"Forget it, Don. Forget it," he said out loud as he drove aimlessly uptown, almost running a red light at Madison and 96th.

He thought of the Ideal Restaurant, the coffee shop-style German restaurant that had closed a few years back. Don's father took him there when he was a little boy. Every time he drove through the German section of the city (Yorkville) he could smell the red cabbage.

Don told himself the joke about the man who came into a bar and said, "Let me have a shot of scotch and a shot of scotch."

"You mean you want a double shot of scotch," answered the bartender.

"No. I want two separate shots of scotch," replied the man, eager to have his drinks in the fashion he ordered them.

The man paid his tab and repeated the same behavior every week, once a week, for several months. Finally, the bartender got up the nerve to ask, "Why do you have your shots in two glasses?"

"I was in the war in Bosnia and watched my buddy leave us. His last words were 'Will ya have one, once a week for me, and once a week for you', and so I have done just that, just what my buddy asked, every week since then."

The bartender was clearly moved by the story. "Here, have one and one on the house. I'm sorry to have asked."

"It's no problem."

That went on for some time until the man came in and ordered, "a shot of scotch."

He needed a shave and his clothes were disheveled.

"You mean a shot of scotch and a shot of scotch," said the bartender.

"No. I mean one shot of scotch," the man said with great remorse. "I stopped drinking."

CHAPTER THIRTY-TWO

Up in the shadowy confines of the condominium, Chessman lay over the young black woman. He was well into the ritual of the evening when he saw a steady flow of blood ooze from her vagina.

Mechanically, he reached for his bag by the bed and inserted two cotton swabs soaked with anticoagulants. The bleeding stopped momentarily. Chessman got a new slide sample ready. He turned his back on the girl and got the biopsy device that scrapped off a sample of skin. In the few brief moments it took to do that, the flow started again. It was now a steady stream of blood. Chessman took a towel and applied pressure.

From inside her anesthetic stupor, the girl said, "What's wrong?"

"Can you hold this?"

Chessman took her hand and pressed it on the towel.

"Steady pressure. That's it."

"Put on this robe. We'll go to my office." Chessman helped her into the robe. She could no longer speak.

What a sight, Chessman supporting the robed woman while waiting for the elevator. Chessman knew that the other apartment on the floor was vacant. He always had management tell him whenever one of the people from the coast was there.

They reached the office without incident. Chessman hurriedly threw on the switches in the office. He was able to maneuver the girl into one of the treatment rooms. After clearing the area with several douches, Chessman did a cursory exam.

"Did you know you were pregnant?"

She was nearly incoherent.

"I am going to help you."

Even in his hallucinatory state, Chessman felt he could easily do an abortion. He had done so many. It would be easy. He wheeled over two tall stainless steel rods with glass bottles and drips. He started an I.V. This would be a snap.

About half-way through the procedure, Chessman no longer had a clear field. He stepped back from the scene. Blood covered the floor. The gown he had draped the girl in was soaked. His own arms were bloodied past the glove line, soaking red into the bright blues and greens of his Turnbull and Asser shirt.

He had hit an artery. Why? There was no artery there. He knew she would die if he waited.

With one hand well inside her body cavity, he applied pressure. With his free hand, he pushed the speakerphone and punched in a number on the wall phone.

Around midnight a nurse walked into a small room off the main hallway. She shook a sleepy Arnie Baer. "Dr. Baer. Dr. Baer." There was panic in her voice.

"Huh? Yeah. What?"

Dysplasia

"Dr. Beitleman is on the telephone for Dr. Gardner. Have you seen Dr. Gardner?"

"He went to the cafeteria to get a coffee."

"Tell him when he comes back to call Dr. Beitleman. I have the number at the desk. He's sending a patient over right now. And he wants to speak to Dr. Gardner."

"Okay. Okay. I got it. What do you think I am, some kind of moron?"

That was precisely what the nurse thought of Arnie. She knew if she didn't tell him something two or three times, he would disregard what she said. She couldn't make up her mind if it was because she was nurse, a woman, or black. At this point in time it didn't matter. She knew his type from years of service at the hospital.

Don's face was maudlin as he walked out of the operating room. He pulled off his bloodied scrubs, went into the dressing area and right to the telephone. He dialed Stu's service.

"Put me through to his home. This is an emergency."

Stu was still awake when Don called. Stu stood outside on the long deck that faced the ocean. He was wearing his summer khakis and a blue V-necked cotton sweater. Inside, three young men were sitting at a bridge table waiting for Stu to come back inside to finish the game.

He answered the remote phone. "Don, how did it go?" Stu asked

"It didn't."

"What? I didn't hear you?" Stu got off his remote phone and picked up a receiver on a regular telephone located outside the screen door.

Don spoke. "She died. She lost a ton of blood before she got here."

Stu's response was immediate. "Just write it up that she was almost dead when you started."

"Stu. It won't be that easy."

"What are you talking about?"

"Damn it, Stu. Someone tried to do an abortion on this girl. I have to put that in the chart."

"No you don't. You simply don't have to do that."

"Who did it?" Don knew it couldn't have been Stu.

"How the fuck should I know? Maybe her boyfriend tried to do it with a coat hanger. Maybe she tried to do it herself."

"Stu. Stop fucking with me. This girl was treated surgically and I want to know by whom."

"Calm down. Look, she's a black girl from who knows where."

"She has I.D. from Columbia University."

Don found Stu's response bizarre. "So what? She's nobody. Just another person in trouble. Write up the report that she arrived in the state she did, and that's all you know. Refer to the internal intervention as a nonmedical source."

It was late at night and Don was physically and emotionally exhausted. Death was not something Don ever got over. He didn't know how some of the other guys did it, but each patient he had ever lost still haunted him in the middle of the night, his pupils fixed on the ceiling, nights where he chastised himself for not doing a little better.

Don caved in. "Okay. I'll say what you said. It's hard for me to do."

"Don, you'll have to trust me. You're doing the right thing. I'm sure whoever tried to do this was trying to help her."

"Stu, her vaginal cavity was abused." Don wasn't thinking. Perhaps she went for an abortion by someone who wasn't qualified. It happened.

"Give it a rest. That's my point. This was not a professional job. Write it up. Go home. And go to sleep. I'll take care of the ambulance guys. They'll say they picked her up outside the dorm. I already spoke to the resident Arnie Baer. He'll back up whatever you write. The Filipino nurses don't know from anything. If they ask them, they'll just read off the chart."

Dysplasia

Of course, kiss ass-show-me-how-to-get-to-the-top Arnie Baer would be ready to help. That was the kind of stuff he always wanted to learn, "the bread and butter," which in this case included one of the most important aspects of medical practice, the ability to cover an ass when called upon in the right circumstances. A favor for Stu Beitleman? Those were the right circumstances for Arnie Baer.

Don was dizzy. He knew what he was doing was wrong, but he didn't want any trouble. He thought about his insurance, how in less than one year he had two malpractice claims. He was confused and had to trust that Stu knew what he was doing, that everything would be okay. Monday afternoon was Don's presentation at the hospital. He had to get some rest. It was already Sunday morning.

Early Sunday morning Congressman Jones sat on a dais between former Governor Mario Cuomo and the Reverend Jesse Jackson. They were attending a breakfast fund-raiser for the party.

An aide whispered into the Congressman's ear.

"Who did you say called?" the Congressman asked.

The aide spoke out loud. "A Dr. Childs from Morningside Hospital."

Congressman Jones wiped his lips with a white linen napkin. He excused himself to return the phone call.

The outside of the Regency Hotel was filled with double-parked limos and Lincoln Sedans with drivers.

Chessman got out of his limo. He was dressed in black tie, an outfit that included a ruby-and-diamond broach in the image of a frog. He walked briskly into the hotel and headed for a reception room.

Chessman would mingle with the fifty or so couples that had anted up some extra bucks to have the privilege of a private cocktail hour. This was a party for Technion, the Israeli equivalent of MIT. Twenty or so hot-shots from Beverly Hills attended the party with the Governor and the Mayor. Chessman knew the crowd well and worked the room in his most deliberate party mode. His mind was preoccupied and he was a little shaky until he downed his first onion martini. After that, he retired to a corner of a room where he could hold court intimidating older men worried about their health by implying that the medical care they were getting was less than perfect.

Suddenly, Chessman checked his wristwatch. He excused himself, working his way out of the small group. "See you in a bit," he said to the group of overly health-conscious executives.

"Hi, how are you?" to the new editor of *The New Yorker.*
"How's the sailing?" to a retired newscaster.
Chessman remarked his way out of the room. Once outside, he went to the nearest telephone, dialed and spoke quietly.
"It's me, Hank. Right. Under no circumstances is he to keep any of his hospital privileges. Is that clear? You also might mention that you will have his overage malpractice insurance at the hospital terminated since this is the third incident this year. His carrier is considering canceling his office insurance as well. Yes. Very sad. I'll be on sabbatical."
Chessman hung up. He walked briskly out of the lobby and into a waiting limousine. The chauffeur held the door for Chessman until he was inside the limo.
"I picked up your bags earlier. Dr. Benjamin told me to tell you that all the other parcels were sent Federal Express."
"Very good. Let's get going."
The chauffeur slammed the door shut and walked around to the driver's side of the limo.
In the back seat was a change of clothes. Chessman removed his tuxedo before the limo pulled out into traffic. As he changed, he

shouted to the driver who was slowly putting up the privacy window. "I have to stop at the hospital before we get going."

Don sat motionless as Dr. Childs read from a printed report. "On top of that, we have done our own brief investigation of what happened here Saturday night. We have found you negligent in the care of this woman. A formal autopsy is being ordered. In the meantime, we had an obligation to notify the police as well as our malpractice insurance carrier. Since the time we discovered who the girl was, we were inundated with calls. We even had a call from President Clinton offering his help with the investigation."

Did Don hear that correctly? "What is going on here?" Don thought he was showing up for the meeting to give his presentation. Did Childs say Clinton?

Dr. Childs wasn't through. "Dr. Gardner, you are hereby relieved of your position in the hospital. We ask that you wait in the cafeteria until we can provide an armed escort to take you out of the building."

"An armed escort. Why?" Don was trembling.

"We're afraid the media has gotten hold of this. We tried to keep this quiet, but the girl was from a well-known family."

Don didn't think. He got up. He didn't hear anything else. Dr. Childs handed Don a letter, reiterating everything he had said, signed with a happy face alongside the signature.

Don would never remember how he got to the cafeteria. When he entered it he saw a dozen or so members of the house staff crowded around the television. The local newscaster was telling the story of Ms. Laurel Carver, a black female student from Columbia University. She lost her life at Morningside Hospital over the weekend. At the urging of local politicians, hospital authorities have conducted an investigation and concluded that she may have been the victim of shoddy medical care.

Don stood behind the other doctors, numb.

The newscaster pointed out that Ms. Carver was president of the campus chapter of the National Black Premedical Students Association. Her father was an active member of the Washington beltway. He once worked as an aide to Colonel Colin Powell.

When Don heard the last part, he realized how this happened almost overnight. If this were another of the noninsurance patients, nothing would have been done. This was an important member of the community. Someone who mattered. Someone who had connections. Someone whose family could demand retribution. Don was set up to take the fall for the death of Laurel Carver. He was now a victim of the same system he was trying to correct.

When the doctors realized that Don was in the room, they awkwardly dispersed, pretending not to see him. One of the doctors turned the television station to CNN, the station that played most of the day. This story was not yet big enough for CNN. CNN was showing the trouble in South Africa.

Three residents from OB-GYN lingered for a few moments, not knowing what to say. Arnie Baer was nowhere. He had taken the day off.

Steve tried to console Don. "Don, it will blow over. Don't worry."

Miles came over to pull Steve away.

Joe walked over with a cup of coffee and handed it to Don.

"Thanks," said Don.

"You're welcome." Joe knew better than to continue the conversation.

Don didn't recall anything that happened in the cafeteria from the time that he walked in until Joe left.

CHAPTER THIRTY-THREE

JUNE, 2000

The elevator ride was one Don had taken thousands of times. He tried for a moment to calculate the exact number of rides, but this proved no easy task with his hands trembling and his mind racing. How had this happened to him? He was a great white doctor. How could he have been so stupid to think he could win over Chessman? He was blindly trying to dig up dirt on Chessman. He realized Chessman was waiting for the right moment to screw up Don's life. He should have seen it coming. The malpractice cases, the false camaraderie. Taking his name off the paper. Chessman had to know what was going on. Don's privileges could not have been taken away without Chessman knowing. Don tried not to blame himself, but he had no one else to blame. At that moment, something deep within Don's soul began to stir that rallied every drop of serotonin in his body to spill forth with an energy surge he had never experienced before. He was not going to let this happen.

Don thought back to when he first entered the meeting room on Monday. He was immediately informed that this was a review to evaluate his performance as a doctor. The heads of three departments stood in judgment, the same men who gave him the go ahead on his project. An independent surgeon was brought in from another hospital, St. Luke's-Roosevelt. Don was told they reviewed his record and his mortality rate was higher than average. They neglected to mention he did more of the non-insurance cases than any other doctor on staff. They also found his handling of the emergency case on the weekend below the standard of care set up by the hospital guidelines. He was being convicted right before his very eyes. Everyone in the room knew this was going to happen. Everyone there had conspired to let Don be the scapegoat.

The elevator shook as it stabilized after hitting the ground floor. Officer Brown opened the old-fashioned mechanical doors and was overwhelmed by a series of flashes accompanied by that annoying whining noise of dozens of cameras advancing at once. Officer Brown jumped between the onslaught of reporters and Don.

"Get out of this man's way." He was firm and his size acted as a mild deterrent as he moved forward with his arm latched firmly to Don's. "Get out the way." Two private security guards on the ground floor took positions in front of and behind Don and Officer Brown. They made a wedge that advanced down the hall and out the side entrance where Don had looked earlier, wondering how he was going to get to his car.

As Don moved out the front door, he forced himself to glance back over his shoulder. What if this was his last time he would ever see the massive concrete archway with the Hippocratic oath engraved over the entrance? The quick glance and self-pity lasted only a fraction of a second. It was quickly interrupted by the shouts of the crowd.

"Gardner is a murderer."

"Baby butcher."

Maybe he would be killed like the doctor at the Planned Parenthood Center.

Dysplasia

The guards picked up the pace and held Don under each arm. He hardly felt his feet touch the ground. The NYC Police already cleared a path. When Don reached the sidewalk, the whole procession slowed down.

"Why are we stopping? What's going on?" Don should have known that even the police cooperated with the media. "Damn," he thought. "I should have called Kronen." Perhaps with an attorney Don would have been treated differently. It was too late.

Before anyone could answer, a microphone was thrust right under Don's nose. "Dr. Gardner. Were you surprised by the decision of the committee?"

Surprised? What an understatement. What would they know about surprise, Don thought.

Don didn't know what to say. He shook his head and tried to move away from the reporters. The security guards held their ground. They weren't instructed to escort Don further than the hospital property.

Officer Brown was already making a statement to a newspaper reporter eagerly taking notes. "Dr. Gardner said he didn't kill that lady and her baby." Ted Koppel could not have done better.

"Do you believe him," the reporter asked, giving his answer the credibility of an expert witness. In today's world of millisecond media, all opinions carry equal weight, and get equal time with the actual experts. Later that week, Officer Brown would talk on the Howard Stern radio show and Hard Ball on MSNBC plus shows with Dr. Childs, an "expert" physician from upstate New York who acted more like a farmer (the producers searched high and low for that expert), and the sister of the deceased, Doreen Carver, who worked in the office of Mike Raptor, a well-known black leader who knew how to position himself in the thick of racial controversy. Mr. Raptor's office managed to have him call in live on every show that covered the story.

Don began a hasty walk to his car. He held up his hand as he passed reporters. He told himself he was a coward. "You just stood there. Coward. You know it wasn't your fault. You have to get to Chessman. He always has answers. What could you do, stand up and yell that you didn't do it?"

Just as Don turned back to look at the crowd, he felt a sharp sting above his eye, like a local anesthetic. A dull, larger pain accompanied the sharp, localized pain almost simultaneously. Don's hand reflexively went to protect the spot on his forehead as the rock left its target and hit the ground. Don brought his hand down to see the bright red mosaic his own blood had painted on the lines of his hands.

"Shit."

"You okay, Doc?" a NYC policeman asked him. "Do you want the paramedics?"

"No. Just get me to my car. Get me to my car."

The policeman said nothing and led the way across the street to the parking lot, where the crowds were well out of reach. Don looked to the hospital windows where the upper floors were lined with doctors, nurses, janitorial staff, and anyone else who could get their face up against one of the small-framed old-fashioned square panes of glass. Don could see the committee room. Childs and two of the doctors, John Safer and Alan Reynolds. What? He thought he spotted a familiar face in the crowd. Chessman?

Don felt his own blood pressure rise, as he was sure the SA node was firing extra jolts at his heart. The epinephrine poured out of every cell causing his body to ready itself for every adrenaline-producing animal's fight-or-flight response. Don stopped berating himself and reminded himself he was going to fight. But he first had to accomplish the simple task of driving away from the hospital.

Two police vehicles blocked the road so Don would eventually be able to drive out safely. Don sat in his car, sandwiched in the parking lot, waiting for the one parking attendant to move the cars that were parked ahead of his. Maybe if Don stopped hating himself so much he could pull his way out of the abyss. He honked his horn. It seemed like it was taking forever.

Don reviewed Childs' words on the papers beside him. "The plaintiff showed failure of clinical judgment that led to errors in selection for surgery and therefore in how the surgical procedure was performed." Childs was already acting as if these were legal interrogatories by the malpractice insurance carrier investigating a lawsuit. "Plaintiff's inter-personal difficulties were becoming significant and problematic. We want to make it clear to all parties present at this meeting and to all authorities responsible for receiving this information under the health codes of the State of New York that this summary suspension is in no way related to his proposed criticism of hospital policy. We make no dispute with Dr. Gardner that until this year he was without criticism from the hospital and he has never had a malpractice claim. Let the record also show that there has been a marked increase in claims made against Dr. Gardner in private practice."

The police escort led Don's vehicle into Central Park at its most northern entrance, very close to the area where the heinous rape and beating of a female jogger took place. Don thought how he used to jog the big loop around the park, occasionally running in a 10K corporate-sponsored race. He thought about the woman who was brutalized. He pictured the scene in his mind, how she was dragged into the bushes and pummeled with a lead pipe. His mind switched quickly to running his fastest time in a 10K, averaging less than seven-minute miles, only to be dragged off the course in the middle of the race and beaten by the same marauding vandals, this time led by their leader Chessman. As the vandals held Don on the ground, Chessman walked over and delivered a brief speech.

"Did you ever think you could fuck with Hank Chessman?" Chessman slapped Don's face hard. "Scalpel," demanded Chessman. A scalpel was slapped into Chessman's hand causing him to smile as he moved the scalpel lower on Don's anatomy. "Action," said Chessman.

One of the vandals had a video camera in hand.

That's it. It had to have been Chessman. That's why Chessman wasn't at the meeting. He turned it all around so that Don would take the fall. Don would disappear from the practice. Chessman could buy his share for a song. The hospital would dump his report in the garbage and everyone would live happily ever after without Don. Don thought about the girl that died, and knew that could not have been planned by anyone. Whoever worked on her, and Don was making the argument that it was Chessman, made an error in the surgery. It was possible not to spot an arteriole anomaly, something that was different, out of its usual place, or sometimes an extra. If the practitioner was sloppy to begin with, he might not be able to stop the bleeding. That's what must have happened and Chessman used the girl's death to set up Don. Lucky for Chessman. Unlucky for Don. Most unlucky for the young woman. That's how Don thought Chessman viewed the whole situation.

Don envisioned the whole scenario. It made sense. Chessman drugged her and got her into the bedroom, like the night Don was there. Chessman didn't know she was pregnant. He caused her to bleed so profusely that he panicked and brought her down to the office. When he realized she was pregnant, he tried to perform an abortion, a D & C.

Dysplasia

ဏ

Of course, with his ego he thought nothing of on-the-spot medical heroics.

The office tape. It ran automatically. Could Chessman have had the foresight to shut off the camera in the treatment room? Maybe Don's life was ruined. God. That Chessman was smart. He knew how to turn every situation into a positive one. He was insane.

Don looked into his rear view mirror and saw the last police car disappear at the 72nd street exit. The police car ahead of him waved for Don to go ahead when they reached the reservoir twenty blocks back. Don was on his own and had been provided police protection for about twenty minutes, the time it took for him to get back into an area of the city where Don was just another faceless person in the crowd. Don looped around Central Park South and exited before the turn uptown on the Eastside and headed north. He headed straight for his office building.

His head was pounding. He could feel that the wound was superficial and the blood had clotted. A rock to the head was not going to stop him. He pushed the night buzzer. He heard Pierre say, "Hey, Doc" over the buzzer that released the lock, letting Don into the building. He went directly to the elevator, got in and pushed his floor.

When he got off on his floor he looked squarely into the overhead camera and half waved to acknowledge that all was well. He turned to the right and then abruptly dropped to his knees. He came up with his back to the wall on the other side of the hall, the same side as the camera. No one could see him now. He moved slowly along the wall under the camera. Then he walked in the opposite direction to the fire doors leading to the stairs. Don entered the stairwell and began a climb to the residential section of the building. He had a second idea. He was heading for Chessman's bedroom. He was going to get the tapes that the perverted Chessman kept on hand. It would be a beginning. Perhaps he would find a tape of the deceased girl with Chessman. As he climbed the stairs he realized it all may be for nothing. Chessman was too smart.

Don used his key to get into the apartment. He made a quick right turn to enter the kitchen. He opened a drawer filled with supplies and pulled out a hammer and screwdriver. No locked door was going to stop him. As he hurried from the kitchen, he planned his method of entry. Whack the screwdriver in the doorjamb. It would have to be hard and take a few strikes. His second method of entry would be to hammer out the lock itself, or try to remove the entire doorknob.

He froze for a second in the hall outside the bedroom. The door was wide open. He flicked his hand across an adjacent wall and stared as the bedroom entry was illuminated. He moved inside slowly. The microscope was gone. The slide box was gone. The nitrous oxide tank was gone. He rummaged through the bedside table drawers. Playing cards. A flashlight. A Bible. Someone went overboard in sanitizing the place. He told himself it was what he should have expected.

Don was more convinced now that Chessman was the killer. Don had to first clear himself. But how? Don stood in the center of the bedroom and looked up at the flat movie screen on the far wall.

The office. Of course. Don's mind was working slowly. He had originally come to check the office tapes. In an emergency, even Chessman would have the sense to turn off the tape but Don wasn't even sure Chessman knew how to do it. It ran all the time when the surgery equipment was activated. Don would give the tape to Jill, who would get it into the proper police hands. After coming up empty in the apartment, he wasn't sure of anything. He kept telling himself that he had to fight back. He had to turn the tables on Chessman. He picked up the telephone in the living room and nervously punched in the numbers.

The voice was cut off as soon as it was barely discernible. Don blurted out his words quickly. "Jill. It's Don. The hospital took away my

Dysplasia

privileges. They reversed the whole thing. I was covering for Chessman and he used it against me."

"What are you talking about?"

"Chessman injured that girl that night."

"How do you know?" It was hard to stay on Don's side.

"I have no direct proof, but I know she had medical care before Stu called me to see her. I knew I was covering for someone. I'm sure now that it was Chessman."

"What medical care? Where are you?"

"She had injury to the genital tract. The cervix was lacerated and so was the vagina. There was a hematoma in the paravaginal and retroperitoneal space."

"Why did she die?"

"Someone began an abortion and hit a rare arteriole anomaly."

"And you tried to do a transcatheter arterial embolization with those sponge things. Like after trauma from birth?"

"Yeah. The gelatin sponge particles. I was too late. She had almost bled to death by the time Stu had her sent to me in the ambulance. If Chessman did this, there may be a tape of part of it in the office."

"Be careful." She believed him. It made sense.

"I will. In case anything happens to me, I wanted someone else to know that Stu Beitleman made the call for the girl and he knows where the patient came from. Maybe your friend Dick can trace the ambulance to Stu."

"I'll try."

"Thanks. I'm going to check the office tapes. Maybe it took place there. I don't know anything anymore. I'm going to get that bastard."

"Don't you think he'd destroy it?"

"I don't know. I've got to try. I've got to find him. If I don't, my whole life is ruined."

"Please don't do anything foolish." The tenderness in Jill's voice made Don hesitate and adjust the volume and speed of his own voice.

"Yeah. Okay. Thanks."

"Where should I call you if I find out anything?"

"Leave a message on the machine at home."

"Okay." She paused. "Don?"

"Yes?"

"I'm sorry you're in this mess."

"It's my own fault."

"Stop beating yourself up. You're not one of the bad guys."

"Yeah, okay." He wasn't listening. "I've got to go."

"Bye."

"Bye."

They hung up.

Jill thought for a moment. The circumstances were overwhelming.

Don ran from Chessman's condo, slamming the front door behind him.

When Don entered his office, he went directly to the main computer station near the front desk area. He could check to see if any tape was made the night he treated Laurel at the hospital. His mind was so jumbled that he didn't notice lights were on in the back rooms of the office, which cast a faint glow in the hallway leading to the front desk.

Don nervously punched in his access code, but instead of checking the tape log file he instinctively went to the CompuServe system and entered the travel reservations program that the office used. It was just a hunch.

There were three travel program itineraries available. He checked the first and it was for all four partners to go to Atlanta for a convention next month. He tried the second and it was Joan Chessman booked for a plane, a cruise and a rental car, originating in Paris. She was flying from Paris to the Mediterranean where she was going to cruise the coast in time for the Cannes Film Festival.

Don wanted to see if Chessman was going out of town. That was his style. Whenever he got someone in hot water, he would lay low. Don paused and thought Joan's trip might be a cover for Chessman. Don abandoned the thought as soon as he got access to the third itinerary. It was for Chessman. He had booked flights to New York, California, Hawaii, Haiti, and London. All returns were open and dated that very same day. Chessman had no intention of being around after the meeting at the hospital. That was it. Chessman set him up. Don exited the travel program, and went to the office files. He pulled up the videotape records from the night Stu sent Laurel Carver to Emergency. He scanned the list. He was interrupted by a familiar female voice that spoke to him calmly.

"Don't bother checking the computer log. There was no session recorded the night you're looking for." It was Tina. She was walking towards the front door with a black case that was used to carry videotapes.

"Tina, what the hell are you doing here?"

"Shouldn't I be asking that of you?"

Don looked at the box. "You have the tape, don't you?"

"No."

Tina kept walking towards the front door.

Don felt his pulse hard in his right temple. His heart started pounding as he rose. He jumped on the desk and slid back the glass windows where patients stood to speak to the receptionist. Tina saw him coming and started to run. Don hit the ground behind Tina, she turned and with both hands took the case high in the air. She guided the case to the side of Don's head, right on the area where the rock had hit him earlier that evening.

"Owww!" Don went down easily. He was tired and he wasn't expecting Tina to be so violently aggressive.

"You're in deep shit, Doc. The tapes in here don't belong to you. They are the personal property of Dr. Chessman."

"Tina, he's covering up. He's a murderer." Don tried to get to his feet, but fell backwards against the wall. He didn't hit the ground. He caught the wall with his hands and managed to support himself. Tina was already out the door.

Don felt weak. He hadn't eaten anything all day. By the time Don got into the hall, all he saw through blurry eyes was a figure holding the elevator door open for Tina. The elevator closed before Don got halfway down the hall. He would never make it down the stairs in time. He stopped and hit the button to summon the elevator with his fist. Hard. Then harder. His face tightened as he tried to think of what to do next.

Don used his car phone to call the office answering service. He would find Harvey or Lou. One of them had to be on call.

"Hello. This is Dr.Gardner. Who's on call tonight?"

"Just a moment," said the operator.

"They never do that," he thought.

"Hello. How can I help you?" It was another voice.

"This is Dr. Gardner. Who is on call tonight?" The anger showed in his voice.

"Don't worry. You don't have call this week. It's either Dr. Gross or Dr. Benjamin. Have a nice evening."

"Wait!" She already hung up. Don was in no state for rational thought. Since most of the operators were black their response was a racial thing. They had heard the news reports. Chessman had Lou or Harvey instruct them to say that. The operators were preoccupied and his thoughts were totally unfounded.

"Jerk. Go find Lou or Harvey." Even Harvey would have to be somewhat sympathetic. He tried Lou first.

Dysplasia

Don stood in the lobby of Lou's building. Lou's wife was home but would not let Don upstairs.

"Vay iz mir! Don't get me involved with this. I told you. Lou is not here. Look at the trouble you've caused." She sounded nervous.

Don was angry but realized it was natural for her to worry about the effect everything would have on the practice.

"Do you know where he is?" asked Don.

"No. You know Lou. He loves to walk around the neighborhood. Try the newsstand or Starbucks. He sometimes gets a pastry there." She sounded more human.

"Okay. Thanks."

Don drove around the streets for a few minutes, looking in the windows of the local places. No Lou.

Don tried the buzzer in the dirty vestibule where Harvey lived. Nobody was home.

"That's right," remembered Don. "He's upstate."

Don got in his car and drove to Harvey's so-called summer home. If no one was there, the ride up and back would give Don a chance to cool down.

He drove through a McDonalds. "A chocolate shake. Two Big Macs. Three apple pies." He needed sugar. He would consume everything on the ride to Harvey's house.

At the gas station, he also bought two cans of Gatorade. "It's the closest thing to an I.V. snack," he often told his residents and patients.

Near the property, he saw lights and knew Harvey was there. Harvey would never leave the lights on. He could see Lou sitting in the living room, his head hung low.

Don didn't go to the front door. He went to the back and entered through the kitchen. Karen was sitting alone on a light wooden rocker.

She rocked ever so slightly while sipping a glass of white wine, reading a book about quilts.

"Hi," she said and smiled, almost in a whisper.

"Hi there, Mrs. Gross." That's what Don always jokingly called her. Don tiptoed across the kitchen.

"They're in the living room. Have fun." Karen rarely got involved with "office business".

They smiled for a second.

Don burst into the living room. "I'm going after him." Don announced calmly. "I have to get that tape. Where did he go? Los Angeles? Paris?"

Nobody was surprised to see Don.

Harvey put his arm on Don's shoulder in an artificial manner, a pretense of "man to man". It's hard to master unless practiced.

"Lou and I have agreed to buy out Hank's share of the practice. He's been planning to retire for some time. We thought it best that you didn't. The money will come from our retirement accounts. We will borrow against it to pay off Hank." Harvey spoke like he was president of Price Waterhouse.

Don pulled Harvey's arm away. It was followed by a firm push in the shoulder.

"You are out of your mind. I'm not giving that murderer one nickel. I'm going to the police with what I know."

Harvey felt confident. "You don't know shit, Don. Everyone knows you don't get along with Hank."

Karen walked slowly out of the kitchen and into the living room.

"Karen. What is it?" asked Harvey. "We're having a meeting."

"This will only take a minute," she answered.

"Could you please go back into the kitchen?" asked Harvey.

"Look, I'm sorry, Harvey." To Don: "I overheard them earlier. Hank went to Haiti. He took some tape with him. The other tapes are still locked in Hank's office drawer—you know, the one that's always locked."

Don realized that those tapes were now in Tina's possession if she hadn't been instructed to destroy them. It wasn't clear to Don whether Tina had Chessman's personal collection of tapes or the office-procedure tapes. Whatever she had, Don could kiss it goodbye. If Chessman did work on Laurel in the office, there was no evidence unless that was the tape Chessman took with him to Haiti. Don wondered why Chessman told Lou and Harvey about the tape. Was Chessman insane enough to make even that into a game? The answer was a clear "yes."

"Stop it, Karen. That's enough," said Harvey.

"Why did you tell me?" Don said to protect Karen. Don could think of a lot of reasons, starting with the fact that Karen was a decent, moral person.

It gave Karen the opening she wanted. "Because I am sick of all you fake, liberal schmucks who masquerade as women's rights advocates. And my husband, the biggest schmuck of them all, is a penny-pinching, controlling bastard who has always pretended to be on the side of women. There is no 'on the side of women'. If you don't get it, then it's too late. And it's too late for us, Harvey. You only cared about the money, not helping women."

"Karen, come on. Not now." Harvey moved towards her.

"It's too late."

"Karen. It's those treatments. You know how they affect you."

"Of course it's the treatments. Of course. It's just another woman's problem."

"I didn't mean it that way."

"You just don't get it." Karen began to cry uncontrollably. She moaned from deep inside her body. She screamed once, a shrill sound, followed by more crying. Harvey tried to comfort her by putting his arm around her. Karen lashed out with her arm and propelled Harvey away. She sunk to her knees.

"Keep the fuck away from me. That's pretty clear, isn't it?"

"Karen, let me get you some water," Lou volunteered.

"I always thought you were the sensitive one, Lou. I thought you understood what we went through. But you're so weak. So weak. I'm sorry for you, Lou, because that's all there is to give to someone as pathetic as you. I'm sorry for you."

By the look on Lou's face, it was clear that Lou didn't feel much differently about himself than Karen did. He hung his head low. Lou was a loser.

Lou looked up at Don. "Hank is not a murderer."

"I can't believe you're still defending him," Karen said as she pulled herself up from the dark-stained hardwood floor. Harvey tried to help her up, but she violently pushed him aside.

Lou continued. "I don't care what you think of Hank or me for that matter, but you must understand that Hank is not a murderer. What happened with that girl was an accident. She had an arteriole anomaly."

"What about the fact that she was pregnant and Chessman was banging away at her with God knows what?" said Don.

"He couldn't have known that. He was on a date. They were alone. What Hank did or did not do will be hard to find out. But deliberate murder. Come on, Don." Lou sounded like he talked to Burns already.

Don shook his head. "I'm out of here."

Harvey looked at Karen. "You realize that if you don't get the tape, the only way you can get off the hook is to get Chessman to testify that he treated her before you." He was trying to sound sympathetic.

"Maybe I can convince him," said Don.

Harvey laughed in a manner that sounded like he was clearing his throat.

Dysplasia

〇

"Yeah. See you guys in court when I get back. Oh. I'm not buying out Chessman. I want out of the practice and I want you guys to pay me a straight twenty-five per cent of the last appraisal," demanded Don.

Harvey's moment of sympathy passed quickly. "Don, don't you realize that you will be sued for malpractice and the possibility of criminal charges against you looks likely? If you leave the country, you will look even more guilty and that would make you a tremendous liability in the office. You will end up paying us for the damage to our business."

Don casually walked to Harvey. With a hard lower palm, Don smashed Harvey as hard as possible in the nose.

Harvey roared in pain, his fingers clasped to the sides of his nostrils. "Owwww! Shit. You broke my nose," screamed Harvey as the blood gushed from his nostrils.

Don turned to walk out of the room, satisfied with his deliberate accomplishment.

Lou raised his head. "Don," Lou said in a loud voice. "Don. Check Hank's house in Petionville. He has things there. Other things."

Harvey stopped and turned to Lou. "What things? What are you talking about, Lou?"

Lou spoke rapidly. "I'm not sure. Things having to do with voodoo. Hank always had weird hobbies. He never let me know exactly what it was. I don't know how it could help. Look. I don't want to see you hurt. I mean that. The office will survive no matter what. I've been covering for Hank for a long time. It was all white-collar stuff. This time it's too much."

"Thanks." Don and Lou shook hands.

"I didn't want to let you down," said Lou. He looked at Don for some sign of approval. Don turned and walked towards the front door.

"Good luck, Don," Karen whispered meekly. She didn't think he had a prayer going up against Chessman. She smiled a little girl's smile. Don smiled back.

Brad Lewis

He made a hasty exit. He ran down the path and got into his BMW. As he drove off, he made a mental picture of the three left in the house. He knew Lou could temporarily fix Harvey's nose. Don still cared about Lou and Karen. He realized by worrying about them he could fend off the great anxieties he held for himself. Petionville. Susan. Of course. Susan. He would get to Susan. He still wasn't thinking straight. He kept forgetting to call Kronen.

The engine began to sputter. He was on the Major Deegan heading south into New York City. He cut over to exit on the little-used 3rd Street Bridge, then cut over a small section of the Bronx that left him off on the Manhattan side where he could connect to the Harlem River Drive, which would become FDR Drive, leading him into the heart of the city. Ever since he read *Bonfire of the Vanities,* he pictured his life ending as his vehicle would be stopped in the crummy, decayed area of the Bronx near the 3rd Street Bridge. The thought never entered his mind that day.

The traffic started to back up. Don saw a small space open up in the middle lane. He gunned the accelerator, but when the car kicked into gear, it lunged into the center lane, hard into a huge pothole. He heard a thud as the wheel jammed into the hole. The right side of the car dipped lower. He swerved to avoid hitting a car that was crawling in the right lane. He hit the brakes and his car skidded into a big old Buick. When the vehicles came to a halt, Don opened his door to run around to the side of his car. The front wheel looked dislocated from the axle and was wedged in the housing of the body of the car. Four black youths were walking slowly from the Buick. To a New Yorker brought up on bigotry, this was not to be a happy exchange.

Dysplasia

Don reached into his pocket and took out some cash and his American Express card. It was a few hundred dollars. He might also have to give up his watch.

"You fucked up," said one.

"You okay, man?" asked the second.

"You want us to get you off to the side?" asked the first.

Don smiled. "I'm okay. Thanks." He was pleasantly relieved.

"Sheet. You coulda been killed. Look at that motha-fuckin-wheel."

Don laughed. "I can't hang around. Here. Take this money. Here's my credit card. Tell the tow guys to charge my card. Just tell them to drop the car at the address on the registration. It's in the glove compartment."

"Why you givin' us money?" asked the heaviest of the four men.

"For the damage to your car."

The heavy guy turned his red wool hunting hat around to inspect the damage to the Buick. He leaned in to take a closer look. He ran his hand over the area where the Buick hit the BMW. "Sheeet. You can't hurt a Buick with dat German toy."

"Here. Take them." Don handed the one nearest him half the money and the card. Don ran across the right lane of traffic, scrambled up an embankment and into the parking lot of a school.

"Damn. That man is crazy or somethin," said the heavy man.

As Don jogged towards First Avenue, his heart pounded fiercely. He had gotten into terrible shape. He slowed down as he approached the avenue. He signaled for a taxi. A gypsy cab, a car and driver that was not registered as a taxi, pulled over.

"Where you goin'?" asked a gray-haired black man with a shiny gold tooth in the front of his mouth.

"Bank Street."

"Fifteen. Cost you fifteen." The gypsies didn't have meters.

"Fine." Don got inside the back of the big maroon Cadillac. He rested his head on the grimy cloth seats.

Don got out of the cab on Bank Street, paid the driver and walked into the vestibule of Susan's building. He pushed the button alongside her nameplate. Hard three times. A voice broke his momentary fervor.

"Who is that? Who is there?" She was home.

"It's Don. Don Gardner. Can I come up?"

The buzzer signified the release of the inner door lock. Don leaned across the vestibule and pushed the door open in time before the buzzer stopped. Then he walked closer to the door, opening it further. Inside he let the door slam and lock behind him.

Don collapsed on a fluffy sofa in the living room, filled with soft, colorful pillows.

"What happened? Are you ill?" She noticed the red bump on his head. "Let me get you a drink. I have some white wine." She walked towards the kitchenette.

"I have to go to Haiti."

Susan stopped and walked back from the kitchenette. She didn't sound surprised or unduly interested. "Why is that?"

"Chessman has gone to Haiti and he has something that I need. I mean, I hope he has something I need."

"I'd better get the wine."

Don raised his voice. "I know I'm not making any sense. This terrible thing has happened. They have kicked me out of the hospital. They think I screwed up on the girl that died."

Don spotted a remote control for the television. He pushed the power button. As soon as he saw an image, he began to scan the local channels.

Dysplasia

Susan brought the wine, one glass in each hand. "What are you looking for?" She handed one glass to Don.

Don gulped the wine. "I'm looking for me. There." He put the remote down at his side. "There I am."

Susan stared in disbelief as she watched footage of Don being led out of the hospital and through the angry mob.

Don changed to another station. There was the hospital again. This segment showed Don being struck in the head by the rock.

"When did this happen?"

"Late this afternoon. Towards evening."

"Let me get some ice for your head," she said.

"No. I'm fine." The area on his head felt numb. His hand felt heavy. "I have to go to Haiti to find Chessman. If I don't, my whole life will be ruined. Can I use your phone?"

"Sure." Susan was cautious.

Don walked to a wall telephone in the kitchenette.

"Here. Use this one." Susan retrieved a cell phone from a black lacquer cabinet.

As he dialed, he noticed four or five objects which looked like wireless transmitters on the shelves.

Don punched in a telephone number.

"Who are you calling so late?" she asked.

"Kronen. I should have called him from the hospital. I was a mess."

"Who is this Kronen?"

"My only friend."

"You mean next to me, don't you?"

Don smiled as Susan put her hand on his shoulder. Don took her hand.

"Damn. There's no answer."

"You can't do anything else tonight. You will think better in the morning."

"I have to get to Haiti." Don put the cell phone down on a coffee table next to the sofa. He felt weak. He sat on the sofa with his head back, inhaling and exhaling deeply and slowly.

"Then you will. If you want to sleep here it is okay. Sleep in my bed. I will sleep on the sofa.

"I'll be fine out here," answered Don. He put his head down in the corner of the sofa. "Sleep," he thought. "Yes. Must sleep."

Susan got some bedding from a nearby closet. He was nodding off by the time she returned. She covered him with a light quilt.

Don would not remember any dreams that night, although he would dream all night, dreams of a tortured mind.

Before Susan went to sleep, she made a phone call. She spoke mostly in French. It was a brief call, maybe two minutes. Then she took one of the communicators from the cabinet. She pushed a button that signaled a remote location. She spoke in a rapid patois, with the tone of someone giving orders.

When Don woke up, he found a note on the coffee table.

"I have a lot of things to do if I am going to Haiti. Leave the information on my voicemail service. LT 8 6470. I need to know for sure that you want to still go. If you changed your mind, just leave the message 'No.'"

Don called Kronen from the phone in the kitchenette. Kronen was already in his office.

"It's me," said Don.

"You looked very nice on television. Where the hell are you?" Kronen exited the program on his computer screen. He clicked on an icon that opened a new program. Kronen kept working while he listened to Don.

Don explained most of what happened since leaving the hospital.

Dysplasia

"What do you want me to do?" Kronen already knew. He thought there was an outside chance Don could be dissuaded.

"I want you to come to Haiti with me," said Don.

Within seconds Kronen had a map of Haiti on his computer screen. "Are you out of your fucking mind? Don't answer, Don. We have to get some people out there protecting your interests. The media is going to murder you on this. And all you can think of is going after the scumbag yourself." Kronen located several telephone numbers from his electronic organizer. He scurried around his office while he talked to Don.

"Yes. I have to get to Chessman."

"We need to start a good foundation to fight this thing. You're going to need to get a hearing to rebuke the hospital's position. Malpractice is a sure avenue and the family might also go after your ass personally."

"That's plan B," said Don.

"What is plan A?" Kronen was busy with papers he was pulling from a desk drawer.

"Chessman. Are you going to help me or not?"

Kronen found a safety deposit box key in a drawer. "Don, Where are you exactly?" Kronen's tone changed abruptly. He was dead serious.

"On Bank Street, north of Hudson."

"Don't tell anyone where you are going. Don't even speak to anyone else. Come up to my office at Matthew Bender. Right now. Do you have any money?"

Don put his hand in his pants pocket. "Yes."

"Enough to get here?"

Don looked at the bills. "Yes."

"Okay. Just come here. I have to call my wife."

"Thanks, Kronen."

"What are you thanking me for? I'm about to really fuck up your life." Kronen hung up.

Brad Lewis

Don stopped at a store on Hudson Street. He bought a large orange juice and a packaged coffee cake. He ate it in the taxi on the way uptown to Kronen.

At Riverside Church, luminaries and public figures, including Congressman Jones and Mike Raptor, gathered in a large hall to pay their respects to the Carver family.

An assistant to an Assistant Secretary of State read a note signed by President Clinton.

CHAPTER THIRTY-FOUR

Barry had been having a great deal of difficulty sleeping recently. Flashes and visions he couldn't put together twisted in his mind. He walked around the apartment at night, trying in vain to discard more of his mother's possessions. All he succeeded in doing was relocating them.

Barry opened a closet, reached up and pulled out a huge cardboard box from the top shelf. He almost went over in a heap from the weight of it and the awkward stance required to get the box. Catching himself with one hand on the side of a very long and old puffy sofa, he let the box falling, its contents of smaller boxes fall to the floor. One box opened and a circular tape rolled out, the kind of tape used on Barry's tape recorder.

Something told Barry that the answer to his sleepless nights, the thoughts about Melinda, would be found on these tapes. From a long time ago, maybe six or seven years. He associated the referral to his office on Fifth Avenue. God. He treated so many people connected with the building in one form or another. Clitoris. Clitoris. A word he heard more than once in his office. Hostility. Rage. Clitoris. Cut off the clitoris. Who was it? When was it? Should he call the police? No. His twisted mind was pulling the thoughts together.

Barry pulled out the oversized case that housed his "portable" Sony. It took two hands to drag the monster close to a table. He put one of his tapes on the reel. Barry pulled out the long cord. He plugged it in and began with the year 1989, starting the arduous task of listening to his session.

"My husband no longer seems interested in sex."

"Why do you think that is so?" asked Barry.

"I'm worried that it might be a medical problem."

Barry recognized the session and knew immediately this was unrelated. He would get through a few tapes before he fell asleep with the side of his head on a pile of tape boxes.

The next day Barry came home early from the office. He called the Manhattan Plaza Racquet Club and told the desk receptionist to give his apologies "to the boys" who were expecting him for his doubles tennis round robin. A lot of creative people played there. Many lived in the surrounding apartments. Regulars included the guys from *60 Minutes*, delightful company but not exactly the fiercest competition. The pace of the games was perfect for Barry. His last MRI showed two herniated discs in his lower back. The Manhattan Plaza was perfect, out-of-work actors and newspeople. But not that day.

He grabbed half a leftover sandwich from Blimpie, a store that specialized in what he preferred to call hero sandwiches, subs as they were known in most places. Barry's mother made him hero sandwiches long before the fast-food companies ever gave it a thought. He consumed it with a ravenous passion along with a bottle of chocolate milk Yoo-Hoo, another delight from his past. The snack would tide him over as he hit the tapes again. He would listen the rest of the day, replenishing himself with bites from the rest of the sandwich and a second bottle of Yoo-Hoo.

Dysplasia

About eight in the evening, Barry was tiring. He took out another reel and started the tape.

"My parents were in the retail business in California. I couldn't take it anymore. My father owned a chain of these drugstores that sold a lot of junk, you know, sort of like Rexall did in New York. All the kids would call me little Miss Save-a-Lot. It was humiliating."

Barry fast-forwarded to the end of that session. He listened while another session started. He could barely hear the voice on the tape. He turned the volume knob. The voice was still unclear. Barry's cat took that moment to speak to Barry in a few melodical meows.

"Shusss, Dr. Freud. Be quiet."

Barry rewound the tape and played it again. The cat jumped in his lap. Barry stroked Dr. Freud while he listened to the tape.

"Shusss, Doctor. Be quiet now. This is very important."

It was a man with an accent.

"I was in the army in my country. I was involved with the detainment and torture of political prisoners."

"You said, 'torture'." Barry said it calmly.

"Yes. All countries do it." He seemed offended.

"Please go on."

"In my country we don't believe in good and evil. We believe the good must exist side by side with evil. It is our way."

The session clicked in Barry's mind. His mouth dropped. He remembered. He listened.

"Why did you come to my office?" asked Barry.

"I am worried." He repeated the words. "I need to continue my work. I need to continue the ritual. I need—" He stopped.

"Yes. Go on. What is it?"

"We had to cut them, you know."

Silence.

"Very often body parts were sacrificed," the man continued.

More silence.

Barry stopped the machine. He pushed Dr. Freud off his lap. "I think this is too X-rated for you." Barry started the tape.

"I am very much afraid that I will do this to someone, a woman perhaps." There was terror in his voice.

"What is it that you fear you will do?" asked Barry.

"I have been thinking about cutting off the most sensitive parts on the woman, like the nipples and the little piece of flesh below the mound."

"Uh-huh."

That was it. Barry shut off the machine. He remembered that guy well. He thought at the time that guy was a copycat who made up the whole thing. Barry had a sense that the man lied about his name and job also. The whole episode struck him as nonthreatening.

Barry was one of the New York psychiatrists who felt doctors were fueling the demonic satanic stuff. They could make some money off the suggestible patients. Barry thought the guy on the tape was convinced by his previous shrink to believe some satanic child abuse, including ritualistic sacrifice. It was an abusive possibility. "Witnessed hundreds of murders." Bullshit. "Committed hundreds of ritualistic murders, including mutilation." Double bullshit. "What if that guy was for real?" Barry asked himself. It happened. Patients slipped through the system all the time. Barry was upset.

He rarely let one slip through. The whole episode sounded like fiction. What if it wasn't?

Just when Barry began to pack up his recorder, he remembered another patient.

Dysplasia

Barry sat in a plain black chair in Dick's office. The Sony tape machine sat on another chair. Barry noticed a picture of Jill and Dick on the wall to the right of the desk.

Dick came in arguing with a female uniformed officer who trailed him. She was brandishing some papers.

"Okay. Okay. I'll rewrite the damn thing," said Dick.

"Dick, it's not me. But you know they like to have the words spelled correctly. And leave out words like 'screw, mucking up, and acted like a bitch.'"

"It's English. They all know the language." Dick took the papers.

The officer left. She stuck her head back inside for a moment to offer Dick a friendly smirk.

Barry got up from his chair. "I don't know if you remember me. I'm Dr. Barry Gruber."

"Yeah, yeah. They told me you were here. What happened, you went through some therapy and you want to be my friend?"

Barry let it go. "I had a patient who told me he wanted to do to a woman what you told me about. A clitoridectomy. It was years ago. I thought he imagined his past."

"Sit down, Doc."

For about twenty minutes, they went back and forth with questions after Barry played the tape for Dick.

Barry had very few answers. "I know the patient was referred to me by Dr. Stuart Beitleman, but it was not one of Beitleman's regular patients. He's always doing favors for someone."

"This name he gave you. Colonel Louis Paul. Did you think he was lying?"

"It was too long ago, but at the time I thought everything he was saying was untrue."

"Thanks for coming in." Dick went over it several times. He felt Barry couldn't be of any further assistance.

- 428 -

"Even if this guy came to me today, it would be difficult to believe him. He said they murdered thousands of people."

"They might have."

"Then where are all the bodies?" asked Barry.

"He didn't say he did it here. It could have been another country. How did you end it with this Colonel guy?"

"I told him I thought he was delusional and referred him to two other psychiatrists who worked with this type of patient, and also gave him the name of a hospital downtown that had a unit where they could treat him."

"Didn't you follow it up?"

"I'm not obligated to do that. Nor did I feel it was necessary." Barry's voice was cracking. He was visibly upset.

"You docs have some racket. I'd lose my job if I didn't follow up every fucking detail."

Barry began to feel responsible for Melinda's death as well as anyone else the murderer may have killed. He knew he shouldn't, so he defended himself as best he could. "Look. I'm not a detective. I'm a psychiatrist. I'm human and therefore I'm not perfect. I hope I've been of some help."

"You have."

"There is one other thing. I didn't think I should bring it up, but I don't know…"

"What is it?"

Barry changed tapes and turned on the machine. Dick listened to Don talking to Barry about his dream.

"I'm having that dream again. I'm in Disneyland with Linda. We're on Space Mountain. Suddenly the lights go out and I'm standing naked on top of the ride. My hands are full of blood and human tissue. Everyone is laughing at me. Then I speak. 'I had to do it. She needed a radical.' Linda is lying lifeless on the rail beside me. A large black circle is over the area where I performed the surgery, the kind of black circle they use on the evening news to block out part of a person or thing."

"Yes. You've had this dream before," said Barry on the tape.

"But this time I check the rest of the cars on the track and there is Melinda, the girl who was mutilated, smiling at me in one of the cars. She asks me why I hate women and I answer that I'm not really sure."

"Is your partner in this new dream?"

"No. That's funny. I haven't dreamt about Chessman for some time. It's always this new way with Melinda."

Barry shut off the machine.

Dick looked troubled, not knowing what to make of this.

"That was Dr. Gardner, right?"

"Yes."

"Boy. He's already in a lot of trouble."

That was the response Barry expected. "Are we through?" asked Barry.

"Yep."

Barry closed the lid on his machine and handed the reel of tape to Dick.

"I guess you want this."

"Yes. Uhm. Doc?"

"Yes?"

"You don't think Dr. Gardner could commit murder, do you?"

"No. I don't and I hope you and your staff don't make any more out of this than you need to. I felt I should bring in the tape since it contained the kind of clap trap you're looking for."

Barry walked out of the office. He felt shaken that he may have some-how let a killer out of his office. He walked slowly down the hall. When he neared the exit doors, he felt someone grab his arm. It was Dick.

"Hey, Doc. I'm sorry. You did your job right."

"Okay." He was surprised to see that Dick was capable of compassion.

"That Colonel guy is a long shot anyway. Thanks for coming in. Again, I'm sorry."

"Thank you." Barry left the building as Dick watched through the glass doors.

For a few moments Dick thought about how Don was so interested in blaming Chessman for the murders, how he pressed Jill to help him. Dick pondered how smart doctors are, some maybe too smart. And why Barry became so cooperative all of a sudden.

CHAPTER THIRTY-FIVE

Jill decided to reconstruct a day in the life of the dead model. Jill started at Melinda's gym, the New York Health and Racquet Club, a chain of several chic chrome-and-glass buildings filled with machines, aerobic instructors, and people who didn't have day jobs or any job at all.

Jill called Dick, fresh from a workout on a Stairmaster. Clad in a pink-and-black Danskin, she stood in a busy hall at a public telephone.

"Maybe I'll run into Chessman here or something."

"Jill. It's not him. Okay? When we get the DNA samples back, that will prove it. Then you and Don will have to find another suspect."

"Why is it taking so long?" asked Jill.

"Ah, come on. You know the system."

"Dick, this is me. I know the system, you are the system. If you asked them to do it, don't they just do it?"

Dick changed the subject. "You know that Don is a suspect. Should we get a sample of his DNA too?"

"What is this bullshit that Don is a suspect? You're just saying that to rile me, aren't you?"

Dick didn't answer. He changed the subject. "Are you on my case because you are on my case?"

Jill knew that Dick had lied, that he hadn't sent in the sample. Jill would have to do it herself.

"Dick, give me the sample and I'll take care of it. I'll send it to Perry upstate."

"Get off my fucking case."

"I'm not on your case."

"Then why do I feel like you are?"

"That's a ridiculous question."

"That's a ridiculous answer."

"Is that it, you feel it's ridiculous?"

"That's exactly it. That's exactly what you do when you are on my case. You twist my words around and use your five-dollar education against my ninety-nine-cent street education. That's how I know you're on me. Get off it. Get off me. Take a break."

"Is that what you want?"

"You can be one irritating—" He stopped.

"I'm irritating?"

"Don't you know when to stop?" Dick hung up.

"He hung up," Jill said to a chubby woman who was leaning in to catch the conversation as she waited for the telephone. Jill handed her the receiver. "Maybe you'll have better luck."

Jill spent that afternoon shopping at Giorgio Armani. Jill thought one of the men in the store was staring at her as she made her way to the front door. He was a handsome, dark-skinned mulatto, impeccably dressed. Maybe he was flirting. He smiled. Jill was too shy to return the smile. She left, thinking that he looked familiar. "No. It couldn't be." She dismissed the thought.

Later she lunched at Tribeca, in Soho. There was a lot of activity around the bar. Jill recognized two actors at a table near hers, Paul Sorvino and Danny Aiello. A little boy asked Danny for his autograph. "Don't you want his autograph, too? He's a big star, Paul Sorvino."

Dysplasia

Jill found eavesdropping boring at best and concentrated on looking around the room as she finished her appetizer of patés. The food was good and that surprised her. She was used to these places being what Dick liked to call "full-of-shit cuisine." He was usually right. She had mashed potatoes and chicken as a main course and was enjoying her food so much she paid little attention to a voice commenting to her as he passed her table that "I had the same thing for lunch. It's great, isn't it?" She looked up and saw a man with his smile slightly off to the side. She thought it was Robert DeNiro.

On her way out the door, she spotted another dark-skinned man. He was wearing a Panama hat and an open-collar shirt. She knew him, didn't she? Or was he the same man she saw at Armani? But he was dressed differently. She only flashed on him for a moment. She didn't want to stare. She was thinking about Don. He didn't answer her calls since the incident at the hospital. She left a message for Lou with Tina at the office, but he didn't return the call.

In the taxi on the way uptown, Jill admitted that her feelings for Don were more than brotherly. It brought a smile to her lips.

Jill decided to work late that night in her office. Several large files were piled high on one side of her desk. Two of them opened, making her raise her hands awkwardly to turn the pages. She spoke into a micro cassette recorder.

"Mr. Manning's chief complaint was pain in the lower right mandible. His dentist referred him to an endodontic specialist for root canal therapy. At first, the pain was thought to be the subsequent failure of the root canal treatment."

She moved a button on the machine and listened for the playback of her dictation. "His dentist referred him—" She fast-forwarded, "—to be the subsequent failure—"

She rewound the tape and rephrased her message. "At first, the pain was attributed to the site of the root surgery. This was unfounded and Mr. Manning was referred to me for differential diagnosis. It appeared that Mr. Manning had a blocked sublingual salivary duct, but after two sessions of 'milking' the duct, I referred Mr. Manning to his internist for blood tests. The swelling may have been related to a node problem."

She flipped forward a few pages and then pulled a letter from a pile of papers on her right. "Enter this diagnosis from Mr. Manning's internist, Dr. Felding. Mr. Manning has been diagnosed with Hodgkin's Disease and I have referred him to Sloan Kettering for treatment and evaluation."

Jill shook her head, disappointed. She turned off the micro cassette recorder and tossed it on the papers. She sighed deeply, running her hands over her face for a few seconds. The electronic sound of a phone ringing interrupted her. She answered by pushing the speakerphone button.

"Hello. Doctor's office," the voice of the answering service said over Jill's own, "Hello, Dr. Stover speaking." "I've got it, Carey," said Jill. "Hello, this is Dr. Stover."

"Jill, it's Perry. Over at the lab. I was going to leave a message for you."

"Hi, Perry. What did you find out?"

"Working late, huh?"

"Yeah. I'm way behind in my charts."

"You know I'm not supposed to be doing this." It was a subtle disclaimer.

"So what else is new?"

"Those cells you gave me do not match the ones from either victim."

"Are you sure?" Jill was already dreading giving the news to Don.

"What is this, a test? Of course I'm sure."

"Thanks, Perry." Her voice dropped off.

"Hey, are you okay?"

Dysplasia

"Fine. Fine. Thanks. I'll talk to you tomorrow."

Jill disconnected the call. She punched in the speed-dialing number for Don.

The telephone rang inside as Don exited his apartment into the hallway.

He had no time to go back inside. He had to get the airport. He continued towards the hall elevator without giving it another thought. Besides, Kronen told him not to talk to anyone. It couldn't have been Kronen.

Jill listened nervously. After fourteen or fifteen rings she lost count and hung up. "Why doesn't anyone have their answering machine on when you need to leave a message?"

Jill gathered up papers that she wanted to take home and stuffed them in a large black briefcase. She turned off the light by touching a plate on the wall near the door and left her office.

CHAPTER THIRTY-SIX

Don got a cab easily. He threw his sports duffel bag into the back seat of the beat-up old yellow Checker cab.

"Kennedy. American Airlines."

"No problem, man," answered the driver.

Don wanted to ask the driver if he was from Haiti or Jamaica, but instead took out the few soft-cover books he found on Haiti at Strands street-side bookstore. He flipped through their pages, hoping some familiarity may reduce his overwhelming anxiety.

Don got out of the cab in plenty of time to make the flight. He gave the driver $35 telling him to keep the change. It was a decent tip, but not a great tip, and even under these extraordinary circumstances he thought maybe he should give the driver another few dollars. "Why are you so insecure?" he berated himself as he slammed the car door. He listened for the sound.

He quickly headed for the American Airlines counter to check in. He was behind a family with two children and a businessman carrying a laptop computer. It only took a few moments and he had the boarding passes. He didn't remember whether he picked smoking or nonsmoking, aisle or window, or anything the pretty, petite, blue-eyed woman had asked.

Dysplasia

"Where is Susan?" He wasn't worried about Kronen, although he felt that Kronen was probably watching him, out of sight, having himself a big laugh at Don's expense. Don walked back to the entrance.

A Lincoln sedan with smoked glass windows pulled up and double-parked outside the terminal. The trunk popped open. A well-built black man in a dark suit and sunglasses got out, walked around the car and opened the back door as another black man, a little more portly, got out of the passenger side of the front of the vehicle. The second man quickly walked inside the terminal, stationing himself a few feet from Don. Don looked outside in time to see Susan helped out of the back seat by the first man. He handed Susan a modest carry-on bag. The two walked inside the terminal.

Don walked immediately towards Susan. The portly black man cut off his path. "That's Don, Jacques," she said.

"Dr. Gardner. We are pleased that you are making this trip on behalf of President Aristide."

Don did not want to argue or discuss the matter. He only wanted to find Kronen and get on the plane. He was on his own goodwill mission, not theirs.

"I'm glad you're pleased." He took Susan's bag. "Is this it?"

She laughed. "I have a lot of clothes waiting for me when we get there."

The thinner black man released Susan's arm and smiled warmly at Don. Don thought back to his trip to Club Med. He found the Haitian people charming. Why was there such political turmoil? Maybe because they were unable to protect themselves from outside influences. Don was far from an expert, but what he read about innate beliefs in the supernatural made them easy prey for the world's corporate and political vultures.

Don and Susan took the escalator up to the departing flights. Perched in the corner, sitting on his Army green duffel bag, was Kronen. He was reading a Hustler magazine so that the cover was in full view to everyone.

"I haven't had a vacation in a long time. This is going to be fun," he said.

"This is Kronen." Don gestured toward him with his hand.

"How do you do?" Susan extended her hand.

"Fine." He got up from his duffel. "She's gorgeous."

"Thank you."

They shook hands.

"Kronen. This is not a vacation."

"Anytime I get away from attorneys, it's a vacation."

They walked towards the departure gate.

"You didn't tell me your friend Kronen was another underdeveloped American male." Susan pointed towards the magazine.

Don shot a wide grin in Kronen's direction. Kronen pushed his lips out, retracted them, brought his lower teeth to his upper lip, and nodded in mock acknowledgment of his position with Susan, as if she was correct.

They sat three across on the plane, Susan in the middle.

Once in flight Kronen dumped the Hustler. It had served its brief purpose. He instead read an article he copied from a recent *Travel & Leisure*, written by a man named Herbert Gold, someone who spent over forty years of his life enamored with Haiti.

"Katie loved Haiti, and all Haiti loved Katie," sang Kronen to the dismay of anyone within earshot.

"Cole Porter must be turning over in his grave," said Susan.

"You know the song?" answered Kronen.

Dysplasia

⌒

"Who doesn't?"

Kronen cleared his throat and pointed at Don. "You never heard of it either," said Don as he reached across and grabbed the magazine from Kronen's hands.

"They're advertising Haiti for tourism?" Don said as he flipped through the short article. "I feel secure in Port-au-Prince, Kenscoff, Jacmel and Cap Haitian, but then I feel safe in San Francisco and New York, too," Don quoted from the article. "I guess it's not as bad as I thought it was going to be."

"Mr. Gold is one of our biggest fans. Can I see what he has written?"

"Sure," Don said as he passed the magazine to Susan.

The plane was surprisingly almost full. Don noticed immediately that this was not the same group that took the flight to Club Med in the '80s with Chessman. A few men in military uniform, a lot of men in plain Brooks Brothers suits, several passengers with laptop computers, and a dozen or so well-dressed people who Don thought were French or Spanish until Susan pointed out they were wealthy Haitians. Business as usual.

Kronen was already into his second Bloody Mary when Susan began a discussion about how great things used to be in Haiti. When she wasn't looking at him, Kronen gestured that he was bored, a big yawn followed by flapping his hand over his mouth. Then he gestured with his hand that Don was being jerked off by Susan. Don shook his head "no" and signaled back by raising his fist at Kronen in a threatening manner. Kronen smiled and pushed the button to release his chair to lean back.

"Noel Coward, Truman Capote, and Irving Berlin would come to Haiti regularly. And of course you've heard of Graham Greene, haven't you?" Susan said as if she felt obligated to give Don a travel log.

"Wasn't that a long time ago?" Don asked.

"Yes. In the '50s."

"I thought everything was going pretty good for a while. Wasn't that Club Med I went to a good money maker?"

"Don, you don't know what Duvalier was like. He let the Club operate by importing everything. The Haitians were slaves to do diddle work."

Don tried to be attentive to Susan, but he knew so little about Haiti. The conversation eventually wore thin. Don finally blurted out, "Look. I'm doing my best. We agreed to help each other. So let's concentrate on what we set out to do."

"Susan, you have to be careful with Don," interrupted Kronen. "He's fragile around women." He started the trip light and silly. He wanted to keep it that way. His more calculated inner thoughts told him this trip wasn't going to be either.

Don's face turned beet red as Susan laughed heartily with Kronen. They were getting along famously.

If he came out of this okay, if he got off the hook and Chessman got what he deserved, he would divorce Linda and date Jill. "One thing at a time," he told himself. He only had the fantasy to look forward to.

Don picked up some of the material he had brought with him to read. He decided to continue with his quick education.

"Voodoo dancers perform at the Oloffson Hotel." It sounded touristy. He read on. "But the intrigue, vendettas and human rights abuses may explode again at any time."

"Great," thought Don. He was going right to hell in some foreign mess that no one in the United States cared less about. Then he had visions of voodoo rituals, like the one he had seen Chessman perform.

He skipped around. "The Toton Macoutes were getting ready to take over." Don knew who they were from Susan. The Macoutes took their name from a Creole word for "bogeyman." They were the dreaded military police controlled by Papa Doc, and very rich. They moved to the Dominican Republic, Canada, and Brazil. Many returned to regain their power and money in Haiti. A government-appointed commission took away any blame from the Macoutes for the massacres during the election. "It is inappropriate to accuse the Army as a whole."

Don dozed off after two Dewars and sodas. His last thought was he was on a wild goose chase with a woman he hardly knows. How would they find Chessman? Maybe Susan exaggerated about her father's capabilities. And maybe Kronen was right "that only a truly insane mother-fucker would keep a tape that would incriminate him in the death of a young black woman." They discussed it in detail that day in Kronen's office. The first time Kronen was trying to play the optimist.

"Sure. The guy is loony tunes. If he is as nuts as you say he is, and he gets his ya-yas by looking at slides of women whose pussy he's snipped, sort of like the snip-of-the-month club, then the motherfucker is crazy enough to keep a tape that might incriminate him in the possible accidental death of a young black girl. Particularly if he is crazy smart, enough to have you locked up to take the fall, crazy smart enough to watch the tape and get off all over again. Crazy smart enough to be one of the sickest people I ever heard of graduating medical school."

Twenty minutes, a cherry Coke, two bags of chips, and one *New York Times* later, Kronen lamented sadly. "We're the crazy ones. We must be fuckin' nuts. Let's not get on the plane with your black babe. Let's tell her that we forgot to feed my cat and call it a day. We will hire the best malpractice attorney in New York. I can call Moskowitz and see if he is in a sympathetic mood. Who knows, maybe he'll see this case as having some value, that is, for his publicity trailer. He loves to go on Larry King. I love to see those two Jews go at it. Larry makes everyone look good, even when Moskowitz is representing a real loser. I might be able to get you hooked up on a retainer, assuming they think you can prove you were set up. We can get damages from the hospital. They must have a deep-pocket insurer. Isn't your friend Jill going to look into the ambulance thing?"

"Kronen?"

"Yeah, Doc."

"Shut up."

"Okay. This is my impression of me saying nothing." He dropped the dialogue completely and explained to Don what he needed to do for the trip.

Don woke up to the sound of the captain making an announcement over the loudspeaker. "It was just announced that the recommendations by the Organization of American States has been accepted by both Lieutenant General Raoul Cédras and ousted president Father Aristide."

The airplane was filled with modest applause and then very quiet conversation. Haiti had little reaction to the news broadcast that morning. Haitians saw many ups and downs in the negotiations since the coup took place that ousted Father Aristide. Ups and downs like a hundred of the President's followers being killed immediately.

This breakthrough occurred after an oil embargo seemed likely. An appeal was even made to the neighboring Dominican Republic. Without oil, Haiti could only exist for six or so weeks.

There were many people in Haiti who wanted Cédras out and all the Lavalas (followers of Aristide) in. Worshipers were still being beaten routinely. Very few Americans were aware that workers were beaten, whipped, and subject to mutilation or sexual abuse. The art associated with Haiti reflected the complicated underlying fabric of the country. Gardere, an artist born in Haiti, made plaster heads that seemed impaled on wooden bodies. The sharp ceramic gave the heads a sense of being cut or mutilated. Mutilation seemed intrinsic to parts of the culture. When Don read that, he thought about the murders. His theories were making more sense.

Susan described to Don that the new plan in Haiti was to get Aristide to nominate a new Prime Minister, adopt an amnesty law to protect soldiers, and get the military high command and police chief to resign so that Aristide could put in a new group. An international mission would help form an independent professional police to replace the existing military police and retrain the Army.

"Fat chance," thought Kronen, who kept his mouth shut.

"I hope you get what you want," Don said.

The plane taxied into position after landing. As it moved along the runway, it passed by another American Airlines jet. The windows were knocked out and the emergency ramps deployed. A fire was evident.

Don signaled to Kronen and Susan to look out the window. Kronen nodded and shrugged his shoulders. It was not a comforting sight to see. Susan appeared unmoved.

As they deplaned, Don glanced across the field at the burnt-out plane. He paused to watch a dozen workers scurry around it. He felt Kronen tug at his arm.

"Don't stare. These people don't like it."

"How do you know that?" asked Don.

"Dickhead. Let's go." Kronen used just enough force to pull Don from his stationary position.

It occurred to Don that perhaps Kronen's experience in the Peace Corps was more extensive.

Things went surprisingly well as they made their way through the Port Au Prince airport. The airport didn't look any worse for wear than any other Caribbean jet strip and "tower", the kind that didn't appear capable of withstanding a decent wind.

They easily went through customs. Kronen was fearless. Susan's command of the patois helped also. The group was treated like a family arriving home. This put Don at ease.

The car rental experience was no more difficult that picking up a car in Honolulu. In fact, it was easier in Haiti. Kronen booked a reservation before they left, given a choice between Avis and Budget.

The people working the rental office were polite and friendly. The Avis car rental company was in the airport terminal. For $617.40 U.S. per week, they rented a four-door sedan with automatic and air. They didn't have a lot of choices.

Kronen kept asking the man behind the counter if he could get him a Jeep. "Believe me, Mr. Klei N. Man." He read the name off Kronen's driver's license. "If I had a Jeep, it would be my pleasure to make special arrangements for you."

Kronen was testing. "Okay. Give us the tin can with the automatic." Kronen knew everything was for sale as well as negotiable. It seemed reasonable that this particular Avis agency did not have access to Jeeps.

Susan wanted to be dropped off in the center of Port Au Prince. She said she would be fine and that she would contact them at the hotel. Don asked if they should book a room for Susan, but she laughed and said, "I am well taken care of here." Don had no idea how far her father's house was or if she made plans to stay with him. Taking Kronen's cue, they dropped Susan off in town.

Dysplasia

Don was anxious to get to the hotel. He looked out the window as they drove past a group of small buildings. Many of the buildings looked to be turn of the century. There were a few modern buildings, but there was no mistaking this for anything but what it was. Haiti.

Haiti had its own character that set it apart from the rest of the Caribbean. The locals used bus-like vehicles called tap-taps. Many of them were painted in elaborate multicolored swirls. Some were made from pick-up trucks and had the backs modified to seat a lot of passengers. They reminded Don of the vehicle used by the Merry Pranksters in the days of Keroac, Burroughs, and Ginsburg.

Kronen seemed to turn with purpose, like he knew where he was going. Don was sure they were heading away from where Susan indicated the hotel was located.

"Okay, let's go to the hotel."

"No way."

"What are you talking about?"

"There. That's what we want." Kronen turned onto a road called Harry Truman Boulevard.

"What are you doing now?"

Kronen didn't answer.

"Kronen. This is not funny. I am not interested in you being funny here."

Kronen stopped the car in front of a building with an American flag, an American soldier at the front door. Don was relieved but still curious.

"We're checking in here first. Then we can check in at the hotel. Do you want to come in or will you wait in the car?"

Don was already out of the car before Kronen finished his sentence.

"I want to let our boys know who we are and where we are staying."

After a brief "registration" at the front desk, Kronen excused himself.

- 446 -

"I have to pee. Can you wait in the lobby or will you feel safer coming in and holding my rod for me?"

"Ha. Ha. I'll wait here."

Don sat down in the lobby and stared at an old-fashioned standing electric fan. He could almost see the individual sections as the fan turned.

Don picked up a leaflet that explained that the State Department did not recommend travel in Haiti. During various periods of unrest Americans were urged to stay indoors until the situation was "clarified and stabilized." Travel at night was not considered very smart. There were attacks by "renegade elements" of the Haitian army. Nonessential personnel were not allowed in Haiti. There was an OAS presence in Haiti and an envoy from the United Nations. Don stared at the fan. He didn't like what he read.

He picked up another sheet marked "Consular Information Sheet", a plain piece of paper designed for quick reference with the name, address, and telephone number of the Embassy. Don noted that they were on Rue Oswald Durant. "Haiti is the poorest country in the Western Hemisphere. Throughout the country, there are disruptions in the flow of goods and services and shortages of gasoline, diesel fuel, propane, and electrical power, owing to the embargo by the Organization of American States. Tourist facilities vary according to price and location and have in many cases suffered because of the embargo." Don skipped down over the Entry Requirements and stopped at "although there does not appear to be a specific threat to U.S. citizens at this time, the potential exists throughout the country for random violence." He skipped ahead to "the police and judiciary are unable to provide adequate levels of security and due process." "Great," thought Don as he put the paper aside. He wondered how much of this Kronen knew.

Dysplasia

Don decided to urinate too since he was bored and felt he would need to by the time they got to the hotel. He walked down the hall to the room marked "gentlemen" and walked inside. It was empty and Don quickly looked under the two stalls even though no feet showed. He never put anything past Kronen, who would play strange tricks at the oddest times. Don opened the stalls. No Kronen.

"Damn."

Don walked outside to the lobby. He asked the woman at the desk if his friend had returned.

"No. I haven't seen him."

"Is there a back exit to the building?"

"Yes. But we keep it locked."

Don began to panic. If Kronen was playing a trick, Don would kill him.

Don decided to take the car and go to the hotel. He went outside and realized he did not have the keys. He reached for the car door, hoping it wasn't locked. It wasn't. He reached inside the glove box to take out the information from the Avis car rental. He walked back inside the Embassy.

Don was directed to use a pay telephone. He didn't have any change. He had some gourdes, the Haitian monetary unit. Most places accepted either the U.S. dollar or the gourdes. Prices were quoted in Haitian dollars or five gourdes. Don returned to the phone armed with a variety of coins.

The phone rang about twenty times. Don pictured the same man who had helped him, taking his time with a customer rather than answering the phone.

"Hello?"

"Yes. Is this the Avis car rental agency?"

"Yes. How can I help you?"

"I lost the keys to my car. Can you come with another set of keys?"

"Sure. I will finish tonight about eight. I will come then. What is your address?"

It was about four in the afternoon. "I need the keys now."

"Sir. I am sorry for you that you lost your keys, but the problem is your problem, not my problem. I am alone here and can't leave until eight this evening."

Don heard a set of keys dangling behind his head. He turned to see Kronen laughing.

"Never mind. I found them in my other pocket."

The man at the Avis agency hung up without giving his conversation with the American another thought.

"Where have you been?" demanded Don.

"Let's go." Kronen was serious, his voice harsh.

It worried Don. "What's wrong?"

Kronen forcibly interlocked his arm with Don's. "Come on. We're getting out of here."

They walked out the door. Kronen wouldn't speak until he had the vehicle moving.

"Chessman is dead," he announced.

"What?" Don was in shock.

"That was his plane on the ground at the airport. The fire was started once the plane hit the ground. They think from the inside and it spread to the outside."

"Did they send the body back?"

"There were five bodies taken from the plane by the military. Chessman was one of them. The State Department has already made a request for Chessman's body to be returned, but they are not getting any cooperation."

Dysplasia

"Shit. The tape was burnt on the plane."

"If he had it with him."

"Shit. I'm screwed."

"We can still go up to his house and snoop around. When we get back, we'll have to go to start plan B. If you want, I can start making some phone calls from here."

Don turned to look at Kronen. "What is the new plan B?"

"This is as good a time as any. By now Morningside Hospital has officially notified the State that they think you screwed up. That's a Public Health law." Kronen turned to Don to make his point stronger. "2803-e."

"Maybe this isn't the best time." Don was in no mood to hear about his impending trials.

Kronen continued. He explained Don's options once they were out of New York. "I'll get some merciless attorney friends to lean on Beitleman to spill what he knows. Beitleman is nobody's fool. He'll cooperate eventually."

"Kronen, come on. Enough." Don covered his ears.

"You can appeal the hospital action. I haven't seen the bylaws but they have to have some clause that allows you to go over what they did in order to give you a chance to show them that you didn't do what they say you did. It's called a proper defense. The hospital's decision will ultimately go before an Appellate Review Committee headed by a County Criminal Judge. If they support the hospital, you're totally fucked. But I don't think they will. The hospital will look bad trying to nail a whistle blower. That's one of the things you have going for you. All this happened when you were about to expose hospital practices that depicted the hospital in a less-than-favorable light."

"Are you saying you can reverse what happened?"

"I don't know. They certainly tried to steam roll over your rights. We can get them on denying your right to due process, 2801-b. But we'll still have problems with the girl's family. They will want your ass on a platter, but if we can keep the charges limited to the scope of malpractice, we can avoid a criminal civil suit. Plus your insurance company has to pick up the whole tab. The family won't be able to get to you personally."

It sounded so cold to Don. "Shit, Kronen. Do you have any idea what I've been going through?"

"No, I don't. And since we're not married, I am not going to sit here and let you explain the depths of your emotional turmoil. Right now we are going to get the fuck over to fucking Oloffson's before it gets fucking dark and some Macoute puts his initials on our heads with his machete. They'll sell them shrunk at the airport with a matching purse and cell phone cover."

Kronen could make Don smile even under the worst conditions. "I need a drink," said Don.

"Daddy will get you as many as you want at the hotel."

"So that's it. We're not married. It's a paternal thing."

"One of us has got to be in charge, it might as well be the one that's stable, brighter, and better looking."

"I would have given you the first two but you're no Robert Redford."

"Is that your yardstick for good looks? The guy's a midget."

"Compared to you, everyone is a midget."

Kronen succeeded in distracting Don just long enough.

Oloffson's Hotel was situated in the center of town. It was old and quaint, possibly the most famous hotel in the entire Caribbean. The endless list of celebrity guests would impress most anyone. One of the last celebrities to make regular holiday there was Mick Jagger and his model wife. Tourism was far from a strong point in Haiti. Many of the hotels closed because of the horrific stories about the widespread murders and mutilations.

Oloffson's was a hotel of only twenty-two rooms, a restaurant and a pool. The grand old Victorian house was originally built as a summer palace only to suffer occupation by American Marines, who used it as a hospital. It was Haiti's first hotel. From the wide and cool verandas, the literary and theatrical greats of the past would sit and stare at the beautiful gardens and the ocean.

Checking in was not a problem. Kronen made reservations from his office. It was easy over the Internet. They were shown to two rooms on an upper floor, which were right off a covered hall that faced an open atrium.

Don and Kronen dumped off their luggage and headed straight for the bar.

"Let's sniff around a little," said Kronen as they made their way downstairs.

Don was impressed with Kronen's "fact-finding" mission at the Embassy, although he thought anyone could have gotten the information. Kronen did everything with such authority.

Don and Kronen socked away drinks at the bar, talking with a UPI reporter named Tony who knew about Chessman's death.

"Your doctor friend was a big shot down here. Too bad."

"Yeah," said Kronen.

"He was my partner," said Don.

"Well, then I guess the partnership is dissolved," said Tony.

Don did not laugh.

Kronen broke into hysterical laughter. "Buy this guy another round."

The bartender obliged.

"Doctor, you ready for another?" asked Kronen.

Don shot down the rest of his drink. "Yeah."

"Did you ever see any real voodoo here?" asked Don.
"Voodoo. If you want to see voodoo, you should have stayed in New York," said Tony.

"What do you mean?" asked Kronen.
"The first international conference on voodoo was recently held in New York City."
"You're shitin' us," said Kronen.

"Fuckin-A. In Brooklyn." Tony was emphatic.
Don's eyes opened wide.
Tony obviously was a reporter that knew his beat. "Brooklyn might seem unlikely to you, but there's something like three hundred thousand Haitians living in New York. They need to improve their P.R. You know they hated that movie about the serpent and the rainbow. They don't like when we write or show that zombie nonsense. Best thing that ever happened is when the Pope recently came out for recognition of vodun."
"Vodun?" Even Kronen was getting interested.

"Vodun. The origin of all religions that worship spirits. That's where they get that voodoo or voodou stuff." Tony tried to get the pronunciations right.

The bulk of the conversation was the same as any three guys getting drunk anywhere in the world. At the end of the evening, when the buzz was waning and sleep was beckoning, Kronen ordered a final round of drinks. The reporter looked worried. His mood had changed. He became somber.

Dysplasia

"Are you okay?" asked Don.

He spoke slowly. "I was in Martiselt, in the south. I watched them gun down seven women who were trying to get at this guy's house. He was a photographer for the police. They were pissed at him. The police shot the women."

"What else have you seen?" asked Don.

"A man bit into the neck of a live rooster the other day. Right in the square. He beat it with the leg of a chair and the mob that was forming tossed it around as the blood flew everywhere. And that was before I had my breakfast."

"Is that part of voodoo?" pressed Don.

"What's your interest in it?"

Don didn't answer.

Tony continued. "Okay. I'll give you the 2.99 course and then I'm going to bed." Tony assumed the tone of an adult telling a scary bedtime story to a child. "Voodoo is a religion. They have a lot of gods called loas. Some good, some bad. The good ones are natural elements—fire, water, or even wind. They also worship the dead. The loa can show up at one of their shindigs and take over someone's body. The show is run by the priest."

"The houngan?" Don showed off his small knowledge of voodoo.

"Yeah. At these deals you have the rada, the mild and helping kind of god, and then you have the petro, the dangerous. They like to throw in graveyard stuff, a coffin or two, bones, shrouds. You get the picture. The priest for this stuff is the bocor. This guy can make your zombie by taking over a dead body. Sleep on that boys. I'm out of here."

"Thanks." Don was fascinated by Tony's knowledge.

"Good night, Tony. We'll see you again," said Kronen.

Tony pulled out a bill from his pocket. "What do I owe here?"

"You're clear," said Kronen.

"Thanks." Tony reached into his knapsack and took out a leaflet that looked like a corporate sales report.

"I just learned what I told you yesterday. It's here in a book. You read, don't you, Doc?"

"Yeah. Don took the pocketbook from Tony.

"So much for mysticism," said Kronen.

"I'll give it to you tomorrow."

"Keep it. It's a compilation of what goes on down here. I read plenty already."

"Thanks."

Tony turned back and said matter-of-factly, "There's some real fine-looking ladies down here, and you won't find that in those papers."

"We'll keep it in mind," said Kronen.

"Thanks," echoed Don. He didn't know about Kronen, but women were the furthest thing from his mind.

As they walked to their rooms, they stopped to listen to a group of guys from CNN.

"The kid was arrested and couldn't get back into the Embassy," said an older man with a moustache, dressed in green khakis.

"Is that the kid they arrested for wearing a Lavalas watch?" said a younger man wearing a Tommy Hilfiger hooded sweatshirt.

"Yeah. Any public support for Aristide was squashed," said the older man.

"When he got home, his parents were missing and they raped his sister. She tried to leave with him and the Coast Guard sent them back. The consulate turned them away."

"Can we get him for the story?"

"I think so. He wants us to use a code name. The guy is afraid they'll kill him next time."

Dysplasia

∞

"Okay. Make the arrangements. We'll shoot some footage."

Don read for about a half-hour. The *New York Times* referred to Jean-Claude, Baby Doc, the installed President for Life, as a technocrat. They were a group of young "chic" Haitians whose taste ran more to cocaine than the previous generation's champagne. They lived in villas in the mountains high above Port-au-Prince. The descriptions reminded Don of Chessman's idea of Hollywood. Enormous parties up in the hills. People building 20,000 and 30,000 square foot houses. It sounded like they were living the same life in Haiti.

Don read of Macoute torture. Forcing men to drink the urine of their captors. Licking their own blood from the floor and having excrement smeared on their faces.

Don was shocked to read that many Haitians were descendants of Jews who were turned away at Ellis Island.

He flipped through the articles quickly, feeling he could read them later in more detail. He stopped briefly to read that Papa Doc cursed President Kennedy with oungas, the curse put on by the priests. When Kennedy was shot, Papa Doc took credit.

As his eyes were closing he caught the words "ritual genital scarification and clitoridectomy" in an article written in the *National Review.* His eyes opened wide. The article discussed how AIDS had made its way from Africa to the Western hemisphere, and pointed out that practices like clitoridectomy and genital scarification were other means of spreading the disease.

Don reviewed the connections of the murders in his mind. It didn't matter. Chessman was dead.

"Poor Chessman," Don thought. It must have been horrible to die in a fire. Don hoped they would find something at the house to help him make his case against Chessman.

Don woke up sweating. There was an enormous noise off in the distance. He went out to the hall where Kronen stood outside, standing in the most ridiculous pair of print boxer shorts imaginable.

"What is it? It sounds like pots and pans clanking," said Don.

"I think that's what it is. The manager was just up here and told me that the people are banging the stuff in the mountains to warn that the army is around," informed Kronen.

"Great."

"Go back to sleep."

"Sure," answered Don sarcastically.

"Do you want to sleep in my room?" Kronen loved to tease Don, even under the most difficult conditions. Somehow, Kronen's sophomoric behavior cut the edge off the terror that showed in Don's eyes. Kronen offered a security of the past, the false security being around old friends.

"I'll take my chances alone." Don smirked.

Kronen went back to his room.

CHAPTER THIRTY-SEVEN

The next morning Kronen was already sifting through the newspapers when Don came downstairs.

The hotel lobby was not very active. There were news people and crew milling about. No one seemed in any particular hurry to do anything.

"There's a tiny little obit for Chessman. Only the *New York Times* has got it." Kronen displayed the newspaper.

"Let me see." Don took the paper from Kronen.

It said that Chessman died in an accident at the Haitian airport. It listed his profession and mentioned his academic titles. It seemed odd to Don that Chessman didn't have one of those "doctor-to-the-stars" obituaries that took up a whole column in the *Times*. Maybe Chessman's wife and children had more class than Chessman.

"Here." Kronen handed Don a note.

"What's this?"

"It's from your Haitian girlfriend."

Kronen spoke as Don read. "She wants us to come up to her house in Petionville."

"Where is it?" Don asked. He shrugged his shoulders and gestured as if to say "why not?"

"I already got directions."

"Then let's go."

"The car is full of gas. There's coffee and pastries in the car."

"Kronen. You are so domesticated."

"I don't want you to whine in the car. The highway system here makes FDR Drive look like it was just paved."

The roads in Haiti were terrible. The two main highways were like country back roads in the United States. The rest of the roads were dangerous at night and a challenge during the day.

Outside the property, the roads were nicely paved. The sight of the main house was breathtaking. It seemed so odd that such exquisite properties were on the same island with the poorest lifestyle in the Western Hemisphere. On the way to Petionville, Don saw impoverished settings that would make a shantytown more desirable.

Two guards stood at the gate. They made no effort to hide their weapons. A shotgun stood ready, leaning against a little booth next to the gate. The man who spoke to them had an automatic weapon hanging by a thin black strap from his neck.

"Yes, sir. A good morning sir. How can I help you, sir?" He was polite and articulate in English.

"I'm Dr. Gardner and this is Mr. Kronen."

"Yes. Mr. Drouin is expecting you. They are near the swimming pool. Drive into the courtyard and leave your vehicle. The man at the house will walk you over. Have a very nice day, gentlemen."

"Thank you." Don answered for both. "Just like in the movies," he thought.

As they drove into the expansive property, Kronen smiled and moved his eyebrows up and down like Groucho Marx.

Dysplasia

∽

"Your girl is rich."

"She's not my girl."

"Get the fuck out of here." Kronen slapped Don on the shoulder.
"What?"
"You never plugged her. Tell me the truth. Right now!"
"I never plugged anyone."
"Okay. You never made love to her."
"I don't want to talk about it."
"So. You did it."
"I did not. She thinks American men don't know how to make love.
She told me I need to learn to be more sensual."
"They always say that and then you go ahead and do what you want
anyway."
"Is that what your wife likes?"
"Leave my wife out of this. I'm talking about sex."
"Very funny, Kronen. Will you quit asking me about Susan?"
"Okay. I'll wait till you get a new girl." Kronen looked at Don to see if
his remark irritated him.
Don shook his head. "Jerk," said Don.
"Maybe," answered Kronen. "But I don't think so."

When they reached the courtyard a uniformed butler waited. He
escorted them to the swimming pool. An outdoor table was set for
lunch. They stood in the bright sun while he took their drink orders.
"Will you be having lobster?" he asked.
"I don't know. Is that what we're having?" asked Don.
"Sir. If you and your friend are having lobster, we need to get the
count. We will send the men out during your appetizer portion to catch
the lobster. That is all."

"Sure. I'll have one," said Don.

"Two," added Kronen.

As the butler left to get drinks, Susan walked from the back of the house with a tall, handsome man. He had mulatto coloring and wore a white shirt. The sleeves billowed in the breeze.

"Don. This is my father, Guy Drouin."

"How do you do, Doctor?" He extended his hand to Don.

They shook.

"Fine. This is my friend, Bob Kronen." Kronen shook hands with Guy.

"Hello. It's nice to meet you, Mr. Drouin. This is quite a place you have." Kronen was in a socially polite mode. He also sensed he was in the company of a very powerful man.

"Thank you. Are you gentlemen hungry? We can begin our meal anytime."

"Sure. We haven't had breakfast," answered Don.

For two hours, Don, Kronen, Susan and Guy dined in luxury, with servants tending to their every need. The ocean was in view in the distance. It was an idyllic setting, ironic on such a troubled island.

Guy Drouin was a manufacturer's representative. He got very wealthy looking out for the interests of American manufacturers. His background was in police work, but after a number of years he became his own company, which would act as a liaison between American business and all affairs Haitian. This included strikes brought on by curses. The solution in those cases was simple. Guy would pay more money to a more powerful houngan who would take away the curse on the factory, and the workers would go back to work.

"My daughter tells me that you have business at the Chessman house." He paused and Susan shook her head, indicating that a response

Dysplasia

∞

would be inappropriate. "I will assist you in going there tomorrow. My men and I will come for you at your hotel. It is not far from here. Now, if you will excuse me." Guy got up from his seat.

Don rose and extended his hand. With his other hand, he swatted Kronen who quickly stood.

"It was nice to meet you," said Don.

"Enjoy your stay in Haiti," said Guy.

"Thanks," said Kronen.

Kronen waited for Guy to be out of sight. "He doesn't seem disappointed that Chessman is dead."

Susan explained. "Many people in this country knew Dr. Chessman. Many liked him and many did not." Susan's mood suddenly changed and tears formed in her eyes. "I'm sorry. I should go inside."

"What's the matter, Susan?" asked Don.

As Susan left, she stated, "Nothing. Nothing. I am sorry."

The butler, standing within earshot at attention walked over to clear the dishes. He spoke clearly and quietly as he picked them up.

"Her mother was the doctor's patient. She die here in the hospital. He call on de phone, say everything is okay. They say if she took de plane to Miami, maybe she live." He walked away, and spoke not looking back. "She die like de poor people."

On the way back, traffic started to crawl. Kronen made his way through the local streets near the hotel. The noise of an angry mob came up suddenly. Don was immediately frightened by dozens of people running in the streets.

"Shit. Let's get out of here." Don was in a panic.

"Where can we go?" shouted Kronen. "Just relax."

- 462 -

Don stuck his head out of the window. In front were one limousine, a Lincoln Town Car, a Buick sedan, and a Caprice station wagon. All were black.

The mob stormed the vehicles. A group of men in business suits exited the Hotel Montana, then immediately ran back inside.

"We're out of here," shouted Kronen.

Don and Kronen abandoned their car and ran in the opposite direction of the mob. They never looked back.

Panting, they made their way into the Oloffson. First stop, the bar. They would learn later that Mr. Caputo, the U.N. envoy, was staying at the Hotel Montana. Demonstrators and the police were attacking the diplomatic vehicles. While the hotel was under siege, they got Mr. Caputo into the home of a U.S. Diplomat. Eventually, Mr. Caputo was sneaked out of the country that evening.

The door opened to Don's room while he was on the phone. Kronen walked in. "You should lock the door," said Kronen.

"I thought I did." He continued the phone conversation. "Yes. That's right. The car is in front of the Hotel Montana. No. We are not going to get it. I don't care how much you charge us. You get the car. You keep it. It is not a safe car. Do you have any Jeeps? Then forget it. Keep the car."

Don hung up.

"You sure can negotiate. Now what do we do for a car?"

"I'm sure Susan can help us. I'll call her after dinner."

Kronen put his hand on Don's shoulder. "How you holding up?"

"Okay, I guess."

"We'll go up to the house, look around tomorrow, then be out of here."

"Yeah." Don couldn't have agreed more.

Dysplasia

"Come on. I'll buy you dinner. I told Tony he could eat with us. You know he likes you."

"Fuck off."

"That's my boy."

They walked out of the room. When Don locked the door, Kronen smiled. "Very flimsy locks," said Kronen.

The night air hit them as they walked through the outdoor hall. In a moment they were downstairs in the dining room.

Over dinner, Kronen grilled Tony for information. Tony was generous.

"Guy Drouin is a very powerful man. He has his own army. He's always in town meeting with the Feds."

"Do you think they will ever restore order here?" asked Don.

"Do you think they'll ever restore law and order in the United States?" answered Tony.

"What? I don't get it?" said Don, annoyed.

"Tell him," Tony said directly to Kronen.

"I think what Tony is trying to intimate is that this place has been problematic so long, there's nothing worth fighting over to straighten it out."

"Something like that," added Tony. Tony's own version was more historically detailed. Kronen and Don spent most of the dinner listening.

The next morning, Guy arrived with an extra Jeep for Don and Kronen. Susan rode with them as they headed to the mountains. Don quickly counted a half-dozen men in other vehicles.

Don stared at the clear blue sky. He thought how well he was holding up, knowing that he was returning home to a ruined life.

Chessman's house was another exquisite oasis of land, swimming pools, outdoor lanai, and a tennis court, perched on a small peak.

Guy stopped the caravan a few hundred yards from the house. He shut the engine. The Jeeps behind them did the same.

"We stop here," he said and made a hand signal to his men. He quickly got out of the car. Don, Susan, and Kronen followed. "You two wait here," he said, pointing to Kronen and Don. They moved to the side of the road.

Kronen reached in his pocket, removed a pistol and unlocked the safety.

"What? What the hell is that? Kronen!"

"It's a weapon," answered Kronen.

"You're doing that to scare me, aren't you? Where did you get that? Do I need one?"

"You great white doctor. You not need weapon."

"Cut it out."

Kronen pointed behind Don. "Don't say cut it out to these guys."

At that moment six tall men swept past them carrying long machetes.

"How did you get through Customs with that?"

"I didn't. There are a few extras floating around the neighborhood."

They waited while Guy and the men made a quick trip around the back of the house. Guy came out the front door.

"It is safe," he proclaimed.

"It's not the way I would have done it, but what the fuck. When in Rome…" added Kronen.

"Not the way he would have done it," thought Don.

Inside, they moved slowly, holding lanterns to illuminate their path. Many of the windows were covered. The house was a decorator's feast. Lifestyles of the rich and famous would be proud to call this one of their own. Robin Leach would get excited about "all the treasures from years of collecting native art."

Kronen turned to Don and asked bluntly, "Exactly what are we looking for? He's croaked. The tape is burnt. Let's get the hell out of here and throw your bones to the legal system in New York."

"Lou said there'd be things in the house." Don's voice let Kronen know they were not leaving.

Don walked towards the master bedroom, an expansive room with a sitting area the size of most living rooms. Kronen and Susan followed while Guy and his men formed loosely around the outside perimeter of the house for surveillance. Don hit a light switch. Power came on in the house. The lights illuminated the marble floors with an eerie reflection of the three figures.

"There's nothing here. Come on," said Kronen.

They went out the far door of the bedroom. It led onto a huge outdoor patio. A little matching building stood about forty feet from the house, much like a pool cabana.

"Let's go in there," said Don.

"Why? You want to see what designer did his towels?" Kronen thought they were wasting time.

"Come on." Don walked towards the cabana.

They followed as Don hurried to the building. The outside door was very thick, as if reinforced with several locks. Don pulled the handle on the door. To everyone's surprise, it was open.

This was no pool cabana. Don recognized the peculiar odor. The room smelled like a pathology laboratory. Formaldehyde. Whew! A most unpleasant stench.

"Somebody died in this place," said Kronen. Kronen tried a light switch. Nothing.

Susan put her lantern to a shelf on the wall. "Many animals died for these."

"What the fuck?" asked Kronen. He picked up one of the jars and held it in the light. "Is this what I think it is? Tell me this hairy set of garbanzos are some animal's balls."

Don took the jar. "You could always spot testicles, couldn't you?"

"These are animals, aren't they?" asked Kronen.

"Don't count on it," answered Susan with an authoritative air that stunned Don and Kronen.

"What are you talking about?" asked Don.

"Your friend Chessman was a bocor, an evil priest. This proves it."

"He wasn't my friend," said Don.

"Let's forget the relationship stuff. What did you say?"

"He was a white witch doctor. They would boil pieces of bodies and utilize that to put a death curse on someone. Chessman would do this so that the competitors of his friends would lose work days when he would curse the factory owners and no one would come to work."

"I told you he was a nut job from the very beginning," said Kronen.

"Holy shit!" shouted Don.

"What is it?" asked Susan.

"Susan, you were right. These are human genitals, parts of a human vagina."

"Oh, God. I'm going to be sick. Let's see if we can drive back to the hotel and get on the next jet home," said Kronen.

"Kronen, don't go soft on me now."

"What do you mean now? I never promised you Rambo. Come on. Let's get the fuck out of here now."

"Don't you see what this means? The murders in New York. The genital mutilation. Chessman. He was the one."

Dysplasia

There was a commotion outside. A few shots were fired. A scream was followed by the sound of running feet shuffling across the terra cotta.

Guy came running towards them. "Quick. Run for the cars. They were waiting in the woods behind the house."

"Who?" asked Don.

"Who cares," added Kronen. He checked his gun.

Susan grabbed one of jars and began to run. Don grabbed another and took off behind her. Kronen reluctantly did the same. This type of evidence would probably be of no value, but there was no time to explain it to Don. Gunfire followed them across the side lawn of the house.

Bullets whizzed by as they ran for the Jeeps. They got there easily and unscathed. Don jumped in the far Jeep. "There's no key here," he shouted.

Susan and Kronen went in the one immediately in front of Don. "No keys. I guess we're staying," shouted Kronen.

"Take it easy and no one will be harmed," said a familiar voice. Dozens of men stepped from behind the Jeeps and walked up the road with weapons drawn. Guy's men disappeared, either because they were outnumbered or because they were in fear. So did Guy.

"The Macoutes," whispered Susan.

A tall figure in a large straw hat stepped forward. He was dressed in tan khaki. The figure was unmistakable. Young men carrying the long curved machetes, the coulines, surrounded the figure.

"Hank Chessman," announced Don in disbelief.

"Welcome to my home." Chessman signaled and said something in Haitian. The guards escorted Don, Susan, and Kronen from the Jeeps. They forcibly escorted them up the road to the main house, in single file formation.

As she walked, Susan talked to the young Haitians in their native language. At one point, they stopped her and a shouting match developed. Chessman stepped between them and pulled Susan ahead by her arm.

"Come on now. That's the problem with people like you. You mix politics in all your activities. This is purely social." He shouted so Don could hear him. "Isn't that right, Junior?"

In the house, most of the guards dispersed, leaving two of the main ones who spoke directly to Chessman. They sat in the living room with Uzis resting on their laps and machetes at their sides. Chessman turned to Susan, Don and Kronen and smiled in an appealing manner.
"Can I get you a drink? A malt scotch, Junior. Your friend, the attorney. We met once or twice?"
"We met," answered Kronen, clearly indicating his dislike for Chessman.
"Kronen," volunteered Don. "Robert Kronen."
"Would you like a drink, Mr. Kronen?" Chessman asked again.
"I don't think so," said Kronen. "I don't think I like your kind of hospitality."

"Sit down, Kronen," ordered Chessman. "You too." Chessman pointed to where he wanted them to sit.

"Oh, yes. Thank you, great white doctor," said Kronen.

Kronen and Susan sat. Don remained standing and stared at Chessman.
"Dear Kronen. I suppose you expect me to come over there and slap you, but I'm afraid it will take more than that to hurt my feelings."

"For a man who's dead, it should take quite a bit to hurt your feelings," suggested Susan.

Chessman smiled. "Susan. You know Haiti. Things change easily. I had to make my retirement a nice one. I don't want to be hassled the way they are going to hassle Junior here."

"You staged your own death. I like that," said Kronen.

"But we know you're alive," blurted out Don.

Two men entered and dumped the group's belongings on the floor in front of Chessman. "Let's see," said Chessman as he opened one of the backpacks. He found the jars. "These are my property, aren't they?"

"Did you cut them off your victims yourself?" asked Kronen.

"The imaginations on you all. Ask Susan. Animal sacrifice is part of our lives in Haiti. It is a religious thing, you might say."

"You sacrifice people," stated Susan.

"A totally ridiculous notion."

"Those are not animal genitalia," Don supplied in almost a whisper.

"Now, now, Junior. What are we going to do with you?" Chessman gestured to his men. "Sit him down. Get them drinks. And tell the others we have honored guests who want to know about voodoo sacrifice. Very nosy honored guests." The men did as asked. Don was escorted to a seat. Chessman spoke as Don walked past. "Junior. I am not a murderer. That was your mistake."

"What about Carver, the girl you butchered and then sent to me?"

"Didn't you read what you wrote in the hospital report? You said she bled to death and you were the treating doctor. You tried to help her. Not much help, were you?"

Don attempted to hit Chessman, but before he could raise his arm, Don was struck in the head by the handle of a machete. He lost consciousness.

The dining room belonged in a museum. It was filled with primitive paintings, two large ceiling-to-floor cabinets compartmentalized with artifacts and bric-a-brac. The table appeared to be finished from one giant piece of wood, the tree knots stained deeply to offset the lighter wood finish.

Don woke up to find himself seated in one of the plush dining room chairs. He stared at the elaborately set dinner table and wondered if the table was mahogany. It was the same color as the wood coat hangers in the doctor's lounge at Morningside Hospital. He had forgotten why he was there.

"Well. Nice to see you again. This could be our last meal. Don't you think we should dig in?"

Don looked across the table at Kronen. Don managed a meek smile of recognition through the throbbing pain on the side of his head. He palpated a bruised area posterior to his right ear lobe, just above the insertion of the sternocleidomastoid muscle. His hand was flaked with dried blood. The area was warm. He tried to remember the cardinal signs of inflammation. Rubor. Dolor. His mind was on hold. Suddenly he felt something cold applied to his head as he counted the number of times his head sustained damage the last few days. Two. No. Three. Four?

"There. This will make it feel better," said Susan. She wrapped a deep-blue dinner napkin with ice and dipped it in water.

"Shall we begin our meal?" asked Chessman. He sat at the other end of the table.

Then Don remembered everything.

No one felt like eating. Guards stood around one side of the table. A commotion was taking place somewhere else in the house. Mumbling and movement could be heard.

Dysplasia

Don nibbled on a few things. After some wine, Kronen got hungry and dug into the magnificent Creole display set before him. Susan stuck to bread and fruits with a skin.

Chessman was drunk and began to slur his words. A look of happiness took over his face as the evening wore on. Chessman signaled to one of the men and the lights in the room were dimmed. "It's time for the entertainment."

"This better be good," said Kronen under his breath. "We didn't have a movie on the plane here."

Chessman was absolutely giddy. "I suppose there's no harm in showing you this as part of your entertainment package. Sort of like those horrendous tour packages they used to offer to bring people from Philadelphia and New Jersey here for a vacation in Haiti."

An electronic screen descended from the ceiling, to Chessman's side. The lights were dimmed further as the generic electronic sounds of the machine coincided with light emanating from the three-colored video source on the other side of the room. All eyes were glued to the screen.

It quickly became apparent that this was no ordinary presentation. The scene opened inside Chessman's bedroom, in his condominium.

"I won't narrate. This type of movie is self-explanatory." A deep gurgle originated somewhere in Chessman's lower stomach, traveled its way up his esophagus and when ready to exit in the form of a belch rushed out combined with a typical Chessman chortle. It was almost funny until one's eyes turned back to stare at the big-screened bare ass of their host/captor.

"The tape," whispered Kronen.

They watched in disbelief. Don was perspired and felt his shirt cling to his chest. Susan threw up the small bits of fruit she managed to eat for sustenance when the girl lay helpless, motionless, obviously intoxicated from one of Chessman's personal valium/demerol cocktails.

Chessman began his prodding, spreading, poking and irritating to the point of causing her life's vital fluid to ooze forth to his ritualistic delight. Susan was similarly repulsed to the point of illness.

Fortunately, Chessman's body got in the way of the camera. The resultant shots seemed no worse than watching a second-rate nude scene. If the girl was Laurel Carver, then Don and Kronen knew that Chessman was deliberately showing them the evidence. It was clear to them that their lives were now reduced to a mere trifle.

Suddenly the movie stopped. The few glitches associated with amateur splicing made their presence known on the screen. White spots, colorful snow, and then the shot went blank briefly darkening the room. The light from the now-white screen lit the room as the scene switched to the office. Yes! Chessman trying to stop the bleeding. Someone spliced the two tapes together.

Kronen watched Chessman working in the office and vomited, his head jerking spasmodically while his cheeks reddened as his breathing almost stopped as the projectile fluid left his mouth in several quick spurts. No one paid much attention.

Kronen allowed himself a humorous thought; "This guy should have gone to film school." Don sat frozen in silence, his arm around Susan as her chest rose and fell spasmodically, like she was having convulsions in slow motion.

Don turned away from the screen. Chessman left the table. Don could hear some ritualistic chanting coming from the living room and realized they were all going to be killed.

They were lifted from their seats by the guards in the group. A loud clap of thunder reverberated throughout the house as they were led into the living room to witness the ongoing voodoo ritual. Each knew they were going to be sacrificed, mutilated in some ungodly horrific way. Don recalled that only a few days ago he thought he was going to die on television and be seen by millions of viewers as an electronic signal dying before their eyes. He couldn't make up his mind which demise was better. He felt like passing out.

They were led near the center of the action where Chessman was chanting from another dimension, unknown to a rational mind. The personalizing of such extremes took years, a time he used to develop his technique. Don recognized it as a form of hypnotherapy or mind control. Despite the circumstances, the depth of the trance impressed Don. Chessman was seeing, thinking, smelling and hearing in a different world.

Herded together, Susan was pushed into the area where Chessman stood. Don looked at Kronen who was slowly unzipping his fly. Kronen had obviously gone over the edge. Unseen was Kronen's hand reaching into his pants as another loud clap of thunder shook the room. A torrential downpour started, sheets and sheets of rain lashed up against the roof and glass windows of the home. The rain was made all the more forceful by the wind.

Kronen had his dick out. Two men waited behind them with automatic weapons. Don had hoped Kronen would think of something. He knew then that Kronen was a fake.

Susan was bound at the hands and strapped to a ceramic dish about ten feet in diameter. Her skirt was now hiked over her thighs and she lay in her stark white panties, which looked more like a surgical wrap than underwear. A series of horrific mutilations crossed Don's mind, ending with the eventual removal of her clitoris, the Chessman way. Would he give her anything to dull the pain?

Suddenly to Don's right a bright yellow stream of liquid arced its way over his head. Don witnessed Kronen shooting his urine as high as any human could, courtesy of leaning back on his heels as far as he could without falling. The guards across the circle found this hysterically funny. Kronen started to laugh and turned around to piss directly on the men with the automatic weapons. They did not find this funny. Before either could register their dislike Kronen had sunk his boot point high into the guy's scrotum. If balls could shatter this guy's were in a million pieces. The agony showed clearly on his face. He screamed as Kronen grabbed his weapon, turning as he began to fire, yelling, "You motherfucking savages are dead." The guard to his right had a second to react before Kronen's leg left the ground like it was made of rubber and connected with the bridge of the black man's nose. Blood splattered as he sunk back against the wall. By then Kronen had shot at least six men who returned fire. Some ran outside as soon as gunfire started. Don never saw a bullet wound. Clothing and flesh spouted open with blood gushing and spurting on furniture, the art, the floor, the ceiling, other people, and Don's face.

Kronen screamed as he jumped into the center of the room, still firing. "Piss on me and I piss on you, you cheap, low-life scumbags." He fired across the room and shattered many of the glass doors and windows.

As if planned, Guy entered the room followed by a dozen black men in uniform, police who sympathized with the government. Seeing the turmoil, Chessman moved to the patio doors and slipped out into the blinding rain. He turned back to look at Don, then disappeared.

Don looked at Kronen. His friend was far from a fake.

Guy untied his daughter.

Don felt himself move very slowly across the room. He zigzagged through the debris and fallen bodies and he fell over a large plush sofa that was torn and tattered by the riddling bullets. He looked outside and saw Chessman's tall figure turn left at a large palm tree. Don started to run.

Dysplasia

~

"Don. Wait!" called Kronen.

Don followed Chessman into an area covered by thick foliage. He saw a muddy path and took off in pursuit. After about twenty yards, the path widened to a road. Chessman was only another twenty yards ahead. Don figured Chessman had a vehicle stashed somewhere, perhaps with more guards.

Don ran as hard as he could to catch up with Chessman. Don tried to grab Chessman around the shoulders and was easily shaken. He tried again. Don caught an elbow in the mouth. He would have to get Chessman off his feet. Don screamed a primal scream that startled Chessman. Don threw his body against Chessman's in a cross-body block. The two hit the mud and rolled several feet to a halt.

Chessman screamed as loud as he could. "I never killed anyone. I never killed anyone. Don't hurt me."

Don used his feet for leverage in order to get his body over Chessman's. Don straddled him to hold him, wanting to strike him.

"You killed that girl."

"I did not. She had an anomaly. You know that."

"You killed Melinda."

"No. I never killed anyone. I swear. Take the tape. You can have it. Please don't hurt me."

"Who killed Melinda if you didn't?"

"Pierre. Pierre."

"Bullshit."

Chessman spoke rapidly. "I would help him with women. I didn't know how crazy he was. She stopped fucking him or something, I don't know. I don't know. I never killed anyone."

Don thought Chessman was stalling. Suddenly his accumulated hatred and revulsion materialized into fists and Don brought them down hard on the side of Chessman's lower jaw. Don was sure he dislocated Chessman's jaw as the other side hung loosely pointed out to the right. He lifted his hands high once again. As he was about to strike Chessman's eustachian tube, two pairs of hands grabbed him from behind and pulled him off Chessman.

Don was relieved to see Guy.

"Go home to your country. Dr. Chessman belongs to us," said Guy.

The men pulled Don back. He wanted to say something, but stopped. His first thought was for mercy.

Two men held Chessman outstretched on the ground. "Donald, listen to me." He didn't call him "Junior."

"You're a killer." Don repeated it. "You're a killer."

"Pierre killed Melinda. I know it."

How odd to pin such a ridiculous thing on the doorman. Don's mind flashed back to the scene on Church Avenue, where Pierre worked as a night security guard.

"Hey, Doc. What the hell brings you to Brooklyn?" Pierre's Caribbean English. He heard this accent continually since arriving in Haiti. Don played the line over several times as Guy's men pulled him down the road, away from Chessman.

The men stretched Chessman's limbs out wide. Chanting came from Chessman's mouth, a chanting Don knew. Chessman was praying in Hebrew: the prayer for the dead, yiskor.

The paradox would stay with Don as long as he lived. Don felt momentary pity for Chessman's twisted mind. It must have been torture for Chessman to live with himself.

The men tried to make Don look straight ahead but he wrestled free and ran a few steps down the road. They had stripped away Chessman's pants. A squat man with no shirt approached with a machete. The two men pulled Don away just as he saw the machete strike downward across Chessman's groin. Chessman's scream accompanied the motion. The rain spread his blood instantaneously over Chessman's lower torso and legs. Another man stooped to pick up something. In his free hand was a jar. The blood from Chessman's body funneled into a neat little stream of rain, a tributary that ran over the muddy road. The blood caught up to Don's feet. The two men and Don watched the blood run past. He turned his head away and stared straight ahead.

Don was sick to his stomach. He wanted to vomit but couldn't.

He didn't remember walking back to the house. When he arrived, there was tremendous activity: bodies were thrown into the foliage, a fire raged in the center of the home, as well as two of the outer buildings. Sporadic gunfire and soldiers in small numbers came up the back side of the hill.

Kronen was in one of the Jeeps. "Let's go. Let's go."

Don pulled himself into the passenger seat. "The tape!" screamed Don.

Kronen reached into his shirt and displayed the VCR tape for Don. Kronen put it back into the drier area of his shirt and put the Jeep into gear.

"What about Susan?"

"She left with her father."

"Did she say anything?"

"Yeah. Get your white asses to the airport."

"That's it."

"I'm sure if you send her a postcard, you two can become pen pals."

The Jeep careened down the road, taking the bumps hard on acceleration while Kronen tried to change gears on the fly. The wind and rain were deafening. Kronen screamed to be heard over nature's muffling downpour. "Did you see Chessman?"

Don paused and said matter-of-factly, "I think they cut off his balls."

"What?"

"I think they cut off his balls," screamed back Don at the top of his lungs.

"Good. They should have cut off his dick, too!"

"I think they did," Don said more quietly, not interested in reviewing the matter any further.

They almost floated down the hill from Chessman's house. The Jeep turned onto the so-called highway, disappearing in the blinding storm.

"I hope we get in before it floods," said Kronen.

The road was deserted. Kronen seemed confident in handling the Jeep. They passed a few tap-taps that went off the road.

When they reached the turn for the hotel, Kronen kept his foot hard on the accelerator.

"Kronen. Where are you going?"

"The airport."

"What about our things?"

"I've got three thousand in cash in the boot of my shoe. If we can't buy our way onto the airline and out of this mixed morality world, we'll never need our things again. Capice, great white doctor?"

"Guy had the police with him."

"Doc. I'm not hanging around here to answer any questions. That's a mess up there. It's not like Chessman's people don't know Guy's, who also happen to work for the police. Everyone knew we were there. Do you want to be part of Tony's next story?"

Don was convinced. "What about our passports?"

Kronen smiled and reached into another flap pocket on his bush jacket. He proudly displayed them.

Don breathed a sigh of relief, one of many he would breath before they would get out of Haiti.

Dysplasia

The Jeep turned into the empty airport. It was a perfect night for Kronen to work more of his magic because there wouldn't be many people around.

They abandoned the Jeep near the entrance to the terminal and walked to the doors.

"Act like we do this everyday. Don't talk or look anyone in the eye," said Kronen.

As they entered they passed a bar where two policemen sat at a small table. The policemen looked squarely at the two soaked and muddied white men, heads held high as they walked towards the counter.

Kronen whispered to Don, "We got caught in the storm. Our Jeep overturned and the bags went over the embankment."

Don was nervous. He realized they might not get a plane. "What if they don't believe us?"

Kronen thought that was funny.

"Why are you laughing? What if they go back to Oloffson's to check?"

Kronen walked towards the men's room. Don followed. Don noticed some people at the far end of the terminal sitting with luggage. Their flights most probably cancelled because of the storm.

Inside the men's room, Kronen checked to make sure they were alone.

"This is for the cops." Kronen sat down on a broken vinyl-backed chair. He unscrewed his boot heel with his pocket knife and took out a soggy wad of one-hundred-dollar bills. "I'm never spending this much for boots again. They leak." Kronen checked in his pants pocket. "I still have my credit cards."

"Me too," said Don.

"The story about the Jeep is in case the airline wants to know why we don't have any return tickets. We lost them with our baggage. The cash is for extras."

"It's the police I'm worried about," said Kronen.

He was right. As soon as they exited the men's room, one of the policemen was waiting.

Kronen took the officer aside and showed him the passports. Kronen reached into yet another pocket and produced a plastic card. The police looked at the card, nodded and handed everything but the card back to Kronen. Don wasn't sure if the policeman pocketed anything from inside the passports. Within minutes, the policeman and Kronen were laughing together.

The policeman put in a call to the airline office for Kronen. An attendant would be there shortly. In twenty minutes, another policeman arrived with proper-sized cotton khakis from the Gap and two Ralph Lauren Polo shirts, in case an extra was needed for the flight. The police couldn't do enough for Kronen.

Kronen bought several rounds of drinks for the police. Kronen was a pro, and Don realized now that whatever job Kronen did for the government, he was damn good at it.

They lucked out. The American Airlines attendant was a thin, older man from Haiti. Kronen stated, "We have a return flight in two days. I believe it is the eighth. Isn't that right, Dr. Gardner?"

"Your name sir?" The attendant looked at the computer screen.

"I'm Robert Kronen and this is Dr. Donald Gardner. We would like very much to get on your next flight to New York or any connecting flights from any other cities. We want to go tonight." As he said the word "tonight", Kronen passed two of the soggy one-hundred-dollar bills across the counter. The man took the bills in one hand. It disappeared below the counter while he continued to operate his keyboard with his other hand. Kronen repeated, "We must leave tonight."

"There is a nonscheduled flight out later tonight to the Dominican Republic. From there you can fly to Miami. It depends on the rain."

"Fine," answered Kronen. He knew that anyone delayed by the storm would also be eager to make connecting flights.

"Six hundred American," said the man. He forced a smile.

Kronen counted out the money.

The man at the desk never asked another question. He prepared two boarding passes and handed them to Kronen, skipping the fancy American Airlines ticket sleeves, and said, "Have a nice trip. I hope you enjoyed your stay here in Haiti."

The boarding passes seemed generic; no names, just numbers hand-written on a prepared form. Don wondered if the man even worked for the airline.

A Saab turbojet prop plane taxied near the terminal sometime in the middle of the night. Don felt someone jostle him awake. He woke up startled, happy to see Kronen. Two black men in business suits carrying attaché cases were already walking towards the little plane.

Once safely on the plane, Don and Kronen drank straight warm vodka, as there was no ice. Don turned to Kronen: "Are you ever going to tell me what you did after law school?"

"No."
"Will you tell me anything?"
"Of course. You're my best friend."

The sarcasm was killing Don. "Okay. The card. You gave the cop a card."

Kronen reached into his pocket, pulled out another card and flipped it to Don: a prepaid phone card.

"That's it?"

"And a lot of cash," added Kronen. "See. Now you know everything I know."

Don sipped his drink. No formal announcement took place before the plane took off.

Kronen grinned ear to ear and downed a shot of vodka in one gulp. He looked around for the stewardess with his glass raised. "Oh, nurse. Could you refill my prescription?" He raised his glass to the two black men in business suits.

"Come on, boys. I'm buying."

Don felt sleep overcoming him. The next thing he knew it was getting light outside. Kronen somehow shaved, put on a clean shirt and looked as fresh as a daisy.

Don whispered to Kronen. "Chessman said he didn't murder Melinda."

"You're surprised he didn't get on his knees and confess?"

"You don't understand. He said he knew who did. He said it was the doorman at our office building."

"Stay out of it. You've got the tape. Let's call it a day."

Don nodded, but continued to think about the Church Avenue meeting with Pierre.

"Did you know that Guy was coming back?" asked Don.

Dysplasia

"No."

"What if he didn't?"

"I was doing okay, wasn't I?" Kronen winked and closed his own eyes to sleep.

The rest of the trip was easy, just two tourists back from holiday.

Don waited for Kronen to finish a telephone call. When he hung up, they walked outside the terminal in New York. Don hailed a cab. Kronen slammed the door shut from the outside after Don got inside.

"Where are you going?"

"Home to my wife. You're in New York. I don't have to watch your ass anymore. Goodbye!"

With that, he tossed some money through the window. Don grabbed the bills and put them in his pocket.

"Kronen?"

"Yes, darling?"

"Thanks."

"Buddy boy, thanks is only a beginning. I am going to manipulate, extort, and if I have to, steal until I feel you've repaid me."

"That could take a long time."

Kronen gave Don his widest grin. "Fuckin'-a. I love to be owed stuff."

The cab pulled away. Kronen lit up a huge cigar, took a few puffs and blew the smoke high into the air. He liked the action. It was something he missed.

CHAPTER THIRTY-EIGHT

Jill opened the window in her office and looked down at the corner of 61st and Fifth. Pierre was helping one of the residents into a waiting limo. She looked at her watch: 7:30.

Jill was too tired to continue. Dick hadn't seen her for almost a week although he called everyday to see how she was doing. They spoke about getting back together, but were still too polarized to make it happen.

She was worried about Don. Rumors floated around the professional community: Drugs. Drinking. Divorce. Bankrupt. Police custody. Suicide.

Manny told Jill that Don might lose his license to practice in New York. "Childs is livid that he can't find Don. You know Childs. He's the kind of guy that can't sleep unless he's ruining someone's life."

Jill walked downstairs. The exit on the doctor's side of the building was locked by this hour. She crossed through the hall to the residential elevators. This area was well lit at night.

Pierre sat in the front of the lobby with his hat off.

Dysplasia

∞

"Of course," thought Jill. "Pierre. He's the guy I saw hanging around all those places." Jill knew about Pierre's reputation for living the "good" life in Manhattan. He looked so different without his uniform.

"Hi, Doc. How are you?" asked Pierre.

"I'm fine. That's you I've been seeing hitting all those hot spots."

"Well, I like to get around." He smiled.

Pierre jumped up from the chair as Jill neared the front door. He extended his arm so that Jill could pass him as he held the door.

"Thanks. Have a good night."

As Jill passed him, he reached his left arm around her waist and held it firmly. She could feel a firm, solid, pointed object in her side.

"Quiet, Doc. Quiet."

"What the—?"

"Don't say a word. Just get into the car."

The advice Jill knew about being mugged, the suggestions about what to do, the calm calculated plans she made in preparation for a crisis were lost. Jill was frozen. Terror spread throughout her body.

Pierre's white Monte Carlo Super Sport was illegally parked in front of the building. Pierre walked Jill to the driver's side and opened the door while standing close to her. He helped her inside, then followed close behind. As she slid to the passenger side, Pierre got in the driver's side.

A few people walked past the car. If someone thought Jill was in trouble, the most Jill could hope for was a phone call to the police, only once the observer was sure of his or her own safety. Jill looked back into the lobby. No one saw what happened. Pierre was always offering people rides. Even if someone saw her get in the vehicle, it still wouldn't seem out of the ordinary.

Jill wanted to scream for help, but the long, stainless steel blade pressed firmly in her side was a clear deterrent. Maybe he had a gun. Any sudden motion might make Pierre lunge with the knife. Jumping out of the car at a light was a possibility. Jill was smart, Jill would think of something.

Pierre started the car with his free hand. He drove off into the night, disappearing in the mix of colorful lights, shadows, and vehicles.

Dick sat in his apartment reading police reports. The telephone rang. "Yeah. What?"

"Hey, Dick."

"Yeah, Tony C. What's up?"

"I forgot to tell you something."

"Okay. Do I have to guess?"

"No. It was on my desk for awhile."

"Is that your final answer?" It was Dick's best Regis impersonation.

"Sorry. I was going through the ding-dongs at 799. You know, the maids, security, and doormen. It took a while, but afterwards I thought I should go out of town on priors. They had a nice little automobile dealership going there at one time."

"Do you have anything?" Dick sounded angry.

"One guy didn't quite check out all the way in the city, so I went out of state."

"What did you dig up?"

"Nothing."

"Did you call to jerk me off or what? If you did, could you wait till I get my shorts down, they irritate my dick when it gets hard."

"No. You don't understand. One guy is a fake. There is no Pierre Dessieux. He ain't from New Orleans or Canada or Bum-Fuck Arkansas or De Butthead, Montana. Everything he is he bought, including his TRW which goes back seven fucking years."

"Can you run his picture against what we've got on file?"

Dysplasia

∽

"That could take a while. We ain't got no fuckin' computer-match bullshit like in the movies."

"I'd better go talk to him again. What's the home address?"

"785 Church Avenue, Brooklyn. He's at the 799 Fifth. It says here he's working tonight."

"Thanks, Tony."

"Do you think this guy is the clit nitwit?"

"I doubt it. It's a long shot. Maybe I'll surprise him tonight. I need to get out of here."

Dick didn't have any leads, but it wasn't unusual for petty criminals, even felons, to have phony I.D. Men trying to avoid paying child support did the same thing.

Dick grabbed a container of Chinese food to eat in the car. He yanked his jacket off the back of the front doorknob and was out the door.

Dick pulled up in front of 799 Fifth Avenue. The lobby was brightly lit although no one was there. Dick walked across the lobby towards the doctors' elevator. As long as he was in the building, he thought he should see Jill. Maybe they could straighten things out.

He took the elevator to Jill's floor. He couldn't see a light under her door. He went back down, this time taking the elevator to the garage.

A garage attendant was watching *Survivor* on a little black-and-white television. Two security guards chatted near the garage entrance.

"Hey. You seen Pierre?"

"He's in the lobby."

"He ain't in the lobby."

"Don't bug me. I'm watchin' here." He said it without looking up.
"The show's a fuckin' fake."
Dick walked out of the garage and used his cell phone to call Jill. He waited for the answering machine to pick up. Dick didn't leave a message. He tried her cell phone.
Pierre heard the cell phone ring in Jill's purse.
"I'd better answer," said Jill.
"No," said Pierre. He pressed on the knife to remind her.
Dick listened to the cyber voice tell him that the customer was not responding or out of range.
Dick drove to Jill's building. He buzzed from downstairs. After a few minutes, he decided to get the superintendent. Dick insisted that the super open Jill's apartment. It was unlikely for Jill to go to sleep before midnight.

The apartment was empty. What if Jill was in trouble? What if Dick was wrong and Don was involved? What about the doorman? What if Jill knew that Don was involved? "That's not logical. She would have told me. Calm down," he told himself.
He used the telephone at Jill's to call Don.

Don was sitting up in bed staring out the window as he sipped a beer.
"Hello?"
"Dr. Gardner?"
"Yeah?"
"Dick Murphy."

- 489 -

Dysplasia

～

"What is it?"

"I'm looking for Jill. Is she with you?"

Don was momentarily flattered. "No. I was going to call you. I think that Dr. Chessman is probably dead."

"What do you mean probably? He died in the airplane fire."

"No. It wasn't him. I saw him alive after that. It's a long story. Where do you think Jill is?"

"Meet me at 785 Church. You like to play cop."

"Church Avenue? In Brooklyn?"

"It's where Pierre Dessieux lives."

"Yes. I know. Pierre! Shit! Chessman told me that he thought Melinda was murdered by Pierre."

"When did Chessman tell you this?"

"Before he died. I'll fill you in later. Do you think Jill is with Pierre?"

The line went dead. Don rolled the thought around in his head. "Pierre is a sweet guy. Even if he was who Chessman says he was, he—"

Don ran full speed to his car. Don's personal hatred for Chessman clouded his vision. Chessman never got his hands dirty. Chessman was telling the truth, at least partially.

Dick Murphy walked around the front of the more dilapidated building on Church Street. There weren't any numbers on the buildings. He passed overturned garbage cans. An old Chevy Malibu filled with gang bangers cruised by. Shops were closed. Rotten fruit lay against the curb. A young Chinese couple walked by at a fast clip. Dick could see the young man clutching tightly at a blunt object inside his jacket. It was probably a gun. Dick hoped it was. He didn't blame any citizen who wanted to protect his turf.

Dick saw a light in the building next door. He went in the front door, stood in the vestibule and looked up and down the names of the tenants. He buzzed a few times until the door unlocked. As he entered the first-floor narrow hallway, a door opened at the opposite end and two large black men bolted down the hall.

"Who the fuck are you?" demanded the first man, his fists flailing.

One of the men threw Dick up against the wall. "Aw, shit. I'm a cop."

Dick reached into his shirt pocket as the second man took a swing at Dick's head. Dick ducked and the man hit his hand on the thin wallboard, taking part of the wall out.

Dick displayed his badge.

"Hey, he is a cop."

"Sorry, man."

"Forget it."

"My wife is in there with my baby. My friend and I don't see many white guys here at night."

"Do you know anyone named Pierre?"

"No. But there is some French dude who has a loft upstairs. I knew that guy was bad."

"French?"

"Yeah. Calls himself an artist."

"Thanks."

"You want us to come with you or something?"

"Just routine." Dick started up the steps.

"You got it, Chief."

"Man. This is like Dick Tracy."

Dysplasia

Dick reached the third-level landing. Moonlight shined in through a skylight. A solid metal door blocked his path. He drew his service revolver from a shoulder holster. Dick pushed the unlocked open door and heard moaning. Someone pulled the door open wider. Dick was startled to see Jill sitting on a cane-backed chair, about thirty feet in front of him, bound, gagged, and naked. A huge bay window was to her right, supplying enough streetlight for Dick to see her clearly.

The side of a machete hit Dick hard on the back of his head. He went down, blood spilling over his face.

Pierre walked to a bulletin board where he kept press clippings of the two murder victims. He had to plan his actions. He would first strike Jill with the handle of the machete.

Jill thought of the autopsy reports. Melinda suffered twenty-three separate injuries. The cause of death was from repeated blows to the head. Semen was found in the vagina, a piece of glass, possibly from a bottle, in her anus. Bits of clothing had bloody handprints. The vaginal labia were neatly cut away in a diamond-shaped lattice outlining the anatomical location of the clitoris. Misty had several sneaker prints on his chest. When Pierre realized he was with a man, he stomped on his chest. The report noted fractured ribs, hemorrhaging of the right lung, vertebral column and the right atrium of the heart. That did not kill him. A ligature, probably rubber tubing, was used to strangle him.

Jill would only be struck with the handle of the machete. Once unconscious, Pierre would then decide how to proceed.

Pierre smiled at Jill. Jill returned a smile out of sheer terror. Jill was beginning to accept the fact that she may die. She trembled as she spoke. "Do you have anything to drink?"

"What does the lady drink?"

"Vodka?" Jill was hoping to anesthetize her body by drinking alcohol. She would at worst pass out.

"I have rum. Would you like some rum?"

"Yes. Thank you very much. I like rum."

Pierre took a bottle of rum from the kitchen counter and two coffee mugs from a cabinet. He walked to Jill and untied one of her hands so she could drink the rum.

"It is good, isn't it?"

"Yes. Thank you."

Don ran to the vacant building first. It was locked. No one was around. He saw the lights in the building next door.

He trembled as he reached for the front door. The two black men, now on the second floor landing, saw Don and walked downstairs to open the door.

"What is it with you cops?"

"Your friend is upstairs."

"Two white guys in one night."

"Damn."

"You wit' the other guy, right?"

"Yeah," said Don.

"He went up to look for some French guy."

Don ran up the stairs as quickly as his tired and sore body would allow. He yelled back, "Call 911. Emergency."

"You got it." The men went inside their apartment.

Dysplasia

Don reached the slightly open door to Pierre's loft. He saw Dick sitting in a chair near the window as he opened the door wide.

"Dick?" Don walked one step towards him and became aware of a sudden movement to his right.

When Don awoke on the floor, Pierre stood over him with the machete.

"Pierre stands across from the Pierre. This was always a thing you thought very funny. Is it still funny?"

"Yeah. Sure. It's still funny. Pierre across from the Pierre." The pain in Don's head was intolerable.

"You think I am a bad man. I am not. It is a thing with you Americans. You don't know good from evil. The problem with you is you don't understand. They exist together. Both are necessary. One is not better than the other."

"Sacrifice me. That's who you want, isn't it?" suggested Jill in a miraculously sincere tone.

"Sacrifice, no. But protect me, yes. That Dr. Chessman. He is a bad man. Did Dr. Chessman turn me in? You know he paid me a lot of money to kill that girl. He is a bad man. He does bad things to women. Bad sex things. I don't like this. He asked me to do many things for him over many years. I did not like to do this. But the girl, she said if he did not pay her another thousand dollars a month, she would go to the television people with photographs of Chessman in his bedroom. She was also evil for doing this."

Don screamed in pain as he rolled to one side. It was as severe an angle he could create while lying flat on his back. That enabled him to bring his head quickly to the right as the machete came down reflexively. The machete caught in the cheap tile, pulling up a square foot tile as Pierre wrestled to regain his weapon.

Seeing the tile stick to the end of the machete, Don charged forward like a linebacker closing the gap off tackle. The momentum of the force carried them across the room, leaving both to roll on the floor as they lost their balance. Don got up on one knee and managed to take his fist to the side of Pierre's face. A trillemellar, he would give him a trillemellar fracture, shattering as many of the fragile bones around the eye socket as he could with one blow. An ugly crunch came from Pierre's skull as Don felt a violent pain in his own hand. He broke his wrist in the process. No more medical jargon. "I broke my fucking wrist," screamed Don as he pulled his hand back. With his left hand, he tried to grab the machete. Pierre had it back in two hands. Pierre kicked Don squarely in the balls, and Don sank to the floor.

Across the room a reddened hand moved slowly down the side of Dick's head, clearing the blood from his eyelids. His trembling hand reached into his shoulder holster to find his gun was gone. He had forgotten what happened. Dick let his body weight pull him off the chair to the floor. He began a slow crawl along the wall. Jill could see him but said nothing, staring in terror. For a second she hoped he was trying to get out alive.

Don was unable to roll completely out of the way. The machete sliced a six-inch gash below his shoulder blades. Don screamed in pain, but knew it could have been worse if it hit the cervical area of the spine. At that moment, Don felt he was going to die. He looked over at Jill, who sat motionless.

"You little wimp. So you got hit in the head. You have a gash in your back muscles. So what? Do you want to die, you wimpy little scum-sucking protozoa?" Don rose to his feet. He could feel the blood run down his back like a warm shower. He ran towards Pierre, who held the machete high above his head. Don was breathing rapidly and felt he was going to pass out.

Dysplasia

∽

A hole opened up in Pierre's chest. Don turned quickly. Dick had fired his gun, somehow from a position flat on his back. The gun fell limp in Dick's hand as he lay motionless.

Pierre came at Don. Don screamed and sidestepped the weapon. Whatever strength Don had he used to throw Pierre off balance. Pierre staggered sideways towards the bay window, the machete lowered, still in his hands. Don dove across the floor and tackled Pierre at the ankles. Pierre fell backwards against the window, hitting his head hard. Don hoped the window would shatter under Pierre's weight, but it only cracked. Pierre fell to the floor. He was still moving.

Don turned back quickly to Jill who was trying to move her foot in the direction of a black bag. Don realized there must be a scalpel and dumped out the contents. Pierre was on his feet, chanting, staggering towards Don. Don clasped his hand on the scalpel as Don ran full force at Pierre. Pierre was knocked off his feet and landed on his back, and Don jumped him. With the addition of his left hand for more force, Don drove the scalpel into Pierre's heart.

Don rolled off to the side, in a state of shock, breathing faster.

Pierre rose, the scalpel implanted firmly between his ribs and picked up speed as he reached the window. He turned his back to the glass, hurling himself through the window.

Don limped to the whimpering Jill to untie her. "You did something right," Don told himself as Jill fell limp in his arms.

Several black-and-white police units arrived at the scene. They were apprehensive as they left their vehicles. Pierre lay twitching on the cracked black top in the street. The first cop walked closer with his gun drawn.

"Okay. Don't move."

An indescribable sound came from Pierre's body, from deep within his soul. The policeman was terrorized as the body flipped over, exposing the scalpel. Pierre's whole body rose for a spasmodic beat, then fell back to the surface. He was dead.

"Get an ambulance," said the young cop, hardly audible, his face covered in sweat.

EPILOGUE

Dick Murphy did not survive his head wound. Neurosurgeons operated for nearly six hours. Jill insisted on waiting in the hospital the entire time despite her own ordeal.

Don was treated successfully. He was told it would take months of physical therapy to raise his arms over his shoulders.

CNN ran the story about every twenty minutes, concentrating on the fact that a prominent doctor from the United States had been killed in Haiti by one of the rival political factions. People still claimed it wasn't Chessman, that he died in the fire.

For the next few weeks, the tabloids had a field day with the mysterious death of Dr. Henry "Call Me Hank" Chessman. It was revealed that Pierre was one of Duvalier's ex-generals, who along with many military men had to leave the country after Papa Doc. Chessman helped relocate Pierre and get him a job. One story had them sharing the same women. By the time the newspapers finished spinning the story, Chessman sounded every bit as ill as Pierre, every bit the murderer, and Pierre knew as much as Chessman about medicine. The truth would be lost, but it wasn't the issue. The media circus that ensued developed a truth all its own.

Dysplasia

Dozens of shows scheduled the cast of characters. The list ranged from Lou, who agreed to speak on television about Hank's career, to a voodoo doctor from New Orleans.

Mike Raptor gave speeches on the steps of Morningside Hospital. "There is nothing hip about ignorance. There is nothing slick about not knowing right from wrong. There is nothing hip or slick about going around killing each other for no good reason. That's why society has a justice system and a prison system. When people learn we have to give them another chance. But our doctors is where we have to demand right from wrong." Mike knew how to work the people.

The circus came to town.

Major publishers bid on the rights to Chessman's life. Joan was eager to move ahead with the project after seeing all the money made from the story about Maxwell, the "English" newspaper owner who "fell" off his boat. The Chessman estate was solvent. Chessman owed no money and his malpractice carrier was stuck footing the bill for whatever damages would arise from claims made by the Carver family.

The Carver family sued the Chessman estate. They got a whopper settlement in an unprecedented case of assault. On Larry King, the lead lawyer explained, "Although she may have consented to sex, she did not consent to the aberrant, torturous, S-&-M style that resulted in her having a miscarriage." The Chessman estate in turn sued the malpractice and umbrella liability insurance carriers. Both refused to pay, citing numerous reasons concerning definitions of coverage. It was estimated that this case would go on for at least three years.

Carol Ann McIntire went public to make a multitude of appearances. She was looking to make her own book deal. She made an excellent witness for the Carver family.

The vacuum created by Chessman's death would include everyone from the main-lining attorneys to the bartender at the Pierre. There was a lot of money to be made. Don said "no" to everyone. He did agree to speak on any show where the topic dealt with "medical abuses to women." He ended up doing a few shows, but the type of show that was more popular was the show that involved discussions about demons, voodoo and sexual mutilation.

Stu made some panicky phone calls the day he found out he might be indicted in connection with the death of Laurel Carver. He squirmed for a few weeks. He nearly was indicted, but the district attorney's office could not determine a charge. He sat through a series of interrogatories and convinced potential prosecuting attorneys that he had no knowledge of the medical condition at the time he made the referral to the hospital. In fact, he sounded like a hero because he described Chessman's voice as being distraught, distant, and hard to comprehend. He knew he had a patient in trouble. By calling the ambulance and delivering the girl to Dr. Gardner, who had an impeccable reputation, Stu reconstructed the scenario to appear professional.

Stu actually received a thank you note from Laurel's brother. The State Board set out to censor Stu for not stepping in to identify the original source of the referral. He made a celebrity-styled appearance and testified that Dr. Gardner wanted to take full responsibility for the care of the girl because Don omitted that the girl had prior surgery. Besides, Stu knew that nobody expected him to question Chessman, a respected member of the medical community. It was an emergency.

In his testimonies, Stu swore he didn't know that Chessman was the physician who began the operation. In the end, the governing bodies found Stu violated several codes of ethics. They told him to be a good boy. Stu would take to his grave the fact that Chessman called him and said, "Let's dump this sick puppy in Junior's lap."

The morning Stu received the modest "censor" letter from the State Board, Sherry buzzed in on the intercom.

Dysplasia

∽

"Dr. Stu. It's the lab."
"Right." He picked up the telephone. "Dr. Beitleman."
"Stu?"
"Yeah, Kenny." There was silence. "Well?"

"I'm sorry. You're positive. Hello? Stu? Stu?"
Stu dropped the phone on his lap and stared. He had regular tests. Why now? All of a sudden he was HIV positive? He paused, took a deep breath, and picked up the phone, pushing the intercom. "Sherry, get me the following people, would you?" Stu ran down his list of partners, probably one of the most medically responsible acts he had done all year. The first one on his list was his wife.

The ambulance drivers lost their licenses. The owners of the business were shut down temporarily. The drivers immediately got jobs working in Nassau County near Northshore Hospital.
Don received a reprimand in the form of a letter from the State of New York because he did not immediately report his suspicion of prior treatment. Pending charges were eventually dropped. The police had no issues with Don. Don did commit malpractice by not reporting the case properly in the chart. The insurance company settled the case.

It was a hot Sunday morning late in August. New York City seemed almost empty, a phenomenon that only takes place a few times a year.
Don sat in the IBM Plaza sipping a soft drink through a straw. It had been a few weeks since he had any hard liquor. He was still drinking an occasional beer or red wine. He wore cut off-jeans, a bright yellow T-shirt, sunglasses, and a New York Mets baseball cap. Don flipped through the Living Arts section of the *New York Times*.
Jill planted a big, affectionate kiss on his cheek. She was also dressed in cut-off jeans and a T-shirt. "What's it gonna be, Doctor?"

"Let's do something disgusting."

"Okay. Let's walk down to the Village and eat one of everything they're selling on each corner."

"Great."

Don hopped to his feet and took Jill's hand. "Do you want to call this a date?" asked Don.

"I don't see why not," was her answer.

Don looked at Jill. She radiated a feeling of happiness and contentment.

The media continued. "Today's show is about a bizarre tale in the world of medicine. It is a tale from our most powerful sector of medical practice in the country. It is about atrocities committed by doctors, the same doctors we put our complete trust in. I hope this makes you wonder about your own medical care and how we trust our lives to these men. I don't know about you but I'm never doing anything without a second opinion. We'll be right back."

A year later Jill and Don moved out of the city. Jill took a job as assistant Chief Medical Examiner in a small city in Vermont. Lou and Harvey bought out Don's share of the practice. Don had enough money to buy a small practice not far from where Jill worked. He had money left over to put towards a house after settling with Linda.

Jill and Don lived in an old, three-room cottage mostly made of stone. There was enough land to add another room later on. Jill decorated the simple cottage with beautiful Early American furniture. She got that second bed she always wanted.

They didn't buy a television. They spoke about getting one with a VCR, so they could watch classic movies.

There wasn't any hurry about anything.

Dysplasia

Jill found a partner she had known as a friend. Don felt reborn. The pair started life anew. Don thought he might try writing again. Jill bought new skis.

Movies could wait.